Oathbreaker

A. J. RETTGER

Acknowledgements

This book would not have happened if not for a few key people. Skye, without your incredible insight, helpful advice, and kind words, this book would not exist, and I am forever indebted to you. All my wonderful beta readers who pointed out the numerous grammatical errors and inconsistencies in my plot, I humbly thank you from the bottom of my heart. I only wish that I could reward you in some way. To the bands and artists who have inspired me, I hope you find the small homages in the book as a sign of my never ending gratitude.

Finally, to my "ride or dies," y'all motherfuckers keep me humble. I love you all.

PROLOGUE

A fresh coat of rebel blood covered the man's helmet. He wiped the visor with his gauntlet; the sound of metal scraping pained his ears. Wiping the blood only smeared it, obscuring his vision more. Frustrated with the lack of progress, he removed his helmet. As it gently blew by, the wind cooled his neck and scalp, which were drenched with sweat from battle. The man scanned the battlefield; all he could see for miles was corpses. Bodies of his enemies and his comrades intertwined with one another. Exhausted from the skirmish, he found a small mound of bodies that looked like a comfortable enough place to catch his breath.

His sword, a glimmering steel work of art at the beginning of the battle, was now stained crimson. He looked down at it, trying to find the original metallic colour of the steel, but it was to no avail; the sword was completely covered with the blood of his enemies. He stabbed the blade deep into the ground and leaned back on the mound of corpses and listened. All he could hear was the wind. No swords clashing, no yelling, no pounding of hooves from the cavalry's horses, no screams of men dying, nothing—only the wind.

This would be quite a peaceful place if a battle had not just taken place here, the man thought to himself as he gazed up at the orange sky. The sweat from his moustache leaked into his mouth. The bitter taste was refreshing since he was completely drained from the battle. Any source of hydration was welcomed by his parched mouth, even if it was his sweat.

I wonder where my horse ran off to? He looked around. The only horses he could find were the ones that had been slain in battle. *Poor things. I hope my Penelope didn't suffer the same fate once I was knocked off her.* He paused his thinking to appreciate the refreshing cool breeze once again. Never in his life did he think a simple summer's breeze could feel so pleasurable; it almost gave him enough energy to get up and search for survivors, almost.

The knight looked far out into the horizon past the battle and saw the sun setting over the dense forest. *One of the damn rebels probably snatched up Penelope in the retreat. Lucky bastard got away with a magnificent mount today.* Just as he finished fantasizing about one of the rebels running away on his former mount, he heard the unmistakable sound of galloping hooves coming closer and closer. His heart leapt up into his throat, for he secretly hoped it was Penelope returning to him after battle. He turned his head to the left and stood up. *If it is one of the commanders, it would not befit them to see me sitting on my arse. They may think I am a layabout.* Once he had his sword back in its scabbard and his helmet resting between his elbow and his torso, he saw, to his disappointment, that the source of the galloping hooves was not Penelope but instead a scout from the army.

"Greetings!" the scout shouted from atop his horse, who was breathing heavily.

A fine steed. A shame this dope is running it straight into the ground. The knight had no love for anyone who rode their animal to death. He was taught that these magnificent creatures were to be respected since they were the only companion a knight would have on the road unless one was lucky enough to have a squire.

"Greetings," the knight grumbled under his breath. Either the scout was a fool or attributed the knight's harsh tone to having just finished a battle because he didn't react.

"Commander Graves asked me to find survivors and report back to camp. How many from your regiment are alive?" the scout asked, with enough authority in his voice to convince a lesser man that he was a high-ranking officer. The knight lifted his arm and pointed to the battlefield, indicating that he was the only survivor. "So, you're saying none of your comrades survived?" the scout said, the authority in his voice wavering slightly.

"No," the knight replied. "They all left already to plough your mother and sister." The knight wasn't sure what the source of his anger was. Was it the idiotic questions that the young scout was asking? Or was it perhaps that he was still upset that this idiot was going to kill his horse when there was no need to run it so hard? Perhaps it was a little bit of both.

"Well . . . head back to camp then and report to Commander Graves," the young scout said with his adolescent voice breaking at the end of the command.

"My horse was lost in battle, so I'll need yours," the knight barked in reply.

"But…but, sir, I need it to check on the other regiments," the scout stammered.

"So, you're saying that you deny a superior his right to a mount?" the knight asked, with his tone remaining as harsh as it was at the start of the conversation.

The scout knew his question was rhetorical and proceeded to dismount his horse, then continued to walk the battlefield to look for survivors. The knight hopped on the horse, patted its sweaty neck, and rode back to camp. At a leisurely pace.

***

The camp roared after a victorious battle. Cheering and the clinking of metal mugs could be heard from a mile away. The knight slowly rode into the camp. None of the battle-weary men paid any attention to him; they were too busy celebrating. Drinking profuse amounts of alcohol, telling stories of their heroics on the battlefield, many of which were no doubt exaggerated, and stories of what they would do once they finally found a woman after the uprising had been quelled. Many of these stories were graphic in detail, with the storyteller often standing up and acting out the physical actions in the air to help him further explain his point.

Brigands. These soldiers have no honour, no code, and are no different than the bandits I put down. Given a chance, they would turn from patriots to cut-throat scoundrels. The knight shook his head bitterly as he rode past the crowd and headed directly to the commander's tent. He dismounted and shouted at a stable boy to give his horse a thorough brushing and lots of water since it had been run sick by the previous rider. The boy complied without a second thought and led the horse away. The knight felt a sort of admiration for the boy, but he was unsure why. Perhaps he reminded him of his son.

Inside the tent, Commander Graves was sitting at his desk, picking what was left of a roast chicken out of his teeth with a small dagger.

"Ah! Sir Deschamps, glad to see those rebel dogs didn't cut you down!" The commander's voice was loud and booming but also slurred.

"I've fought tougher men than that rabble," the knight responded quickly without trying to sound too boisterous.

"Bloody right, you have!" the commander barked back. "Your deeds are well known, and you are renowned for your bravery. Glad they were able to convince you to serve your country," the commander slurred and swayed drunkenly, almost knocking the contents of his desk on the floor.

"No convincing was needed. I live to serve and protect the people of this great kingdom." The knight knew how important modesty was in these types of situations.

"Come! Come! Join me and the fellow officers tonight. We'd be honoured to have such a distinguished guest join us at our table." It seemed impossible for the commander to stand upright at this point, as his torso swayed from left to right the entire time he was talking.

"Gladly." The knight begrudgingly obliged; he had about as much respect for army officers as he did for the bandit leaders he was used to cutting down.

The commander and the knight walked toward the table that was filled with four men and a dwarf. Each of them had a frothy mug of ale in their hands. Deschamps recognized a few of them. The dwarf, Finley Graeme, had a long red beard and a fat cherry-like nose. His face was completely black, no doubt from working the smithy all day, trying to keep up with the army's demand for new or repaired weapons and armour. *I ought to get that dwarf to re-sharpen my blade. Gods know how dulled it got in battle today.* Sebastian Archambault, a twenty-year-old officer with shaggy and matted dirty blonde hair, also sat at the table, along with Theodore Clague, whose crimson red hair was slicked back from sweat not from battle but from this terribly hot day. He had a thin patchy red beard, which made him look unseemly. Next sat Reginald Letchings. His grey beard and short grey hair were neatly trimmed, making him the only officer that looked dignified and suitable for such a high rank. But there was one man who Deschamps did not recognize sitting at the table—a man with long black hair and a small beard. He was the only one who had bloodstains on his armour. *Officers rarely see battle; perhaps this is another "distinguished guest."*

They both sat down at the table, and the commander loudly yelled, "Gentlemen, and Sir Dwarf, allow me to introduce our guest. The living, breathing hero: Sir Pablo Deschamps of Rougge!" The commander sounded more like a herald at a play rather than a commander of an army.

"So, Sir Deschamps," Sebastian Archambault began, "how did today's battle compare to your legendary deeds at Rougge?"

"Actually, I'm from Rougge, my first deed was completed in Weston Hill," the knight corrected, then took a sip from the mug in front of him.

Sebastian's face instantly blushed. Deschamps didn't seem to notice, though; he was too busy being distracted by the officer's unprofessional appearance. *A man of such high rank ought to look dignified*, Deschamps thought to himself, but he attributed the man's dishevelled look to the ignorance of his youth. *A wonder how he was able to achieve the rank of an officer so quickly.*

"Gentlemen, I was informed that the king himself is coming down to congratulate all of you on such an astounding victory today," the commander boomed, interrupting Deschamps' train of thought.

The mood at the table instantly changed. Both Theodore Clague and Reginald Letchings drank to soothe their nerves. Sebastian Archambault failed to hide his excitement and was as giddy as a child about to receive a gift. Finley Graeme immediately tried to wipe off the black soot that was caked on his face. *Funny. The dwarf knows more about the skills of grooming and looking presentable than most of these officers.* The man with the blood-stained armour didn't seem affected by the news. Instead, his piercing grey eyes continued to stare at the knight. Deschamps could tell they were full of contempt.

"Forgive me, but I don't believe I've had the honour of making your acquaintance," Deschamps spoke, trying to break the tension with the man in the blood-stained armour. The man remained silent, taking a drink from his mug, but his grey eyes did not move off the knight.

Finley Graeme finally spoke up, breaking the awkward silence that had fallen over the table. "This here is the commander of the mercenary unit, Ewald of Four Trees."

"Of Four Trees?" Deschamps asked. "I was there a few years ago, a lovely piece of the countryside." He paused for a brief drink. "I had heard reports that a group of bandits were attacking villagers and stealing livestock." He paused once again to build suspense; this was not the first time he had told a tale about his knightly heroics.

"What did you do?" asked Sebastian, leaning forward and knocking over his semi-empty mug in the process. He had been fascinated by the tales of knightly heroics ever since he was a boy. Unfortunately, he was not born into the right family to become a knight; one could only become a knight if his father was one. Instead, he joined the army hoping that one day the king would bestow a knighthood on him.

"Naturally, I cut them down like the scum they were. A bunch of farmers with swords is all they were, but they refused to surrender and let the proper authorities punish them, so my sword and I had to do the punishing," Deschamps replied, speaking more and more valiantly as he went along, his modesty fading. Perhaps it was a result of the ale; perhaps it was because of the awestruck stares from everyone at the table, except Ewald, who just kept staring at him with those piercing grey eyes.

"Aye, I remember those bandits," Ewald finally croaked. His voice was deep and menacing, more menacing than his eyes. "Sure, they took from villagers and farmers, but they also protected them from the ravenous beasts that lurked in the forests. Some say it was a fair price to pay for peace of mind." His eyes didn't leave Deschamps'. They stared so deeply that Deschamps' hair stood on the back of his neck.

"If they were such noble protectors, why were they attacking the villagers then?"

"If the king's treasury stopped paying you for protecting the people, would you still risk your neck every day knowing that you wouldn't get compensated?" Ewald's voice trembled; the entire table could tell rage was consuming him.

"Of course, I would! For it is the noble and admirable thing to do!"

"You knights think everything is so black and white, blinded by your chivalrous code and brainwashed by those radiant virtues. You'd probably not know your head from your arse!"

"My good sir! Need I remind you that you are speaking to an *ordo equestris*. Change your tone!" Deschamps slammed his clenched fist onto the table to emphasize the anger this blatant disrespect had caused.

"Fuck you! You and I both know that who you are in the presence of these buffoons and royal dignitaries is different from who you are out on the road when it is just you and your horse!" At this point, Ewald stood up, his veins protruding from his neck and bulging from his forehead.

"I challenge you to a duel, you rapscallion!"

"Don't bother. I was informed that my company and I are being shifted to the Eastern Front, and I think it's high time we set off." Ewald turned on his heels sharply and left the table in what can only be described as an angry march.

The table fell silent; not a single person dared to breathe until he was far from earshot in fear that he'd come back and duel the knight.

"Well, I never!" slurred Commander Graves. "Don't worry, my dear Pablo. I will report him for such vile and inappropriate behaviour to a man as distinguished as yourself."

"No need. I'm sure he is just pained by the men he lost today. We all are." Deschamps punctuated his statement with a solemn drink from his almost empty mug.

Commander Graves suddenly turned his attention to the boy who had been carrying pitchers back and forth to the infantrymen all evening. "Boy! Bring us more ale!"

"But, sir . . . the soldiers are demanding more and more ale; I'm already three pitchers behind!"

"Does it look like I care? We are the officers, and you will serve us first!" Graves' tone was harsh, harsher than what was needed. The rest of the table roared in laughter as the young boy scuttled away, except for Deschamps and the dwarf.

"How many men did you lose today?" Finley asked once the laughter had died down.

"Too many, Master Dwarf. Too damn many," Deschamps replied solemnly, finishing his mug.

"Were they all knights such as yourself?" Sebastian asked, hoping to hear more stories of knightly deeds.

"No, as far as I know only a few of us knights answered the call to battle," Deschamps stated. "The rest decided to keep protecting the people from the ne'er do wells. With many of the men gone to battle, the women and children are left vulnerable."

"Are you aware of which ones answered the call to action? Reginald Letchings asked.

"Well . . ." Deschamps paused as if he needed a moment to think, but he knew very well which knights were brave enough to answer the call to action. "I believe there was a new knight fresh out of his graduation that joined the cause; I believe his name was Marcus Con-something or other. Then there was a dear friend of mine whom I trained and occasionally fought with in our youth, Sir Franz Hibblehart—a man with so much honour and bravery that the minstrels will be writing songs about him for centuries. And finally, there was

Sir James Tholomew, a hero in his own right. It was he who slew the Giant of Broken Grove."

"No way!" Sebastian slammed his mug onto the table. "A giant? Really?" His eyes widened.

"According to the tales," Deschamps stated, coyly brushing off the young officer's enthusiasm.

"Wait, isn't that the Order of the Swords responsibility? You knights protect people from the worst of men, and they deal with the magical beast and monsters? Things that go bump in the night?" Theodore Clague said mid-sip of his ale.

"Gods, Clague, are you daft!?" shouted Commander Graves. "The Order of the Swords hasn't been around for centuries. They're all sell-swords like our dear Ewald, who departed not long ago. That order fell from grace a long, long time ago." The Commander slammed back the rest of his mug before pouring himself another one.

"Now, now, there's no need for insults, my friends," Deschamps said after finishing his own mug of ale. "Although it is true the Order of the Swords was created to defend the people from things that go bump in the night, such as vampires, werewolves, giants, corpse-eaters, and other ghastly beasts. The problem is that they had no loyalty, no king to keep them in check. They were free to roam kingdom to kingdom like vagabonds. Unfortunately, mercenary work pays a lot more than slaying monsters." He paused to pour himself another mug; the table kept silent while he did so. "Fortunately for the rest of us, the order is almost dead, as they stopped taking recruits years ago. Some sort of inhumane experiments were being conducted, and the whole order imploded, or so I've been told."

"Good riddance!" Commander Graves slurred. "The only thing worse than fuckin' sell-swords is godsforsaken mages!"

"Cheers to that!" shouted Theodore Clague. The entire table lifted their mugs and clinked them together, except for Finley.

"After the tragedy that happened at Caspula, I'm glad the kings in the North allied themselves together and banned magic from being practised both at court and privately," Reginald managed to say while fighting off a few hiccups.

"What happened at Caspula?" Sebastian asked, to which he was greeted with stares of disbelief.

"Do you not know boy?" Reginald snapped back.

"Forgive him, Reginald, he was only a wee lad when it happened. It was ten years ago already and he's only twenty," Clague spoke after pouring himself another mug of ale.

Deschamps couldn't help but be lost in thought about the young army officer. *He must have some family connections to become an officer at such a young age, but the name Archambault doesn't stand out to me. Perhaps it's a fake name, as to not draw attention to himself.* His thoughts were suddenly interrupted by Commander Graves' drunken slurring of the story of Caspula.

" . . .Mages were the left hand of every king. They handled things that spies, generals, and ministers couldn't handle themselves, ya know? The magical stuff, like stopping bastards from being born, making sure the queen has a boy instead of a girl, curing impotence, ya know, kingly matters." It was at this point that he paused to take another big drink from his mug, even though all of the members of the table would have agreed that he had had more than enough to drink so far. "Then one day, King Leon of Keten denied his mage some supplies that were 'needed' to conduct some magical experiment or whatever."

"What happened next?" Sebastian asked eagerly.

"If you let me finish my damned drink, I'll tell you!" the commander barked before he finished what was yet another mug of ale. "Well, them their mage went fuckin' ballistic. He threw a tantrum that would rival even the most spoiled tyke. He damn near levelled half of the city of Caspula because the king said no. Damned scroll-stuffer thought he was the one in power instead of the king. If it wasn't for some brave lad with a crossbow who shot him dead in the heart, the whole city would've been destroyed."

"Wait, how did he shoot him with a crossbow? Wouldn't the mage see him and stop the crossbow with magic?"

"No," Theodore Clague spoke up since the commander was mid-drink. "It is said that the crossbow bolt's head was forged with pixie dust, and as you may or may not know, Sebastian, human magic doesn't affect fey magic. And thus, the mage was helpless against this specific crossbow."

"Why is that?" Finley said finally breaking his long-time silence.

"How the fuck should I know?" barked Clague. "I ain't no fuckin' scholar. Go ask some bookworm."

For a bit after that, no one spoke but rather took drinks of various sizes from their respective mugs. Some getting more drunk than others. The drunkest was Commander Graves and Theodore Clague, who had their arms wrapped around each other in a brotherly embrace, while Finley Graeme and Pablo Deschamps remained almost stone sober.

"I'll tell you what, those damned rebels put up a hell of a fight today," Reginald said, finally breaking the silence.

"Yes, they were a worthy opponent," stated Deschamps as he took a small sip from his mug, trying to prevent himself from getting too drunk.

"How many did you cut down, Sir Knight?" asked Sebastian eagerly.

"I didn't have time to count. I was focused on staying alive," Deschamps answered with a subtle hint of distaste that such a question would be asked.

"Well, I cut down twenty," Clague retorted as he pulled out a necklace of severed elf ears from inside his gambeson. The necklace was greeted by either awe or disgust. The only ones with disgust were the two individuals who were not officers of the army.

"Damned, knife-ears," barked Commander Graves as he finished his drink. "Fuckin' non-humans are good for nothing the 'ole lot of 'em!"

Finley Graeme's gaze met the commander's and an awkward silence fell over the table. Nobody had a clue what to say.

"No offence, Master Dwarf," Commander Graves finally said, swallowing his pride.

"None taken," Finley replied, with a clenched fist. Luckily, nobody noticed such minute things in their state of inebriation.

"The dwarves have got it right!" shouted Sebastian Archambault. "They stay neutral and forge our weapons and armour, and thus help our cause!"

"And getting filthy rich off of it," mumbled Theodore Clague under his breath. Luckily, nobody heard him as there was shouting coming from the camp.

"Sirs! Sirs!" shouted the boy who brought them more pitchers of ale earlier in the night. "The king has arrived!"

"Gods blast it!" shouted Sebastian as he stood up with such excitement that he knocked over the pitchers of ale and several mugs that were on the table.

"C'mon, gents, let's go greet His Royal Highness," Commander Graves slurred, who looked like he was in no condition to meet royalty.

The table got up and walked down the hill to greet the royal caravan, each at their own pace. Deschamps noticed that Sebastian was almost at a full jog going down the hill. *No doubt eager to meet the king and do some bootlicking.* He also noticed that Commander Graves and Clague were staggering down the hill, arms embracing one another for balance. Reginald and Finley walked on either side of the knight.

***

The carriages in the caravan were a perfect visual representation of the wealth divide between the king and his subjects. Each carriage was pulled by four pure-bred draft horses with the finest tack gold could buy: dark leather bridles, golden bits, and nosebands that had been bedazzled by rubies, sapphires, and emeralds. The interior of each carriage was something out of every commoner's imagination. Satin blinds, leather seats, and blankets made from the finest silk. *Obviously, discretion isn't a priority for this new king. His father would have never wasted resources on such a spectacle.* The parade of magnificent carriages passed the knight, each more regal than the last. Finally, the convoy stopped. A hush fell over the crowd of drunken soldiers, as this would likely be the last time they would ever get so close to royalty.

Suddenly, a door to one of the carriages swung open. A golden crown emerged from behind the satin blinds and revealed itself to the masses of inebriated soldiers. After what seemed like an eternity of silence, the king raised his hand and waved to his subjects. The camp erupted. Never before had a king been greeted with such enthusiasm. The personal guards of the king were instructed to part the sea of soldiers to make room for his highness to walk through the camp. However, this was no easy task, as the drunken enthusiasm of the masses made them ignore many of the guard's commands.

Seeing that the crowd would not respond to his guards, the king decided to calm the mob with a speech. "My good men! What you have accomplished here today has not gone unnoticed! You have fought hard, and long. You've given your blood, sweat, and tears for your country. And I, on behalf of all of your fellow countrymen, thank you."

The crowd exploded with cheers and screams.

The king raised his hand again, quieting the soldiers. "Your names will not be lost in the annals of time, and each and every one of you will be graciously rewarded for your bravery!"

The crowd roared again with enthusiasm, even though kings have been making similar empty promises for generations.

"I will speak and shake hands with every one of you fine men, but first I must meet with your commanders."

This time when the king's guards went to separate a walkway in the crowd, the soldiers were much more obedient. The king walked with his nose to the sky. Guards surrounded him on every side, and the small boy who kept the king's cape from dragging in the mud struggled to keep up with the long strides of royalty. The soldiers pushed against one another trying to get as close to the king as they could, many reaching out and touching the king's shoulder or hand and exclaiming that they managed to touch nobility.

When His Royal Highness managed to finally reach the officers, he paused for a minute. Everyone held their breath with anxiousness. The king looked at Commander Graves and Theodore Clague and spoke, "Enjoying your victory, I see." His voice was deep and commanding and conveyed a sense of authority.

"Aye . . .I mean, yes, Your Highness," Commander Graves managed to slur out while almost falling on his face during his bow.

"You, sir," the king said to Theodore Clague, ignoring the commander's drunken buffoonery, "what's your name?"

"Theodore Clague, Your Highness. Officer of the 23rd Regiment."

"I see you've been celebrating your victory."

"I have been, milord."

The king made a hand gesture, and a young servant carrying a satchel full of parchment quickly scurried out of the mass of people.

"Yes, Your Highness?" the page timidly asked.

"Please make a note that the 23rd Regiment commanded by Officer Theodore Clague is to be relocated to the Eastern Front. They are to mobilize at sun up," the king stated with an expression that can only be described as bored.

"Yes, Your Grace," the servant said.

Everyone could tell that this was not a reward but instead a punishment for being drunk in the presence of a king. Theodore Clague bowed to the king to thank him. The king briefly shook hands with Reginald Letchings and

Sebastian Archambault and exchanged courtesies. Finley Graeme, however, was completely ignored by the king and was even pushed over by one of the king's guards, although nobody seemed to notice.

"Ah, Sir Pablo Deschamps!" the king said with a wide smile on his face. "Let us take a walk. We've a matter to discuss privately."

"Of course, Your Grace," Deschamps answered while executing a flawless bow. He followed the king and the royal guards away from the camp while Theodore Clague went to go inform his men that they were to march out at first light. Reginald Letchings, Commander Graves, and Sebastian Archambault went back to their table and resumed drinking. Once again, nobody noticed the dwarven blacksmith; covered in mud and sulking, he slowly walked back towards his forge.

***

"That Commander Graves is a buffoon!" the king exclaimed, finally breaking the lengthy silence of the walk. Deschamps said nothing, for he knew his knightly protocol clearly stated not to speak to a king unless directly asked a question. "I'll have him stationed in the Far North, freezing his balls off for his disrespect! So drunk that he can't even stand when he meets a king, inexcusable!" The king's voice grew louder and louder. Deschamps could see veins starting to protrude from his neck. He had never known a king to get so upset over such a petty matter. "That Letchings seems to be a veteran. Perhaps I'll make him commander, or maybe even that Archambault; he seems competent."

A twenty-year-old commander?

"Tell me, Deschamps, do you enjoy being a knight?" the king finally asked, interrupting the knight's thoughts after he seemingly calmed down.

"I do, Your Grace."

"What made you choose this life?"

"You see, Your Grace, you must be born into becoming an *ordo equestris*. My father was a knight and my grandfather was a knight as was his and as was his. It has been a tradition in my family for generations. Although we technically do have a choice, we all become knights. The reward is too great to pass up."

"I suppose I'm the one who is supposed to bestow those rewards upon you."

"Yes, Your Grace. Your father knighted me almost twenty years ago once I completed my first deed at Weston Hill. As his successor, tradition dictates that you must fulfill his side of the agreement." Deschamps tried to word his phrase in as respectable a manner as possible but he fell short.

The king stopped in his tracks and looked at him coldly. "What are these rewards?" the king finally drawled out, maintaining his angered look.

"The standard agreement is once a knight's thirty years of service is complete, he shall be rewarded with his own private estate and a monthly pension for the rest of his life from the king's treasury," Deschamps said while meeting the king's sinister gaze, not out of an abandonment of fear, but simply because he was trained to always meet a gaze, even if he didn't want to.

After a lengthy silence, the king asked, "Who was your father?" Then he resumed walking. Deschamps and the royal guard followed suit.

"Antonio Deschamps. It is an unwritten rule in the order, but a son must always outperform his father's greatest deed."

"What was his?"

"He fought in the War of the Frost, particularly the Battle of Frozen Lake. Once the commanders had been killed by some of Keten's soldiers, he rallied the troops and retook the lake from Keten. A deed that is often credited to turning the tide of the war."

"A great deed indeed. I remember my grandmother telling me stories of the battle when I was a prince. I'm glad you come from a long line of patriots."

"Thank you, sire."

"I hear that before you joined the cause to fight the elves, you were called the 'Scourge of Bandits' and that you've taken out more bandits than anyone else. Is this true?"

"Yes, Your Grace. However, fighting bandits isn't what it is all cracked up to be. Most are only intimidating when they are fighting a farmer with a rake or a woman with a broom. As soon as they meet a real swordsman, they're unmatched."

"And the rebels?"

"Same thing, men and women who are often unskilled with a weapon. The only thing I worry about going into battle is the sheer numbers, and their ability to shoot an arrow."

The king nodded in an agreement, for he knew how dangerous an elf could be with an arrow since the aftermath of an elven assassin was why he became a king at such a young age.

"I've been told that in order to become a knight you have to take an oath on some radiant virtues or whatever. What virtues exactly do you swear to?" the king asked.

"Well, there are four and all *ordo equestris* must live by these virtues at all times, and each is as important as the last. First, bravery—we swear to always demonstrate bravery and never display cowardice, for it would humiliate ourselves, our families, and the order. Then, there is honesty. Always be honest when conversing with the people and to yourself. Integrity—act with integrity in any and all difficult situations and avoid bringing shame onto the order. And finally, loyalty to your brothers of the order. One must never harm another brother of the order, and if one is in need, you must not deny them aid."

"Do you have a son? Do you hope he will follow in your footsteps and become an *ordo equestris*?"

"Yes, he is thirteen and is back home in Rougge with his mother, and I am certain he will join the knightly order. It is in his blood."

"Well, he will have a hard time living up to your legacy, especially with what I am about to ask of you."

Deschamps froze; he had never been given a mission from a king before. His body filled with anticipation—half out of excitement, half out of fear.

"We can end the uprising in the next week provided you continue serving your king. My spies have uncovered that there is a small village about a day's ride from here; they have been aiding the rebels by providing them with food, shelter, and medical attention. I want you to go there and cut them down."

"Your Grace, you must be joking. They are your subjects!"

"They are traitors! I forgave your insolence once during this conversation, but I will not do so again! You will not tell me what I must and mustn't do! I am your king! I am King Dryden III!"

Deschamps dared not say more, as the gravity of his situation donned on him. This was an order he couldn't refuse, not if he wanted to maintain his family's legacy.

"There, now that we have reached an understanding, you will ride out at once."

"Yes, Your Grace." Deschamps bowed low and began walking towards the stables to grab a horse so he could begin his mission. The king turned around and saw that the young boy holding his cape had heard everything and looked shocked that the king would give such an order to a noble knight.

"Guards, cut out the boy's tongue; he must not disclose what he heard here tonight," the king ordered.

Deschamps shook his head in disgust at his king, but mainly in himself. He hated being powerless and wished desperately that he could have saved the boy from his punishment.

On the night of Dudurn 27, 1175, the legendary knight Sir Pablo Deschamps of Rougge stormed an elven stronghold and cut down every last rebel himself. It is wildly accepted that this single deed ended the Elven Uprising of 1170. However, Sir Deschamps did not live out the remainder of his days in glorious retirement (too few knights do). Instead, he ended up disappearing mysteriously in the Caenun of 1175.

Lucas Pius,
Chronicles of Legendary Knights, III Edition

CHAPTER ONE

The sound of boots hitting the stone floor echoed throughout the halls of the Knight College. It was still early, and nobody was awake yet, except for one recruit, who had woken up early to reminisce about his time in the college before his graduation ceremony. The recruit went past the southwest window that overlooked the small town of Redfern, the college situated on its outskirts, and went down the small spiral staircase to the East Wing. He had to be extra stealthy in this part of the college because this was where the headmaster's quarters were. The headmaster was almost always in a sour mood and looked for any excuse to yell at the students.

The recruit stopped halfway through the East Wing and looked down at the dirt courtyard through a stained-glass window. He recalled all the countless hours of training he had endured at the college. He remembered the heat of the sun beating down on his neck while he practised his swordsmanship; he remembered the distinct taste of dirt mixed with blood. He remembered the pain of an instructor's sword striking him in the ribs, arms, or legs. He looked back on all of these memories fondly. He was grateful for what these gruelling lessons had taught him and was eager to use this knowledge outside of the college.

The recruit continued to walk around the college, day-dreaming about his future life as an *ordo equestris*. He dreamed of fighting bandits, slaying dragons, protecting the innocent from the wicked, and, of course, rescuing damsels in distress. During his absent-minded walking, he quickly found himself in the West Corridor. This corridor was well known to every recruit because of the giant oil paintings of famous knights that hung there. Every recruit dreamed that someday their painting would hang on the wall and join the illustrious company of knights that had the honour of adorning the wall. During his free time at the college, the recruit frequently found himself in the West Corridor because there, on the wall, hung a painting of his father—Sir Pablo Deschamps.

"I wish you could join me at the graduation ceremony, Father," Mario said aloud. The painful memory of learning of his father's disappearance five years ago surged back into his mind. He would've given anything to have his father attend. Suddenly, Mario heard the creaking of plate armour to his right and quickly turned his head only to see a familiar face staring back at him.

"I knew you'd be here," said the knight in full-plate armour.

"Yes, Sir Augustine."

"Please, Mario, you're a knight now! Call me Brother Augustine!"

Mario knew this was a huge compliment. Even though he wouldn't officially be a knight until after he completed his first deed, it meant a lot to him that his mentor would find him an equal. Sir Pedro Augustine looked like he came straight out of a fairy tale. He was strong with broad shoulders; women from town swooned over him whenever he'd head to the market to buy something. His long, luscious, blonde hair was of great envy to many women, and some men. But his eyes, most would say his greatest feature, were as blue as the ocean, and a person could get lost in them just as easily. It was unusual that a man so young would be an instructor at the college; however, Sir Augustine valued education. He saw it as part of his vow of loyalty to the order.

"For the record, I wish your father was here to see you graduate as well," Augustine said, smiling at Mario.

"Thank you, Brother Augustine."

"Brother? What nonsense are you filling that boy's head with now?" barked another voice from behind Mario. He could tell from the gravelly tone and the anger in the voice that it belonged to another instructor, Sir Darius Withers.

"Mario is graduating today Darius. That means he is the newest member of the order. Whether you like it or not," Augustine snapped.

"Newest member . . . the boy hasn't even completed his first deed yet," Sir Darius growled back.

Sir Darius Withers was easily recognizable; four large claw marks had cut across his entire face. The scars, about half an inch deep, distracted from the other features of his face. It was only after about two years at the college that Mario realized that Darius' eyes were yellow and that the only hair on his head was a small moustache and goatee.

Although Sir Withers was never the embodiment of kindness, he was easily one of the bravest knights to ever serve the order. It was told that a gang of bandits he was fighting kept a tarraq as a pet. Mario had never seen a tarraq in person, but he had seen drawings of them in books. They were ravenous creatures, about as big as a man that walked on all fours, similar to a gorilla. Their arms had long razor-sharp claws at the end, about three inches long and retractable. Depending on the sub-species of tarraq, the sharp spines on the back could either be venomous or not. As if the gods thought that this wasn't enough when creating such a beast, they decided to fill its maw with sixty-four dagger-like teeth, each about a quarter of an inch long. Unless one was trained in fighting monsters, fighting a tarraq meant certain death — which made it all that more impressive that Sir Darius walked away from the fight alive, albeit scarred for life.

"Mario, go to town and get food for the banquet after your graduation ceremony today, and take Tiberius with you," Sir Darius said without breaking eye contact with Sir Augustine.

"Yes, sir," Mario muttered and quickly shuffled away back towards the recruit quarters to grab Tiberius. *A poor start to my big day, but hopefully hitting the town with my best friend will turn it around.*

Mario's mind filled with completing great deeds and other illusions of grandeur as he walked back to the quarters, unaware of what the town of Redfern had in store for him that fateful day. In fact, he was so busy day-dreaming, that he didn't notice the foot sticking out into the hallway. Mario immediately fell face first onto the stone floor. His nose began to bleed.

"Watch where you're going, clumsy!" the owner of the foot exclaimed. It took a while for Mario's eyes to focus, but when they did, he saw that the person standing over him was Tiberius, and he was offering him a hand back up.

"Tiberius! You could've knocked all my teeth out!" Mario shouted.

"I was trying to make you as handsome as our good instructor Sir Darius Withers. Ladies love a man with scars, you know."

"Always were a jokester. Come on, we have to go into town and get supplies."

"What for?"

"You seriously don't know what today is?"

"No, I am well aware. I just wanted to get a rise out of you. Now shut up about it. I've heard you talk about this day non-stop for five years."

"I know, I know, I just want to . . ."

"Live up to your father's legacy. The great Pablo Deschamps! The Scourge of Bandits and Slayer of Elves. Hero of the Elven Uprising. I've heard it all before. Now can we go already?"

"Gladly." Mario smiled while pinching off his bleeding nose.

***

The town was wide awake. People were going about their daily lives: the devout entered the temples to pray to the various gods for various blessings, men were kicked out of their houses for their philandering the night before, guards had already fallen asleep during the early morning shift, children ran through the streets with sticks playing "knights and bandits," merchants were setting up their stands in the market, and of course, people flocked to the nearest tavern. This had only been the third time Mario had set foot in Redfern since joining the Knight College. Recruits had an extremely strict tutelage schedule that was always to be adhered to, but the air always smelled better in town than in the college. Today was no different. The second Mario's foot left the drawbridge and hit the dirt of the town he felt the rush of freedom surge throughout him. Anxiousness filled his body when he realized that his freedom was only a couple of hours away.

"Well, come on! We don't have all day!" Tiberius mocked. Mario quickly hurried to catch up with his friend and went straight to the market to buy the supplies.

"Gods, blast it! Looks like they're still setting up their stands," Tiberius said, his voice flooded with sarcasm. "Looks like there is nothing to do now but head to the nearest tavern."

"I'm not sure that's a good idea, Tiberius . . ."

"Oh, come on! One ale won't hurt! Plus, who knows when we will be seeing each other again since I'm not graduating today." Mario could hear the subtle disappointment in Tiberius' voice.

It pained Mario that Tiberius wasn't graduating with him today. In fact, no one was. He was this year's lone graduate. Every recruit had to spend a mandatory five years in the college but couldn't graduate until every teacher agreed that they were ready to become a knight. It had been Mario's plan since a small child to graduate in the least amount of time, just like his father. "Alright," he muttered, letting his pity for Tiberius get the better of him. "Just one though. I don't want to get expelled on my graduation day."

Since Tiberius and Mario were unfamiliar with the town, it took some time before they found a tavern. Eventually they found one, a run-down establishment by the name of The Crooked Leg. Upon entering, the name seemed to be quite fitting. The walls were less than ninety degrees with the floor, and the floorboards were bowed and curved, making it uneven and difficult to walk on. Bowls slid across the slanted tables into patrons' laps, and a smell that could only be associated with an infected leg filled the room.

"Gods, it's worse than our quarters in the college!" Tiberius exclaimed.

"Still want that drink, or do you want to go back to the market?" Mario asked, hoping his friend would forget about his quest, but he should've known it would be no use; Tiberius never gave up.

"Two ales barkeep!" Tiberius shouted after sitting at the least crooked table he could find. Before Mario had a chance to find a suitable chair, two mugs were already on the table. He decided to cut his losses and just enjoy the beverage.

"Thankfully the ale tastes better than this place looks!" Mario exclaimed after taking a big gulp. He then realized that Tiberius hadn't even taken a sip from his mug yet; he was too busy admiring the barmaid. "I swear, that's the whole reason you joined the order."

"Mario, I'm offended!" Tiberius said in his most posh voice. "I wanted to follow in my family's footsteps and protect the good people of our kingdom from the wicked and vile that hides in the streets."

Mario shook his head. "So, this is your big plan? Take me out to get an ale and watch you fail at courting barmaids?" he asked, taking another sizeable drink. The sooner he could get back to the task at hand, the happier he'd be.

"You used to be fun, Mario," Tiberius answered, completely ignoring the question asked. "Remember when we snuck out in our third year to go race horses along the riverside?"

"I do, but do you remember the thrashing we got when we were caught sneaking back into the college?"

"That's the part that makes it a good story!"

"Well, hopefully today doesn't end up the same. I want to start being a knight as soon as possible."

"Yes, yes, I know. What was your father's first deed again?"

"It was in Weston Hill. He answered a notice that some villagers put up. Apparently, some people had been stealing grain and livestock from the village folk. So, he rode in, fully clad in armour, and tracked down the people capable of the foul deed."

"How many did he cut down?" Tiberius asked, taking a small sip from his mug while still making eye contact with the waitress at the bar.

"None. He ended up arresting the bandit outfit and took them to the local guards, who then carried out the punishment."

"Ah, a perfect first deed. The wicked punished with no bloodshed. If you're trying to beat that, well then you're fucked."

"Tiberius! That language isn't very fitting of a knight!"

"Well, technically, I'm still a recruit, so I can still curse all I want. Damnit." Tiberius' coy smile made Mario burst out laughing.

"What did your father do for his first deed?" Mario asked, almost finishing his ale.

"Oh, that's a great tale, full of romance, drama, and action. Unfortunately, it's too long to tell over ONE round of drinks." Tiberius winked while taking another sip from his mug. Mario cursed under his breath but ultimately agreed to another round.

Once again, the service was quick and prompt. Out of the corner of his eye, Mario noticed the barmaid give a subtle wink in his direction while serving the drinks. Mario smiled politely. He was used to women lingering their eyes on him. Like Sir Augustine, Mario was widely regarded as handsome, and was often considered as the best-looking recruit.

"Now where were we . . ." Tiberius paused to take a lengthy drink from his freshly filled mug. "Ah yes! My father's first deed. It was on the border of Keten and Drussdell. There was a wandering clan of elves, which made the local villagers nervous. So, my father went to disperse the elves, fully expecting a fight, only to find the love of his life, my mother."

Mario had almost forgotten that Tiberius was a half-elf. He always wore a red bandanna covering his head, which, by design, covered the tops of his slightly curved ears to avoid prejudice. Even the instructors at the academy didn't find out he was a half-breed until part way through his studies, and by then, they couldn't deny him entrance nor expel him simply because of his race, as that was before the Elven Uprising when animosity towards elves wasn't as high.

"So, there they were, my mother and father. Star-crossed lovers. One, a nomadic elf who had lived off the land her entire life. The other, a high-class

25

knight, born of privilege and bound by tradition. A bard couldn't come up with a better love story!" Tiberius took another drink, this time almost finishing his mug. "My mom left her clan, and her and my father built a small homestead by Gravenport, on the far eastern edge of the kingdom far from disapproving and judgemental eyes."

"Did you see him often?" Mario said, finishing his second ale in thirty minutes.

"I suspect as much as you saw yours. The life of a knight is lonely—travelling all across the kingdom never seeing your family, all to protect the innocents. What a life." The resentment was obvious in Tiberius' voice. Perhaps it was the reason he wasn't graduating with Mario today. Or perhaps it was because of his race.

"At least your dad got to retire and is now living with your mother. Mine never came home."

"When was the last time you saw him?"

"Right before the uprising started. I was eleven at the time. Once I heard that he ended the uprising single-handedly, I expected him home within a month, but he never showed." Tears began to form in Mario's eyes.

"Let's go get those supplies, huh? It's your graduation day!" Tiberius suddenly exclaimed. Mario nodded in agreement.

The sun's heat berated their necks as they walk through the streets. They could hear the shouting and haggling from the marketplace a few streets away. Mario took the time to observe the people of Redfern while he walked. He saw children chase after one another fighting with wooden swords. He saw women cleaning their porches, trying to make it look as pristine as possible for when their husbands came home from work. He saw an old man lying in the gutter with a rusty sword and wearing what appeared to be a tarnished army uniform. He couldn't help but wonder how an army veteran could end up so destitute. Perhaps he had a gambling problem or was a little too fond of the drink. Mario's thoughts about the old man were interrupted when Tiberius stopped dead in his tracks, looking down a side alley. There, in the alley, were two men armed with broom handles beating an elf, who was hunched in the fetal position trying to protect his head with his hands.

"Tiberius, let it go. We have already been out for too long, and we shouldn't get in more trouble," Mario suggested, although he knew it would be to no avail.

"Isn't this why you became a knight?" Tiberius' voice shook with anger as his hands gripped the handle of his sword. "To protect the downtrodden, those who can't protect themselves!? Or do you only want to protect them when it is convenient for you!" Tiberius scolded, glaring angrily at Mario.

"We could summon the guards, and I just don't want to get in trouble with Headmaster—"

"The guards won't do anything; they'll see a 'knife-ear' getting berated and will sit back and watch or even join in if nobody is around to see it. Look, if you're so worried about getting in trouble, just go to the market. I'll meet you there . . . after I handle this." Tiberius marched towards the alley, still gripping his sword. Mario watched in stunned silence as his best friend marched angrily towards the alley. His conscience begged him to follow Tiberius, but his legs wouldn't obey. Instead, he stood there frozen in place, unable to take a step towards the elf and his attackers.

Mario continued on his way to the market, although he wasn't sure why. Tiberius was one of his best friends, who he would do anything for, but when it came time to actually do a knightly deed and help someone in need, he couldn't commit all because it may result in him not graduating today. The walk to the market was a long and somber one. Mario was ashamed of what he had done and began doubting if he really had the mettle to be a knight.

What if I'm on the road and see the same thing? Will I intervene then or will I turn tail and run like I did today? Was it because it was an elf? Would I have intervened if it was a human? These thoughts and more plagued Mario's mind, so much so, that he lost track of where he was and walked right into a fruit merchant's stand. After the necessary apologies, Mario managed to wrangle his thoughts and went around and bought all the supplies needed for the banquet: eggs, flour, bread, fruit, and some meat. Mario paid and tipped graciously since the merchants had agreed to bring the goods to the college, although it was mainly because he wanted to ease his guilt-ridden conscience.

On the way out of the market, Mario saw Tiberius, leaning on the wall of the entrance, covered in blood. He knew that it was not his blood. Mario didn't acknowledge him; instead, he looked at the ground and walked back towards the college.

"Tiberius, I'm sorr—"

"Don't. It's fine," Tiberius interjected, his voice was cold and harsh, which was unusual for him but understandable given the situation. Tiberius took a deep breath and continued, "I'll jump in the moat by the college and wash off, you know, so you don't get in trouble."

Mario nodded his head in acknowledgement. The rest of their walk was in silence.

***

"By the gods, Tiberius! You're soaking wet!" the headmaster shouted when he saw the two recruits come back from town.

"Well, I wouldn't be if I hadn't lost a bet," Tiberius grumbled. How well he could lie amazed Mario, even if it was not very knightly.

"What bet?" the headmaster questioned.

"I bet Mario that I could run to the market faster than him. He disagreed. So, the stakes were that the loser had to jump in the moat. The winner is clearly obvious," Tiberius said, flawlessly playing the role of a sore loser.

The headmaster sighed exasperatedly. "Bloody children . . . Well, get changed, Tiberius, and, Mario, come with me. It's time for your ceremony."

Mario complied and gave a nod to Tiberius as a thank-you. Tiberius replied with a cold stare. Shivers ran down Mario's spine, still in disbelief that he didn't help his friend.

For an old man, the headmaster could move quite quickly, as he was already several paces ahead of Mario. They walked through the winding hallways of the college, their footsteps echoing. The silence was palpable. Mario knew the headmaster was going to say something, perhaps he just hadn't found the right words yet.

Finally breaking the excruciating silence, the headmaster spoke. "Was there really a bet? Or did Tiberius just lie as a cover for even more asinine behaviour?"

Mario gulped, for this was going to be the first time he lied to an authority figure. "Yes, that's exactly what happened. I'm just glad I was faster so I wouldn't be soaking for my ceremony." Mario hoped that his lie was as convincing as Tiberius'.

For some time, the headmaster did not speak, obviously considering if Mario was telling the truth or not. Once again, he broke the lengthy silence. "I hope you are going to bring more professionalism and maturity to your knightly duties once you graduate."

"Absolutely, sir," Mario promptly replied, relieved that he was not asked any more questions about the incident.

The hall where the ceremony was held was so large that the entire town of Redfern could have gathered there for the banquet. Instead, twelve knights, ten recruits, and one headmaster were the only people present. The hall's architecture was based off of triangles: triangular windows instead of square ones, triangular doors in place of traditional square doors, the walls curving toward the roof to meet at a single, centre focal point. Clearly influenced by the elven architecture of the east, which was ironic since there had never been an elf to serve the order, and most knights secretly disliked non-humans. The room was lit by torches on the wall and a few key braziers on the floor to eliminate any and all shadows present.

Mario and the headmaster walked side-by-side down the middle of the room and up the steps to the platform where the ceremony took place. There were two instructors per step, one on either side. Finally, the headmaster donned the ceremonial robes, indicating to everyone watching that the ceremony was about to start.

"We have gathered here to witness one of the greatest moments in a young knight's life," the headmaster began, his voice echoing off the stone walls and filling the room. "Today, I'm proud to say we have one of the most gifted students I've seen in a long-time graduate. In fact, the last student I saw with your amount of talent and skill was your father, Sir Pablo Deschamps of Rougge. I think I speak for all of your instructors when I say you have a bright future ahead of you, if you choose to stay on the righteous path of knighthood. Now, do you solemnly swear to protect all those that are in your kingdom? To uphold the four virtues of bravery, honesty, integrity, and loyalty while you do so?"

"I swear it," Mario responded, his voice trembling with excitement.

"Then I hereby dub you *ordo equestris pro tem* until the moment you complete your first deed and until the king himself knights you. At which time, you will become an *ordo equestris*."

Mario stood, shook the headmaster's hand and turned to see the smiling faces of all his instructors and peers—except for Tiberius and the always scowling Sir Darius Withers. Mario was filled with joy. This was the moment he had worked his whole life for. He thought about each of the virtues he swore to and promised himself that he would uphold all of the virtues until his dying breath, no matter the cost. Little did he know that in under a year's time, he would break that promise.

A knight's first deed can be a trying time. For the first time in your young life, you have total authority over your decisions—to choose which tasks are beneath a knight of your ranking, which should be left to the common guard, and which tasks require the delicate touch of a trained professional. There is no shortage of evil, but an honourable knight should not waste his time tracking down the thief of a sweet roll. This would be a waste of his knightly abilities, and therefore, a waste of the king's gold.

Unknown,
The Knight's Handbook, XIV Edition

CHAPTER TWO

The banquet hall was unsurprisingly empty after the ceremony. It was no secret that Mario wasn't the most popular of the boys, and since attendance wasn't mandatory, many of the other students were absent. The lackluster attendance pained Mario's heart and injured his ego. When he had dreamed of this day as a boy, he pictured both the ceremony and the banquet to be full of his peers and mentors. In reality, it was only him and the instructors that didn't have to teach courses. Mario was playing with the piece of meat on his plate, sulking about the abysmal attendance of his banquet, when he felt a bony hand on his shoulder. He turned his head to see the headmaster's surprisingly sympathetic gaze.

"It's time for you to start your journey. Sir Darius is awaiting you in the armoury."

"Thank you, I'll head there right away." Mario struggled to put a smile on his face.

The walk from the banquet hall to the armoury was a fairly long one, but Mario didn't mind. He used the time in solitude to recollect his thoughts and cheer himself up. *I'm going on my first quest today. Who cares if nobody showed up to my banquet. I'm a knight!* As the idea of superiority consumed him, he couldn't help but continue his walk with swagger and his head held high.

The armoury was full of weapons and armour from throughout the centuries. Rays of sunlight glistened off the steel plates and swords as they seeped through the cracked and splintered walls. Mario always thought that the armoury smelled better than the rest of the keep. Tanned leather, freshly formed metal, and a subtle hint of burnt hickory filled his nose whenever he walked into the ten-by-fifteen-foot room. When he was a young recruit, he would often sneak into the armoury at night just to breathe in the smells and give his nose a break from the stench that was the recruit quarters.

"Hurry up and don your new armour," Sir Darius Withers barked.

Mario felt like a child on its birthday, he quickly ran and grabbed a set of plate armour that looked just like his father's. Sir Darius helped him don the plate armour, as it was usually a two-person job. The silence was unbearable.

"Do you think you will ever leave the college and resume your duties as a travelling knight one day?" Mario asked, unable to withstand the silence anymore.

"How does that feel?" Darius asked while tightening Mario's breastplate.

"Good. Do you know where I am heading for my first mission?" Mario continued, trying to avoid having to sit in excruciating silence.

"Listen, I am not your mum. Don't mistake me as someone who holds you dear to their heart. To me, you're just another student who will most likely be cut down within a year."

Mario gulped. *What could have made Darius such a jaded man? Perhaps he lost someone close to him while he was a knight, or maybe he regrets an ill-advised decision he made as a young man.*

As if able to read Mario's thoughts, Darius explained, "Young knights are often regaled as the bravest and most courageous of all the knights. The truth of the matter is that they are the most reckless, impulsive, and fool-hearty of the bunch."

"So, what—"

"My advice?" Darius asked, once again anticipating his question. "Trust what I taught you. Resist your impulses. Let your muscles guide you. The worst thing you could do in battle is let your mind cloud your judgement."

Mario sat in his teacher's advice for some time while Darius finished helping him don the rest of his armour. *Let my muscles guide me. Let my muscles guide me.* Mario repeated the veteran's words over and over in his head to ensure his brain would remember them in the heat of battle.

"A standard sword for a standard knight," Darius scoffed while holding a mundane sword. The hilt was in the shape of a cross and wrapped in brown leather for an easier grip; emerging from it, a double-edged blade, thirty-three inches long. Both blade and hilt were forged out of steel. "Go to the stables. Sir Augustine is waiting for you and will give you a horse. And don't forget your shield."

Mario nodded and hastily made his way to the stables trying to conceal his excitement. *Darius always was a cold man. I know Sir Augustine will give me a warm farewell.* His steel boots clanged off the stone floor of the college as he walked, echoing throughout the halls like thunder bellowing in an open field. He passed several of his former classmates on his way to the stables. They gave him stares of envy or indifference. Mario then spotted Tiberius walking to class.

"Hey! Tiberius!" Mario shouted, hoping that he would hear him.

Tiberius stopped, let out a sigh and made eye contact with Mario.

"I didn't see you at the ceremony or the banquet."

"I had to dry off remember?" Tiberius' tone was still harsh and cold.

"Well, I hope we will meet one day on the road. Who knows, maybe we will even fight some bandits together!"

"Sure, take care, Mario." Tiberius turned away and continued walking to class.

"Tiberius, wait!" Mario shouted.

Once again, Tiberius stopped, let out a sigh and turned to face Mario.

"I don't want us to part like this. You have been my best friend for the last five years. . . . I'm sorry for not helping you in town."

"Mario . . . not only did you not help me in town, but you also didn't help that elf. Hopefully, with your new armour and sword, you'll act like a knight. I have to get to class." Tiberius turned and walked away in a hurry.

Mario stood there, basking in the weight of the words of his former best friend. As he continued walking alone in the empty hallway, Mario promised to himself that he would help the next elf he saw in need, no matter the circumstances.

Unlike the armoury, the stables had no pleasant smells. The large wooden barn was filled exclusively with the smells of moulding hay, old oats, piss, and shit. Even in this environment, however, Sir Augustine still managed to look magnificent. Long blonde hair blowing in the wind at the end of the barn. He was holding the reins of a majestic brown mare, who had already been saddled and was just as eager as Mario to start their adventure.

"Sir Mario Deschamps!" Augustine cheerfully called out.

"I'm not a knight yet, Sir Augustine. I still have to complete my first deed. . . ."

"I judge from your tone that Sir Darius spoke to you about young knights dying. Pay no mind to him, Mario. You're one of the most gifted recruits I've had in years, and I know the headmaster feels the same. You are every recruit's better when it comes to sword work, you know the Knight's Handbook like the back of your hand, and you are the only recruit to pass the gauntlet on the first try."

Memories of enduring the gauntlet flooded Mario's mind. It was easily the hardest test every recruit had to pass. One had to survive an onslaught of arrows, dodge swinging logs that were determined to knock a person down on their arse, and successfully parry, block, and counter an instructor's attacks—all while wearing full-plate armour in the hottest month of the year. He remembered how sore he was after finishing it, and the relentless stinging in his muscles in the following days. He also remembered the burning of his throat as he vomited into his steel helmet upon completion.

"I know you'll bring honour to the order and your father's legacy," Sir Augustine said, interrupting the young knight's thoughts.

Mario's eyes welled with tears, but he managed to pull himself together in front of his mentor. "Is this my mount? What is her name?"

"That's for you to decide. A knight should always choose the name of his mount himself." Augustine smiled, pretending not to notice the tears in Mario's eyes.

Mario hopped on the horse and patted the mare's neck. The mare nickered in response to the touch of the metal gauntlet on her neck. "I think I'll name her Priscilla."

"Priscilla? May I inquire as to why?"

"Well my father's horse was Penelope, and my grandfather's horse was Persephone. So, it's somewhat of a Deschamps family tradition."

"Keeping with tradition, I like it," Augustine said as he looked up to Mario with a glowing smile.

"So where is my first mission?" Mario asked eagerly.

"You know I can't tell you. An *ordo equestris pro tem* must find their first deed on their own. But I'll give you some advice. I have heard that the people of Eulway are in need of a knight. Perhaps, that will be a good place to start."

"I thank you, Sir Augustine. I will head there now. I hope to see you in a few months once I have completed my first deed."

"I know you will, just remember what we taught you," Augustine said as he waved goodbye to the fresh-faced recruit, who rode off on his new horse towards the village of Eulway. This was the last time Mario saw his mentor.

***

The first day of travel was exactly how Mario imagined it. The landscape was breathtaking, and he made sure to ride at a leisurely pace so he could appreciate its beauty properly. In the fields beside the road, peasants were already harvesting the golden-brown wheat. Every town he rode through was filled with people who were ecstatic to see him. Women cried and swooned as he rode past, and men scrambled to try and touch his suit of armour. In one of the towns, Mario tossed a few coins to the awestruck children, who stared in amazement as he rode by. A smile broke across his lips. As he travelled further west, the landscape changed from golden fields of brown to luscious green hills, and then into a forest of orange, red, and yellow. As he laid his head down for the night, underneath the stars, he couldn't help but smile as he thought about the day's events. *This is the life.*

On the second day, monotony set in. The landscape gradually turned from beautiful to dull; the townsfolk went from excited to cold indifference. When he first left the college, he thought that adventure would be around every corner and that there would be no shortage of heroics and great deeds. However, the second day proved that this was not the norm; in fact, the life of a knight was quite lonely and boring. Throughout the day, Mario found himself daydreaming or recalling memories from his time in the college, and this lulled him into a state of inattentiveness. On the night of his second day, Mario had to stretch his saddle-sore body before he adjourned to his bedroll. Even the ground proved to be less comfortable than the first night. He tossed and turned all night long and barely got a few hours of sleep.

On the morning of the third day, Mario heard faint screaming coming from down the road. "Come on, Priscilla! Heeyaw!" Mario exclaimed as he spurred his horse to a gallop. Priscilla's hooves sounded like thunder as they pounded against the dirt road. The wind pierced through his armour, cooling the sweat under his armpits and on his neck. Mario thought back to the tales his mother used to tell him as a child. The tales where evil spectres chased naughty children with steeds faster than the wind. *I am sure Priscilla could outrun those horses.* A smile crept onto his face as he thought about racing one of the mythical spectres with his new horse.

Mario could see a large shadow on the side of the road, and the screaming had become more distinct. "Help! Somebody in the name of the gods help me!"

Mario urged Priscilla further, pushing her to her limits of speed. She let out a heavy snort every time her hooves would thud against the dirt. Mario could begin to see that the shadow was a tipped over wagon. He pulled back on his reins and slowly trotted to the fallen wagon.

"Hello? Is someone there?" a voice called out from beneath the wagon.

Mario remembered that knights were supposed to conduct themselves in a distinguished and civilized manner, especially when dealing with commoners. "Yes! It is I, Mario Deschamps! An *ordo equestris pro tem!*" Mario exclaimed, hoping his voice would sound regal and knightly.

"Oh, praise to the gods! A knight, just what I need! Please, help me. I'm stuck under this wagon," the voice exclaimed.

Mario dismounted and walked around to the other side of the wagon and saw that the source of the voice was a man pinned underneath it. The middle-aged man was wearing a leather cap, and dirt covered his face. *Nothing like a merchant, but perhaps he is a farmer or just some hired muscle to protect the cart from bandits.*

"What happened here?" Mario asked.

"Some bandits attacked us! They were able to flip the cart, and before I could run away, it fell on my leg! Please, it hurts so bad!" the man called out, his voice reflecting his pain.

"Where is the rest of your party? And how did they manage to flip the wagon on you?"

"How the hell should I know! I was just walking beside it, and the next thing I know the damn wagon flipped on my leg! Please help!"

"No matter, I will assist you, fair citizen. Then we shall get to the bottom of this." Mario approached the man, and as he went to place his hands where the stranger's leg was stuck, he noticed that there was a groove carved out in the wagon right where the leg was positioned.

Suddenly, Mario heard Priscilla whinny. He looked up and saw another man riding away on her back. "Stop, you scoundrel!" he shouted. Mario then felt a cold, piercing sensation on the left side of his ribcage. He looked down and saw that the man had pulled his leg out from under the wagon and stuck him with a dagger. The man adeptly pulled Mario's sword from his scabbard and shoved him to the ground. Mario clutched his side as blood poured from underneath his armour.

"Thanks for the help, Sir Deschamps!" the bandits cackled as they rode away on Priscilla.

I'm going to die. Not even three days as a knight, and I'm going to die. Hoodwinked like a common fool. Sir Darius was right. Mario struggled to stand up, but he knew he had to at least move to the other side of the wagon so he was visible to travellers on the road. *Hopefully, a good Samaritan will pass by.* Mario knew that this was a fool's thought. In all likelihood, he would bleed out on the side of that road.

With great effort, Mario managed to crawl to the other side. He leaned his back against the wagon. "And now, let us hope for a miracle," he said aloud as he began to lose consciousness.

***

Mario awoke to the bouncing movement and the sound of a cart's wheels turning on stones and dirt. Every jostle of the cart sent shockwaves of pain shooting up his spine. He opened his eyes and saw only the moonlight and the stars overhead. He let out a groan of pain when the cart hit a hole in the road.

"Will you drive straight!" a voice shouted.

"I cannae see a bloody thing! 'Tis darker than a fuckin' gold mine," another voice barked in response.

"I thought dwarves were supposed to be good at seeing in the dark?" asked a third voice.

"Oi? What good are ye halflings, then? Fuzz-footed bastards . . ." the second voice retorted.

"Enough!" the first voice shouted. "If we don't hurry, this man will die. Gods know how long he was on that road for. He was as pale as snow when we found him."

The only response was another crack of the reins. Mario didn't have the energy to thank his saviours. He didn't even have the strength to move his head to look them in the eyes. All he could do was stare at the night sky until he lost consciousness again.

***

The cracking of the fire woke Mario. His side ached, albeit far less than it did when he awoke in the cart. He turned his head to see a dwarf and halfling playing cards, illuminated by a fireplace. He looked around the small wooden hut and saw that it was filled with jars containing strange herbs, fluids, or insects. He let out a groan as he shifted his body weight to the side.

"Oi! He's awake!" shouted the dwarf.

Mario had so many questions, but his mouth wouldn't open. The only sound he could utter were moans of pain.

"Everybody out!" a fourth voice called as their silhouette entered the hut. The voice was feminine but exuded authority.

Mario saw the dwarf and the halfling leave the hut and watched as the silhouette of the woman approached him.

"Don't worry. You'll be okay," the figure said. Although she was mere inches from Mario's face, he still could not make out a single feature. "You need rest." The figure's voice was strangely soothing and comforting. Suddenly, she raised her hand to Mario's face and said, *"Glavus cairen."* A blinding blue light erupted from her hand, briefly illuminating her face. Mario quickly lost consciousness once again.

This time when Mario awoke there was no firelight. Instead, sunlight was pouring through the cracks of the hut's wooden exterior. As Mario began to sit up, he was surprised to realize the pain in his side was gone. He looked down at his ribcage and saw a large scar that had been healed over. No stitches, no cauterization, only magic. Mario pulled himself out of bed and walked towards the door of the hut. When he opened the door, the sunlight blinded him, instinctively he raised his left hand to shield his eyes. Once again, he was surprised by the lack of pain he felt—the only sensation, a small tingling by the scar.

"Look who's back from the dead!" the halfling shouted as his four saviours were crowded by a small campfire eating some food.

"Yeah, an' he's bloody naked! Put your meat tassel away boy!" the dwarf snickered.

Mario looked down and, to his horror, realized he wasn't wearing any pants. Mario quickly ran to a nearby clothesline and wrapped some cloth around his waist. The rest of the camp chuckled.

"I owe you all a great debt of gratitude," Mario said, trying to not dwell on his indecency.

"Don't worry, I'm a healer. It's what I do," the woman said as she tried to keep eye contact with Mario.

Mario could feel his face turn red as he began sweating even though it was a cool summer morning. "What . . . What do I call you?" Mario asked, trying to eliminate some of the awkwardness.

The halfling spoke first. "Well, I'm Roger Bumblefoot." Roger had a small beard and a head of curly light brown hair. He wore a small grey woollen coat with brown pants. Like most halflings, he was barefoot, exposing his hairy feet for all the world to see. "This here is Miles Thaler." Roger pointed towards the male human, who was eating a cooked squirrel. Miles looked about thirty-six years old. His long brown hair was tied up into a ponytail, and he wore a head-band around his forehead. He was quite lean, not an ounce of fat on him, but by no means a strongman. "This crotchety old bastard is Finnegan Graeme." This time Roger pointed toward the dwarf, who was riddled with crumbs and had grass tangled in his greyish beard.

"Who ya calling a bastard, ya feather-footed prick!" Finnegan snapped back.

"Gentlemen, please! I'm sure the knight doesn't want to hear you two bicker!" Miles Thaler spoke up.

"How do you know I'm a knight?"

"Well, how do you think, lad? 'Tis not every day ya see someone in full-plate armour who's not a knight," Finnegan said as he took a bite out of the cooked squirrel.

"Where is my armour?"

"In my hut," the woman answered. "But I must know, is the college sending knights without horses and swords now? The king must have stopped viewing your order as an essential service." Her voice was riddled with sarcasm and a smile cracked over her lips.

"You're . . . you're a witch?" Mario questioned, even though he very well knew the answer.

"I hate that term. People say witch and immediately think I'm tricking gullible children into an oven in a house made of sweets. But if you mean a woman who practises magic in solitude, then, yes, I'm a witch." Her smile remained on her face, but the tone of her voice was much less playful than before. For someone who lived in solitude, she did appear to be quite civilized. Fashionable clothes, short blonde hair, tasteful makeup, and even some bejewelled earrings.

"If we didn't bring you to Marian, you surely would've died. No common surgeon could've saved you. You lost too much blood," explained Miles.

"How far of a journey is it to Eulway?" Mario asked.

"About half a day ride, why?" Roger Bumblefoot answered.

"I was told to go there. It's where my first deed is to be completed."

"Well, we're heading there anyway, so we'd be happy to travel with you," Miles replied.

"If he can handle the journey," retorted Roger, while looking towards Marian for reassurance.

Marian eyed Mario from top to bottom and, after a while, finally spoke. "Yes, I'm sure a man of his build is ready for that journey. Just take it slow." A coy smile spread across her face. Mario instantly recognized it as the same smile the barmaid had when she looked at him at the tavern in Redfern.

"I should get dressed." Mario shyly walked back into the hut.

"Take your time, lad! I still got half a squirrel to finish!" Finnegan called from outside the hut.

The hut smelled of ash as the embers from the fireplace were still smouldering from the night before. Mario dropped his improvised loincloth and began to find his clothes so he could don his armour. Suddenly, the door swung open and Mario spun around, covering his unmentionables with his helmet. Standing in the doorway and giggling was Marian. She shut the door behind her.

"Let me help you with that," she said with a smile.

"Um . . . dear madam, I don't think—"

"Madam!? A few seconds ago, I was a witch, and now I'm a madam? How I've moved up in the world!" Marian laughed.

"I . . . um . . ."

"Relax. I won't bite. Believe it or not, I know donning armour is a two-person job. Now let me help you."

Marian's hands felt as soft as silk. The armour seemed to glide on with ease, no doubt with the help of her magic. Mario couldn't help but admire her beauty. He kept getting lost in her deep blue eyes whenever they made eye contact with his. *This must be how the townswomen feel when they see Sir Augustine.* Once Mario was fully covered in armour, save for his helmet, she took a step back and admired him. He did the same to her.

"My, you look exquisite in that armour." Her eyes met with Mario's.

"You . . . um, look fine yourself."

Marian let out a hearty laugh. "Thank you, but you're not my type. A little young for my taste."

Mario could feel his face turning red again, but he decided to quickly change the subject. "Why did you help me?"

"Like you, I set off to help people. Unlike knights, however, magic is looked down upon, and some people will try to lynch or even burn those who practise it. All because of one power-hungry man at Caspula."

Mario nodded; he knew the tale of Caspula very well. His mother had often told him the story of the evil sorcerer and heroic boy who killed him. "Thank you. It's nice to know that not all mages are evil." Both Marian and Mario exited the hut.

Outside, Finnegan Graeme was sitting on the cart, which was already hooked up to a horse. Miles Thaler and Roger Bumblefoot were finishing up with loading supplies in the back.

"Are you ready to head towards Eulway?" Roger asked.

"Ready as I'll ever be," Mario retorted.

"Sorry, lad, you'll have to walk. No more room in the back. But I'll keep it nice and slow for ya," Finnegan explained.

"I'm fine with that. I could use a bit of exercise."

"Marian your payment," Miles said, handing the mage a small burlap pouch.

"Thank you, Miles. And do take it easy."

"We will. Until next time."

As the four unlikely travel companions departed, Mario looked back at the witch's hut in the small clearing of the forest. He also couldn't help taking one last look at Marian, who was just as stunning from a distance as she was up close.

The fair folk of Eulway have seen hard times for generations. It was as if the gods themselves hated that small village. Constantly plagued by war, famine, disease, droughts, floods, and infestations of monsters. The people of this town have seen, and more importantly, endured through all. A testament to their willpower.

Master Aegius Laramonde,
History of Settlements in the Kingdom of Drussdell

CHAPTER THREE

By mid-afternoon, the sun was hot and unforgiving. Mario's freshly cleaned clothes were already soaked in sweat. The visor of his helmet was lifted so that the stench could escape and not be trapped underneath his plate armour. The main road offered little shade; most of the trees had been cut down so that wagons could easily travel. Roger and Miles both sat in the back of the cart. Miles was whittling a small figurine out of a piece of wood he found near the witch's hut, while Roger complained about the heat, fanning himself with his hand. Finnegan Graeme drove the cart, occasionally grumbling under his breath at Roger's complaints.

"We never got ya name, lad. What do we call ya?" Finnegan said, finally taking a break from his angry grumbling.

"I'm Mario. Mario Deschamps."

"A Deschamps? You're shittin' me! Me brother met one while he was the army blacksmith during the Elven Uprising."

"A Pablo!?"

"Aye, that's the one. Me brother said he was a right prick."

"Oh . . ." Mario's shoulders slouched, and he looked down at the ground.

"Don't take it personally, kid. Me brother is an insufferable bastard. Ya could give him a pouch of gold, and he would still say something awful 'bout ya."

Mario lifted his head to meet Finnegan's stare.

"Was he your father?"

"Yes . . ."

"What's it like having a knight as a father?" Roger Bumblefoot said, taking a break from his whining.

Mario went on to tell his new companions the whole story. That his father had left when he was thirteen to fight in the Elven Uprising. How he had heard tales that his father single-handedly ended the Elven Uprising, and that a few months after hearing these tales, he had expected his father home. Mario also told his companions that his father never did return.

"Ah, that's a tough break, lad. I'm sorry," Finnegan stated.

"What about you three? You saved my life, yet I truly don't know much about you."

"Well—" Finnegan started.

"I am the youngest of five!" Roger interrupted. "I grew up in the Kingdom of Keten, in the small settlement of Andreshire, primarily a halfling settlement. Ever since I was a young age, I craved to see the world, so when I met Miles, I immediately joined him."

"What is it that you do exactly?"

"We are cobblers. Travelling around fixing people's shoes," Miles explained. "It's not a glamorous job, and it won't make you rich, but it's a living."

"Bloody ironic that a halfling is a cobbler. Doesn't even wear shoes himself!" Finnegan snorted from the front of the cart.

"What about you, Finnegan? Are you not a cobbler?"

"Gods no! I wouldn't be caught dead in such a boring profession. I'm . . . uh . . . I'm . . . Miles, what's my job title again?"

"Transport and defence extraordinaire."

"Aye, right, or in common tongue—the muscle." Finnegan grinned, flexing his bicep.

"And our driver!" Roger Bumblefoot added.

Finnegan grumbled under his breath and gripped the reins even tighter, so much so that his knuckles began to turn white.

"Why didn't you become a blacksmith like your brother?" Mario inquired.

"Truth be told, the forge never interested me. I was never good at shaping and heatin' metals, let alone being put in tight spaces and breathin' in all that shite. I'd much rather be above ground, and only in front of a fire to heat me grub," Finnegan explained, scratching the bits of cooked squirrel and bread out of his tangled beard.

"So, tell me, Mario, how did someone manage to get the better of a knight?" Miles asked curiously.

Mario felt his face go red. He silently cursed to himself underneath his helmet. He could hear the sound of Sir Darius' harsh voice mocking him in the back of his head. "I thought someone was in need of assistance. . . . Turns out it was a simple trap, and I was blinded by my naivety."

Miles shook his head, "Nonsense, you thought someone was in trouble and went to their aid. A willingness to help people isn't a curse, Mario. It's a gift."

His words rang in Mario's head. He felt the colour of his face return to its normal complexion. Whenever you made an error in the college, Mario was used to being berated by his instructors. But for some reason, Miles' praise filled his body with a warm sensation. A smile broke across his lips.

"Besides," Miles interrupted Mario's thoughts, "I'm sure your father would say the same thing."

Mario barely managed to stifle his tears at the compliment. He quickly, and stiffly, nodded his head in thanks and turned his head forward to avoid Miles' friendly gaze. Otherwise he would've burst into tears. "How do you know Marian?" he asked, eager to change the subject.

"I've known her years," Miles responded. "We've been in and out of each other's lives so much that it's hard to remember how we first met. I think I first saw her in the capital when she was a royal mage, and I was just starting my cobbling business."

"There were royal mages?" Roger asked in complete disbelief.

"Oh yes. At one point, every king had a retinue of mages at their disposal. One that dealt with infertility, one for reading omens, one for disease, one for poor crop yields, and so on." Miles paused briefly; the sound of his knife cutting into the small wooden figurine filled the void. "Then it all came crashing down because of that damned mage at Caspula. Because of one bad apple, mages like Marian had to flee and go into hiding."

"I'm sorry," Mario apologized, though he did not know why. He knew Miles was angry but could not think of anything else to say.

"What're you whittling there, Miles?" Roger asked, once again changing the subject of the long hot walk.

"A griffon. It's for my son; he loves them. I hope to give it to him as a present when I see him again." Miles' voice was calm, but Mario noticed it had a subtle hint of regret in it.

"How old is he?" Mario asked.

"He's six . . . was six. He passed away two years ago. Some sickness gripped him. And neither the doctors nor the mages could save him." Miles' voice trailed off. Tears began to run down his face. "Worst part is I was on the road when it happened. I wasn't even there to bury my son," his voice cracked.

The party was shocked. Nobody knew about Miles' son. Not Roger, Finnegan, and especially not Mario. They let the pain of their comrade sink in. The only sound heard was the jingling of the horse's tack and the sound of the wheels of the cart crushing the dirt of the road as it rolled.

"I'm . . . I'm truly sorry, Miles. I didn't know," Roger said.

"How could you? You are the first people I've told since I found out about it. In fact, that's the first time I've even acknowledged his death aloud. I just hope that the gods are taking care of him now and that he forgives me for not being there when he needed me." Miles dropped his knife and stared at the half-carved griffon figurine.

The party walked in silence for a good part of the journey after that; the cracking of the reins, the chirping of the birds, the sound of the wagon moving, and the occasional cough or clearing of the throat were all that could be heard.

After a few hours of travelling this way, the party came across an old man sitting on the side of the road. He was wearing long black robes, with gold seams and cuffs. Stitched in the middle of his chest was a large golden sun. However, you could barely tell it was a sun since most of it was covered by his long grey beard that went down to his knees. Once the old man spotted the party, he erupted into a fit of anger, and rage.

"Begone! Travel no further! Your kind are not welcome in the village of Eulway! These are decent people who will not be corrupted by your wicked ways, for they are under the protection of the Golden Sun, whose light shines brightly on all noble creatures," the old man shouted while pointing at Finnegan Graeme.

"Sod off, you damned heretic," Finnegan sharply replied.

"Heretic!? The Golden Sun will smite you for your blasphemous tongue! For his light warms the souls of the righteous and burns those of the damned!"

"You must've stayed in the shade then because you're as rotten as they come!" Roger Bumblefoot retorted as he lifted his head from the back of the cart.

"A halfling and a dwarf!? What they say is true: 'Evil comes in pairs.' Begone! I shall let you pass no further! The good people of Eulway have accepted the Golden Sun as their saviour and have suffered enough. Your kind, you . . . you non-humans, only bring suffering, disease, and evil upon decent, noble people!"

"And what am I if not one of those noble creatures?" Mario sharply interjected.

"Golden Sun have mercy! They've corrupted a knight!? Does your evil know no bounds!" the old man screamed. "Listen, my child, it is not too late for you. Accept the Golden Sun as your saviour, and you can still be redeemed. Repent your blasphemous ways and come into the light! The Golden Sun forgives all and only asks that you serve and help others bask in his glorious light,'" the priest said to Mario, gripping him by the shoulders of his plate armour.

"Listen, old man," Miles said while standing up in the back of the cart. "These two 'non-humans,' as you put it, are my employees, and I will not have them cursed at. And this knight is a dear friend of whom I'm escorting to Eulway, for he has business there. So, go and spread your filth elsewhere to ears more gullible than ours." His voice was harsh and cutting. There was no trace of the man who was crying in the back of the cart only a few hours ago. This man was angry and willing to defend his friends no matter the cost.

The priest let go of Mario's shoulders as they pressed into to town. "You'll see, you'll all see! When the day of reckoning comes and the Golden Sun does not shine on you, only then will you see the error of your ways!" the priest called out as they continued to make their way towards Eulway.

***

Smoke filled the muddy narrow streets of Eulway, and the smell of burnt flesh filled the village. The smoke burned Mario's eyes and vomit filled his mouth as he walked down the cramped, overflowing streets. Everywhere he looked people were either dead or dying. Almost all had black dots on their skin. Their eyes were milky and bloodshot; the colour of their irises, a sickly white. *Gods, what happened here? This is nothing like the town of Redfern.*

"Bring out your dead!" yelled a man as he rang a bell. He was pulling a wagon loaded with bodies. Most of the people on the wagon were either elderly or children. All were dead.

"Aren't these people protected by the Golden Sun?" Finnegan muttered sarcastically.

"Now's not the time for that Mr. Graeme," Miles scolded. "These people are sick, and I'm afraid even the likes of Marian's magic can't save them."

"What makes you say that?" Roger asked.

"She's quite powerful for a mage, but you would need a master sorcerer to combat a plague like this. The only thing we can do for them now is pray."

Mario didn't like feeling so helpless. He joined the order so he could help people, not stand by and watch them suffer as they slowly approached an agonizing death. *Unfortunately, there are some problems that a sword cannot fix.*

"Keep an eye out for a guardsman or the sheriff. That's who you'll need to talk to in order to find out if there is work for you here," Miles said, almost unaffected by the horrendous sight that surrounded him.

As they progressed through the streets, Mario felt like the villagers were glaring at him. Everywhere he looked a dying person stared at him angrily through their dying eyes. *What do they want me to do? I'm no cleric, no healer. I'm just a knight!*

Suddenly, a middle-aged woman approached them carrying a baby. Her head was wrapped in a dirty cloth, but Mario could still see the black splotches on her skin and her sickening milky eyes.

"Please! Please! Take my baby! Spare it from this curse!" the woman begged, extending her child towards Mario.

"I . . . I'm sorry, ma'am. I cannot," Mario solemnly answered. He felt a lump in his throat as he saw the woman's eyes swell with tears.

"Best keep your distance, Mario. Lest you want to suffer from the same blight as these folks," Miles warned, his voice not wavering in the slightest.

Mario nodded and made sure to keep a distance of at least three feet from the woman as he walked by her. They could hear her sorrow-filled wails all the way down the street.

"There! At the end of the street! Look!" Roger Bumblefoot cried out from the back of the cart.

Mario looked where Roger was pointing and saw a grizzled, middle-aged man wearing a guard gambeson. The man was answering the dying pleas from the citizens of Eulway, doing his best to remain calm, but he was clearly frustrated with the number of people he was trying to talk to. Mario decided to approach him.

"Excuse me, good sir. My name is Mario Deschamps, and I am an *ordo equestris pro tem.* I heard that you may be in the need of a knight." His noble voice overpowered and deafened the cries for help from the peasants.

"Aye, we's could use an extra hand dealing with this lot," the guard said while pointing towards the crowd of people that surrounded him with his head.

"Although, somethin' tells me that a task like that is beneath yous." The guard spat on the ground.

"I am not much of a healer, unfortunately," Mario replied. He could feel sweat drip down the back of his neck underneath his helmet and chainmail.

The guard stood silent for a while, ignoring the pleas of the peasants surrounding him. "Walk with me," he said, pushing his way through the crowd. "We's have heard tales of some bandits attacking a few local farmers, kidnapping the womenfolk, the usual. We's been so busy trying to keep order that we's haven't had a chance to investigate."

"When did these reports happen?" Mario asked.

"Hmm . . . about three months ago, maybe four."

"The plague has been going on for four months! Why have you not sent for aid?"

"The plague started just under a month ago."

"Why didn't you investigate the claims when they happened?" Mario's voice was beginning to shake with anger.

"We's don't have time to investigate every claim when they come in. Hell, most of them are fake."

Mario stared at the guard silently for some time, trying to quell the anger that was boiling within him. Once he regained his composure, he continued, "Tell me all the significant events in the past few months."

The guard snorted his nose and spat on the ground. "Well, about five months ago, bandits were attacking the nearby villages of Yulga and Creighton. So we's increased our diligence and what not. Then about four months ago, the bandits attacked us. Murdering, stealing, raping, and pillaging. Gods blast it. I've been a guard for fifteen years, and I ain't never seen bandits like these before. Theys ruthless, cruel, bloodthirsty savages! Usually, bandits try to extort coin or give a ransom of some kind, but not these. Theys focus solely on destruction. Then after our eighth bandit raid on the village's surrounding farms, some priests came to town. Preaching some new God that was benevolent and would protect us from these attacks."

"The Golden Sun?" Mario interrupted.

"Aye, those are the cunts," the guard said. "At first we's paid them no mind. Theys were preaching that the raids were happening cause we's was corrupt and in need of cleansing, but the raids kept happening. Finally, the mayor allowed them to use an abandoned house for their temple. A few weeks later, the raids stopped, with only the occasional missing cow or burned down barn. The people began to believe in this 'Golden Sun' and left the old gods for this new fancier one." The guard spat on the ground and shook his head. "These priests, preaching that the non-humans are the cause of all misery. Folks started believing them and started exiling their neighbours; people that they've known for years! We's lost our blacksmith, a few elven families, and our doctor. We's sure could use her now the plague has shown up, and these priests claiming it's a 'cleansing,' saying it will only affect those who are corrupt and interacted with the non-humans!" The guard's voice started to shake.

"I'm sorry, I met one of those priests on my travels to Eulway. I'll look into these bandits for you, but I can't do anything about the clergy men," Mario said, removing his helmet so the guard could see his face.

"That'd be great, although yous would need a guide who knows the area like the back of his hand."

"You said you've been a guard for fifteen years. How about you?"

"I'm just a guard . . . I . . ."

A smile spread across Mario's face as he recalled a rule that he had learned about while in the Knight's College. "Sir," he began, "as a vassal to the king, you must aid me when requested. Failure to do so will result with you being charged for treason."

The guard stood there shocked. It seemed as if Mario's words had taken all the wind out of his lungs. The guard swallowed and said, "Fine, let's go now."

"Not yet. I need to requisition a sword from your blacksmith. Point me in his direction."

"Did yous not listen? He's been kicked out of the village 'cause of those priests!"

"My mistake. . . ." Mario's face began to turn red, making him regret taking off his helmet. "What about the guards? Surely you have an armoury I can use."

"Aye, we's do. . . . Follow me."

"Meet me back here. I must say farewell to my companions, for I fear this is where we will part ways."

The guard nodded and walked away, grumbling under his breath. Mario put on his helmet and walked back into town to find Roger, Miles, and Finnegan. It didn't take him long to find his companions, as the town of Eulway was quite small. He saw Miles buying some supplies from a vendor and Roger loading them into the cart.

"Are you departing?" Mario asked, already knowing the answer.

"Yes, there is no place for us here," Miles replied. "We will head to the town of Riverwell. There's always a need for a cobbler there."

"Will you be joining us?" Roger eagerly asked.

"Unfortunately, no. The people need me here. They've been plagued by more than disease recently." Mario tried to hide the disappointment in his voice.

"Well, if you're ever in Riverwell, lad, be sure to check if we're still there. I'll show you how dwarves drink!" Finnegan said before letting out a hearty laugh.

Mario nodded his head and smiled. "I will friends. So long."

With a crack of the reins, the cart set off. Finnegan Graeme drove with Roger Bumblefoot and Miles Thaler sitting in the back. Mario turned away and walked towards where he to meet the guard. Although Mario was sad to leave his new friends' side, deep down, he knew he would see them again.

Standing near the outskirts of town stood the guard holding a second sword in his hand. "Shall we set off?" the guard asked in a grizzled voice.

"Before we do, what do I call you, good man?"

"Hamish, my name's Hamish."

"Well, Hamish, let us not tarry any longer. We have some bandits to track down."

The Eeragwia Forest is fraught with dangers. Full of beasts of all kinds. Wolves, bears, boars, and, of course, monsters. Those who travel there are either fools or have a death sentence, for only a few men have ever returned from venturing deep into the bowels of this forest.

Samuel Kumar,
Memoir of an Explorer

The Golden Sun shines only on man, for he is the only one befitting to rule this world. Dwarves, elves, and halflings only have one goal: to corrupt the purity of man.

The Book of the Golden Sun

INTERLUDE

Lukas Aurelius was an ordinary man with no distinguishing features. He was of average height and build, and he always wore generic, bland colourless clothing. However, this was part of his gift. He could blend into a crowd of people and always remain invisible. This was the reason he was the emperor's best spy.

Sunlight leaked into the emperor's war room from the east-facing balcony, which overlooked the capital of the Valerian empire, Kaspyia. The sounds of the city poured into the room.

"Gods! Will that rabble ever quite down!" Minister of Finance Plutarch Segerius exclaimed.

"You've lived here for half a century, Plutarch. I would think you would be used to it by now," General Gaius Corvus scoffed.

"Or is your new estate far enough from the city that you can't hear the noise anymore?" Minister of Foreign Affairs Simian Perculus sneered.

"And where is your estate, Simian? Oh right, you've wasted all your coin on adultery," Plutarch retorted.

"At least he has fun . . ." Minister of Magic Constatine Aegius interjected, "unlike some of us." He gestured to Lukas Aurelius, who was listening from the shadows of the room.

"Do you ever stop working, Lukas?" Constantine asked.

"As a spy, you always have to be working; otherwise, you'll end up stabbed in the back," Lukas answered, keeping his face hidden in the shadows.

"Even amongst friends like us?" Plutarch Segerius asked.

"Especially amongst friends. How else would I protect our dear emperor from domestic threats? You see, I find it interesting that you have built a brandnew estate when only a few months ago you filed for bankruptcy." Lukas Aurelius lifted his face so his dagger-like eyes could meet with Plutarch's. A bead of sweat ran down the minister's face. "You complain about the noise, but what you hear as noise Plutarch, I hear as information. And information is power."

The war room fell silent. Every minister looked down at the floor and didn't dare to utter another word. Suddenly, the doors to the room swung open, and the angry footsteps of the emperor echoed as he marched across the cold marble floor. Everyone stood at attention when he entered, not only out of protocol, but out of fear as well. The emperor was rarely in a good mood and would easily replace anyone if they upset him in any way.

"Hail V!" shouted Minister of Finance Plutarch Segerius. The remaining advisors made a sharp salute with their arms and shouted, "Hail V!" in unison.

Emperor Vesuvius Vladimir Valerius was the fifth of his name and by far the cruellest. His appearance conveyed an aura of authority that everyone obeyed. His pale, steely eyes caused men's heart to fill with fear. Although Lukas Aurelius was completely loyal to the emperor, he still felt uneasy that he could never decipher the emperor's thoughts by examining his face. The emperor was stoic and expressionless, making it difficult for anyone to gain insight on him.

"Leave us," the emperor croaked in his trademark monotone voice.

"But, Your Excellency, we have matters to discuss. . . ." Minister of Foreign Affairs Simian Perculus started.

"Guards, feed Minister Perculus to the dogs and have someone find me a replacement by lunch," the emperor said while picking at some dirt stuck under his fingernail.

"Wait! No!" Perculus pleaded before he was dragged out of the room by three ebony armoured guards. The rest of the ministers quickly exited the war room without uttering a single word.

"What have you found out for me, Aurelius?" the emperor said while looking at the world map, which rested on the pedestal in the middle of the room.

"Everything is going according to plan, Your Excellency," Lukas Aurelius quickly answered.

"Specifics, please." The emperor continued to avoid eye contact with the spy in the shadows of the room.

"Well . . ." Lukas Aurelius approached the pedestal. "The northern kingdoms are at each other's throats. Without the common enemy of the elves, their alliance has dissolved and they have begun to squabble with each other once again."

"Excellent. Continue."

"In the western most Kingdom of Artanzia, King Tryton is trying to combat a fierce famine. However, because of his lack of aid during the Elven Uprising, the other northern kings are not keen in giving him support. This means he is desperate for an ally, which also means we would have great leverage on him if you decide to make an alliance with him, Your Excellency."

"I agree. It will be the first task I assign to my new foreign affairs minister when I meet him."

"The kingdom of the Far North, Keten, is quietly biding their time. They are moving their forces to their west and southeast borders. According to my sources, they plan to invade and conquer Artanzia once the famine has made them weak, and then launch a campaign against the Kingdom of Drussdell."

The emperor let out a small snort of air. Lukas Aurelius knew that this meant to continue with the debriefing.

"The rumours we heard were true. King Dryden III of Drussdell is nothing like his father. He is young, impulsive, and above all, clueless on how his kingdom is run. Our plan to incite chaos in his kingdom should go off without any problems."

"We should quickly ally ourselves with Artanzia so that Keten will put all their forces along their southern border and invade Drussdell. This will incite further chaos in the Kingdom of Drussdell, and once they are weak from the Keten invasion, we will invade and destroy both of the battle-weary forces, thus, effectively trapping the Kingdom of Keten between us and one of our allies."

"I could not agree more, sire. Shall I move on to phase two of our plan?"

"Yes, and make sure our agents receive all the resources they need to make sure our plan is a success."

Chapter Four

The trees were like mountains. Their enormous branches teemed with leaves, blocking all sunlight from reaching the forest floor. Hundreds of ravens had perched themselves on these sturdy branches. Their foreboding caws and croaks warned all heroes to dare not enter this forest. Mario and Hamish did not heed the ravens' warnings.

"I's don't like the looks of this forest," Hamish muttered from under his breath.

"Nonsense! With your experience as a guard and my training as a knight, we will be fine," Mario said boisterously.

Mario's plate armour clanked with every step he took, alerting all the creatures in the forest where he was at all times. Hamish's chainmail rattled under his gambeson with every wheezing breath. Fallen leaves crunched beneath their every step, making it difficult to venture deeper into the forest stealthily. The only other noise came from the ravens. Their menacing black eyes followed the two travellers with malicious intrigue. Once the larger predators had eaten their fill, the ravens would feast on the remains.

Despite the trees blocking out the sunlight, the heat from the sun's rays found a way to penetrate the forest floor. Sweat dripped down from Mario's forehead and into his eyes. Every drop of sweat stung and made him blink repeatedly to try and ease the pain, only to have more sweat drop in.

"What makes you think that the bandits have a camp in this forest?" Mario asked as he lifted his visor to wipe his sweat-ridden brow.

"I's saw them retreat behind the treeline after one of their raids. Figured the bastards' camp would be in here somewhere."

"What can you tell me of this place?"

"The Eeragwia Forest is rumoured to be cursed."

Mario scoffed at such a ridiculous idea. *How could an entire forest be cursed? And who is powerful enough to bestow such a curse? These commoners will believe anything.* "What makes you say that?" Mario politely asked, barely able to hide his skepticism.

Hamish cleared his throat as he scanned the dark and ominous trees for hidden threats. "Tales tell of a woodman who went mad and butchered his family with his own axe. Their blood has forever stained the soil of this forest, and their spirits still haunt it."

Mario struggled to keep a straight face, but once he caught a glimpse of Hamish's judgemental gaze, he managed to stifle his laughter. "Who was this woodsman?"

"I's dunno. Always just been legend around town. Probably just to scare the little ones so they don't wander into the forest."

Mario never believed in old wives' tales or legends about curses. However, he couldn't shake the feeling that he was being watched by something. An unknown beast lurking deep in the shadows of the forest, patiently waiting to pounce on its prey. The trees began to take on a sinister appearance as Mario imagined them growing out of a pool of blood. The ravens suddenly became more ominous as their coal-like eyes watched him.

"Look! Over there!" Hamish shouted suddenly, pointing to a body lying beside the path.

Mario removed his helmet and wiped his eyes only to gasp in horror once he saw the grotesque sight. In front of him was the mangled corpse of a man wearing a small leather jacket stained with blood. Long, deep cuts including one over his jugular vein dissected his body. Animals had chewed away at the corpse's fingers, arms and legs leaving nothing but the bones. The worst part was his head, which had been crushed like a watermelon.

"What . . . what kind of creature is capable of such a thing!" Mario exclaimed, trying to keep from vomiting.

"A monster," Hamish answered plainly.

"How . . . how could such a creature even exist!" Mario stated, ignoring Hamish's thoughtless answer.

"I's told yous. I's don't have a good feeling about this forest."

"Let's just hope whatever killed this poor soul ate its fill."

"Nay, the only things that ate this man were the animals. Wolves, foxes, and ravens. Whatever killed this feller . . . didn't do it for food." Hamish pointed at the different wounds on the corpse.

"What other possible reason is there!?" Mario asked in disbelief.

"For sport." Hamish spat on the ground.

Suddenly, Mario felt uneasy. The self-assured feeling that filled his body when he first started his journey had faded. Instead, fear took its place and gripped Mario's body tightly. He slowly looked up at the ravens above, and they glared at him with menace. *Perhaps we can turn back? Perhaps there is a safer path where the likelihood of meeting monsters isn't so great.*

A crack of a twig breaking snapped Mario back into focus. He spun on his heels to see what made the sound, but all he could see was the ominous-looking foliage of the forest.

"Did theys train yous knights to fight monsters?" Hamish asked, unbothered by the sound behind him.

"No, that job is left for members who belong to the Order of the Swords. Unfortunately, there aren't many of their ilk around anymore. And I have a feeling we may need one," Mario answered, still scanning the forest for any potential threats.

"This looks like one of the bandits that raided Eulway. Bastard got what he deserved," Hamish grumbled while slowly rising to his feet.

"Then let us not tarry any longer," Mario said. "Hopefully, we will catch up with his comrades once we are free of this godsforsaken forest."

Mario and Hamish continued walking along the forest path. The fallen dead leaves suddenly crunching louder than before. Mario felt his nerves begin to get the better of him. He had never been this scared before; perhaps it was the gruesome story that Hamish told that unnerved him so much, or perhaps his body was trying to warn him of the dangers he'd face in this cursed forest. The ravens continued to follow them, flying from one branch to another, trying to keep their future meal in sight. *Please, gods, do not let us get lost in this forest. Allow us to not stay a moment more than we need to here.* Suddenly, Hamish stopped in his tracks.

"What is it?"

"Look." Hamish pointed to his breath, which was now visible.

A shiver ran down Mario's spine as he realized the dramatic drop in temperature. The hair on his neck stood up on end as the cold air pierced through his armour like a dagger.

"Gods . . . the ravens," Hamish muttered, staring at the trees.

Mario looked up and to his disbelief saw that the tree branches, once teeming with ravens, were now barren. They had all fled.

"Something is here . . ."

A rustle of a bush forced Mario's head to snap to the right, but it was already too late. A long tentacle had shot from the undergrowth of the forest and struck Mario right in the chest. The force of the blow launched Mario five feet back. The impact of the ground stole the air from Mario's lungs. He wheezed and coughed, struggling to get air into his lungs. He fumbled for his sword and desperately tried to rise to his feet. Mario saw that Hamish was already hacking away at some of the large vine-like tentacles that surrounded him. He gripped his sword and shield tightly and valiantly charged to give aid to his new ally.

Another tentacle erupted from the foliage of the forest, surging towards Mario. This time, however, Mario was able to do a quick pirouette on his toes and avoid the devastating blow. He swung his sword down into the tentacle, managing to chop it in half. Green ooze sprayed from the severed limb, staining Mario's plate armour a dark green.

A loud, bellowing roar emerged from the forest. Trees began to topple over and the ground started to shake—the source of the tentacles was approaching. The beast exploded from the underbrush and let out another bone-chilling roar. The beast must've been at least twenty feet tall. Its body looked identical to a large mound of shrubbery. The only difference was its large circular mouth, which was filled with razor-sharp, spinning teeth.

Mario gasped as he took in the monstrous appearance of the beast that stood before him. "By the gods . . ."

"How do we's kill the cursed thing!" Hamish screamed as he chopped at a tentacle.

Mario paused to think, a costly mistake to make in the midst of a battle. A tentacle swung from Mario's blindside and struck him on the side of the head. He could feel the steel of his helmet puncture his skin and pierce the bones of his skull. His vision blurred and he tried to remove his helmet, but every pull of his helmet forced the caved in steel to scrape against the side of his head. Pain shot down Mario's spine, and he let out a horrible, wailing cry. He stabbed his sword deep into the dirt and leaned his weight on it so he could stand up.

Another tentacle swung from the side, this time striking Hamish in the back. The strength of the blow sent him flying, and he landed right next to the corpse of the bandit. Mario finally had an idea.

"Fire!" he shouted.

"What!"

"We have to light it on fire! We can't fight all of these tentacles!"

Hamish reached into his satchel and pulled out a piece of steel and some flint. He quickly stood up and charged towards the ungodly beast. Mario charged as well. Although his vision was skewed and the pain from his collapsed helmet pained him, he still charged forward screaming a ferocious battle cry that would strike fear in the heart of every living creature—except the monster.

Two tentacles swung at Mario from opposite directions: the left one swept his legs from under him and the right tentacle struck him just below his shoulder, forcing Mario to fall prone. The left side of his head bounced off the dirt, and the pieces of steel that were lodged inside his skull vibrated painfully. He tried to let out a groan of pain but couldn't. He felt the monster's tentacles constrict around his body, forcing the air out of his lungs.

Mario gasped for air, but every time he tried to inhale, more of his breath exited his body. His vision was slowly fading to hazy darkness. Death was fast approaching, and there was nothing Mario could do to stop it.

A blood-curdling scream filled Mario's eardrums. The tentacles squeezing the life out of his body loosened abruptly. Mario opened his eyes and saw that the gargantuan creature was alight in flames. He looked and saw Hamish hacking at the tentacles of the burning monster as it tried to make its escape. A few seconds later, the large monster collapsed, shaking the entire forest, the remnants of its body still burning.

Mario could feel Hamish's hands lift his head; every movement sent him into agonizing pain. *What I wouldn't give to be back at Marian's shack right now.*

"We's got to leave here. The forest will go up in flames!" Hamish shouted, trying to get Mario to stand up. But it was to no avail. Mario's mind had already slipped into unconsciousness.

***

The sharp stinging pain on the left side of his face woke Mario. It felt as if someone was slowly chiselling the left side of his head. He was breathing heavy, but every breath brought great pain. Mario looked down at his ribs, and although there was little light in the room, he could see that the whole midsection of his torso was bruised. He lifted his hand to the left side of his head and realized that someone had bandaged his wounds. *Gods, I wish it was Marian taking care of me. Then I wouldn't be in so much pain.* With great effort, Mario lay back down and stared at the thatch roof of the building he had awakened in.

"Yous still alive?" Hamish's voice asked, seemingly uninterested in the answer.

"Yes, although I'm not sure how," Mario answered, clutching his ribs while he talked.

"Well, I's dragged you out the forest after the battle. The forest was on fire, and it didn't seem right to let yous burn along with that beast."

"Did you also apply the bandages to my head and look after my wounds?"

"Nay, I's came across these people, and now we's here."

"Who would be in a place like this?"

Mario's question was interrupted when the dark room was flooded by moonlight as the door suddenly swung open. Mario instinctively raised his hand to cover his eyes, only to cry out in pain when he moved. He blinked his eyes several times so that his pupils would readjust to the new light. Once his vision became clear again, he realized that Hamish was sitting across the room with his hands bound. Standing in the doorway was an elven woman armed with a bow.

"So, you're the *dahrenn* who is responsible for killing our guardian and destroying our forest."

Mario remembered back to when Tiberius was teaching him elven curse words during their first few years at the college. He remembered that *dahrenn* was a slur for humans meaning "unworthy one."

"It was going to kill us. We's had no choice . . ." Hamish started.

The elf whipped her head around and glared at Hamish. The elf slowly paced towards him and leaned down so her face was only inches away from his.

"You made your choice when you trespassed into our forest." Her voice was cold and harsh. Hamish avoided eye contact with her.

The elf's presence unnerved Mario. He had never seen a woman assert such dominance and authority over anyone. The only women that he thought were capable of such character were the shieldmaidens from the Mjältön Isles in the

Far North. It was clear that the elf shared the same temperament as those fierce women warriors.

"Please forgive us. We are only trying to protect our people," Mario uttered with great difficulty.

"Your people do not deserve protection!" the elf snapped as she focused her attention on the bedridden Mario. Her ferocious glare made the hair on his neck stand on end. "Your people have done nothing but kill and defile the land that they have settled on. You destroy anything that refuses to conform to your idealistic, hypocritical morals! You grind pixies into dust in order to make magic-invulnerable weapons, you tear down the sacred homes of creatures that have lived there long before humanity even emerged on this world, and the way you treat the other races . . . dwarves, elves, and halflings are all treated as if they are inferior even though we were on these lands long before you!"

The elf's eyes filled with tears. Her nostrils flared and the veins of her neck and forehead protruded. She clenched her fists so hard that her knuckles cracked and began to turn white. All the muscles in her legs, back and arms were fully tensed, waiting to spring into action.

"I'm sorry . . . but I was just trying to do what was needed to survive," Mario pleaded as fear of what the elf might do gripped his heart.

"So were we . . . till your people slaughtered us," the elf growled, then she stormed out of the hut.

"Are all elves that bitter?" Mario looked at Hamish, who had turned a sickly pale.

"Ever since the uprising. I's always treated non-humans with decency. Guess we's all the same to the elves," Hamish muttered, staring at his feet.

Mario didn't respond. He wondered if he could say the same. Outside the hut, he saw the shadows of elves. He listened attentively, trying to figure out what they had planned for himself and Hamish. He heard the stacking of wood, the striking of flint and steel, the crickets of the forest chirping. He heard elves whispering to one another in their own tongue, but most obviously, he heard the unmistakable croons of the ravens.

Mario tried to look around the hut, but it was pitch black. The only illumination was the small, feeble rays of moonlight seeping through the cracked wooden door. Mario leaned further out of bed, trying to eavesdrop on the elves' conversations. He heard two voices approaching the hut. He could make out that one of the voices belonged to the angry female elf from earlier; the other belonged to a different female elf. The second voice was calm and soothing. Mario leaned further out of his bed, every muscle in his sore torso screamed with agony, but it was worth it in order to get a better listen on the conversation.

Before Mario could hear anything of value, his tired muscles gave out on him, and he fell onto the floor. The thud was loud and clearly alerted the camp outside the hut, as everything had suddenly become silent. Mario wanted to scream in agony, but the fall knocked the wind out of him, and all he was able to utter was a barely audible wheeze.

"Yous okay?" Hamish asked from the darkness.

Mario gasped, still fighting for air. "No . . ."

"Well, one of the elves will probably come to check on yous now after a loud fall like that."

"Hooray . . ."

The door to the hut swung open. Every feature of the elf standing in the doorway was hidden as rays of moonlight shined into the hut from behind them. But Mario knew that the elf at the door was the same angry she-elf from before. He recognized her rigid, seething posture.

"What did you do *dahrenn*?" she asked with a voice as cold as a gust of winter air.

Mario gasped for enough air so that he could respond in a full sentence. "I . . . fell . . . off the bed."

"Were you trying to escape?" Her voice rose in volume as she approached Mario, who was lying on the ground like a helpless worm.

"Enough, Deidre," another voice called from the doorway of the hut. The she-elf stopped in her tracks and looked at the shadowy figure standing in the doorway.

Mario recognized the voice. It was the calming voice from before. A sense of relief fell over him. Whoever this elf was he was grateful that she stopped Deidre from reaching his helpless body.

Deidre walked past the shadowy figure outside the hut, clearly upset. Then the figure said something in elvish, and three more figures entered the hut. Two approached Mario's helpless body, and one walked in the general direction of Hamish. Mario felt the pair of strong hands lift his tender body and start to carry him outside the hut.

The cool night breeze kissed his bruised chest. He had not felt such a soothing sensation since Marian used her magic on him. Mario looked up and saw
that two young male elves were carrying him towards a large bonfire. They were
almost identical: both had coppery-red hair, emerald green eyes, and skinny,
sunken faces.

Almost fifty elves were gathered in a circle surrounding the fire. Each elf
clutched a small sheaf of grass closely. The two elves set Mario down gently in
front of the fire. He looked around the circle and saw that every elf was looking
at him, some with sympathy and some with anger.

"So, you entered our forest, burned it to the ground, and killed our guardian,"
spoke the soothing voice beside Mario.

He slowly turned his head to see the source of such a majestic voice. The
firelight illuminated the elf's features: her sharp triangular jawline, her skinny
pointed nose, her long silvery hair, which cascaded over her shoulders and past
her breasts to finally stop just above her waist. She was skinny, the norm for elven
women, but not sickly. As Deidre, she commanded attention with her presence
but in a different way. She was given attention out of respect and admiration,
not fear.

"I had to survive . . ." Mario started, still mesmerized by the elf standing
beside him.

"But you entered our forest uninvited. If someone were to enter your farm-
yard uninvited, would you greet them with open arms?" A cunning smile spread
slowly across her face.

"No, but I would also not greet them with certain death."

"True, yet when humans come uninvited into our homes, it almost always
means certain death," the elf replied.

Mario gulped and said nothing. He knew it was not the time nor the place to
defend humanity's actions of the past.

"Our friends have been watching you." The elf pointed to the trees, where
hundreds of ravens rested on their branches. "They are my diligent lookouts,
letting me know who enters my forest and what they do."

Mario gulped again. The presence of so many ravens made him feel uneasy.
Perhaps it was because he was taught that ravens were omens of impending
doom, and being surrounded by this many only meant that his death would
come soon.

"We captured you and your friend after you killed our guardian. It is only fair that you are held on trial for your offences against the clan." She widened her smile so that her teeth were showing.

"Is this meant to be my trial?" Mario asked.

"No."

"Wait . . . what?"

"While you rested, the clan decided your fate. It was close, but the majority voted that we should heal you and escort you out of our forest on the promise that you never return."

Relief spread through Mario's body. *I won't die in this damned forest!* Mario was unable to contain the smile on his face.

"I take it that you agree to these terms?" the elf asked, already knowing the answer to her question.

"Yes! Absolutely!"

"Very well."

One of the elves in the crowd handed the leader a large curved leaf that was holding a liquid in the middle of it.

"Drink this. You will fall asleep and awake refreshed and healed."

Mario eagerly clutched the leaf and slurped all of the magical liquid down. Suddenly, he felt hazy and woozy. His eyes started to feel heavy, and quickly, he slipped into a deep sleep.

***

The sounds of an argument awoke Mario from his magically induced slumber. He sat up instantly and, to his relief, felt no pain in his torso. He looked down and saw that all the bruising had disappeared. *Good as new. Looks like the elves are as talented with magic as Marian is.* Mario groggily got out of his bed and stretched his bed-sore body. *Soon I will be back on the path, tracking down these bandits and bringing order upon the land once again.* A smile broke on Mario's face. He rubbed his eyes, but his hands froze when he felt bumps on the left side of his face. Mario frantically examined the unknown lesions. He then realized where the marks came from. *My helmet.* Mario started breathing hysterically. His heart felt like it would burst right out of his chest. He fell down onto the bed, trying to get his breathing under control. The door to the hut swung open, and Hamish lazily entered the hut. Mario sprung from the bed like an arrow launched from a bow and gripped Hamish by the collar of his gambeson.

"How bad is it!" Mario screamed.

"What?"

"The scars! How bad are my scars?" Mario's voice began to crack.

"Theys . . . um . . . are noticeable," Hamish awkwardly replied.

Mario's grip loosened. He felt weak at the knees. *I was a fool for fighting that monster. Now look at me. I'm disfigured for life. Every day I'll be reminded of the time I thought I could fight a monster.* At that moment, Mario realized why Sir Darius was always bitter. *His scars remind him of the foolish mistake he made . . . the same one I made.*

"Yous alright? Yous look a little pale," Hamish said, interrupting Mario's thoughts.

"Yes, just trying to come to terms with my new appearance."

"Well, yous better get used to it 'cause that helmet is fucked."

"What do you mean?"

"I's watched the elves try to pry it off yous. The damned thing was embedded in your skull. Theys said it was a miracle yous lived, and that theys didn't have the magic to remove the helmet without leaving scars."

"It was that bad?"

"Kid, I's was surprised to see yous get back up after taking that hit."

I didn't think it was that bad; perhaps in the middle of the battle, I didn't notice as much. At least it doesn't hurt anymore, even if I do look grotesque. Mario's heart sank as he realized that he would no longer catch the flirtatious eyes of women. A lump formed in his chest at the thought of living out the rest of his life looking horrifically scarred. "What is the commotion outside all about?" Mario asked, quickly changing the subject and distracting himself from his thoughts.

"Yous will never guess who's been chosen for our escort," Hamish replied; a coy smile spread across his thin chapped lips.

Outside the hut, Deidre and the elven leader were facing each other with the rest of the clan watching. Deidre was screaming and yelling at the elven leader, like a child throwing a tantrum. While the elven leader, like the mother of a temperamental child, remained calm and stoic.

"Why me!" Deidre cried out, veins protruding from her neck, her hands clenched so tightly in fists that her knuckles were turning from white to blue.

"You know why, my child," the leader said softly. "You are my best tracker and most gifted archer. You are the only chance these two humans have to escape the forest in one piece."

"But I don't want them to! They're *dahrenn*. They don't deserve to leave here alive!"

The elven leader turned her head and made eye contact with Mario and Hamish. She swiftly turned her head back to Deidre and spoke in elvish to her. This time, however, her voice was not soothing, but instead shrill and harsh. Deidre fell silent. She nodded her head and walked away. The elven leader approached Mario and Hamish as the rest of the elves dispersed to carry out their daily routines.

"Apologies for that display. Deidre will be back soon, and then she will guide you safely out of our forest."

"Doubt it. We's most likely to get shot by her arrows," Hamish muttered under his breath.

"Thank you," Mario said, quickly trying to cover up his companion's rude remark. "Where are my things? I would like to leave as soon as possible and not remain an inconvenience to you or your people."

A smile broke across the elven leader's face. "Hamish already packed them while you rested."

Mario bowed politely and thanked the elven leader again for her hospitality and generosity. As they waited for Deidre to return, Mario examined his damaged helmet once he had adorned his armour. *How did I ever survive such a blow? The gods must've looked kindly on me at that moment.*

"You might as well throw that piece of scrap metal away. It's about as useful as a drunken archer," Deidre snapped.

"It can be fixed," Mario said optimistically, ignoring her snide tone.

"Mario, she's right," Hamish started. "The only use for that helmet is to smelt it down and forge another."

"Come on, we're losing precious daylight. The forest is a place you don't want to be trapped in at night," Deidre interrupted. She was already walking into the forest, leaving Mario and Hamish behind.

Mario tucked the helmet away in his bag and followed Deidre into the forest.

Fathers shall not be put to death for their sons, nor shall sons be put to death for their fathers; everyone shall be put to death for his own sin.

Deuteronomy 24:16

Chapter Five

M ario was breathing heavily, although not as heavily as Hamish, who sounded like he was moments away from death. Deidre was about twenty feet ahead of them, and she showed no signs of fatigue. *Deidre certainly moves fast for someone who is supposed to be guiding us. Also, now I know why knights always ride horses . . . because plate armour is impossible to walk in.* Mario stopped to lean on a tree while Hamish collapsed at his feet.

"We need to rest." Mario gasped. "We've been walking hard for five hours."

"Trust me, you do not want to be here at night," Deidre warned. "Now, let's keep going."

"I's not taking another step till we's rest!" Hamish exclaimed, lying on the cold dirt floor of the forest.

"Then you'll die, *dahrenn.*"

"Please, Deidre, we need rest. Ten minutes—that's all we ask."

Deidre let out an exasperated sigh and walked back to regroup with Mario and Hamish.

"What happens at night that makes this place so dangerous?" Mario wiped the sweat off of his brow.

"Monsters. Bloodthirsty creatures that love killing anything they come across," Deidre answered coldly while gazing into the forest.

"Why live in such a place then?" Hamish asked, finally able to catch his breath and stop wheezing.

"Who better to protect us from the real monsters?" Deidre said sarcastically.

"What is more dangerous than those creatures?"

"I'm sitting with two right now," Deidre answered coldly.

Both Mario and Hamish went silent. Neither wanted to utter a sound and set off Deidre's vicious temper. It was clear that she despised humans; she couldn't even talk about them without clenching her jaw.

Mario stared at Deidre while she wasn't looking. He looked at her flowing long golden blonde hair that ran down to the middle of her back. He looked at her slender, sinewy body. He admired her pale, blueish-grey eyes whenever he had the chance to look at them. *How can someone so beautiful be so full of hatred?*

"Time's up," Deidre said as she stood up already beginning to walk away at full speed. Mario and Hamish begrudgingly got up and ran to catch up with her. The party of three walked for another three hours before Deidre suddenly walked off of the path heading deeper into the forest.

"Wait, yous is leaving the path," Hamish called.

"The path is a decoy and doesn't lead anywhere," Deidre answered without stopping.

"That's not true. I's seen the other end on the other side of this forest." Hamish jogged to catch up with Deidre, who was not going to stop for any reason.

"Both trails lead to a dead end, *dahrenn*," Deidre barked.

"Why do you hate us, Deidre?" Mario asked, finally addressing the elephant in the room.

"You mean besides burning down a part of our forest and killing our guardian?"

"Yes."

"Because humans always cause pain, wherever they go. They don't care who they hurt, as long as they get what they want."

"You don't know us. We've never done anything bad towards elves."

"Let me ask you this, have you heard of the tale of Pablo Deschamps?"

"Yes, he's my father," Mario announced out of habit, and without thinking.

Deidre stopped dead in her tracks. Her whole body went stiff and her hands clenched into fists. "Your father?" she asked, voice shaking.

Mario and Hamish looked at one another awkwardly before Mario decided to answer once again, knowing he'd regret it. "Yes."

"Your father is Sir Pablo Deschamps!?" Deidre screamed as she sharply turned on her heels to make eye contact with Mario.

Mario nodded and looked at the ground. He knew that he would have to answer for his father's sins.

"You're the son of the *dahrenn* who slaughtered my people!? The man who is regaled as a hero by your kind because of how well he killed us!"

In one fluid motion, Deidre had her bow in her hand and an arrow nocked and aimed at Mario's head.

"Easy! Easy!" Hamish cried as he tried to get in between the two, but it was too late.

Mario heard the twang of the bowstring and waited for death. But it never came. He opened his eyes and saw that Deidre had another arrow nocked, but it was aimed at the side of Mario's head. Another twang came from the bow, and Mario could feel the wind brush his cheek as the arrow flew past his head.

A guttural cry came from the bushes behind them, a cry of a man who had just been struck by an arrow. Deidre pulled out her dagger and walked past Mario, making sure to bump him harshly with her shoulder.

"Please no!" the man cried as Deidre towered over him, dagger in hand.

"Deidre, wait . . ." Mario started.

"Back off, *dahrenn!*" Deidre shouted. "You're lucky these arrows aren't in your skull."

"Wait! He's one of them!" Hamish pointed at the wounded man.

"One of who?" Deidre asked, annoyed by the constant interruptions in her execution.

"The bandits we's are after. He has the same clothes as the feller we's found by your guardian."

Deidre's head whipped around, and she glared at the wounded man. "There are more of you? How many? And what are you doing in my forest? Speak now or I'll gut you like a deer."

Even though her threats weren't directed at him, Mario still felt a shiver run down his spine.

"We . . . we come in here to fetch elven girls," the man said, coughing up blood as he did so.

"And do what with them?" Deidre's voice was shaking. Her face had turned red with rage.

"Sell 'em as slaves mostly . . . after we have our fun with 'em," the man cackled. "Hell . . . I'm sure you'd be fun to take a roll in the hay with."

Before anyone could blink, Deidre's dagger swung down and slit the bandit's throat. A fountain of red sprayed across the shrubbery. The once emerald bushes were now dyed a dark crimson. The entire forest was quiet, except for the sounds of the bandit gargling as he choked on his own blood.

"Bastards . . ." Hamish muttered.

"Deidre, I'm—" Mario started.

"Don't. You said you two are after these men? Well, I'm joining. Girls have gone missing from our clan for a few weeks now. I figured something attacked them in the forest, or they just left the clan. But not this. . . . They'll pay for what they've done."

"What about the monsters?" Mario asked.

"Nothing is more dangerous than an elf who has had her kin taken away. Not even humans."

"Lead the way."

***

When night fell on the forest, it transformed its appearance from ominous to sinister. The lack of light was playing tricks on Mario's mind. Every branch, bush, and tree appeared to be some monster waiting to attack its unsuspecting prey. Even the ravens looked more menacing in the darkness. They were almost invisible; Mario was only able to see them when they moved their head suddenly or flapped their wings. He flinched every time. *Gods, what will happen if we come across something worse than the guardian? I pray Deidre will protect us, although I wouldn't be surprised if she left me to die on account of who I am.* Mario tried to remain diligent and look for threats that were cloaked by the darkness of the forest, but it was no use. His human eyes could not compete with the superior elven vision of Deidre. Even Hamish seemed to have better vision than him. This place made Mario feel uneasy; every fibre of his being screamed for him to leave this place. It warned him that something bad was going to happen.

"I can't believe these swine have been able to survive in our forest for this long," Deidre whispered to the group.

"I's told yous. These aren't ordinary bandits," Hamish answered in an equally hushed tone.

"But they'll die like they are." Deidre grimaced, gripping her bow tighter in her hands.

"What's that over there?" Mario asked, pointing towards a faint green glow in the distance.

"Probably some godsforsaken monster," Hamish grumbled quietly.

"Shh, follow me," Deidre whispered as she slowly approached the mysterious light. When they got closer to the source, she stood up and her body relaxed. "It's a lichenite," she said, extending her hand out towards the light.

"A what?" Mario asked.

"A lichenite. They're small magical creatures that are harmless to us. They are able to change the chemical compounds of the dirt, making the soil more fertile for plants." Deidre held the small creature in her hand.

The green light dimmed, and Mario was able to see the unique features of this strange creature. It was no bigger than a gold coin. It had a thick mossy coat covering its whole body, making it appear no different from regular moss, except for its shimmering green glow, of which the brightness the creature could control. It had two small legs and two small arms, similar to a human, but had no distinguishable hands or feet. It had three eyes, each as black as coal. However, these eyes were not stationary; instead, they flowed and rotated around its body in a small triangular pattern.

Mario gasped as he stared at the small creature in Deidre's hand. "Remarkable."

"These are the types of creatures that humanity destroys," Deidre replied coldly.

Suddenly, the lichenite started running in circles in Deidre's hand. It acted as if it had urgent news to tell the three travellers but was unable to communicate to them through speaking.

"What does it want?" Hamish asked bluntly.

"I'm not sure, but it seems important," Deidre replied. She set the little creature on the ground, and it took off running into the depths of the forest. "Follow it!" she exclaimed as she sprinted after the little green light. Mario and Hamish quickly followed.

While pursuing the lichenite through the pitch-black forest, Mario somehow felt more at ease. The forest didn't appear as evil as it did earlier in the night. The speedy green light gave Mario a sense of giddiness; he felt like a child chasing after a butterfly. Fear had left his body as curiosity and joy took over for the first time in a long time. After a few minutes of pursuit, the green glow of the lichenite was overwhelmed by the large orange glow of a nearby campfire. Deidre, Hamish, and Mario approached the campsite stealthily and observed, hidden by the dark foliage of the forest.

There were five men in the camp, sitting around the fire. Three were heavily intoxicated, while the other two were asleep. The pleasing aroma of cooked venison graced Mario's nose. The scent made him salivate instantly. *What I wouldn't give for a piece of that meat right now.* In the far corner of the camp, chained to a tree were three elven girls. They were almost identical. Long blonde hair, green eyes, and a pale complexion that was covered with freckles. The three girls were holding each other's hands. *Sisters.*

Deidre pulled an arrow from her quiver and nocked it in her bow. She began to take aim.

"What are you doing?" Mario whispered.

"What does it look like?" Deidre quietly snapped back.

"If you shoot now, you'll give away the element of surprise. We don't know if they are by themselves or if they have companions nearby."

"Then we better kill these five and leave."

"But if others are nearby, they could hear the sounds of fighting and come rush to help. We should wait and see if more show up and then attack stealthily."

"Mario's right, Deidre. We's don't know how many of them are in this forest. We's could be overwhelmed if we's attack now," Hamish interjected.

"Fine, we sit and wait," Deidre huffed as she put her bow down.

"Thank you," Mario replied, with all the sincerity he could muster.

"*Bloede dahrenn,*" Deidre cursed under her breath.

The drunken bandits were quite entertaining to watch. They were singing songs, hugging each other, trying to out drink one another, and making complete fools of themselves. Mario could've sworn that he saw a smile on Deidre's face. *That's probably the first time she's smiled at a human. Glad to know she can enjoy their drunken foolishness as much as I do. Or perhaps she's smiling at the thought of what she is going to do to them once we finally attack.* A chill ran down Mario's spine at the sickening thought of Deidre experiencing pleasure through mutilating humans.

"Listen, Gaspard! How many fuckin' knife ear we got 'ere?" one of the bandits slurred.

"I sees six of 'em, but I only remember catching three," the second bandit replied, rubbing the temples of his head as he drunkenly swayed from side to side.

"You're seeing ploughin' double!" the third one exclaimed. "There's three there, George, why?"

"Me's thinkin' of havin' some fun with one of 'em," the first bandit replied as a sickening grin spread across his drunken face.

"You heard Henry. He said no more rapin'. It's bringing down their prices," the second bandit replied, still trying to sober up.

"Fuck Henry," the first bandit replied. "We'll just say one tried to escape, and we had to rough 'er up a li'l. He'll never know." The first bandit rose to his feet and looked at the chained elves with malicious intent. "Unchain that middle one for me, Oscar, and help me pin 'er down."

The third bandit rose to his feet and slowly started walking towards the chained elven girls.

Mario was torn. *If we attack now, there's a good chance we will get surrounded and overrun by their friends. On the other hand, if we don't do anything, they'll rape that elven girl, and we will be just as bad as those bandits.* Mario started to bite his bottom lip; this was the hardest decision of his life. For the first time, there was no correct answer. Both outcomes were terrible, and Mario didn't have the luxury of time to contemplate his decision. It needed to be made in the moment. Suddenly, Mario remembered his promise to Tiberius before leaving the college. That he would not be another bystander when an elf needed his aid.

Mario leapt from the undergrowth, unsheathed his blade, and let out a blood-curdling battle cry. Hamish quickly followed suit. As the two charged into the camp, they could feel the wind from Deidre's arrows brush their cheeks. Before Mario had even made it ten feet into the camp, the third bandit, Oscar, already had an arrow through the back of his head. Blood sprayed from his mouth and covered the elven girls, who screamed in terror.

The first bandit, George, drunkenly turned around, but by the time he did, it was too late. Mario had already swung his sword at his neck. His head flew three feet into the air. Blood erupted from his severed neck like a volcano. The campsite was painted crimson with the bandit's blood. His headless body convulsed and writhed on the ground.

Mario turned his head and saw that by the time the second bandit, Gaspard, had grabbed his sword, Hamish had already driven his sword through the bandit's ribcage puncturing his heart. The bandit coughed and sprayed his blood across Hamish's face. Hamish gave a sharp twist of his sword, and Gaspard screamed in agony. With his left hand, Hamish pulled out his dagger and drove it deep into Gaspard's right temple, making his body shake uncontrollably.

The two sleeping bandits didn't have an opportunity to wake. Deidre expertly shot her arrows at their brain stems, killing them instantly.

The whole encounter took less than fifteen seconds. Mario wiped the blood from his eyes and realized the severity of the slaughter that had just occurred. His stomach churned as he looked down at the headless body of George. *An entire life . . . ended in the blink of an eye.* Mario's lips began to tremble and his cheeks began to quiver. Mario felt his skin go pale. He leaned on his sword for balance and tried not to vomit. He looked over at the three elven girls, who were covered in Oscar's blood. *I imagine I have the same terrified look on my face.*

"Not bad, *dahrenn.*" Emerging from the bush with her bow slung across her back, Deidre smiled.

"Let's just unchain them and get out of here," Mario replied, still queasy from taking his first life.

"Yeah, we's weren't exactly stealthy." Hamish wiped the Gaspard's blood off of his face.

Deidre and Mario hurried over to the three elven girls. Mario fiddled with the lock while Deidre tried to calm the girls.

"I hear horses," Deidre interjected.

"Fuck!" Mario screamed as he couldn't unlock the chain.

Hamish quickly marched over and struck the lock and broke it in half with a mighty blow. "Run!" he screamed at the elven girls as they scattered into the forest. "We's will have to hold off the bandits so they can escape." He readied his sword for more enemies.

"Agreed," Deidre said, already nocking another arrow in her bow.

"Go in the centre of the camp and form a circle," Mario ordered.

In only a few moments, they were surrounded by about twenty bandits. The bandits rode around the three heroes in circles, cackling and lobbing insults at them but never attacking. The bandits reminded Mario of a pack of rabid dogs—trapping their prey, circling it, creating fear, waiting for the opportune time to strike.

Suddenly, the bandits grew quiet as a man riding a giant black mare emerged from the forest. He was wearing a small tricorne cap, with the feather of a woodpecker sticking out of it. He wore a thick leather coat and carried a large war hammer on his back.

"So, what do we have here?" the man boasted. The rest of the bandits howled as they prepared for a spectacle. All three heroes turned to face the enigmatic bandit leader. "Tell me," the leader continued, "why on earth would a free elf travel with a knight and a town guard?"

"Perhaps she's their whore!" one of the bandits shouted from the crowd. The rest of the bandits erupted in laughter.

The bandit leader smiled. "Is that true? Is she your sex slave that you two share on a nightly basis? My, what a sight to see. But that wouldn't be very fitting of a knight, now, would it?"

Deidre gripped her bow tightly and glared at the bandit leader.

"I think she wants to shoot me!" the bandit leader exclaimed. The horde of bandits cheered and hollered with enthusiasm. The charismatic bandit leader dismounted his horse and walked towards her. "Go on then," the leader continued, spreading his arms out wide, exposing his torso to Deidre. "Take your best shot."

Without hesitation, Deidre pulled the bow and loosed an arrow at the bandit leader. To her surprise, he expertly sidestepped out of the way, and her arrow flew harmlessly into the forest.

"You elves are so predictable." The bandit leader chuckled as he unsheathed his war hammer. "Now tell me, why did you kill my men? I have done no harm to you two. The elf, I understand, but what wrongdoing have I done to you because whatever I did, I'll right it." The bandit leader's voice was captivating, and his elegant, complex hand movements entranced Mario.

"Yous attacked my village," Hamish growled, gripping his sword. "Yous hurt innocent people, people I's sworn to protect."

"But I need to make a living too," the leader quickly countered. "Is being a bandit any different from any other occupation? I do what I am good at in order to survive. No different from a farmer or a tradesman."

"Your kind is a plague on this kingdom, and you should be cut down like the rats you are." Mario snarled, readying his shield and his sword.

"Whoa! Look at the mighty knight we have in front of us, lads! Tell me, how did you get that scar on your head? You must be a fierce warrior to receive a memento such as that," the bandit leader replied playfully, giving more elegant hand movements to his men.

"If you must know—" Mario started.

"Never mind, I'm bored with this. Go ahead, boys." The bandit leader waved his hand as he walked back to his horse.

Before Mario could turn around, he heard three distinct, loud thuds. One to his left, one to his right, and one from behind him. After hitting the forest floor, the last thing he felt before going unconscious was his nose breaking.

The Order of the Swords was a school that taught men how to fight monsters. These men underwent rigorous training. As a result, they were the best warriors that gold could buy. A single member from the Order of the Swords could cut down twenty armed opponents with ease. Because of this expert swordsmanship, many of the order's members turned to mercenary work since it paid better than monster hunting. The order's recruit numbers declined after rumours that Headmaster Lazarus Snagglefort performed demented blood transfusion experiments on the students spread.

Ulysses Ikyma,
Master Ulysses' Guide to Everything

CHAPTER SIX

The convoy of bandits that were escorting the party of three took pleasure in the prisoners' suffering. The two in the front of the wagon would often hurl insults at Mario and Hamish and throw derogatory, racial slurs at Deidre. The two other bandits, who were on horseback, took joy in causing physical pain rather than emotional. Whenever they were bored, they whipped one of the prisoners or tripped them so that when they fell, they were dragged behind the wagon. However, even that didn't seem to satiate their boredom. Whenever the leader of the convoy, Pascal, got tired of the monotony, he would order the convoy to stop. This usually meant that Deidre was going to suffer the most. Sometimes he would only beat her; sometimes he would do more.

Mario was oblivious to all of this. He didn't think about the pain in his broken nose. He didn't think about the suffering he and his comrades were enduring. He didn't even think of the blisters on his feet that were painfully filled with pus. Mario was lost in a state of numb indifference. The only thing he looked at was his blood-stained armour in the back of the bandit's wagon, and the only thing he could think about was taking George's life.

I ended that man's life. Was he beyond redemption? Was he so vile that he couldn't do good if given a chance? Did I needlessly take a life from this world? How am I any better than them? What if we could have captured them instead? Mario's head was spinning. Every time he closed his eyes, he was haunted by the image of George's head being cleaved from his neck. Blood had exploded from the bandit's severed neck covering the entire camp in red. Mario shuddered when he remembered how the headless body of the bandit squirmed and convulsed after the brutal decapitation. Mario had not slept since the slaughter.

"Where are yous taking us?" Hamish asked, hoping that this time he would get an answer.

"Be quiet or next time I'll take you into the brush instead of her," Pascal barked, pointing to Deidre.

Deidre walked with her head down, staring at her feet. Her cheekbones were broken, her face was bruised, and her bruised groin forced her to walk with a limp. When Pascal would first stop the convoy, she would kick and scream and fight with all of her might, but now, defeated, she'd just let it happen.

"Why not just fucking kill us?" Hamish pleaded as he grimaced from the pain in his feet and back.

"Why would I!?" Pascal exclaimed. "We're barely surviving on what we get from selling young elvish girls as slaves. Imagine the takings for an elven woman and a knight. Hell, his armour has to be worth a couple hundred gold itself! Granted, I know we won't get much for you, but something is better than nothing." A twisted smile spread across his face.

Pascal's appearance matched his temperament perfectly. His skinny triangular face was riddled with scars. His auburn eyes were filled with evil. Whenever a thought of committing an atrocious, sadistic act came into his head, he would smile enough to show the crooked, rotten yellow teeth underneath his curly black moustache. He was a beast of a man.

"Hey, boss, where are we meeting up with Henry and the others?" one of the bandits in the front of the wagon called back.

"Henry and company are moving on from the forest," Pascal answered, maliciously eyeing up Deidre. "We are to meet John and Gianluca just north of Riverwell."

"I thought we was goin' to rescue Arthur?" asked the other bandit on the horse.

"Arthur's an idiot. If he is stupid enough to be captured and taken to Kartaga, then fuck him. I'm not risking my neck to save his sorry ass," Pascal snapped, no longer eyeing Deidre sinisterly but now eyeing his own men.

"It can't be that hard to bust him out of a prison," muttered the driver of the wagon.

"Kartaga has been the prison capital of the empire for centuries. Nobody has ever invaded it, and nobody has ever escaped. The only people that are allowed into the city are members of the prisoner convoy. They're a puppet state for the empire. All the prisoners get sent there, and in return, the city-state gets financial backing from the emperor," the other bandit in the front of the wagon replied.

"I once heard from a feller that they carry out the most vile and sadistic punishments imaginable. Even for something as little as stealing bread," the other bandit on the horse chimed in.

"If nobody has ever escaped and only the convoy is allowed in, how the hell would he know what punishments are carried out there?" Pascal asked angrily.

"I . . . uh . . . I dunno," the bandit confessed.

Pascal's horse started rearing and neighing uncontrollably. Her feet started to prance on the spot as she fought against her master's commands. The mare's nostrils flared, and her eyes widened. She sensed the impending threat that nobody else did. Pascal curled his hand in a fist and punched the mare right in the jawbone. "Fuckin' animal!" he screamed. "I'll teach you to listen." The mare's teeth rattled, and she stopped behaving wildly, knowing that nobody was going to heed her warnings.

"So, tell me, Knight. What did you do to get that scar? Must be one hell of a warrior," Pascal asked, grinning viciously at Mario.

Mario didn't answer. He didn't even hear the question. His mind was trapped in a cruel cycle of flashbacks and guilt. *Perhaps I'm not man enough to be a knight. I should've never tried to live up to my dad.* A hard punch dropped Mario to his knees. The forest floor cut his face open as he was dragged behind the cart. The pain didn't even register to Mario. In fact, he didn't even realize he had been knocked to the ground.

"Stop!" Pascal yelled as he dismounted his horse. Deidre flinched out of habit. He walked over to Mario and lifted him up by the scruff of his neck and gave him another punch right in the teeth.

Blood filled Mario's mouth, and the sudden shock to his teeth made him snap back into reality.

"I asked you a question boy!" Pascal growled, clutching Mario by his throat. "Where did you get that scar?"

"A . . . uh . . . monster gave it to me," Mario stammered, trying to focus on the question so he wouldn't be hit again.

"A monster?" Pascal laughed. "We have a hero in our midst!" The rest of the bandits cackled and howled at Pascal's sarcastic tone. "What was it? A werewolf? A vampire? A giant?" Pascal asked mockingly as he wiped the tears from his eyes.

"I'm . . . not sure what it was," Mario stated, his head still hazy from the two punches.

"Perhaps it was a squirrel!" a bandits at the front of the wagon called out. The bandits erupted in laughter. They continued for quite some time to name harmless animals that could've left Mario disfigured. Mario just stood there, head down, taking the abuse.

"That's enough." Pascal gasped, hyperventilating from his fit of laughter. "I thought you knights were supposed to come from great families. Your father must have been some sorry sack of shit to have you as a son."

Mario snapped his head up and glared at Pascal angrily. He ground his bloody teeth. His body filled with rage. The convoy leader had his full attention now.

"Look at that! A little bit of fire in this one's belly!" Pascal cried as he pointed at the clearly agitated Mario. "Are you upset I made fun of your daddy? Are you going to cry?" Pascal asked mockingly.

Mario stood silently. Seething. His eyes did not move from Pascal's.

"The way he's lookin' at you, boss, I'd say he wants to kiss you," the other bandit from the horse yelled out.

"Is that so?" Pascal laughed, his eyes gleaming with evil intent. "A fucking cock jockey for a knight. That's bloody rich! Tell you what, go ahead give me a smooch."

While the bandits laughed at Mario's expense, nobody noticed the movement in the brush behind the convoy. Even the horses didn't notice it this time. It was invisible, slowly biding its time, waiting for the perfect opportunity to strike. Death would come.

Pascal cocked his fist back and, in a flash, punched Mario right in the throat. Mario dropped to his knees, wheezing and coughing up blood. Hamish took a step towards his injured comrade.

"Take one more step, and I'll slit your throat and fuck your corpse into oblivion!" Pascal growled, glaring at Hamish.

Hamish immediately took a step back and averted his gaze.

"Come on, we're losing daylight. Let's go!" Pascal cried out.

With a crack of the reins, the wagon began to move again, Mario dragging behind it. With great effort, he spun around so that his rear was dragging across the floor of the forest. After taking a deep breath, he dug his heels into the dirt so the wagon would drag him into an upright position and he could walk again.

Mario looked over at Hamish and gave a nod to reassure his comrade that he was okay. *I've ruined these people's lives. Hamish would be in Eulway, living an uneventful life as a guard, and Deidre would be safe with her fellow elves. I'm the reason they're here. It's my fault.*

The convoy kept marching forward till they reached the edge of the forest. The path dipped down to cross a small ravine. The sides of the path were fifteen feet high, making the path more like a trench than a road. The chasm-like path was barely wide enough for the wagon to pass through—the perfect spot for an ambush.

"Should we go around?" asked the driver of the wagon.

"And lose more time? Nonsense, go through it. I've gone through this path a hundred times before," Pascal reassured his men.

Reluctantly, the reins cracked, and the wagon slowly moved forward into the passage. The bandits squeezed together so that they could fit through the narrow passage as a whole unit.

Suddenly, a twig snapped on the righthand side of the path. Mario snapped his head to look, but all he saw was a grey blur fly past his face. A choking scream came from behind him. He darted his head around to see that the other bandit riding the horse had his throat sliced open. A scream came from the front of the wagon. Mario looked forward, but all he saw were the two decapitated heads of the bandits falling to the ground.

"What is going on!?" Pascal cried, looking left to right, trying to find his unknown assailant.

Whatever beast this is, it's fast. Too fast to be human. Mario didn't see what caused Pascal to fall to the ground, but he heard his captor's body thud against the dirt floor of the forest. The arrogant, evil look that seemed to be permanently glued to Pascal's face was gone. In its place was the pale look of horror. Pascal slowly tried to crawl away from his unseen attacker. Mario heard another thud slightly ahead of him. He turned to see, to his surprise, a hooded man. *Another group of bandits? The elves?*

The hooded man slowly approached the crawling Pascal, who was begging to be spared. The hooded man spoke no word, seemingly unphased by the bandit's pathetic pleas. When Pascal stood up to fight, the man struck Pascal in the forehead. Mario could hear the bandit's skull crack.

Pascal started the crawl away again. The hooded man stabbed his sword deep into the dirt and pulled out a butcher's hook. A smile spread across Deidre's bruised face. Hamish closed his eyes and looked away. Mario watched on with horror. His eyes glued to the spectacle that was taking place.

The hooded man stabbed the hook deep into Pascal's shoulder. Pascal screamed in pain; tears ran down his face as he sobbed pitifully for his life. The stranger refused to say anything; the only response Pascal received was a series of punches to the face. Bones shattered with every hit. In less than five punches, he was unconscious.

The stranger reached into his satchel and pulled out a small syringe. He stabbed it directly into the bandit's heart. To everyone's surprise, Pascal regained consciousness and screamed in agony. The hooded man ripped Pascal's shirt open and pulled out a small knife from his boot and pressed the blade to Pascal's chest.

Mario watched in horror as the man started to carve something into Pascal's body. He wanted to look away, but he couldn't move his body. He was paralyzed in a state of shock.

In about two minutes, the hooded man stood up while Pascal screamed and writhed in pain. The stranger grabbed the hook out of the bandit's shoulder and drove it deep into his forehead. Everything went silent.

The stranger reached for a small bundle of rope from under his cloak. He tied an end to the hook embedded in Pascal's head and threw the other end over a high tree branch. The stranger pulled and hoisted the corpse of Pascal so that anyone entering the forest could read his warning. The words "SLAVERS DIE" were carved prominently and legibly across Pascal's bare chest. After hanging the corpse, the hooded man focused his attention on the three tied up prisoners.

Mario gulped. Dread filled his body. His mind was racing at the thought of what this man might do to him and his companions. The hooded man grabbed his sword out of the ground and continued to approach. When the man was only a few feet from Mario, he raised his sword high above his head and swung. Mario closed his eyes, but when he heard the sound of rope being cut instead of flesh, he opened his eyes to see his bonds undone.

"You alright?" the man asked in a nasally voice.

Mario was speechless; his mouth felt dry and his tongue didn't work. He looked at Hamish, who was rubbing his raw, rope-burned wrists. He then looked at Deidre, who was gently touching her swollen, bruised cheeks.

"Are you alright? Do you speak common? *Eludir?*" the man asked again.

Mario nodded. His face still white from fear.

"Alright then," the stranger stated and began to walk away.

"Wait!" Deidre called out.

The man stopped in his tracks and turned around. His face still hidden by his hood.

"Where are your comrades?" Deidre asked.

"I have none."

"Yous mean to tell us yous did this all by yourself?" Hamish gasped in disbelief.

"No human is that fast," Deidre added.

"Not one you've ever met," the man stated dryly.

"What's your name?" Mario asked, still trying to see his saviour's face.

The stranger let out a sigh and lifted his hood. He was nothing like Mario imagined. He was young, too young to be that good with a sword; he couldn't have been more than twenty years old. His face was skinny with a thin, patchy brown beard. Mario stared into the stranger's hazel eyes. He saw pain and suffering, more than someone his age should've seen.

"Call me Flint," the man stated.

"Why did you save us?" Deidre asked, still touching her cheek tenderly.

"I've been hunting these bandits for a while. You were just here."

"Why not wait for a knight to take care of it?" Hamish inquired.

"Because I know a knight will try to arrest them. These monsters deserve to be butchered," Flint said angrily.

"*Blais'navaal*," Deidre agreed.

"Well, thank you," Mario said begrudgingly. "We are hunting them as well if you would like to join. We know where their comrades are."

"It's best if I work alone . . ." the man started but suddenly shifted his focus to Hamish. As quick as lightning, Flint reached into his satchel and threw a coin at Hamish's face.

Hamish immediately grabbed his face and howled in terror as smoke rose from his cheek.

"What did you do!?" Deidre cried out.

"Silver, your companion is a changeling. Silver burns them at the touch, just like werewolves," Flint stated calmly.

"How did you know?" Mario asked, looking curiously at the screaming Hamish, whose appearance began to change before his eyes.

"I didn't. I just suspected it. If he wasn't a changeling, the coin would've bounced off his face harmlessly. Most changelings kill someone then assume their identity. They can't create an appearance, only imitate it." Flint reached for his sword.

"Wait!" Hamish screamed in a distorted voice. His body began to morph and change before their very eyes. The sounds of bones breaking filled their ears as his appearance was torn apart and a new one took form.

In the place of Hamish stood a featureless solid black creature. It was close to seven feet tall and had long, gangly arms that touched the ground. The back of the creature was hunched so that its head was a full foot in front of its torso. "I didn't kill him!" the creature spoke in a layered, distorted voice. "I found him on the battlefield. He was already dead! You don't know what it's like for us changelings. We were hunted to near extinction by the Order of the Swords. I just wanted to live peacefully among humans. I didn't deserve to be hunted. Please! I've never killed anyone."

"I believe him," Mario stated.

"Then you're an idiot," Flint said angrily, still holding his sword in his hand.

"He could've killed me, but instead he brought me to Deidre's people who healed me. He's not evil!" Mario argued.

"Move aside," Flint commanded.

"If you want to kill him, you'll have to cut me down as well," Mario said, standing between Flint and the creature.

"And me," Deidre added, who had retrieved her bow from the wagon and had an arrow nocked and aimed at Flint already.

Flint looked at Mario, then the creature, then Deidre. He begrudgingly sheathed his sword and let out a sigh. "Fine, but the moment I catch him doing anything nefarious, I'll kill him."

"We're almost out of the forest, we can camp by the river. Then Riverwell is only a day's walk from there," Deidre suggested.

The creature changed shape before Mario's eyes; the process of the creature's metamorphosis was haunting and made Mario's stomach churn. This time, Hamish took the shape of a handsome, middle-aged man with fine clothes. He had a cul-de-sac of short brown hair around the top of his head and a neatly trimmed beard. His eyes were as black as the creature's original form. They stuck out of the pudgy face like coals in the snow. Although the creature's new face was fat, the rest of his body was lean and fairly muscular.

Mario quickly went to gather his things and followed Deidre to the new camp. He froze when he picked up his blood-stained armour. The memory of beheading George instantly rushed back into his head. A shiver ran down his spine.

***

The clearing was picturesque. Moonlight reflected off of the river. Birds happily chirped, and fireflies buzzed about the campsite. The ominous aura of the forest had been left behind. Mario had fallen asleep by the campfire; he tossed and turned as nightmares haunted him. The sight of George's headless, wriggling body was burned into his mind.

"No!" Mario sat up screaming. He looked around and saw that nobody was by the fire with him. Hamish was skipping rocks into the river, Flint was leaning against a tree, sticking to the shadows, and Deidre was nowhere to be seen. Mario slowly got up and walked towards Flint. *Perhaps a killer of his magnitude can give me some advice in dealing with these dreams.*

"How'd you get the scar?" Flint asked without looking up at Mario.

"It's a long story," Mario answered, hoping he wouldn't have to tell the tale.

"It's a long night," Flint answered, still not making eye contact with Mario.

Begrudgingly, Mario sat down beside Flint. He told the tale to the best of his recollection. How the beast ambushed Hamish and him in the forest, how his helmet caved into his skull, how he they killed it, and how Deidre's people healed him. While Mario was talking, Flint didn't make a sound; he didn't even make eye contact with Mario. He just sat motionless, leaning against the tree, like a statue.

"You're lucky," Flint finally said after a lengthy silence.

"Why?"

"From what you've described, that sounds like you fought a ghillie. They are ancient beings and are highly territorial. You're lucky you got away with just a scar."

"How do you know all this?"

"Books."

They sat in the silence while Mario tried to think of the right way to word his question. But he was distracted by his insulted pride. *Will I be like Sir Darius? The first thing people will notice about me from now on will be the scars?* "Can I ask you something?" Mario said after finally finding the right words.

"If you must."

"How many people have you killed?"

"Lots."

"Do you sleep okay? How do you get the images out of your head?"

"You don't."

"But I can't sleep. All I see is the man I killed there . . ."

Flint sighed, and for the first time since the start of their conversation, he made eye contact with Mario. "Listen," he began, "it doesn't get easier. Every time you kill someone that weight sticks with you, and it doesn't go away until you go in the ground. My advice, take solace in the fact that the bastard deserved it."

Mario sighed, although unsatisfied with Flint's answer. He thanked him and walked away. *I'm sure Sir Darius and Flint would get along well. Both don't seem to mince their words.* While walking back to the campfire, Mario heard a barely audible sound coming from behind a tree. Mario decided to stealthily investigate. To his surprise, he saw that behind the oak tree was Deidre sobbing in the fetal position.

Mario froze. This was a Deidre that he had never seen before. The confident, angry, ferocious elven archer that he met less than a week ago had vanished. In her place was a defeated, battered, and broken elf whose innocence was stolen. *What do I do? Should I say anything? How would I even go about comforting her?* Mario decided to do nothing and instead grant her privacy.

Mario walked absentmindedly. His mind was preoccupied with replaying the gruesome death of George over and over again. *Why can't I get this out of my head? Am I meant to be cursed with this thought till I die? Is Flint right? How did dad cope with it?* Mario looked up to the moon in search of answers. *Dad, I wish you were here with me. I don't know what to do. Ever since I left the college, I don't feel like I should be a knight anymore. I wish I never took my vows.* "Then I could abandon this fucking quest."

"What quest?" Hamish asked.

Mario hadn't realized that he said the last part of his thought aloud. He also hadn't realized Hamish had been standing beside him for some time. The unexpected response made him jump.

"Nothing," Mario lied, for the first time since taking his vows.

"From my knowledge, you knights aren't supposed to swear . . . or lie," Hamish said, expertly sensing Mario's dishonesty.

"I can't get the thought of killing that bandit out of my head," Mario answered, preparing for a painful conversation.

"I can only imagine what killing your own kind would do to someone." Hamish stared deep into Mario's eyes. "I hadn't harmed a living thing until I joined you."

So, I corrupted you. I forced you to become something you are not.

Hamish put his hand on Mario's shoulder. "We are in this together, Mario." Hamish smiled.

Mario was at a loss for words. He turned his head and looked at his reflection in the river. He saw his scarred face, and his blood-stained armour. *A grim sight.* "Help me take this armour off. I want to wash it."

It took only a few minutes for them to remove his armour and scrub it clean. Mario decided to let it dry near the campfire and spend the night in his linens. The wind cut through the thin layer of clothes; it was invigorating. Without the weight of his armour, Mario felt free, free of his responsibilities, oaths, protocols, and duties—and also free of the troubling memories.

Mario decided to walk back to the clearing where he saw Deidre crying before. *Perhaps I just need to do what Hamish did for me. Just let her know that we are here for her.* Once he got to the clearing, Mario froze in horror. He saw that Deidre had hung herself from the oak tree.

"Flint! Hamish! Come quick!" Mario cried as he ran up to Deidre's legs and lifted them to take the weight off her neck.

Flint was the first to arrive. When he saw what had happened, he quickly threw his dagger at the noose and cut it in half. Deidre fell to the ground with a hard thud.

Hamish, Flint, and Mario stood around Deidre's motionless body in silence. Hamish and Mario were stunned. Their mouths agape. Flint's face remained emotionless, his brown eyes staring stoically at Deidre's lifeless body. Suddenly, Deidre started coughing.

"Oh, thank the gods!" Hamish cried out.

"You should've let me die, *dahrenn.*" Deidre spat as she grabbed the noose from around her neck.

"Deidre, it will be okay. . . ." Mario started.

"How would you know!?" Deidre snapped. Tears filled her swollen eyes.

The three men were not sure of what to do or say. Finally, Flint kneeled down on the ground beside Deidre.

"*Turiel dah'brereen. Sae'ashaal murin.*" Flint's voice was strong but quiet. It spread an aura of calmness amongst the group.

Deidre nodded slightly and wiped the tears from her face.

"Leave us," Flint stated calmly.

"But . . ." Mario started once again.

"Now's not the time," Flint said firmly, glaring at the others.

Reluctantly, Mario and Hamish left to sit by the campfire. Neither said a word while they waited. They sat in silence, staring into the reeds on the other side of the river, listening to the crackling of the fire and the slow, gentle lapping of the river. After about an hour of silence, Flint sat down beside them at the campfire. Mario and Hamish both looked at him, Flint gave a subtle nod. No words needed to be said. Relief coursed through Mario's body.

***

The following day was beautiful. The sun was shining, the birds were singing their lovely songs, and the skies didn't have a single cloud in them. The party of four departed early in the morning and marched silently until about noon when they stopped for a quick rest by the riverbed.

"Why did you change form?" Deidre asked Hamish, speaking for the first time since the previous night.

"The same reason you change clothes; a skin can get tiring and boring after a while," Hamish answered uninterestedly.

"You're talking differently now," Deidre observed.

"I don't just take on the appearance of the person; I take on all their mannerisms. Their appearance, their voice, even their speech impediments. Everything. The only thing that I can't replicate is their personality," Hamish informed.

Mario wasn't listening to any of the conversation between Deidre and Hamish. He was too busy looking down at his newly-cleaned armour. Even though the bloodstains were no longer visible on the armour, it still felt like they were there. *This damned armour. Even after washing away the evidence of the memory, it still lingers.*

"We should continue. We can rest at the inn in Riverwell," Flint said, bringing Mario's attention back to the task at hand.

An idea shot into Mario's head. "Hey, the people I was travelling with before I met Hamish were going to Riverwell. Perhaps they'll be there!" Enthusiasm filled his voice at the thought of reuniting with his old companions. The exciting thought also took Mario's mind off of the horrors of the past.

"Was that the dwarf, halfling, and human?" Hamish asked.

"Yes. They were cobblers." Mario picked up his sword and shield off the ground.

"You travelled with non-humans?" Deidre asked in disbelief.

"Of course. They saved my life. I hope that one day I can return the favour." Mario smiled.

Deidre had no reply. She quickly grabbed her bow and left to catch up with Flint, who was already walking down the road. Mario and Hamish quickly followed suit.

The road to Riverwell was abandoned. Not a single person was on it, except for the party of four. The road was a well-known trade route, so it was uncommon for it to be deserted. *Something is off.* It wasn't long after that Mario saw what was wrong. Along the roadside, walked a man wearing familiar black and gold robes, with a large golden sun embroidered in the middle.

"Oh no," Mario said.

"What is it?" Flint asked.

"The Church of the Golden Sun. One of their priests walks along the road," Hamish continued sourly.

"So? Why should we fear a clergyman?" Flint asked ignorantly.

"They aren't fond of non-humans . . ." Mario looked at Deidre.

Deidre looked up and saw Mario's eyes on her. They were filled with empathy and sadness. Deidre frowned and asked, "So, what? Not the first *dahrenn* I've met that didn't like elves. Won't be the last either."

"They blame the non-humans for all the problems facing humans. Disease, war, famine, everything is somehow the non-humans' fault," Hamish explained.

"So, no different than the rest of the uneducated filth that makes up the human race." Flint scowled.

Mario was shocked. *He sounds like Deidre. Perhaps they bonded over their hatred of humans. That doesn't make sense though. Flint is human. How can he hate us so much? What kind of person despises their own kind?* When they walked past the priest, Mario's body tensed. He feared what would happen.

"Stop!" The priest yelled. "No non-humans may enter the human sanctuary of Riverwell!" This priest was much younger than the one in Eulway. His hair was a vibrant blonde, and his face was clean-shaven, save for a small amount of peach fuzz on his chin.

"We have business there," Mario answered.

"There is no business for an elf in Riverwell! You blasphemers will be struck down by the Golden Sun for your heresy. May the Golden Sun show you no mercy, and may your bodies know an eternity of suffering in the next world!" the priest yelled, pointing a skinny finger at the group.

"Save your breath, kid. Unless you are going to stop us . . . which I highly discourage," Flint stated, his hand already on the pommel of his sword.

"I can do nothing. I am a man of peace, just know that the Golden Sun will cut you down! You and your elven whore . . ."

Before the priest could finish his sentence, Deidre had shot an arrow directly between the priest's eyes. The priest's body fell limp on the side of the road as blood began to pool on the ground.

Mario turned his head to look at Deidre. Her face was remorseless. It was the same face she made when she killed the bandits in the forest. This time, however, tears were running down her bruised cheeks, not tears of sadness or joy, but tears of anger. Mario placed his hand on her shoulder, but she quickly shrugged him off and stormed down the path. Flint looked at the corpse of the priest and spat on it. He glared at Mario and Hamish, then continued down the road and caught up with Deidre. Mario and Hamish followed. Nobody said a word for the remainder of the journey.

***

The town of Riverwell was teeming with life. It resembled more of a city than a town. Behind the giant stone walls of the town was a metropolis of diversity. Elves, dwarves, halflings, and humans all congregated in the streets and went about their lives. *This doesn't look like a "human sanctuary." Perhaps the priest was wrong. This looks like a utopia, free of racial discrimination.* Mario didn't realize how wrong his observation was.

In the middle of the town sat a giant fountain, the top adorned with a golden statue of Peslius, God of the Sun. Depicted as an old man, Peslius held a bundle of wheat in one hand and an hourglass in the other. People crowded the fountain and tossed whatever coins they had into it in hopes that their prayers would be answered. Guards patrolled the area and kept a diligent watch, making sure nothing happened to the monument.

Beyond the fountain square, a series of walkways over the river led them to the middle of the market where the deafening sounds of bartering filled the air. People were screaming at one another trying to get the best deal. Mario began to feel overwhelmed; there were too many people in one area. He felt like he was going to drown in the sea of noise.

"Do you see your friends!" Hamish yelled, trying to cut through the wall of sound.

"No!" Mario replied, barely hearing his own voice.

"There are no non-humans here!" Flint yelled.

Mario looked around and realized that Flint was right. Everyone in the marketplace was human. Deidre was the only elf. It didn't take the town guards long to notice either, and soon, they were surrounded.

"That thing can't be here! This is a human's only district!" one of the guards yelled from behind his steel helmet.

"She's with us," Mario explained.

"Do you have a permit?" another guard asked.

"A what!?" Hamish yelled.

"A permit!" the guard repeated.

"No!" Mario replied as his voice began to go hoarse.

"I'm sorry, but we'll have to escort you back to your homes," the guard replied.

"We're not from here!" Mario corrected.

"Then we'll have to escort you out of town," the guard said.

"Hey! They're with me!" a familiar voice called in the distance.

Mario turned his head and saw Miles storming over to the rescue. He cut through the sea of people with ease, quickly and acrobatically turning and shifting his weight to navigate the narrow spaces between person to person.

"Here's my permit," Miles said upon reaching the guards.

"Very well, but take them back to your stall," the guard replied harshly.

"What was that about?" Mario asked.

"I'll explain once we're safe," Miles replied calmly.

Miles' stand was located in a back alley behind a local inn called The Laughing Minstrel. The smell of raw sewage and rotten food filled the alley. Mario could see that business had been abysmal due to the poor location. Finnegan Graeme had almost finished packing up the cart.

"This town's gone to bloody shite," Finnegan cursed as he lifted another heavy box onto the cart.

"I had to get a permit due to having non-human employees. And because of Finnegan and Roger's race, we were given this location," Miles explained, clearly frustrated.

"At least they still worship the old gods," Hamish added.

"Fuckin' hell they do. 'Tis only a matter of time before that cocksuckin' statue is taken down and a big bright Golden Sun takes its place," Finnegan explained.

"The church is getting some serious support across the kingdom," Roger explained. "Riverwell is now segregated, and only certain people can visit certain shops, and non-human shopkeepers have to charge a non-human tax, making their products more expensive."

"Giving human shopkeepers an economic advantage," Flint added.

"Exactly," Miles answered sombrely.

"Soon, only humans will populate Riverwell," Roger said.

"I'm sorry," Mario said.

"Nothing you can do; 'tis the times. But tell us, how have you been? Looks like you got one hell of a scar!" Finnegan roared.

Mario winced at the mention of his scar. He took a deep breath in and then went on to tell the painful and lengthy tale of the past few weeks. His march into the Eeragwia Forest with Hamish, who was actually a changeling disguised as a guard, and their battle with a giant beast that almost killed him. His encounter with the elven colony and Deidre, who was tasked to escort them safely out of the forest but stayed to hunt down the bandits with them. Their ambush that rescued three elven girls, but resulted in the bandits capturing them instead. Then finally how Flint saved them from their captors.

"Gods," Miles said, "Sounds like you've been through a lot."

"It has definitely tried my will," Mario replied. Unable to shake the image of the bandit's death out of his head after retelling it.

"Well, let us get right shit-faced tonight!" Finnegan exclaimed. "Luckily, this place accepts everyone as long as you pay. So, let's get drunk off our asses!"

A smile spread across Mario's face; it had been a while since he could relax. *We deserve a night off.*

The inside of the inn was a sight for sore eyes. The smell of roast chicken filled the room. On the north side of the building was a small stage, and on the stage was a quartet of minstrels singing songs about dragons, knights, and heroes of yore. Mario saw that the patrons were mainly non-humans. They greeted Miles, Hamish, Mario, and Flint with looks of distaste.

Miles found the biggest table and ordered a round of ale for everyone. It didn't take long for the two parties to start befriending one another. Finnegan was trying to convince Hamish to change his face into ridiculous things. His requests were ludicrous and juvenile. He demanded that Hamish change his face to a badger's head, a pot of gold, and a pair of weighty breasts. Hamish refused to participate but was entertained by the drunken creativity of the dwarf.

Miles and Flint were in a deep, philosophical debate. They discussed a plethora of topics. Some of the more interesting topics included: the morality of historical controversies, the various flaws in the global political systems, the impact the Church of the Golden Sun will have on the kingdom, and how cobbling wasn't so different from mercenary work. Their discussion was more of a monologue, as Flint only replied with head movements or one-word answers.

Roger was talking the head off of Deidre. He was telling the tale of how they found Mario and the story of how he became a cobbler, and, of course, telling hundreds of jokes. To Mario's surprise, Deidre was smiling and, for one of the jokes, even laughed. *We all needed this.* Mario took a sip of ale and enjoyed the music of the minstrels.

Suddenly, the doors of the inn flew open. A sweating, blood-covered dwarf stood in the doorway panting and gasping for air.

"There's a riot! Everyone—"

Before he could finish, he collapsed on the inn's wooden floor, a hand-axe embedded in the back of his skull.

The riots in Riverwell in 1177 were one of the most brutal and violent pogroms the world had ever seen. Very few people managed to escape the city with their lives and even fewer escaped unscarred. It is truly a blight on our otherwise flawless history..

Adam Talbot,
A Comprehensive look at Drussdell's History

CHAPTER SEVEN

The door slammed shut before anyone could react. The bartender had closed it and was putting all of his weight against the door to prevent it from being reopened. A couple of the other patrons quickly started stacking chairs and tables against the entrance, trying to create a makeshift barricade. This was not their first pogrom. Although the barricade of tables and chairs was structurally sturdy, it did nothing to block the noise that was coming from outside. The sounds of weapons clanging, women screaming, houses burning, and people dying leaked through the inn's rickety thin walls.

There was a bang at the front door. The patrons could hear muffled orders being barked from outside the walls. Another bang; this time the barricade shifted half a foot back away from the door. A couple of dwarves instinctively used their body weight to reinforce the barricade. All of the regular patrons' faces were pale with worry, fearing what would happen to them if the barricade should fall.

Mario looked at his companions. Roger and Finnegan were both pale, much like the other patrons. Deidre's complexion was no paler than usual; however, she had a look of worry. Another bang at the door. Mario looked at Flint, who seemed to be unaware that the inn was trying to be broken into. Flint's stoic, expressionless face irritated him. Mario could feel his face flush red with anger. Another bang. Mario turned his head to see Hamish's reaction, but Hamish had already leapt from the table and was lending his weight to help reinforce the barricade. Another bang at the door; this time it knocked one of the dwarves reinforcing the barricade on his back.

"Is there another exit?" Miles yelled at the bartender.

"Ummm . . . I . . . uh . . ." the bartender stammered.

"We need to know now!" Miles barked, his voice booming throughout the inn.

"There's the door that leads to the sewers, but it isn't very pleasant," the bartender said hesitantly.

"Trust me, it's more pleasant than what you will find out there," Flint said plainly while continuing to seem unbothered by the whole situation.

"Take everyone else down into the sewers and get them somewhere safe. We will hold off the mob," Miles instructed with authority.

The bartender complied and led the patrons down into the sewers. Mario was impressed with Miles' ability to take charge in a critical moment. He also wished that he would've acted in the same way sooner.

"You better head into the sewers. We can take care of ourselves," Miles instructed the dwarves holding the door.

"Fuck off!" the first dwarf barked.

"Any dwarf worth his beard never shies away from a good fight!" the second dwarf added.

Finnegan quickly rose to his feet and joined his brethren in reinforcing the door. "These lads are right, Miles. And we could use all the help we can get."

Miles reluctantly nodded and turned his focus to Roger. "You better go with the others; we will find you when this is all over," his voice shaking.

"I can help . . ." Roger began.

"Listen here, fuzz-foot," Finnegan barked while leaning against the barricade. "I like you, you're a good lad, but you're absolute shite in a fight. You'll be about as useful as a knitted sword."

Finnegan's words seemed to cut Roger deep, deeper than intended. Roger's head sank down so that he was looking at his feet. Miles kneeled beside him and lifted his chin with his right hand and handed Roger a dagger with his left.

"Don't listen to ol' Finn. I need you to go and protect the others. They aren't warriors, and they need someone to protect them." Miles' voice was soothing, similar to Marian's. Mario was impressed by how easily Miles could change his tone from authoritative and commanding to soothing, calming, and almost motherly. Roger seemed to cheer up, and he ran to catch up with the patrons. Miles stood up on the table and looked around the inn. Once again, he had assumed control of the situation.

"We won't hold that door for much longer. They will breach this inn, and we will have to fight our way out of here. They must not get to the sewers; we have to protect that exit at all costs. Deidre, I want you to stand on the stage and cover us using your bow. Mario and Hamish, I want you to be our first line of defence. You two are the most skilled with a sword. . . ."

"I better join them." Flint nonchalantly rose from the table drawing his sword.

"Right. Finnegan and the other dwarves will join me in barricading the sewer exit. Once we have that fortified, we will help out you three at the door."

"What if Roger and the others need to escape the sewers?" Hamish asked, teeth-gritting as he leaned all his weight against the barricade.

"Unfortunately, that won't be an option for them. They'll have to push forward . . . or die," Miles replied. "Everyone clear about what they are doing?"

Everyone nodded, and nobody seemed to object with any of the assigned duties. They quickly sprang into action and began carrying out their orders. Deidre took her position on the stage behind a flipped table, an arrow was already knocked and ready. Finnegan, the dwarves, and Miles were taking whatever wasn't being used for the front barricade and piled it on top of the sewer hatch, making it difficult for anyone to pursue after the others. Hamish, Flint, and Mario leaned against the door with all their might. Each bang against the door grew stronger than the last. Mario lost his footing every time.

In a few minutes, the door flew open, and the three men barricading the door fell on their backs. The outsiders flooded into the tavern like a sea of rats funnelling through a small crack in a wall. Deidre quickly shot her arrows into the mass of enemies. Her first shot was so powerful that it went through two men before finally stopping in a third's chest. Flint was the first to his feet. His sword seemed to sing as he swung it through the air, performing a macabre dance between him and his foes. Every turn or shift of Flint's bodyweight sent heads flying, staining the inn's wooden floors red.

Mario rose to his feet and began pushing back the rabble with his shield. The nightmarish thought of beheading George was not in his mind. The only thing he was thinking about was surviving. As he was hacking, slashing, and mutilating each attacker, he noticed that most of these men were not armed with swords. Many had makeshift weapons like scythes, sickles, pitchforks, or hammers. Mario even saw one man wielding a piece of lumber and trying to use it as a club. Mario also saw Flint effortlessly sever the man's jugular. Mario's face went pale. *These are commoners. The people I'm sworn to protect.* . . .

Mario's lack of focus caused him to not notice the commoner charging at him from the side, tackling him to the ground. Mario wheezed as the hard wooden floor knocked all the air out of his lungs. Mario looked up in horror as he saw the man hold a hammer above his head, about to swing it down to crush Mario's skull. Mario closed his eyes, but instead of hearing the sound of steel crushing his bones, he heard blood-curdling screams of horror. He opened his eyes and saw a large, gangly black hand had torn the man's head right off his neck.

Hamish had reverted back to his monstrous natural form. Using his nightmarishly long arms as a pendulum, knocking over the horde with each swing. Hamish let out an ear-splitting, distorted scream as a spear punctured his leg. He grabbed the man wielding the spear and lifted him into the air with ease. The man screamed and begged for help, but it was too late. Hamish squeezed the man like one would squeeze an orange or a peach, and the man popped. His innards spewed out of his mouth and blood leaked from the eyes. Mario could hear the sounds of his ribs breaking under the force of Hamish's monstrous hand.

Mario got on all fours and began to stand up but was immediately pushed down again. He turned his head up and saw that the three dwarves were using his back as a springboard, catapulting themselves into the horde of enemies, with weapons drawn. Each dwarf let out a terrifying battle cry as they landed in the middle of the crowd. Mario lost sight of each of them as they got sucked into the mass of bodies. He felt a hand on his shoulder and felt himself being lifted to his feet. He turned his head and saw Miles. His face covered in blood. Mario nodded his head and began to focus on the enemies barrelling into the inn. Instinctively, he assumed a battering position with his shield. Every time an enemy would crash into his shield, he would push them back, slash with his sword, then reset his position waiting for the next enemy.

In less than two minutes, the horde of rioters began to retreat. Screams of "Monster!" could be heard in the streets. Mario turned his head and saw Hamish had already reverted back into the form of the handsome man with the fat face. Blood poured out of his leg from where the lance hit.

"We have to put a tourniquet on you," Mario stated, looking concerned at Hamish's knee.

"It's nothing. We have to get out of here; then we can worry about licking our wounds." Hamish grimaced as he limped over to regroup with the rest of the party.

"Where's Finnegan?" Miles asked in a panicked voice.

The mound of corpses began to shake. A small hand burst through the top of the corpses and a muffled scream could be heard from underneath. Mario and Miles quickly began throwing bodies off the pile and uncovered an exhausted, blood-soaked Finnegan Graeme.

"Soddin' hell! Thought I was done for," Finnegan growled, wiping the blood off his face.

"Where are the other dwarves?" Miles asked.

"I saw one get cut down, but the other . . ." Finnegan trailed off.

"There's no time to look for him. We have to get out of here now." Flint casually wiped the blood off of his blade.

"But—" Mario started.

"No, he's right. We have to leave," Miles said somberly.

They exited the inn and walked into the street. Mario was shocked. It looked like the world was set ablaze. Everything was glowing red from fires, and the sky was black with smoke. The deafening sound of screaming could be heard throughout the town. *This is going to be talked about for centuries. . . .*

"Quickly, to the river! That's where the runoff from the sewer goes, and that's where Roger will be," Miles instructed.

They ran down the street as fast as they could. When they turned the corner to head toward the river, they froze in terror. In the middle of the street was a bloodbath. Non-humans and humans were engaged in a bloody brawl. Men were being cut down like dogs, women were being dragged into side alleys while they screamed, and children were butchering their peers with whatever they could find. Deidre shot an arrow at a man who was dragging a small elven girl into a side alley. As if it was a cue for battle, the rest of the party charged forward ready to engage in another fight.

This time Mario crashed into the crowd, breaking up the brawl. He stood up and began to swing his sword, slicing anything that got in its way. While keeping his focus on the battle, Mario saw that Hamish had decided to stay back and protect Deidre, not that she needed protecting. He saw Finnegan Graeme splitting heads open with his hand axe, their brains covering the street. Mario turned his head and saw a man swing his scythe at Flint's abdomen. Mario saw Flint's intestines slide out of his stomach and onto the street.

"No!" a cry from behind Mario shouted.

Mario turned on his heels and saw that Miles was surrounded, overwhelmed by the number of weapons attacking him. Mario sprinted across the street as fast as his feet could carry him. He knocked over one of the men and stabbed him in the chest while he was prone. The young knight then did a quick pirouette and chopped the head off another one of Miles' attackers. Mario could hear an assailant behind him swing. Instinctively, he ducked and spun on his toes and thrusted his sword up through the lower jaw of the man. Mario saw that a few of the other attackers had arrows sticking out of their bodies. He looked at Deidre and gave a slight nod of the head as a thank-you.

Miles was sitting on the ground with his back against the foundation of a building. Mario kneeled and began to examine his friend's wounds. The most serious was a cut that was right below the heart that was about six inches deep. Blood was flowing like a river from the wound. The next serious injury was a two-inch-deep cut in his upper right thigh. *Hopefully, they missed the artery.* Mario quickly cut a piece of clothing off of one of the corpses and began to fashion a tourniquet around Miles' wounded leg.

"Mario . . ." Miles struggled as he coughed up blood.

"Save your breath, Miles. You'll be fine." Mario tried to wrap Miles' leg as best he could.

"No, Mario . . ." Miles began, coughing up more blood this time.

"Miles! Stop it, you'll be fine!" Mario snapped angrily.

Suddenly, Mario felt a sharp, cold pain right under his left armpit. Mario swung his elbow back impulsively; it connected with something hard. He heard his attacker begin to stand up again. Mario gripped his sword with his right hand and blindly swung around hoping to hit his attacker before they had a chance to regain their posture. Mario turned and saw that his attacker was not a man, but a boy. A young boy no older than eight years old. He was holding a small knife in his hand, his face covered in ash and blood. His green eyes were staring at Mario full of shock. Mario looked down and saw that his sword had sliced through the boy's midsection. The boy's upper half slowly began to fall backwards as his lower half fell forwards. The only thing holding the boy together was his partially severed spine.

Mario instantly vomited. He collapsed on his hands and knees and puked profusely. A shockwave of pain spread throughout his body every time his stomach gave an excruciating heave. His esophagus burned with pain as the contents of his stomach surged up his throat, through his mouth and onto the street. Tears began to fill Mario's eyes, some out of pain and some out of disgust. Mario could feel the blood vessels underneath his eyes rupturing from the amount of force behind each heave. Mario looked down at his vomit-covered gauntlets; they were shaking uncontrollably.

Mario's comrades were still fighting, but he could not hear the sounds of the battle. Instead, all Mario heard was a deafening ring, muffling all of the sounds of the outside world. *What have I done? I just killed a child . . . a child! A knight should never harm a child. This armour, this sword, and shield; they bring out the worst in me. They turn me into a . . . monster.*

Mario felt a hand touch his shoulder. He closed his eyes and prayed that it was an enemy, that it was someone who would take his life and free him of his guilt-ridden conscience. When the fatal blow never came, Mario turned his head and saw Deidre, her bow slung across her shoulder. With her help, Mario slowly got back up to his feet. To his surprise, she quickly and tightly pulled Mario into an embrace. More tears leaked out of Mario's eyes; it had been so long since someone held him. It had been so long since another person hugged him and made him feel that sense of hope and security.

"Miles is dead . . ." Deidre whispered into Mario's ear solemnly.

Mario quickly tore himself from Deidre's embrace and knelt beside his fallen comrade. A thick pool of blood surrounded Miles' corpse. His skin had already begun turning pale.

"The wounds were too serious. Even if a surgeon was here, it would have been a miracle to save him," Flint said from behind the group.

Mario spun around on his heels and looked at Flint astonished. "How're you . . .? I thought . . . I saw you die!"

"You didn't," Flint stated plainly.

"I did!" Mario exclaimed this time standing up to meet Flint's eyes. "I saw that man with the scythe. He sliced you in the stomach, and I saw your guts fall out."

"You're welcome to check." Flint parted his coat.

Mario examined Flint's abdomen carefully. His shirt had clearly been sliced by a scythe, yet there was no wound. There was barely a scar. Blood was soaked into all of Flint's clothes, but it was impossible to tell if it was his or the others'.

"We don't have time for this. We have to get to the river," Finnegan said, somewhat angrily.

Mario stood up and sighed. "Fine. Hamish, you and I will carry Miles' corpse. Deidre will cover us while Flint and Finnegan take point." *I can't let any more of these people die . . . not because of me.*

"Like hell, we're bringing that!" Flint pointed at Miles' lifeless husk.

"We have to give him a proper burial!" Mario screamed.

"We will be lucky if we make it out of here alive by ourselves. It will be impossible for us to escape while we are hauling his corpse around. I'm sorry Mario, but he will just slow us down."

"I can't believe this! He is my friend and doesn't deserve to rot in the streets!"

"We cannot jeopardize the group for a fucking corpse!"

Finnegan cleared his throat. "Mario, he's right. I loved Miles, more than me own brother. But if we take him with us . . . we'll rot in these streets alongside him." A single tear ran down Finnegan's cheek before his dry, bushy beard absorbed it.

Mario looked around the group; it seemed that everyone was in agreement. They had to leave Miles behind. Defeated, Mario whispered, "Fine."

"Quickly, to the river. Maybe we can grab a boat!" Hamish yelled. The party took off running down the street towards the dock district.

As they were running, Mario turned his head back towards the carnage that he narrowly survived. He looked at Miles' pale body sitting in the pool of his own blood. He remembered when Miles saved his life and brought him to Marian when he was on death's doorstep. *Goodbye, my friend. I'm sorry I couldn't pay back my debt to you.*

Mario then focused on the mutilated corpse of the young boy. He had to fight every muscle in his body in order to keep himself from puking again. He saw that the boy's emerald eyes had already started turning grey. He saw that the look of shock and horror was still frozen on the child's face. *I'm sorry that I stole your life. I'm sorry for what I've become.*

The streets to the dock district were narrow and winding. Every corner presented the opportunity for another fight. Another massacre. Fortunately for the battle-wearied group, most of the fighting had moved to the centre of the town. Mario could hear the screaming and could see the firelight reflecting off of the golden statue of Peslius. Suddenly, and without warning, the giant golden statue teetered to one side and began to fall like a giant oak cut down in a forest. Mario could hear cheering coming from the centre of town once the statue crashed into the streets. *The old gods are dead.*

"Look a boat!" Hamish pointed at a small canoe that was still moored at the docks.

"Quickly!" Flint called as he waved people past him.

Three men came running down the dockside, screaming at the heroes as they crammed themselves in the small boat. Deidre began to ready her bow once again.

"Deidre don't," Mario pleaded, grabbing her arm.

Deidre reluctantly lowered her bow and severed the rope connecting the boat to the dock with her knife.

As they were slowly grabbed by the current of the river, Mario could hear the fading cries of the three men in the distance.

"Stop! That's our boat! Thieves!"

Mario pulled his knees tight to his chest and buried his face in his hands. He wept for the rest of the night.

Kartaga is an evil and a vile place. Prisoners from all across the empire are sent there for their punishment. No matter the crime, whether it be adultery, theft, or murder; all wicked souls are sent to Kartaga.

Gracus Valenicus IV,
The Fool's Guide to the Empire

Demons are quite curious creatures. Most demons require something to bind them to a person. Usually that "something" is a state of being. Certain emotions beckon to certain demons, and the demons usually exploit those emotions in order to sustain themselves. Some of the most common emotions that draw demons are: gluttony, lust, envy, rage, and pride. Although there have been a few reports of demons sustaining themselves off of more complex emotions such as regret, guilt, and even joy.

Professor Hanubis Moretz,
A Beginner's Guide to Demonology

INTERLUDE

The war room was chaotic as advisors argued with one another and servants rushed in and out for more food and drink. Bored, the king stared listlessly at the scene happening before him. Lukas Aurelius remained hidden in the shadows of the enemy's hostile war room. Nobody saw him; this was his gift—to blend in and remain invisible, no matter the environment.

"Your Highness, please listen! We are on the verge of a crisis!" one advisor beseeched King Dryden.

"Crisis? It is just a little riot. Sire, it is nothing to worry about. Do not concern yourself with such petty manners," another advisor retorted in an arrogant tone.

"I shall decide what is worthy of my attention not you!" the king said, his voice cutting through the noise in the room like a knife cutting through butter.

"Yes, Your Grace." The advisor bowed graciously, trying to hide his cherry-red face.

A wonder how anything can be accomplished with leaders as incompetent as this. A wonder that these Northmen are able to have kingdoms at all. I'd expect them to lead nomadic tribes of barbarians by the way they act. Lukas Aurelius snickered quietly at his own thoughts, still carefully spying on the enemy king and his advisors.

"Please, Wallace, what's this about a riot?" King Dryden III said softly.

"Well, Your Grace, reports say that the town of Riverwell has suffered from a civil uprising, a race riot if rumours are to be believed," Advisor Wallace stated nervously.

"Rumours are nothing but the absent-minded gossip of bored milkmaids and town drunkards. Please, Your Grace, I beseech you, don't listen to this nonsense!" the other advisor interrupted.

"Interrupt Advisor Wallace again, Hector, and I promise you it will have grave consequences," the king said menacingly. The ambiguity of the king's threat made Advisor Hector gulp. "Continue Wallace."

"As I was saying . . . the rumours are that a group of elves have started the riots. They call themselves 'The Resistance.' Apparently, they are a group of elves that are still trying to keep the Elven Uprising alive. The same uprising you crushed years ago," Wallace continued, sweating and blinking profusely as he did so.

"How accurate are these rumours?" the king asked, clearly bored with the conversation.

"Very accurate, sire. It has been reported that they have torn down the golden statue of Peslius that was in the middle of the town."

Interesting. There is civil unrest and a lack of faith in the old northern gods. The king is already losing control over his kingdom. One cannot rule on family legacy alone.

"Blast it! When will these fucking elves learn!"

"Sire, there are ladies present." Advisor Hector pointed at some of the female servants bringing in wine. King Dryden shot daggers at his advisor. Hector knew that he had made a grave mistake.

"I am the king! I have been ordained by the gods to rule over this kingdom until my dying breath! If I wish to curse in my own fucking war room, then I'll bloody do so! And damned if there are ladies present! Wolves do not concern themselves with the opinion of sheep!" the king's voice boomed, veins protruding from his neck. He took a deep breath and wiped the hair out of his eyes, then said calmly, "Perhaps the other advisors would care to know what you were doing last week in the slums."

Hector's face went pale. His eyes widened as he started to sweat profusely. "Please, Your Grace . . . I won't utter another sound . . . you have my word. . . ." Hector's voice cracked.

The king eyed his advisor viciously. He saw that Hector's eyes were filled with desperation, silently pleading that the king did not reveal his secret to his peers. Fortunately, the king woke up feeling merciful. "Do not forget, Hector, that you were not born a noble, and without me, you would still be laying in that piss-covered hovel you called home."

Hector nodded anxiously and timidly walked across the room to rejoin his fellow advisors. He quietly let out a sigh of relief.

The rumours are true. The king's temper has not cooled since his coronation. However, it appears his violent outbursts have stopped. Instead, he prefers to humiliate and manipulate his noblemen. The lack of respect he has for his advisors will be his downfall.

"Send in some of the army to control this rabble," the king ordered.

"How many shall I send, sire?" General Atticus replied, stepping forward from the crowd of advisors.

"Take a quarter of your forces from the southern border. The empire won't attack any time soon. Keten is our biggest threat at the moment, and these elves are a close second," the king replied.

A wicked smile spread across the hidden face of Lukas Aurelius.

"I thought I destroyed these elves' spirit when I sent that knight Pedro Dechamplain—"

"Pablo Deschamps, sire," one of the advisors interjected and immediately regretted it.

The king stared at him coldly and slowly replied, "Thank you," while gritting his teeth. "Too bad he's not here. We could use him to dispatch the elves once again."

"What happened to him, Your Grace?" another advisor asked after sensing it was safe to ask questions again.

"I sent him to slaughter the traitors who were giving aid to the elves during the uprising. Because of the . . . let us say delicate matter of the mission, we had to make sure he didn't spread the word. He is now buried in an unmarked grave in the mountains of the Far North."

So, the king ordered a knight, Pablo Deschamps, to kill his own subjects and then had the knight killed in order to keep the news from spreading to the populace. Not the most important information I've learned today, but perhaps we can use it as a nasty rumour to sow discontent with the king.

While the advisors were debriefing the king on other, more trivial matters, Lukas Aurelius stealthily exited the war room and made his way down the spiral staircase. Nobody seemed to notice him.

CHAPTER EIGHT

The campsite was flooded. Rain assaulted the roof of the makeshift shelter that Deidre and Finnegan had assembled. Hamish and Flint tried to get a fire going, but all the wood was drenched from the rain. Eventually, they gave up and decided to huddle together under the shelter for warmth.

Mario sat outside in the rain. He stared absently at his gauntlets, hoping that the rain would clean the blood that had stained them. But it was no use; the only thing the rain washed away was the tears streaming down his cheeks. Even though they were a few miles downriver, Mario could still smell the smoke bellowing from Riverwell. The cold, wet wind pierced through his armour like a spear. Goosebumps covered his entire body, but he failed to notice. His mind was preoccupied with replaying the vicious flashbacks of the atrocities that occurred in Riverwell.

"You alright?" Hamish asked, slowly sitting down beside Mario.

Mario didn't answer; instead, he just kept staring at his blood-covered hands.

"You've been out here for over an hour. . . . You'll catch a chill." Hamish placed his hand on Mario's shoulder.

"Perhaps I deserve it, Hamish. . . . Ever since leaving the college, I've turned into a monster," Mario's voice wavered as he talked; the lump in his throat made it difficult to breathe.

"You're not a monster . . . I am," Hamish answered sombrely. Mario raised his head and looked at Hamish. His eyes were full of regret. "I've never had to harm a human in my entire life, but now . . . it's one thing to plunge a sword through somebody's chest or slice their necks open with a blade . . . but what I did . . . *that* was truly monstrous."

Mario remembered the sight of Hamish's gangly, black hand tearing the head of a man clean from his body. He also remembered how Hamish squeezed a man so hard his innards spewed out his mouth. A chill ran down Mario's spine. "You did what you had to in order to survive."

"So did you."

Although Mario knew that Hamish was right, he found very little comfort in facts. Even though it was a matter of life and death, Mario still regretted killing that boy, and he regretted not being able to save Miles. The guilt was eating him alive regardless. "How's the leg?" he asked, only now remembering that Hamish was wounded in the riots.

"Sore," Hamish replied, looking down at his bandaged leg. "Deidre made a poultice, and Finnegan used a piece of his shirt for the cloth. I should be fine, only a few days of limping. How's the arm?"

Mario had forgotten that he had been stabbed. He gingerly touched the fresh wound under his left armpit. A sensation of pain filled his body as the cold chain mail touched the sensitive wound. He winced, hoping that Hamish wouldn't notice. "It's fine, just a tad tender."

Hamish didn't respond. Instead, he just looked at the young knight curiously, then stood up. "You need to come into the shelter. We'll look at your wound in the morning."

"I'm fine," Mario replied, his voice as cold as the night air.

Hamish stood up and walked back to the shelter, shaking his head. Finnegan exited the shelter and patted Hamish on the back, then joined Mario outside in the rain.

"Hey, lad . . . how're ya feelin'?"

"Terrible."

"I know . . . a right shame what happened back there. We're all dreadfully sorry for what happened, but we can't take back the past."

Mario scoffed at the cliché. "So I should just accept the atrocities that I've committed and move on with my day?" Mario snapped, his voice a lot harsher than he intended it to be.

Finnegan sighed deeply and sat down in the mud beside Mario. "Listen, lad, we all did things back there we wish we could take back."

"What do you regret? Not getting drunker before the battle? Or not having enough time to finish your last ale?"

The rain obscured Mario's vision so he didn't see Finnegan's meaty fist fly at him. He was suddenly greeted by the crunch of his nose as the hefty, dwarven knuckles smashed into it. Blood started to pour out of Mario's nose and fall onto his already blood-soaked armour.

"You whinin' li'l shite!" Finnegan stood up in anger, his face bright red. "You fuckin' talk to me like that again and I'll kick your damned teeth in!"

Mario rubbed his throbbing, aching nose. "I'm sorry, Finnegan. That was uncalled for. I'm not myself . . ."

Finnegan took another deep breath and placed his hand on Mario's knee. "I know, lad . . . I know. Truth is, I don't think anyone is themselves after that mess."

"What do you mean?"

"Like I said, we all did things we regret. Hamish regrets for turnin' into a monster, you regret killing that boy, and me . . . I regret how I acted." Mario lifted his head and saw that Finnegan had tears swelling in his eyes. "I was a right coward. Left me only friends behind. Miles is rottin' in those soddin' streets, and Roger is gods know where . . . probably rottin' not too far from Miles."

"He probably got out just like we did. . . ."

"I hope so . . . but I have to know for sure. That's why come mornin' . . . I'm headin' back."

Mario's eyes widened, and he leapt to his feet. "You can't go back! They'll kill you!"

"I have to know for sure. . . . Those lads deserve better than what they got. I'm sorry, Mario, but me mind's made up."

Mario didn't know what to say; he just gave Finnegan a slight nod of his head and hoped that Finnegan knew what he wanted to say. It seemed to work, as the dwarf smiled in response and walked back to the shelter.

Mario sat back down and allowed his mind to wander. Although it didn't wander far, he could only think about the same three things: the guilt of killing the boy, the regret of leaving Miles' body behind, and being a disappointment to his father and the college.

"Mario! Get in here!" Deidre barked sharply from underneath the cover.

Mario begrudgingly stood up, hocked his bloody snot across the ground, and walked toward the others. The shelter was nothing special, a typical wilderness lean-to designed to do one thing: keep the inhabitants dry. The frame was made out of branches from the nearby birch trees, and the roof was made of dirt and leaves. Mario looked at the unappealing shelter and laughed quietly to himself. *A fitting place to sleep for a knight of my stature.* He lay down slowly, placed his head against the soft ground, and let the sensation of sleep consume him.

***

A shiver ran up Mario's spine. Adrenaline quickly surged through his veins, and he immediately sat up from his slumber. Danger was nearby. He looked at his companions and saw that they were all still sleeping soundly. He looked outside of the lean-to and saw an eerie thick fog had covered the ground. Mario couldn't see the river that was less than fifteen feet away from him, but he could still hear the gentle lapping. He walked out of the shelter and the only thing he could see were his shins. His boots, his feet, and the ground were completely submerged in this supernatural fog. He turned around and saw that the shelter was gone. It had vanished without a trace.

"Great, another fucking nightmare," Mario cursed, "as if being awake wasn't enough of a nightmare."

A distinct sound pricked Mario's ears and made his whole body go stiff. The ominous jingling of bells in the distance. Mario whipped his head around to see where the sound was coming from, but every time he moved his head, the sound moved in the opposite direction. The bells seemed to be coming from every direction. With every jingle, the bells grew louder. Closer. Mario was spinning in circles, trying to find the elusive source. When the bells seemed to be right next to him, they finally stopped. Then, silence. An unnatural silence. No birds, no wind, no sound, nothing. Suddenly, Mario felt the warm air of somebody's breath on the nape of his neck. He froze, too scared to move.

"Mario . . ." the ghastly voice whispered in his ear.

***

Mario sat up suddenly. His body was drenched in sweat. His chest was heaving; his lungs were out of air. Everyone else was already awake and sitting around a freshly made fire. Mario walked towards the fire; his body felt ice cold.

"Well look who's— Ya feelin' alright, lad? You're as pale as snow," Finnegan asked.

"Yeah, just had some bad dreams," Mario answered.

"Must've been some dreams," Flint replied completely uninterested in the conversation.

Flint's tone aggravated Mario, but he just nodded politely and sat down beside the fire, trying to absorb as much heat as possible.

"Finnegan says he's leaving," Hamish remarked.

"I owe it to Roger. I need to be sure if he survived or not," Finnegan replied sternly.

"I can guarantee you that he died in those sewers," Flint added, seemingly bored with this conversation as well.

"I have to bloody well try! Else I'll never forgive meself." Finnegan's face was beginning to turn red as his anger rose in his body.

"I think we should go with him," Mario interjected, silencing the whole group.

"Are you mad?" Deidre asked in disbelief.

"We barely got out of there with our lives last time, and you want to go back into that mess?" Hamish added.

"Like Finnegan said, we owe it to Roger," Mario replied, standing firm.

"I joined you so we could find and kill these bandits together, and I doubt they survived that slaughter. There is nothing left in Riverwell. We have to find a new lead," Flint interjected angrily, this time fully engaged in the conversation.

"Mario, it's fine. Ya don't have to come with me. . . . In fact, this is something I have to do on me own," Finnegan added solemnly.

Mario was at a loss for words. He wanted to do the right thing and go back and search for Roger, but the others had a point. It would be dangerous, and it would mean abandoning his mission, albeit temporarily. Mario begrudgingly nodded his head. "We'll meet again, once this is all over." He placed his hand on Finnegan's shoulder.

"Thanks, lad, I'm sure we will," Finnegan replied unconvincingly.

Deidre, Flint, Hamish, and Mario stood around the fire as they watched Finnegan walk into the forest back towards the smoldering ruins of Riverwell. Mario couldn't help but feel regret as he watched his friend disappear amongst the trees.

"Now what?" Flint said. "We have no leads, and these bastards could be anywhere."

"Kartaga," Deidre interjected.

"What did you say!?" Flint exclaimed, his entire body stiffening.

"You know it?" Hamish asked.

Flint gulped and wiped his sweaty brow, his hazel eyes not moving from Deidre's. "I've heard of it. Why do you bring it up?".

"The bandits in the forest said that there was another comrade of theirs that is being held there," Mario replied.

"We could go there," Deidre added, staring back at Flint.

"We will have to cross the border into the empire. You would be leaving your post, Mario," Flint said.

"I'm afraid I have to see this through now no matter where it takes me. For Roger, Miles, and Finnegan's sake as well as my own," Mario retorted as he stood up from the fire.

Flint sighed and began to ready the boat.

The cool morning breeze stung Mario's bare chest as they sailed along the river. Hamish had insisted that he remove his breastplate so his wound could be tended to. The river was calm, which made stitching Mario's wound that much easier. Mario stared at his reflection in the passing water. He saw a scarred man staring back at him. He couldn't take his eyes off the scar; it was a constant reminder of all the awful things he'd done since leaving the college. Mario also noticed that a thin, patchy beard was growing on his face. If it was a few weeks ago, that would've bothered him, but now, it seemed fitting. *A dishevelled appearance for a disgraced knight.*

Something hard hit the side of the boat. Deidre almost rolled out, but Flint grabbed her by the collar of her shirt. Everyone looked around nervously.

"What was that? A rock?" Hamish asked, his hand already on his sword.

"No," Flint replied, still looking forward, seeming unbothered by the source of the disturbance.

"What the hell is it then?" Deidre exclaimed.

"A kappa," Flint replied calmly.

"A what?"

"A kappa. They're mischievous creatures that live in rivers, and they're usually harmless."

"Usually," Deidre replied sarcastically.

"They have a bubble on the top of their head. If you hit that, you'll be fine. But if you want to stay on the safe side, don't look them directly in the eyes."

Mario watched the unholy creature swim beside the boat. It was about the size of a dog but had appendages like a human and had the head of a frog. It was covered with shiny, green scales and had a shell on its back like a turtle. Mario watched in amazement at the bizarre creature. Even though the kappa had arms and legs like a human, it chose to swim like a fish, perfectly matching the boat's speed.

"How do you know so much about monsters, Flint?" Hamish asked. "You could tell I was a changeling almost immediately, and now you know what this creature is without even looking at it. Where did you learn so much?"

"I've read a lot of books. Monsters always fascinated me as a child," Flint mumbled.

"Will it be hard to sneak across the empire's border?" Deidre asked, bored with the grotesque creature beside the boat.

"If we snuck through on foot, it could be challenging, but that's why we are following the river in the boat. It is usually less guarded, which means less trouble for us."

Mario didn't hear any of the conversation; he was too busy being fascinated by the kappa beside the boat. The creature would swim up and pop its head out of the water, then dive back under and disappear in the murky river. After a couple of seconds, the creature would repeat the pattern again.

"I think it wants to play," Mario cut in, still staring at the creature in awe.

Annoyed, Flint responded, "Doubt it. Like I said, kappa's are mischievous and like to make fools out of humans. It's probably trying to find a way to trick you."

Mario shook his head in disbelief. The kappa seemed harmless and so playful; it reminded him of the small lichenite that he saw in the forest. A creature that, by all definitions, was a monster, except in behaviour.

Once again, the kappa dove underwater, rendering itself completely hidden from Mario's eyes. He waited for a few seconds for his new friend to return, but it didn't. He waited for a few more seconds and still nothing. Finally, after what felt like an eternity, Mario saw a stream of blood flow past the boat.

"Hey, Flint . . ." Mario started, but before he could finish, an explosion of water behind the boat knocked everyone onto their backs.

Mario was the first to stand up and saw a giant eel-like creature looming above their boat. Its mouth was circular and filled with round, but sharp teeth.

In the middle of the creature's mouth was a forked tongue. The creature let out a shrill, high-pitched squeal as it crashed back down into the river.

"Shit!" Flint exclaimed.

"What is it?" Mario asked.

"A petromyzon. It's going to try and knock you out of the boat. Hold on!"

Before anyone could react, the beast hit the boat with its body. The boat flew about five feet in the air before it came crashing down again on the river. Everyone fell hard against the wooden floor. Mario was sure he could feel a tooth get knocked loose.

"Good." Flint breathed as he regained his posture.

"How the hell is this good!?" Mario yelled, wiping the river water out of his eyes.

"It's toying with us, which means it doesn't want to eat us right away."

"So what do we do? You're the one who's read all the books on monsters!" Hamish yelled while trying to regain his footing.

Before Flint could answer, a barbed tail exploded from the murky depths of the river and missed Mario's neck by only a few inches. Instinctively, Mario pinned the powerful tail to the deck of the boat underneath his body weight. Mario could feel the tail pushing against his ribs; it was too powerful for one person to pin down.

Suddenly, Mario felt the tail of the beast being pushed down further. He turned his head to his left and saw that Flint was also laying on the tail, pinning it against the deck.

"Good thinking." Flint gasped. "Hamish! Cut this fucking tail off!"

Hamish immediately sprang into action. His sword jumped from the scabbard at incredible speed. The sunlight glistened off the blade as it hissed through the air. The first strike went halfway through the tail. A green liquid shot from the wound, covering everyone in the boat.

The head of the creature emerged from the water and let out another high-pitched wail. This time, Deidre was ready for it. In about three seconds, she shot five arrows right into the midsection of the monster. Every time the arrow hit, more green liquid exploded from underneath the beast's oily, black skin.

Hamish raised his sword one more time and, with a tremendous yell, swung downwards at the tail once again. This time completely severing it from the monster's body. The beast cried once more and dove back into the water.

Flint gasped as he rolled off of the tail. "It's done."

"Is it dead?" Deidre asked.

"No, but petromyzons hate having to work for their food. They prefer something with less fight in them. And I think we proved that we are no easy meal," Flint explained as he wiped the sweat from his brow.

"We're sinking!" Mario cried as he noticed water pouring over the sides of the boat.

"We're too damn heavy!" Hamish yelled, "Quick grab the tail and throw it overboard!"

The tail of the beast was heavier than it appeared. It required all four of them to lift and throw the tail in the river. Even with the beast's appendage discarded, water kept pouring in.

"Take off your shoes!" Deidre barked as she began removing her own. Without question, the rest of the group followed her lead. Everyone knew what she intended to do with them. Everyone began bailing out the boat with their boots. The smell of wet leather filled Mario's nose. With four of them working together, it took only a few minutes before they could float with ease again.

Everyone rolled back and caught their breath. Mario wanted to wash the green blood off of his face, but he was afraid of what other horrors could be lurking in the river.

"Everyone okay?" Deidre asked while slipping her wet shoe back on her foot.

Hamish gasped as he wiped the green blood off his face with his sleeve. "I think so."

"How much longer?" Mario asked curiously.

"We'll be there tomorrow night. Unless we hit more trouble," Flint answered.

Mario leaned over the side of the boat to stare at his reflection once again. This time there was a scarred man covered in green blood staring back at him. Mario's stomach began to churn as all the other blood-soaked memories began to return. The feelings of guilt and regret slowly engulfed his body.

"Mario . . ." a ghastly voice whispered, as though right beside his ear.

Mario's body stiffened. He quickly turned around and looked at his companions.

"Did you not hear that voice!?" Mario asked as he began to break out into a sweat.

"What voice, Mario?" Deidre replied, confused.

Mario's eyes darted around the boat, everyone seemed to share her confusion. He tried to relax his body and leaned against the side of the boat. "I guess I'm hearing things, probably just from a lack of sleep."

"Well feel free to catch up. The rest of us will keep watch while you rest. You're looking pretty pale," Hamish responded.

Mario closed his eyes and tried to sleep, but he knew it would be of no use. Not only was he haunted by the memories of his past, but now he had this ghostly voice lingering from his nightmares. He feared that he would never be able to sleep again.

The cool air from the river caressed Mario's cheek as the party slowly made their way down the soothing river. Occasionally, Mario would open his eyes and see the landscape of the riverbank gradually changing. Dense forests turned into open grasslands, and the grasslands slowly transformed into golden brown fields. The temperature subtly started to rise, but the wind from the river cooled them off and made the rise in heat almost imperceptible.

Suddenly, Flint's monotonous paddling stopped. Mario leaned forward and opened his eyes. His hand already on his sword. He scanned the riverbank, looking for more potential threats.

"What is it?" Mario asked after not being able to see any danger.

"The border," Flint replied stalely.

Mario stood up carefully. Ahead of him was nothing, just a slightly murky river about a hundred yards wide, with a bland riverbank full of wet dirt and brown shrubbery. Mario felt underwhelmed.

"This is the border? Doesn't look like much," Deidre complained as she removed her bow from her shoulder.

"Exactly," Flint replied as he let the boat silently coast along the river, its current slowly pushing them toward their destination.

"Why is it unguarded?" Hamish asked as he examined the riverbeds.

"I don't know," Flint replied. The party waited tensely, anticipating an ambush or attack that never came. After about three minutes of coasting, Flint grabbed his oar and resumed paddling down the river. "Welcome to the empire," he said, cracking a sarcastic smile.

Mario looked back up the river. Even though the riverbanks on the north side of the border were identical to those on the south side, Mario felt a sense of familiarity when he stared back towards the North. He knew nothing of the people, culture, animals, or the environment of the empire. All he knew was that it was south. Everything he ever knew and loved was back in the northern kingdoms. But a feeling of hopefulness washed over him. Perhaps all the guilt and regret that was following him would be left behind in the North as well. *This could be a blessing in disguise. I can start again and repair my reputation as a knight, leaving all my mistakes behind.* Unfortunately, guilt and regret recognize no borders. Mario felt the boat's back end begin to turn. He saw that it was slowly turning so that the body of the boat was perpendicular to the river.

"Fuck!" Flint screamed as he swung his oar, attacking the river with it.

"What's going on?" Hamish asked, confused as to why the boat was turning in such an unnatural way.

"Kappas! They're turning the boat so we capsize . . . or we miss our turn," Flint said gravely.

"Why?" Deidre asked as she aimed her bow into the water, waiting for the opportune time to strike.

"As I said, they like to make humans look like fools. They are mischievous fucks," Flint growled as he smacked the water once again with his oar, hoping to hit one of the kappas that were turning the boat.

"What turn?" Mario yelled as he slashed at the kappas swimming by his side of the boat.

"There's a fork in the river up ahead. If we go left, we go down some mild rapids and will be at Kartaga by tomorrow night." Flint angrily scanned the water.

"And if we go right?" Hamish asked hesitantly.

"We go down a waterfall and our bodies will be at Kartaga by midnight."

Everyone's face went pale. This river and its unholy inhabitants could be their demise. Everyone attacked the kappas with a sense of urgency. Mario looked downriver between his slashes and saw that the fork in the river was just over fifty yards away. He attacked the water vehemently with his sword. However, every swing seemed to miss its mark. The kappas were more elusive than they first appeared. Every once in a while, one of the kappas would pop their heads up out of the water and nudge the boat in the direction of the waterfall.

"*Diabhal!*" Deidre shouted as another one of her arrows missed the elusive monsters.

Hamish and Flint were just as unsuccessful. Every swing tipped the boat, forcing them to regain their balance. The lack of balance combined with the kappas' speed created a challenge that nobody could overcome. Before they knew it, the boat had drifted down the right fork towards the waterfall.

The boat began to straighten out as the kappas swam away back towards safety. Their devious work was done. Defeated, Flint sat silently as he pulled his oar out of the water. The river was eerily quiet as the party drifted slowly to their impending doom.

"What do we do now?" Mario asked nervously.

"We wait," Flint said calmly. In the distance, the roaring of the waterfall could be heard. The current of the river was stronger and the boat began to pick up speed.

"So, do nothing? That's your big plan?" Deidre snapped as she stared menacingly at Flint.

"We won't be able to reach the shore. In about a minute, we will be at the waterfall. My suggestion, start praying to your gods. Our best chance of living through this is to go over the waterfall head-on instead of sideways," Flint explained, his tone more grim than usual.

Mario's feelings of guilt and regret came surging back into his body with renewed fervour now that his death was likely upon him. His hands became clammy, a lump grew in his throat, making it difficult to breathe, and sweat began to drip into his eyes. He looked around nervously at his companions. Deidre was on her knees and her hands folded over in prayer. Mario could hear her whispering in elvish. Hamish vomited over the side of the boat, his skin tone slowly turning darker and darker as they approached the waterfall. Flint sat at the back of the boat, oar in his lap and his eyes closed, patiently waiting to go over the waterfall.

Mario got down on his knees and clasped his hands. *Desperate times . . .* "Gods, if you're listening, I've come to ask a favour of you. I know I haven't been the most devout man, but I'm desperate . . ." The roar of the water began to drown out Mario's voice, but he continued to whisper his prayer. ". . . none of these people deserve to die because of me. I'm the only reason any of them are here. Have mercy in your hearts. Don't let me die with more guilt than I already have. Please, I beg that you allow me and my friends to survive this fall."

"Deal," a ghastly voice whispered in Mario's ear.

Mario's eyes shot open to see the source of the voice, but it was too late. He was already over the waterfall, plummeting back down towards the earth.

*Vampires are mindless beasts. They are no different than the wolves
and bears that growl at our doors every night. They are governed by
their ravenous hunger and not by logic as we humans are. As a result,
they will be a species of beast that will be easily eradicated. A wooden
stake and cloves of garlic are the best defences against vampires. All
vampires are terrified of the stuff, just like the wolves and the bears are
terrified of our torches and swords.*

Professor Ivan Hellasin,
Hellasin's Guide to Monsters

*Anyone who listens to Hellasin's hogwash is risking their lives believ-
ing superstitions and myths. Professor Hellasin has never even seen
a vampire, let alone killed one. Truth is, vampires come in a variety
of subspecies. The mindless beasts that Hellasin is referring to are
called sasabonsams. But actual vampires are similar to humans and
are governed by logic and emotions and are even capable of forming
societies. Also, wooden stakes and garlic are about as useful as a boat
with a hole in it. Your best defence is to find a member of the Order of
the Swords.*

David Günne,
Debunking Monster Myths

Chapter Nine

The mud on the shoreline was smooth and cool to the touch. It stuck to everything it came in contact with, Mario's face being no exception. Mario coughed painfully, trying to expel the water that had filled his lungs after going over the top of the waterfall. He tried to wipe his wet, muck-covered face, but only managed to further smear the sludge. He gingerly crawled back towards the river and plunged his head into the water. It was ice cold. He could still hear the muffled sound of the haunting voice talking to him even underneath the water.

Mario lifted his head and began to take in his surroundings. He realized he had washed up along a gloomy small beach covered in black sand. The beach had flat plains on the eastern bank, but on the western bank, where he found himself, there was a steep embankment blocking the view of what was west of the river. He also noticed that the air was heavy with humidity. It felt like a lead blanket was resting on the top of his head. He saw the rest of his friends had miraculously washed up on the same beach. Hamish was coughing up water, Flint was dumping water out of his boots, and Deidre was wringing out her soaked hair.

"Looks like we're all in one piece," Flint said as he picked at a few kernels of sand stuck in his teeth.

Hamish wheezed as he tried to catch his breath. "By all accounts—a miracle."

Mario's face quickly lost its colour. He realized that it was no miracle. It dawned on him that he had just made a deal with someone, or something, and they had intervened to save their lives. The only question left to ask was: Why?

"Where are we?" Deidre asked, interrupting Mario's thoughts.

All of their heads turned to Flint, who seemed to know the most about the empire. Flint looked around the beach and gave an unsure shrug. "I'm not sure," he muttered as he rose to his feet. "Let's get on top of this hill and see what we can see."

Begrudgingly, they rose to their feet and began the arduous task of climbing the embankment. Their wet shoes slipped on the dew-covered grass, making the climb that much more difficult. After the third slip, Mario began stabbing his sword and shield into the soft earth for traction. He noticed everyone else was doing the same with whatever equipment they had managed to keep with them after the waterfall. At the start of the climb, everyone's clothes were soaked with river water. About halfway through, their clothes had dried. By the end of the climb, their clothes were soaked with sweat instead of water.

Atop the embankment, they stopped to catch their breath. Mario and Hamish collapsed on their backs upon reaching the summit, while Deidre and Flint elected to take a knee instead.

"Gods, why is it so hot?" Hamish complained as he heaved to catch his breath once again.

"It's the empire," Flint stated. "It's known for two things: the heat and the cruelty."

"*Diabhal!*" Deidre gasped as she wiped her sweat-soaked hair out of her eyes.

Mario and Hamish both sat up to see what had made Deidre gasp in awe and then they too were awestruck. In the distance, surrounded by golden brown fields, they saw a city with a colossal castle that was illuminated solely by moonlight. The palace had conical towers along the walls of the city.

"Woah," Mario uttered, his mouth still agape in amazement.

"That . . . is Kartaga," Flint said with a hint of remorse in his voice.

"Doesn't it look a little . . . ominous to anyone?" Hamish asked timidly.

"If that is where the bandit is, that's where I'm going," Deidre said as she rose to her feet and stormed across the fields towards the castle. The others struggled to keep up with her pace.

As they approached the city, Mario realized Hamish was right. Something was off about this place, but he couldn't figure out what. The hair on the back of his neck stood up. The whole area seemed to be lacking in life. No flies in the air, no crickets chirping, no mice running through the fields—it was as if all living creatures stayed away from this place.

Once they approached the main gate of the castle, Mario realized what was off about the city. There were no torches. The entire city appeared to be illuminated by the moon. The absence of torchlight added to the city's sinister appearance. *Perhaps it doesn't get as cloudy in the empire as it does in the North.*

"Will they even let us in?" Hamish asked as he stopped at the gate.

"They will," Flint replied.

Before anyone could question Flint's certainty, the gates of the city swung open and a swarm of armed guards rushed out and surrounded the party. They were decorated in black plate armour, and their helmets were forged in the shape of a skull. The guards looked ready to attack but hesitated once they saw Flint.

"The countess will want to see you," one of the guards said in a muffled voice from behind his helmet.

Before anyone could inquire, the guards forcefully escorted them inside the city walls and towards the castle. The city of Kartaga was extraordinary. The streets were made of smooth and polished cobblestone. Every building appeared to be made of stone, even the huts and the shops. All of them had a hint of elven architecture: triangle doorways, triangular windows, and, of course, triangular frames. However, something was off. It wasn't completely elvish; it had its own unique twist to it. Mario struggled to put his finger on it.

Despite it being the middle of the night, the city was teeming with life. People were shopping, visiting, and working, as if it was midday. Children were playing in the street or jumping in and drinking from the river that flowed through the city. *Strange, I didn't see a river flow from the city walls when we approached.*

The castle was atop a steep hill, looking down on the city. A massive winding staircase connected the castle's doors to the city streets. Even though the city's appearance was breathtaking, Mario couldn't stop staring at the people. They had pale white skin, paler than anyone in the North. He saw that they all had light coloured eyes. Light blues, light yellows, and a few that were completely white, except for the pupil. *This doesn't look like the prison capital of the empire. This city is breathtaking.*

The doors of the castle swung open and exposed a beautiful throne room. The white marble floor glistened from the moonlight entering through the triangular windows on either side. There were two series of pillars that equally divided the room into thirds, each as black as the night sky and approximately fifty feet tall. At the end of the throne room sat a beautiful woman atop a magnificent throne that appeared to be forged out of blackened steel. As they approached, Mario noticed that she had a pale complexion similar to her subjects. Her thin frame was accented by the elegant black and red gown that she was wearing; it swept the floor behind her as she approached them. Her jet-black hair and her sharp, distinct cheekbones accented her piercing, light blue eyes, eyes that couldn't stop staring at Flint.

"Andronikus! How good of you to return. How long has it been? It feels like centuries." Her dark voice echoed throughout the empty throne room.

Everyone looked around confused. Nobody knew who she was addressing. Suddenly, Flint stepped forward and away from the guards.

"Greetings, Alexandria, nice to see you again."

The countess licked her lips as she approached Flint. "I see you've brought friends. They look delicious." She smiled, baring her fangs.

"She's . . . she's a vampire," Deidre stammered.

"I know," Flint answered shamefully.

"Wait, how do you know so much about this place? Who the hell is Andronikus?" Hamish yelled confused.

The countess turned and looked at Flint slyly. "They don't know?" she said, her voice teeming with excitement.

"Know what?" Mario asked with frustration.

Flint took a deep breath and looked at each of his comrades in the eye. "My real name is Andronikus. When I was a boy, I was conscripted into the Order of the Swords, the monster-hunting guild. I was the top student both in theory and in practice," he admitted bashfully. "When I was young, I came here looking for work. Once I met the countess, I decided to stay for a while and we . . . became intimate." Flint's voice was riddled with shame and regret.

Everyone's jaw dropped, except for the countess'; she continued to smile from ear to ear. Silence filled the majestic throne room. Nobody could believe the words they were hearing.

"Wait, you're telling me that you . . . and her . . ." Deidre stammered.

"We fucked dear . . . try to keep up," Alexandria snidely interjected.

"And you didn't fucking trust me!?" Hamish screamed as he marched forward so he was face to face with Andronikus. "You slept with a fucking vampire, but you wanted to cut me down the moment you found out I was a changeling!? I'll fucking kill you!" Hamish's voice began to distort as he yelled.

"Doubt it," Alexandria remarked sarcastically.

Hamish's head turned sharply, and he stared angrily at the vampire. His chest heaved, and he clenched his hands into fists. Mario could see the complexion of Hamish's skin grow darker. He knew that Hamish was about to revert to his natural form.

"Well, that seems like enough excitement for tonight," Alexandria said, ignoring the fuming Hamish. "You're welcome to stay as long as you want. Any friends of Andronikus are friends of mine."

Mario felt uneasy by her tone, although it was warm and welcoming. Her smile seemed malicious and sinister.

"Craven, show them to their rooms," Alexandria said, carelessly waving her arm.

Silently from the shadows emerged an equally pale man. He was tall and had short black hair. His irises were completely white, and he had an empty, soulless stare. Without a word, the man motioned for everyone to follow him and noiselessly began walking down a side hallway. They cautiously followed behind, unsure if the countess could be trusted. Andronikus brought up the rear, sulking in shame.

"Not you," the countess called out, pointing at Andronikus. "You will join me tonight. We have a lot of catching up to do." A vicious smile spread across her pale lips.

The rooms were exquisite. The beds were decorated with the finest linens, almost everything was gold plated, and giant oil paintings of the countess hung on all the walls. The party was split up into three rooms. Deidre opted to have her own room, Hamish and Mario decided to share one together, and Andronikus joined the countess.

"I can't fucking believe him!" Hamish exclaimed as he paced angrily across the room, wearing out the artisanal rug that decorated the floor.

"Try to calm down . . ." Mario said, not knowing what to say.

"Calm down? Calm down!? He tried to kill me, Mario! I can forgive ignorance or hesitancy in trusting a monster, but after you've shared a bed with one? That I cannot abide. Fucking hypocrite!" Hamish's voice became more and more distorted the angrier he got. His true form was beginning to appear.

"We don't know the whole story, Hamish. He seemed pretty ashamed once he revealed everything to us. Perhaps he regrets what he did. We've all done things that we wish we could take back." Mario paused, realizing that he had just repeated the same words of advice that Finnegan gave him that morning.

Hamish stopped mid-pace. His rushed breathing began to slow down, and his skin complexion began to return to normal. He took a few deep breaths and turned to face Mario. "You're right. He's had plenty of opportunities to kill me. I should at least give him the benefit of the doubt."

Mario was relieved to hear that Hamish's voice had returned to normal, partly because he was scared of sharing a room with him while he was in his natural form.

"I still don't trust this countess though. . . . I think we should take shifts watching the door, in case they try to drink our blood tonight," Hamish whispered as he eyed the door cautiously.

Mario looked at the door, and underneath it, he could see the shadows of two feet standing on the other side. *Craven's most likely.* "Agreed. I'll take the first shift," Mario said, his eyes locked on Craven's shadow.

Hamish begrudgingly agreed and climbed into the soft, luxurious bed. He let out an involuntary moan of comfort as he laid his head down.

"Gods, this feels amazing. . . ." Hamish mumbled as he stretched himself onto the bed.

"Don't get too comfortable. I may need you to wake up and back me up should the need arise," Mario said. He turned his head and saw that Hamish had already fallen fast asleep.

***

The countess' room had every luxury known to man: a golden bathtub, a nickel washbasin, a bed that took up half of the room, with sheets made from the finest silks. There was a large, triangular window facing north that looked down onto the city. It was probably the most breathtaking view in the empire. Three oil paintings adorned her walls. One of her, one of Kartaga, and one of Andronikus.

"Help yourself to a cup," Alexandria said as she pointed towards a pitcher on the table that was full of a sticky red liquid.

"Joke never gets old," Andronikus remarked dryly.

"Lighten up. It's been ages since we've seen one another. I have to bring back some of our classics for a reunion such as this."

Andronikus shivered as the vampiress caressed his shoulder. He stared out the window overlooking the city, wishing he was somewhere else.

"Excuse me while I slip into something a little more comfortable," Alexandria said as she seductively walked behind the silk curtain in the corner of the room.

Andronikus began to take off his various weapons, knowing that they would be of no use to him here.

"Your friends seem nice, although I remember you being more of a lone wolf type."

"I've changed."

"Not that much clearly. You're still a man of few words, and you haven't aged a day."

Andronikus laughed aloud. "That tends to happen when you're immortal." He turned his head and saw the shadow of Alexandria changing from behind the curtain illuminated by the moonlight. The sight of her slender yet supple figure filled his body with excitement. Excitement and shame.

"Who's the one with the scar? I can smell the blood on him. I can tell he still doesn't have a taste for it yet. Reminds me a little of you."

"If you touch him . . ." Andronikus began.

"Relax, you know I only feed off the prisoners . . . and you."

"You only feed off me because my blood gets you drunk. It doesn't nourish you at all."

"A lovely side-effect of that exquisite bloodline of yours," Alexandria retorted as she emerged from behind the curtain in a near-transparent, black robe. It was barely dark enough to cover her most intimate features.

Andronikus couldn't help but laugh at the countess' comments. "Who would've thought that the child of a pixie and a human would become immortal."

"You know that is my favourite painting in the whole castle." Alexandria pointed to the portrait of Andronikus on the wall.

"How can you like such an awful painting. It's an abomination." Andronikus said, while trying to ignore the attractive sight beside him.

Silently, Alexandria wisped across the room and clung to his neck with both arms. She stared up at him admirably with her piercing blue eyes. Andronikus kept his eyes focused on the painting.

"A shame nobody ever got to see it. You would've made a lovely count."

Andronikus laughed. "Yeah, a monster hunter ruling over a city of vampires."

Alexandria's grip tightened. "You almost did. In fact, I thought you would until you disappeared all those centuries ago."

Andronikus pushed away from the vampire and stared at her awe-inspiring blue eyes. "You know we never would've lasted."

"Why?" Alexandria snapped as she placed her hands on her hips. "When we first met, you were barely a century old. I helped turn you into the killing machine that you are. Without me, you'd just be some bumbling immortal constantly dying and reviving from every monster you didn't have the skills to kill. Thanks to me, I made you the most dangerous man with a sword. . . . Together we could've conquered the world."

Andronikus shook his head. He took a deep breath to control his rising level of anger. "You know why I left." His voice was harsh and shaking with rage.

Alexandria let out a sigh and walked towards Andronikus. Out of instinct, he stepped back. "I know, because of her."

Andronikus' anger instantly left his body; instead, it was replaced by sadness and regret. "How is she?" he asked somberly.

"Still doesn't want to see you . . ." Alexandria's words cut him like a dagger.

Andronikus sighed and placed his hands on the small mahogany end table in front of him. A single tear streamed down his face.

"And who can blame her?" the countess continued. "You turned her into a monster," she hissed as her venomous blue eyes watched Andronikus' tear roll down his cheek.

"I tried to save her!" Andronikus yelled as he turned to face the vampire. "She would've died if you didn't turn her." His voice cracked as he struggled to say the words.

"And now she is a vampire, forced to live under my rule if she wants to stay alive. Otherwise she's have to go and kill innocents in order to get the blood she needs to live," Alexandria coldly reminded.

Andronikus' fists clenched. He gritted his teeth as he struggled to contain his emotions. His hands began shaking uncontrollably.

"You know . . ." the countess began, "if you ever run away again for another few hundred years, I'll banish her from my city." Alexandria's voice was as cold as ice.

As soon as the vampiress' words hit Andronikus' ear, he froze. He knew that this was not an idle threat. "I won't . . . I just have to finish my business with the bandits then I'll be back . . . for good."

While Andronikus was consumed by the throws of regret, Alexandria was able to wrap her body around his. Her mouth right beside his left ear. "Good, and I know you have to go and stretch your legs every once in a while. But remember our agreement . . ." Alexandria reminded.

"I remember," Andronikus replied. "Every year I'm on my own, is another five I have to spend here . . . with you."

The vampiress' grip tightened. She took a sharp, excited inhale and bared her dagger-like fangs.

Andronikus took a deep breath, not because he needed to calm down, but because he knew what would happen next. In the blink of an eye, Alexandria sunk her fangs deep into his neck. He remembered the first time he was bitten; it was so painful. The venom burned his entire body as it coursed through him. But now he was used to it; he was used to pain in general. Everything caused him pain, and as a result, he was numb to it all.

Alexandria removed her fangs and took a deep breath. She took a cloth from the table and wiped her blood-covered mouth with it. Her pupils began to dilate as the mutated blood began to take effect. As Andronikus wiped the blood from his neck, the two fang marks had already healed.

"You see that's what I love about you," Alexandria slurred as she stumbled towards the bed. "You heal so quickly that there is no mess, and your heightened immune system quickly destroys my toxins, preventing you from becoming a vampire."

Andronikus shook his head out of frustration. "You also 'love' me because my blood gets you drunk off your ass."

Alexandria gave a playful shrug as she collapsed on the luxurious bed. She rolled over onto her hip and propped her head up with one arm. With the other arm, she removed the strap holding her near-transparent black robe together, exposing her naked body for Andronikus.

"Come, lay with me. For old time's sake."

Andronikus sighed and begrudgingly began to remove his clothing, knowing it would be no use to argue.

***

There was a heavy pounding at the door. Mario sat up quickly and instinctively reached for his sword. He saw that Hamish had fallen asleep on the small chair in the corner of the room when he was supposed to be keeping watch. Mario sighed and threw a pillow at Hamish, waking him up. Mario rose to his feet and groggily walked towards the heavy wooden door.

"Yeah?" Mario slurred as he opened the door while still rubbing the crust from his eyes.

"Breakfast," Craven said stalely.

"Sure, just give us a few minutes," Mario said as he closed the door on Craven's face.

Mario slowly walked back and collapsed face down onto the soft, luxurious bed. It felt like all of Mario's stress and the tension in his muscles were absorbed by the fine fabric of the bedsheets. This was the most relaxed he'd felt in months.

"What's going on?" Hamish garbled while wiping the drool from his face.

Mario quickly rolled onto his back and stared at the stone ceiling. "I see you kept a diligent watch," he teased sarcastically. Hamish's face began to turn red and he began to scratch the back of his neck shyly. "Time for breakfast," Mario continued.

"Gods, I don't even want to know what the countess will make us eat for breakfast."

"One way to find out."

Outside the door, Craven was silently waiting for them. With a nod of the head, he sharply turned on his heels and began to escort them down a narrow winding staircase that led to a giant mess hall. The hall could've easily housed the entire town of Redfern. In the middle was a humongous oak table that looked like it would sit about thirty people comfortably. Thick, black, velvet curtains draped the east side on the room. On the west side, two giant triangular wooden doors led to the kitchen area where servants could be heard preparing their meals.

Deidre was already sitting at the table eating an apple when Mario and Hamish arrived. Without a word, Craven gestured for them to take a seat and then went back up the spiral staircase. It was eerie how silently he moved.

Mario sat down across from Deidre, and Hamish sat beside him. Mario's body felt stiff; he secretly wished he could've had his breakfast brought to him in bed.

"How did you sleep?" Deidre asked, breaking the silence.

"We took turns keeping watch," Hamish answered, picking the crust out of his eyes.

"What about you?" Mario asked.

"I tried to keep watch, but I ended up passing out in the bed," Deidre responded while taking a bite from the apple. There was a hint of shame in her voice.

"There's something with those beds, right?" Hamish asked excitedly. "I've never known comfort like that."

"Royalty has its perks I guess," Mario stated sarcastically.

Mario heard the sound of faint footsteps coming down the staircase. He turned around and saw Andronikus shamefully entering the hall. His head hung low, and he avoided eye contact with everyone. He quietly sat beside Deidre and continued to avoid eye contact.

"Morning," Hamish growled resentfully.

"Morning," Andronikus mumbled.

"How'd you sleep?" Mario asked, hoping that he would lift his head.

"I didn't really . . ." Andronikus began.

"Ah! Good morning, everyone! How're we feeling today?" the countess boisterously exclaimed as she entered the hall.

Before anyone could answer she walked towards the east wall and pulled back the curtains. Sunlight filled the darkroom and nearly blinded everyone. The countess stood there in her black robe basking the bright sunlight. "There, isn't that better?" she asked cheerfully.

"I thought vampires couldn't go into the sunlight?" Mario asked as he shielded his eyes from the onslaught of bright rays coming in through the window.

"You see, Alexandria isn't a typical vampire. She's what we call an upir," Andronikus informed.

"A what?" Deidre asked.

"An upir, dear," Alexandria interjected, her voice riddled with condescension. "You see, most humans confuse vampires with creatures called sasabonsams. Like us, they feed off humans, but they are more bestial and have no control over their impulses. Vampires, on the other hand, are civilized and are able to govern themselves like humans."

"So, what are sasabonsams exactly?" Hamish asked as he cautiously stared down the countess.

"They typically look more like beasts and can rarely change form. Some resemble giant bats; others resemble shadows. It varies on the species. Some examples are adze, nachzehrers, ekimmous, or gakis. Vampires look like humans and can blend into human society with ease," Andronikus informed.

"Wait, you mean to say that there are vampires living amongst humans?" Mario asked bewildered.

"Yes," Andronikus answered coolly. "In my experience, most are gravediggers."

As everyone sat in the wealth of knowledge that had just been dumped on them, the wooden doors on the other side of the room swung open. Servants completely cloaked in protective, black robes entered the room carrying various dishes. The aroma of freshly cooked bacon, fried hash browns, baked buns, and cooked eggs filled the hall. Mario's stomach instantly started to grumble as soon as the smell hit his nose. His mouth began to water; he knew that this was going to be the best meal he would have in a long time.

Even the serving plates in the castle were ornate. They appeared to be crafted from solid gold. The luminous tableware made the food look even more appealing.

"Dig in!" The countess exclaimed as she clapped her hands.

The food was exquisite. Every bite made Mario's mouth salivate and desire more. It was almost as if he was tasting this food for the first time. He turned his head and watched the servants scuttle back into the kitchen under their protective robes. "Are they not upirs?" Mario asked as he stuffed his mouth full of hash browns.

"No. Unfortunately, upirs are quite rare, and the only way to make more of them is to be bitten by one," Alexandria informed as she took a sip from a glass chalice that was filled with a red liquid.

"Kartaga is called the prison capital of the empire. Why is that?" Hamish asked as he slurped up the yolk from his egg.

"Because all of the empire's prisoners are sent here," Alexandria replied as she played with the lone grape on her plate.

"We came here looking for a bandit. He goes by the name of Arthur; we heard he was taken here," Deidre said, asserting herself as she eyed the countess.

The vampiress looked back at Deidre, annoyingly, through her piercing blue eyes. "We can certainly check," she said through gritted teeth.

With a clap of the countess' hands, Craven silently emerged from the shadows. The sudden, unexpected emergence of Craven made Mario jump in his seat.

"Craven, take us down to the dungeons. Our new friends want to check our prisoners," Alexandria instructed as she took another sip from her transparent chalice.

Craven nodded his head and gave an arm motion for everyone to follow as he opened a door along the north wall, which led to a descending spiral staircase. Mario and the others quickly stuffed their starving mouths with the remaining food before following the mysterious servant.

The stairwell down to the dungeon seemed out of place compared to the rest of the castle. Everything Mario had seen so far had been the epitome of luxury, pampering, and excessive wealth. But the stairwell was none of these things. It was dark, muggy, and full of dust. The smell of blood filled the stairwell. Mario's stomach began to churn. The malodorous air reminded him of the riot in Riverwell.

At the bottom of the staircase were two rectangular steel doors. The doors were about ten feet tall and were covered with bloody handprints. A bead of sweat ran off Mario's forehead and down his cheek. *Nothing good is behind this door.* Although Mario anticipated the worst, nothing could prepare him for the actual horrors beyond the door.

When the doors swung open, Deidre, Hamish, and Mario gasped in horror. The dungeons were filled with prisoners who were chained in their cells, most screaming in agony. As they walked down the hallway, Mario looked at each of the prisoners in the cages. Some were old; some were young. Some men, and some women. But almost all of them were in unspeakable pain. Aside from being chained to the walls in their cells, each prisoner had tubes coming out of their arms, legs, and neck. The tubes ran from the prisoners' body and into the floor of the dungeon.

"You're draining their blood," Deidre said, astonished.

"Of course, how else do you think a city of vampire survives?" Alexandria replied coldly.

"This isn't right. . . ." Mario began.

"Don't feel sorry for these monsters. They're all rapists, murderers, and thieves. They deserve this." Alexandria's voice was harsh and unwavering.

"How can you say they are the monsters when you do this to them?" Hamish growled angrily.

The countess' head snapped back, and her piercing blue eyes narrowed at Hamish. She pursed her lips and clenched her teeth. Suddenly, her face relaxed. "Believe it or not, humans are a resource. Your blood is a resource." She paused to take a few steps towards Hamish so that they were face to face. "What is a better use of resources? Having these guilty executed so that their blood stains the streets and is later washed in the gutter? Or is it better that they support a city of people that have never harmed an innocent person."

"You're not people," Mario stated coldly.

Alexandria's head slowly turned back towards Mario. He saw that her menacing glare had returned. Mario gulped nervously.

"How aren't we people? Because we have fangs? Because some of us can't go into the sun? Or do you believe that only humans qualify as 'people'? That elves, dwarves, and halflings also can't be considered 'people'? Go out in the city and ask the children what flows through their streets and where it comes from. Most won't be able to tell you that it comes from humans. We have done nothing wrong."

Mario froze; he didn't know what to say. To his disbelief, the vampiress made a compelling argument. Once again, he gulped nervously.

"Let's just talk to this bandit and leave," Andronikus said quietly.

"Agreed," Alexandria huffed, and she quickly stormed down the hallway.

Being in the dungeon unnerved Mario. The constant screaming, the smell, everything about this place made him sick. He wished that it would be over soon, that he would be able to leave this nightmare. Finally, they came to the cell. Inside, the prisoner looked more like a skeleton that still had skin on it rather than a man. He looked up towards the cell gates and wheezed, "Help me. . . ."

"Craven is this the right one?" Alexandria barked. Craven nodded his head. "Then open the door."

With a swift turn of the key, the cell's door swung open. It stunk like shit, piss, and blood. Mario almost vomited as soon as he crossed the threshold into the cell. Deidre quickly marched up to the prisoner and grabbed him by the throat.

"Where's your leader?" She snarled as her grip tightened around Arthur's throat.

"Feisty, isn't she?" Alexandria sarcastically remarked.

"Tell me!" Deidre screamed, ignoring the countess' comment.

"Hen . . .'enry? You lookin' fuh 'enry?" Arthur gasped, his face beginning to turn blue.

"Deidre, that's enough," Hamish said, taking another step into the cell.

Reluctantly, Deidre released her iron grip from around Arthur's throat. The bandit immediately began coughing and wheezing. "Talk," Deidre growled.

"I dunno where 'e is! I swears!" the bandit said once he finally caught his breath.

"Allow us, dear," Alexandria interjected. "Craven, if you don't mind."

Silently, Craven entered the room and walked behind Arthur. Suddenly, Craven's fingers on his left hand turned into claws. As quick as lightning, he plunged his claws deep into the left shoulder of Arthur. Arthur screamed a sound so hideous that it wrenched Mario's stomach.

"Tell them," Alexandria ordered as she stepped into the cell. Her voice was deep and dark, adding an aura of grave seriousness to the situation.

"I 'onestly dun—" Arthur started but before he could finish his sentence, Craven twisted his claws deeper into the bandit's body.

"We can do this all day," Alexandria taunted menacingly.

"I know nothin'!" Arthur screamed through clenched teeth.

With a sharp twist of his wrist, Craven's claws spun inside Arthur's body. The bandit screamed in agony at the top of his lungs, but even that wasn't enough to drown out the sounds of his ribs breaking from the force of Craven's claws. Arthur gritted his teeth to stifle a scream. Blood began to squirt out of his mouth between the gaps in his teeth. Craven's claws were puncturing vital organs. Every breath seemed laboured for the bandit. Every time he exhaled, a soft wheezing sound escaped his body. Finally, Arthur took a deep breath and screamed, "I'll never tell ye!"

Alexandria approached the chained man threateningly. She brought her bright red lips close to his ear. She took a sharp breath in and whispered, "So you *do* know something."

Arthur's eyes widened. Mario could see Arthur had come to the realization that his choice in words had doomed him. Mario also saw that the two vampires realized this as well. Their sinister smiles alluded to the hell that was about to befall Arthur.

"That's enough, Craven," Alexandria said playfully. Her icy blue eyes glimmering sadistically.

Craven did as he was commanded and violently removed his claws from Arthur's body. The bandit's blood flew across the room and splattered the walls of the cell red.

"If he won't tell us, perhaps he'll talk to Gregor." Alexandria's tone was dark and ominous, yet her vicious smile never left her face.

Without uttering a word, Craven exited the cell and made his way down the hallway of the dungeon and through another set of giant steel doors. Alexandria casually gestured everyone to exit the cell with her supple hand. They all backed away from the cell and stared at the steel doors at the opposite end of the hallway. Nobody knew or could have predicted what horror Craven would return with.

A loud, bellowing roar could be heard from behind the steel doors. Andronikus' body straightened and stiffened suddenly. The hair on the back of his neck stood up. He slowly turned his neck and glared at Alexandria angrily. His hands were clenched into fists.

"You didn't," Andronikus snarled.

"Oh, but I did," Alexandria coyly replied while winking at her former lover.

Suddenly, the steel doors busted open and the most grotesque creature Mario ever witnessed leapt from the shadows. Craven was controlling it by a chain that was tied around the creature's neck. The creature was as big as a horse and walked on all four. The beast resembled a bat that had been left in water for a few days and was now beginning to bloat. The beast's body was covered in loose olive-toned skin. Its dark red eyes darted around the room quickly, scanning for potential prey.

With a stamp of its feet, the creature bellowed out another roar. This time, a five-foot-long black tongue rocketed out of the beast's gaping maw. The tongue had a small mouth that was located at the tip. The tongue's mouth was filled with small spiral teeth. It wagged across the room, behaving as if it had a mind of its own.

"What in the gods is that!?" Hamish exclaimed as he stumbled backwards and fell onto his back, unable to stop staring at the monster in front of him.

"That is Gregor . . . our interrogation specialist," Alexandria informed as she exuded an aura of pride.

"That is an ekimmou. A sasabonsam," Andronikus stated angrily.

"What's it going to do?" Deidre asked as she reached down to grab the dagger in her boot in case things went awry.

"He is going to get you the information you want," Alexandria replied coldly. The countess took a few steps towards the beast and began caressing its cheek. After whispering into its ear, the countess led the beast into Arthur's cage and slammed the door behind it.

Arthur was still groggy from the amount of blood he lost during Craven's interrogation, and as a result, it took him a while to realize that he was trapped in a cage with such a monster. Arthur screamed once the gravity of his situation dawned on him. He began to writhe in his chains as the snarling beast slowly approached him.

Mario's stomach began to gurgle. He felt his skin go pale from the unholy spectacle before him. Mario wished he hadn't come to this place. He closed his eyes and prayed for it all to end when suddenly he felt someone's warm breath on the nape of his neck.

"Watch. This is all because of you," that ghastly voice whispered into his ear.

Mario stood up straight and opened his eyes. Unfortunately, he did not see the source of the voice, but he did see the atrocities of Gregor's interrogation taking place. He saw the ekimmou's tongue peeling the skin off of Arthur's face. He saw the bandit squirm in agony. Mario turned his head to see that Alexandria and Craven were smiling at the spectacle. He saw Hamish staring at the monster with horror but was unable to take his eyes away. He saw Andronikus staring at his feet while his hands covered his ears. Mario also saw that Deidre watched the mutilation with morbid curiosity. He could've sworn she had a grin on her face. . . .

Finally, Mario's breakfast made good on its earlier threats as it forcefully exited his mouth and onto the floor. He could still taste the hash browns and the eggs as they passed by his tongue for the second time that morning. Tears began to swell in Mario's eyes, and his head shook violently. Once his empty stomach painfully heaved one last time, Mario wiped his mouth and quickly exited the dungeon and went back up the spiral staircase.

As Mario ascended the staircase alone, he couldn't help but regret his choice in coming here. He desperately wanted to escape this awful city and return to the North. He wished he could abandon his mission and get away from all the smells, the sights, the slaughter, the atrocities, and the monsters. He wished he could escape the guilt and regret that came with being a knight.

One has to pay dearly for immortality; one has to die several times while one is still alive.

Friedrich Nietzsche

CHAPTER TEN

The stone walls of the castle were cold and unforgiving. The screams of Arthur could still be heard, even though he was behind two giant steel doors. Mario sat on the stairs and put his hands over his ears to try and block out the sound, but it was no use. It was just too loud, and the empty stairwell only amplified the screams of agony. The smell of blood began to seep into his nose, forcing his stomach to heave once again. Every now and then the screaming would stop just long enough for Mario to think it was over and uncover his ears, only to have it start again. Mario could feel his body begin to shake uncontrollably. His muscles tensed and his teeth were clenched so hard that he thought that they might crack.

Suddenly, he felt a hand on his shoulder. He looked up and saw a beautiful young pale woman standing above him. She had hair as white as snow and mesmerizing grey eyes. She was thin, with barely any meat on her bones. Mario could see the scars of bite marks on the left side of her neck. As if reading his thoughts, the woman gave a friendly smile, which displayed her fangs.

"Are you okay?" the woman asked sincerely.

"It's been a long day. . . ." Mario sighed.

"A long day? It's still morning. Come with me."

The woman gripped Mario's hand tightly and pulled him up the stairwell. She pulled him through the kitchen where he had eaten his breakfast that morning. She pulled him down numerous long, winding hallways each one identical to the last. Mario couldn't stop but stare at the back of the young vampire's head. There was a sense of innocence to her, a quality he admired and wished that he still possessed. The woman was filled with juvenile enthusiasm, laughing and giggling as she dragged Mario, who was struggling to keep up, down the hallways of the castle.

Finally, they came to a stop. They were in front of a set of giant triangular glass doors. Beyond the doors was a beautiful garden full of lush vegetation and exquisite flowers. The vampiress slowly pushed the door open, and almost instantly, Mario felt cleansed as the stench of blood that filled his nose was replaced by the lovely aroma of flowers in bloom. He slowly crossed the threshold into the garden and felt his worries melt away. Even in his wildest dreams, Mario could not have imagined a garden more beautiful than this.

The woman grabbed Mario by the hand again and dragged him to a small bench in the middle of the garden. Mario sat down and began to admire the garden's beauty. He admired the two poplar trees on either side of the bench. He was awestruck at how the branches from both trees came together and formed a natural arch above the bench. He noticed the small stream of water that flowed inches in front of his feet. He closed his eyes and allowed the smells of the garden and the soothing lapping sound of the stream to relax him. Sensing this, the woman placed her hand on Mario's shoulder. He opened his eyes and saw her lovely grey eyes staring back at him.

"Better?"

"Much, thank you." Mario gulped, for one of the few times in his life he was at a loss for words. "Who are you?"

"They call me Bianca," the woman replied, her voice only adding to the soothing aura of the garden. "You seemed upset so I brought you here. It's where I come when I'm feeling overwhelmed and need to relax."

"Thank you." Mario could feel the butterflies begin to flutter around in his chest as he stared into Bianca's enthralling eyes. *I wish Tiberius was here with me. He would know what to say to her.*

The two of them sat comfortably in the silence, just staring into the garden and admiring its splendour. Bianca seemed content, staring at all the awe-inspiring exotic flowers that populated the garden, while Mario secretly panicked, trying to think of a conversation starter.

"What are you doing in Kartaga?" Bianca asked, finally breaking the ice for him.

"I'm here with some friends. We are in search of some bandits and—"

"Ah, the source of the screams in the dungeon, say no more."

Mario's nerves finally got the best of him, and he asked the first question that popped into his head. "What's it like?"

"What's what like?"

"Being a vampire."

Bianca giggled and began to stare into Mario's eyes once more. "Want me to show you?" Her eyes focused on Mario's neck, and her body began leaning forward towards his.

Mario froze. He wanted to tell her no, he wanted to stand up and run away, but every muscle in his body ignored his commands. Instead, he just sat there, frozen in fear.

Bianca instantly pulled back and erupted into laughter. "You ... you should've seen your face!"

Mario laughed along nervously.

Bianca took a deep breath and wiped the tears from her eyes. "You really want to know?"

Mario nodded his head and waited with bated breath.

Suddenly, Bianca's smile vanished, and she let out a forlorn sigh. "Truth is, I miss being a human. I miss being able to hug my mom every day. I miss my friends ... I miss being hungry for something other than blood."

Without realizing, Mario reached his hand out and grabbed Bianca's. Her hand squeezed in response.

"How did you become a vampire?"

"I was born in a small town along the border of Artanzia and Keten called Midway. My father abandoned my mother and me when I was born, forcing my mother to raise and care for me by herself. When I was about eighteen, a sickness stormed the village. It infected everybody. First, you came down with a fever, then black boils would cover your skin, and finally, you died."

Mario squeezed Bianca's hand tighter. She moved her body closer to his.

"As a girl, my job was to tend to the sick. I had managed to stay healthy until my mom fell ill."

"I'm sorry. . . ."

"Once she became sick, taking care of her was my only duty. I didn't care about anything else. I felt it was only fair to care for her since she had done so much for me growing up. Unfortunately, the sickness took her quickly, and there was nothing I could do. I still remember how delusional she was from the fever. She rattled on and on about how my father was coming back to save me and how I wouldn't die from this sickness. I didn't believe it. My father never cared for me or my mother. If he did, he would've helped raise me." A tear began to roll down Bianca's cheek.

The idea of a vampire crying struck Mario as odd, but he shook the thought out of his head. He continued to nod his head and listen to her story attentively.

"Then one day, a strange man appeared on my doorstep. I had just finished burying my mother, and at that point, the fever had already begun to grip me. My whole world was gone. . . . I didn't care about anything anymore. All I wanted to do was just die, so I could be with my mom again."

This time, a tear began to roll down Mario's cheek. The way Bianca's voice shook as she recalled the story made his heart ache. He regretted bringing up such a painful memory for her.

"The man claimed to be my father and told me that he had returned to save me. I didn't believe him obviously. I thought he was just another charlatan who was trying to take advantage of the sick and weary."

"What happened next?"

"Next thing I know, I'm over this man's shoulder and he's carrying me to his horse. Because of the sickness, I was too weak to fight back. So, I just sat there, hoping that when this man was done with me that he would just kill me and put me out of my misery."

Bianca and Mario's shoulders were touching at this point. Her long white hair tickled his neck, and her hot breath caressed his cheek. Their hands remained tightly interlocked.

"But he never did anything, instead we just kept riding south. We rode for what seemed like months. Then finally, we arrived here. He carried me up the castle steps, my body riddled with hideous black boils and brought me to the countess. They argued for some time but ultimately, she agreed to save my life by turning me into a vampire. When I awoke the next morning, my fever was gone and my boils had vanished. I felt like a brand-new person . . . except I felt hungry. I remember gorging myself on bread, meat, and fruit, but nothing seemed to sate my hunger. Finally, the countess explained to me what had transpired. She explained that I was now a vampire and needed to feed off of the blood of the living in order to survive."

Bianca inched closer to Mario and placed her right hand on Mario's left thigh. "Ever since then I've been stuck here. I used to come to this garden when I had trouble coming to terms with what I had become. Now when I see someone upset, I bring them here and hope that it helps them in the same way that it helped me."

Mario didn't know what to say; he sat there staring at the vampiress. He was amazed by how beautiful she was; he was amazed by how attracted to her he was. *I now see how Andronikus could fall for a vampire.*

"What about you? What's your story?"

The sound of Bianca's voice made Mario's skin tingle. Every fibre of his being was filled with excitement and anxiety. He took a few seconds to calm himself. "It's a long story," Mario began.

"I've got the time." Bianca smiled. This time, Mario wasn't put off by the sight of her fangs. Instead, he found them strangely appealing.

He took a deep breath and began to tell her his story. He started his story by talking about his dad, Pablo Deschamps, the great knight who is regaled in the North for his incredible deeds. He told her that his father stopped an elven uprising and saved the North from certain disaster, but never returned home. He then told her his own story: his time at the Knight's College in Redfern, how he met his companions on his quest to track down the bandits, how he got his disfiguring scar in the Eeragwia Forest and barely made out of the pogroms in Riverwell. He even told her that he was having second thoughts about being a knight.

"That's quite a story . . ."

"Yeah." Mario sighed. "I have a feeling that it isn't even close to being done yet though."

"Perhaps, but every good story needs a happy ending." Bianca wrapped her arms around Mario's neck.

Mario's body stiffened with anticipation. Slowly, they leaned toward one another and their lips almost touched.

"Bianca! What the fuck are you doing!?" a voice screamed from behind them.

Mario and Bianca turned around and saw Hamish, Deidre, Alexandria, and a fuming Andronikus standing in the doorway of the garden.

"You know each other?" Mario asked, blinking uncontrollably.

"She's my fucking daughter! If you hurt her, I swear I'll . . ."

In the blink of an eye, Bianca had shot up from the bench and grabbed her father by the throat and slammed him into the stone wall. "If *he* hurt me!?

Nobody could do anything worse than what you did to me!" She snarled, her grip tightened and Andronikus' face began to turn purple.

"Come now, child . . ." Alexandria said as she took a step forward.

Bianca's anger suddenly shifted, and she shot daggers at the countess with her eyes. "If you touch me, I'll rip you to shreds, you fucking hag!"

The garden was quiet. Mario no longer felt calm and relaxed. Instead, all of his anxiety and stress came rushing back into his body tenfold. His muscles tightened and his mouth became dry. He swallowed, hoping that it would grant him the courage to say something. "Bianca . . ." he squeaked.

Bianca's head turned sharply towards him. He could see that her eyes welled with tears. Bianca grimaced and closed her eyes, and with great speed and strength, she threw Andronikus across the garden. His body flailed as he bounced off of the hard ground and tumbled through the vegetation. He came to a hard, sudden stop when he crashed into a tree trunk. Mario could've sworn that he heard ribs breaking.

Bianca ran from the room, crying with her hands over her face. Andronikus slowly stood up, brushing the dirt and dust off as he did so. Without showing any sign of pain, he followed Bianca out of the doorway without uttering a word.

The group fell silent. Even the cunning countess was rendered speechless. Everyone just stood in shocked silence, not sure how to react to the situation they had just witnessed. They avoided eye contact with one another, not able to find the words to express their discomfort. Instead, everyone decided to leave the garden while an awkward aura hung in the air.

***

The wind was howling at the top of the battlements on the walls surrounding the city. It was a cold and unforgiving wind. *A fitting place for a bastard like me.* Andronikus thought to himself as he stared out into the countryside. The barren fields surrounding the city of Kartaga only added to Andronikus' already dreary mood. For a brief moment, he thought about jumping from the castle walls, but he knew it would be of no use. *It would take more than a little fall to kill an immortal like me.* He heard quick footsteps approaching from his left side, but he didn't acknowledge them. He already knew who they belonged to.

"Well, that was . . . eventful," the countess remarked as she joined her lover on the stone battlements of her city.

"You were right. She still hates me."

"I mean, it is kind of your fault," Alexandria added venomously, hoping her words would destroy the last remnants of humanity left in Andronikus' heart.

"It's not just that. She hates me because she thinks I abandoned her and her mother all those years ago."

"Didn't you?" The countess' toxic fingers caressed Andronikus' tense neck as he stared solemnly out from the castle walls.

Instinctively, he shrugged them off. "No," he retorted. "Her mother asked me to leave them. She knew what I was . . . she knew everything about me. She thought it would be best if I didn't outlive my little girl. So she sent me away, trying to spare me from heartache. But once she fell ill, she sent letters for me, hoping that one would find my hands. She knew Bianca would get sick from the plague, and she begged me to come back so Bianca wouldn't suffer the same fate as her. I just wish Bianca would give me the chance to explain this to her."

"Too bad she is busy being used by that knight," the countess muttered passively.

Andronikus' head snapped up and stared at the countess menacingly.

She knew she had touched a nerve. She knew she had him right where she wanted him. "I mean did you see how she was eating out of his grubby little hands?" she continued. "I'm surprised she didn't ask him to fuck her right there on the spot!"

Andronikus' face was red with rage. His muscles tense and his fists clenched so hard that his knuckles turned white and popped from the pressure.

The countess smiled, her pearly white fangs glistening in the sunlight. She slowly wrapped her arms around Andronikus' neck and gazed up into his cold, angry eyes. "You see what would happen to her if it wasn't for our deal? The humans would either hunt her, chase her to the ends of the world, like a monster, or they would try to fuck her, treat her as a novelty and nothing more." Alexandria could hear Andronikus' teeth begin to crack from his clenched jaw. "Here, behind my walls, she is at least safe and is treated with respect. Out there, she would be used and passed around more than a communal washcloth . . . and Mario would be the first in line."

"I'll wring that bastard's neck!" Andronikus screamed as the veins began to bulge out from his neck and forehead.

"Go and find him then."

In a fury, Andronikus sprinted down from the battlements in search of Mario. The countess stood on top of the battlements, quietly laughing to herself and basking in the sunlight.

***

By late afternoon, Deidre, Hamish, and Mario had begun packing their things. Mario had learned that Gregor proved useful, as he successfully extracted multiple bits of key information from his interrogation with Arthur. First, Mario learned that the bandits' main camp was on the northern part of Drussdell, right beside the Drussdell and Keten border. He also learned that the bandits were not operating alone. Arthur confessed that the bandits would receive letters that contained instructions. The letters instructed the bandits when to raid, where to raid, and for how long. Unfortunately, Arthur succumbed to his wounds before he could give the name behind the person sending the letters.

Mario was tying his shield to the saddle of one of the four horses provided by the countess. He looked up and down the streets of Kartaga, but there was no sign of Andronikus or Bianca. There was a lump in Mario's stomach. He hoped that he would be able to see Bianca again and kiss her before he continued on his journey. However, he also feared what Andronikus would do to him once he reunited with the group.

Suddenly, Mario heard footsteps approaching him from a side street behind him. His heart leapt up into his throat; he hoped it would be the beautiful vampiress, with her flowing white hair billowing in the wind. But to his dismay, he saw that it was a visibly angry Andronikus marching towards him, sword in hand.

Mario quickly turned to pull his sword out of his scabbard, but his hand slipped off of the handle. Andronikus picked Mario up by the collar of his shirt and lifted him into the air. He brought his mouth close and whispered into Mario's ear, "If you ever even look at my daughter again, I'll gut you like a fuckin' carp." Andronikus violently shoved Mario to the ground and continued to walk towards his horse.

"Hey!" Hamish exclaimed as he offered a hand up to Mario.

"Let's leave. We have to reach the mountains by nightfall," Andronikus ordered, paying no mind to the fallen Mario.

"Why the mountains? Why can't we just follow the river again?" Deidre asked as she restrung her bow.

"Alexandria got a report that both sides are increasing patrols around that area. It will be even riskier to cross the border that way this time."

"What's in the mountains?" Mario asked.

Andronikus' head snapped, and he glared at Mario menacingly. "A series of caves we are going to use to sneak back into the North," he growled through gritted teeth.

"Is it safe?" asked Hamish, who responded with a glare of his own.

"There's a reason I suggested the river before the caves, but we're left with no other option now."

No one spoke, as they thought of what dangers awaited them in the caves. Before anyone could ask more questions about their path, Andronikus spurred his horse and galloped out of the city. The others begrudgingly followed and hurried to catch up with their guide.

It had been so long since Mario had been in a saddle. As soon as his horse reached a gallop, he felt as if a forgotten part of himself returned. The cool touch of the wind on his cheek, the way his horse's hooves pounded against the solid earth as she ran, how her breathing was perfectly in time with his own—all reminded him of simpler times. Times where his only concern was whether or not Sir Darius was in a foul mood that day. How he wished he could go back to those days.

After a few hours of hard riding, they stopped their horses at the foot of a mountain. The mountain disappeared as it ascended into the clouds. A feeling of insignificance and inferiority took over Mario as he stared up at the gargantuan rock formation in front of him. He gulped nervously, knowing that he was going to have to scale that mountain.

"Single file," Andronikus instructed. "The paths are pretty narrow, so watch your footing." He spurred his horse on and took the lead. Deidre quickly followed him, with Hamish and Mario taking up the rear.

The mountain pass was riddled with loose shale and the horses' hooves constantly slipped out from underneath them. Mario was worried that it was only a matter of time before one of the horses would slip and fall over the edge of the path and down the side of the mountain, taking its rider with it.

"So, what are these caves exactly?" Mario asked, finally breaking the long, excruciating silence.

"They used to belong to a dwarven city called Mnildrom," Andronikus informed as he kept his eyes on the dangerous path. "They were said to be the most technologically advanced civilization the world has ever seen. There were even tales that they had weapons that could shoot fire, similar to a dragon's breath."

"Is any of it true?"

"Supposedly."

"What happened to them?" Deidre asked.

"Dunno," Andronikus added stalely. "One day they just disappeared. Vanished without a trace. The empire explored their abandoned city and found blueprints, diagrams, and craftsmen's notes, but unfortunately, nobody could understand them. They were too complex for anyone else to recreate."

"Your vampire tell you that?" Hamish growled.

Andronikus swiftly pulled up on the reins of his horse bringing it to a sudden stop. "Do we have a problem changeling?" He snarled as he dismounted his horse.

"I don't know, do we?" Hamish snapped back as his voice began to turn distorted.

With a quick flourish, Andronikus pulled out his sword. "Then maybe we should solve it."

Hamish jumped off his horse, and Mario could see that his hands had begun to grow in size and change colour. He knew that unless somebody did something, it was going to get bloody.

"Everybody just calm down!" Mario shouted at the top of his lungs.

Andronikus' eyes darted up at Mario. Before Mario could react, Andronikus quickly picked up a rock and hurled it at Mario's face. The stone hit Mario at the peak of his nose, and he heard the bones break. Mario screamed in pain and covered his face with his hands. After the initial wave of pain subsided, Mario lifted his bloody face from his hands and glared towards Andronikus. He slowly removed his sword from his scabbard.

Suddenly Deidre pulled out her bow and shot an arrow at the feet of Andronikus and Hamish and readied another arrow pointing directly at Mario's broken nose. "Enough!" she screamed. All eyes immediately focused on her. "I'm tired of all of your bitching! You're acting like children when we have a job to do!" Her eyes glared at Hamish, who had turned pale out of surprise. "So what if he wanted to kill you when he first met you? He didn't. In fact, you two fought beside each other several times since then. You think someone who wanted you dead would do that?"

"No," Hamish replied sheepishly, his eyes cast down on the ground.

Deidre's eyes darted towards Andronikus, whose mouth was agape. "And you!" she screamed. "He almost kissed your daughter, big deal. Get over it and stop acting like a child! She is a grown person and can make her own fucking choices!"

Andronikus gave no reply. He just hung his head in uncomfortable shame.

"If you three can't grow up and help me track down these bandits then fine, I'll do it myself!"

"But I . . ." Mario started.

"You . . ." Deidre snarled, clearly still not done with her tantrum. Mario saw that her eyes widened suddenly, and her fingers let go of her bowstring. The arrow shot past Mario's face. He turned his head to see, on the ledge above him, a giant lizard-like beast. The monster spread its colossal wings and jumped from its perch. It grabbed Hamish's horse with its legs and flew out over the side of the mountain. The beast's sharp talons dug into the horse's stomach and streams of blood and bile began to pour out of the creature's body. The horse let out a whinny in pain, a sound that sent a shiver down Mario's spine. The monster then threw the horse into the air with a mighty swing of its legs. The horse's body helplessly flailed in the air as it fell back down toward the monster's gaping maw. In the blink of an eye, the entire horse disappeared inside the monstrous gullet.

"A wyvern!" Andronikus yelled as he hurried back onto his horse.

Hamish instinctively hopped on the back of Deidre's horse, and they galloped up the narrow mountain pass at a dangerous pace. The wyvern let out an ear-splitting caw and swooped down to give pursuit. Mario spurred his horse to go faster, but he feared it would be of no use. The horse was already breathing heavy and every step was a further invitation for the creature to slip and fall down the mountain. Mario could feel the wind from the wyvern's wings on the back of his neck. He knew it was close.

Another arrow whizzed by Mario's face once more. This time the arrow hit its mark. Mario felt the creature's warm, sticky, blood spray all over his face. Once more, the wyvern let out a wail and, this time, flew up the side of the mountain and disappeared amongst the clouds.

"Where'd it go?" Hamish asked, his head darting side to side, waiting for the ambush.

"Just keep riding!" Andronikus yelled as he spurred his horse further up the mountain.

With a fear-inducing cry, the wyvern dove from above and burst through the thick layer of clouds. This time it attacked the front of the line. The wyvern had miscalculated its swoop and was too high to reach Andronikus, Deidre, or Hamish. But it was the perfect height to attack Mario. Mario froze as he stared at the gaping maw of the lizard rapidly approaching him. He saw the rows of dagger-like teeth, eagerly waiting to tear him into shreds. Mario closed his eyes and waited for death.

Luckily, his horse's hooves finally slipped on the loose shale of the mountain path. The fall sent Mario flying from his saddle and into the mountain while his horse tumbled down its side, along with his shield and his supplies.

The wyvern, frustrated by its lack of success, let out a cry and swooped once more towards Mario. Reactively, Mario pulled out his sword and collapsed to his knees while he pointed his sword straight up into the air. By the time the wyvern saw what was happening, it was too late. The creature's soft underbelly was no match for his sharp sword. As the wyvern flew over top of Mario, the sword's point punctured its chest and gutted the monster, using its own momentum.

A shower of blood, guts, and gore poured on top of Mario as the wyvern's corpse crashed over into the side of the mountain. Mario stared at his blood-covered body and knew that this was as bloody as he had ever been. However, this time he did not feel regret or guilt at the sight of the blood. Instead, he felt a sense of pride. *I just killed a wyvern!* Mario wiped his face and stared at his companions, whose mouths were open in shock. After a lengthy silence, Andronikus burst into laughter. Deidre and Hamish also joined in. Mario even chuckled himself as he stared at his body, which was completely red with carnage.

"Look at you!" Andronikus said between his laughs, gasping for air as he did so.

"Well, someone had to do something," Mario joked. He walked towards Andronikus' horse, and the monster hunter lent him a hand up onto its back.

For the rest of the day, the four companions joked, laughed and had fun at Mario's expense. But he didn't mind; in fact, he enjoyed it. He felt like they needed something like this to bring them closer together. This was the most he'd laughed in a long time. It was nightfall when Andronikus had stopped his horse outside the mouth of a cave. With a swift hand signal, everybody dismounted. "This is it. We'll have to leave the horses here," he instructed.

Mario looked deep into the cave and wondered what unspeakable horrors lurked inside them, waiting to attack any foolhardy adventurers. But he was not afraid. He felt that if Andronikus, Deidre, and Hamish were by his side . . . they would be unstoppable.

Caves. I fucking hate caves. Every cave I have ever entered has either been full of monsters or one sneeze away from imploding on itself. Unfortunately, I fear that I am in one that is both. This fucking shithole looks like it'll collapse on me at any moment, and I can't get any sleep because of the ungodly creatures that stalk me. My only saving grace is that if this cave collapses, it'll take some of those fuckers with me.

Excerpt from *Diary of an Unknown Explorer*

CHAPTER ELEVEN

D*rip. Drip. Drip.* Every once in a while, a drop of water would fall out of the darkness and hit Mario's face. The cool water was refreshing, as the caves were oddly hot, and the temperature only seemed to rise the deeper they ventured into them. The entire cavern was surrounded in a blanket of darkness—an unforgiving, unnerving blackness, with the only source of light being the faint glow from Andronikus' torch.

Mario felt the gentle pull of the rope around his waist. He quickly caught up with the others. *If it wasn't for this rope tethering me to the others, one would easily get lost in this place.*

"Do you know where you are going?" Hamish called out, his voice echoing throughout the mighty cavern.

"No," Andronikus answered stalely.

Mario's stomach grew uneasy. It worried him that Andronikus had no idea where he was leading them. Mario wasn't even sure if he could see at the front of the line. However, that wasn't Mario's greatest concern. He felt as if someone or something was watching them as they walked further into the cave. Something that was hidden by the thick cover of darkness.

Suddenly, there was a low, resonant rumbling coming from deep within the cave. The noise shook the walls of the cave violently. Stalactites plummeted towards the ground with fiendish speed. Mario quickly adjusted his position for better balance and prayed that none of the stalactites would fall on him. The loose earth underneath him gave way, and he felt his footing slip. Mario instinctively dug his sword deep into the soft earth. The rope around his waist tightened. He could feel his right foot dangle helplessly over the abyss of nothingness that was waiting to engulf him below. As quickly as it began, the rumbling stopped.

"What's going on?" Andronikus called out gruffly.

"I slipped."

"Are you hurt?"

"No, I'm fine," Mario said as he pulled himself back on the narrow pathway.

"The hell was that?" Hamish asked, trying to conceal the fear in his voice.

"I don't know," Andronikus replied once again.

Mario kept his head on a swivel as they continued to descend deeper and deeper into the caves. Every step they took seemed to increase the temperature of the caves. After half an hour, Mario's body was coated in a thick layer of sweat. The sour liquid stung his eyes as it dripped down from his forehead. After an hour, Mario's vision was blurred by sweat droplets, and he felt as if he was about to collapse from exhaustion. His heavy plate armour was weighing him down. Every heaving breath he took burned his already broken nose.

"We're here," Andronikus cried out suddenly. Mario wiped the sweat from his eyes, the metal gauntlets scratching his face as he did so. In front of them, illuminated by Andronikus' faint torchlight, were two massive stone doors with strange runes written all over them. One of the doors had an enormous hole in it that looked like it was made with explosives.

"What do they say?" Deidre asked, eyeing the colossal stone doors in front of her.

"I dunno," Andronikus replied. "I can't read Dwarvish. I assume it was a spell of some kind sealing the doors shut to prevent intruders."

"What about that hole?" Hamish replied, pointing to the giant hole in the bottom of the left door.

"Probably how the empire got in."

Cautiously, Andronikus led them through the hole in the door. Mario couldn't take his eyes off of the stone doors. It baffled him how someone could build something so big. He examined the strange writing as he walked by, unable to decipher its warning.

Inside the doors lay an ancient city. Everyone was rendered speechless, even Andronikus. Every building was larger than the palace at Kartaga. In fact, Mario couldn't even see the roofs of the buildings as they were swallowed by the darkness of the cave.

"Anyone smell oil?" Hamish asked.

Mario took a deep breath and immediately winced in pain. It felt like someone had shoved daggers up his nose. His whole body reacted to the pain and every muscle tensed. He took a few seconds to take a few deep breaths, making sure to breathe through the mouth, and regained his composure.

"I smell it," Deidre interjected.

Andronikus slowly bent down and examined the floor of the cave. Right below his feet was a small gutter that was carved into the stone. The drain appeared to be filled with something. Andronikus dropped the torch in the gutter, and the substance ignited.

The small stream of fire rushed towards the city centre, fuelled by the oil in the gutter. The little river of fire was faster than an arrow and illuminated the entire city. In the middle of the city, the small stream of fire exploded into a mighty inferno. Mario could now see that the tops of the buildings went all the way to the roof of the caves. He guessed they were about five hundred feet above him.

Deidre gasped, staring at the enormous city that sat before them. "Whoa."

"The oil still works?" A puzzled expression was glued on Hamish's face as he carefully examined the fire.

"It's dwarven oil," Andronikus replied while untying the ropes around their waists. "It will be here long after we are dead."

The city streets were wide enough to comfortably fit twelve wagons side by side while still having enough room for a group of people to walk on either side. Every building was made entirely of stone. Each building had a personification of a dwarf beside it, and every statue was carved meticulously and in great detail. Wrinkles, blemishes, even each individual hair of the dwarf was visible through the carving. *These statues look so lifelike. They almost look like real dwarves.* Mario reached out and gently poked one of the statues on the nose, secretly expecting that it would come to life. If the statue was alive, it did not react.

"This is the biggest city I've ever seen," Andronikus mumbled as they approached the giant cauldron of fire in the centre of town.

The cauldron appeared to be a workshop of some kind. The edges were littered with anvils, benches, scrolls, and tools. The tools that Mario recognized were the ones that he had seen around the blacksmith forge back at the Knight's College. Hammers, tongs, chisels, and punches. However, for every tool he recognized, there were three that he did not.

"What is all this stuff?" Mario asked aloud, picking up one of the strange tools.

"I have no idea," Andronikus answered. "My best guess is that they were used by alchemists or mages."

"Hey, look what I found!" Hamish exclaimed. In his hand was a small, black porous rock. There was a faint blue glow radiating from inside the rock.

"Put that down! You don't know what it is!" Deidre barked.

Hamish scoffed, staring intently at the fist-sized rock in his hand. "Loosen up, Deidre," he said. "Imagine the things we could learn from this place if—"

Suddenly, the rock began to shake violently in Hamish's hand. The faint blue glow from within the rock now became a blinding white light. It was as if Hamish held the sun in the palm of his hand.

Mario closed his eyes and put his hands in front of his face to help shield himself from eye-burning brightness. "Toss it into the fire!"

"No!" Andronikus cried out, but it was too late. Hamish had already thrown the small orb of light into the inferno in front of them.

Another low rumbling came from within the cave; only this time, it was much closer. The vibrations from the sound knocked everyone on their backs. Mario looked up and saw that the air was swirling with an eerie blue smoke. The smoke slithered through the air like a snake and separated itself into a hundred smaller pieces. Each piece darted toward the outskirts of the city in a different direction. Just as before, the sound stopped suddenly, and the cave went eerily quiet.

Deidre stood up and dusted herself off. "Let's get out of here."

"Agreed, the only question is how?" Andronikus scratched his patchy beard in frustration.

"Umm guys," Hamish interjected nervously.

Mario turned in the direction of Hamish and saw that an army of dwarven statues was marching down the street towards them. All of the statues were perfectly in sync with one another. The sound of their stone feet hitting the stone roads echoed throughout the caves. It was like a curtain of thunder bellowing towards them. Mario instinctively drew his sword.

"They're coming from everywhere!" Deidre cried out.

"Fuck," Andronikus added.

A sinking feeling of despair gripped Mario's throat. He knew they would never be able to survive this. The sea of the moving statues was endless. Every time Mario thought he saw the end of the army, more would appear and fall into line. Once the dwarven army had surrounded them, blocking off all escape routes, they stopped fifteen feet away from the cauldron of fire.

"What're they waiting for?" Deidre growled.

"Ask them," Andronikus answered calmly, yet sarcastically.

Finally, a lone statue stepped forward. Mario could see that the eyes of each statue glowed with the same blue light that was inside the rock.

"Who awakens us?" the statue said softly in a deep, gravelly voice.

Mario could see that the statue talking was the one that he had poked in the nose earlier. His cheeks began to turn red with embarrassment. The statue had a long beard and appeared to be wearing plate armour. He was brandishing a great axe as he glared menacingly towards the group.

"It was him," Deidre answered, pointing towards Hamish.

The statue craned his neck, and an expression of confusion took over his face once he saw Hamish. "*You* have awoken us? But you are not a dwarf; none of you are dwarves."

In one swift motion, the entire dwarven army shifted into an attacking position. Mario looked around at his comrades nervously. Everyone, apart from Andronikus, looked scared shitless. Mario cleared his throat. "Please, we mean you no harm. We only wanted to pass through your caves to get back home."

The statue slowly turned his neck towards Mario and glared savagely at him. It began to walk menacingly towards Mario, gripping his great axe tightly the entire time. When the statue was only a few inches away from him, it stopped. The statue's right hand let go of his great axe, and he slowly raised it and gently poked Mario in the nose. Mario silently winced in pain as the cold, stone hand touched his broken nose. A small smile appeared on the statue's lips. "Very well, you may pass."

"We don't know where to go," Mario retorted.

"Up," one of the statues called from the crowd. The entire army of statues exploded with laughter.

"Great idea, which street leads to *up*?" Andronikus replied.

"You will want to take the left-most street and through the old tunnels," the main statue said. "But beware of the obzen."

"The what?" Andronikus asked angrily.

"The obzen," the statue replied. "It is why we were created. We were made to protect the dwarves of this city from them."

"What are they?" Mario asked, fearing he already knew the answer.

"Terrible monsters that hunt in bloodthirsty hordes," the statue said. "If you see one, it is already too late; in a few seconds, there will be thousands."

"How do we kill them?" Deidre snapped.

"You don't," the statue replied calmly. "Every time you kill one, two more appear in its place."

"How were you supposed to protect the dwarves of Mnildrom if you can't kill these things?" Hamish interjected.

"We were meant to serve as a distraction. To fend off the obzen while our people escaped."

Mario gulped nervously. He felt a bead of sweat rush down the side of his face. He looked around to each of the streets and could not imagine a monster capable of fighting such an army. *I pray we never see these beasts.*

"Let's get going," Andronikus barked as he made his way towards the left-most street.

"Thank you," Mario said to the statue and quickly followed behind the others. The sea of statues parted as they made their way down the street and out of the city.

The cave became cooler the further they walked away from the circle of fire in the centre of the city. Mario began to feel more and more comfortable as his profuse sweating began to slow down. Soon the only source of light was Andronikus' measly torch. The uneasy feeling in Mario's stomach slowly returned. He felt the bile bubble and pop with every step he took. It felt like the eyes of the mysterious obzen were watching him, hidden from the shadows.

Suddenly, a bright speck of light darted in front of Mario's eyes. Mario shook his head, convinced he was seeing things. The little speck of light shot past his eyes once more. Mario slowly reached down towards his sword, hoping he would be ready the next time the pest would fly by his eyes. As if sensing his anticipation, the speck of light flashed by once more, this time in front of Deidre. Reactively, she came to a sudden stop.

"What was that?" she blurted out as she readied her bow.

"What was what?" Andronikus repeated. The dart of light instantly shot past Andronikus' eyes, as if it was waiting for a cue. "Fuck."

"What is it?" Hamish asked his sword already in hand.

"A nuisance." Andronikus sighed as he eyed the little dot of light carefully. "A pixie."

"So, what do we do?" Mario asked.

"We ignore it and keep walking."

Mario, Deidre, and Hamish relaxed their bodies in unison and sheathed their weapons, although they did not take their eyes off of the pixie. They watched it cautiously as it danced around their faces, as if it was trying to get their attention.

"What in the devil does it want?" Hamish growled as he waved his hand in front of his face, as if he was swatting away a mosquito.

"Probably to piss us off." Andronikus scowled as he eyed the floating ball of light.

"Can we get rid of it?" Deidre asked, clearly annoyed by the small creature buzzing around her face.

"No." Andronikus snarled. "Pixies aren't from this world; they're fey. Because of that, they aren't bound to the same laws as we are. The only way to capture or, even better, kill the little bastards is with a Balazar snare."

"A what?" Mario asked, confused as he touched his nose gingerly.

"A device specifically designed to capture fey. It's named after the wizard who was the first person to successfully capture a pixie, Balazar Tanis."

"How does it work?"

"No clue. But hopefully, it makes the little piss ants suffer." Andronikus growled as he tried to bat the ball of light out of the air.

Mario stared at Andronikus' face curiously. He couldn't help but wonder why someone like Andronikus had such animosity towards a creature such as a pixie. *Sure, the little devil is annoying. But there are far greater nuisances in the world.*

Suddenly, they came to a stop. In front of them was a cramped small dark mining tunnel. Mario felt a warm breath on the inside of his ear. Goosebumps covered his body, and all of his muscles froze in place. "Death is near," the voice whispered in his ear. Mario began to sweat profusely once again.

"Hey, guys, are we sure this is the safest route?" Mario asked, scratching his neck nervously.

"This is where the statues told us to go. Are you scared?" Deidre teased.

Deidre's words cut Mario like a knife. He felt his cheeks turn red from his wounded pride. "Pfft, I'm not scared. You're the one who's scared," Mario scoffed, his chest puffed out with false bravado.

"Good, then you won't mind leading us through the tunnels then." Andronikus smiled from ahead.

Mario swallowed nervously. *Me and my big fucking mouth.* Reluctantly, he sauntered over and grabbed the torch from Andronikus' hands and took a step towards the tunnel. Suddenly, the pixie darted away from the tunnel and back into the darkness of the caves. *It almost looks scared.*

"Good riddance," Andronikus growled.

The tunnels were five feet wide and about six feet high. Mario and Deidre were the only ones who could stand upright in the tunnels, while Andronikus and Hamish had to duck or squat to avoid hitting their heads on the supports. The smell of the rotting wood from the old supports filled the tunnels. Mario coughed as the smoke from the torch rose into his face. His eyes began to tear, and the smoke burned his already irritated sinuses.

"I wish that pixie was here so it could give us some light." Mario coughed.

"And I wish all those little bastards would rot like these boards," Andronikus replied sourly from the very back of the line.

"Anyone else seeing these little holes branching off the main tunnel?" Deidre said, changing the subject.

Mario looked on either side of him and saw what Deidre was talking about. Each of the holes were about four feet in diameter and were black as coal. Staring into the holes filled Mario's body with the sense of impending doom. "Leave. Now," a voice whispered in Mario's ear.

"Maybe it was the dwarves branching off when they were mining," Mario added casually, completely disregarding the warning from the voice in his head out of fear.

No one answered. Perhaps, like Mario, they knew that was not true. Some*thing* had made these holes, not some*one*, and Mario would wager that it was something sinister that wanted to eat them.

Mario's torch began to flicker and wave. A gust of wind blew down the tunnel, covering them in a cloud of dust. Mario closed his eyes as his face was assaulted with tiny pebbles. The smell of rot hung in the air.

"We must be getting close to outside," Hamish remarked once the dust finally settled.

"Smells like a corpse up ahead," Andronikus replied as he readied his sword.

Mario nodded and cautiously pressed on. He moved the torch to his left hand, so his right hand was free to use his sword. The smell of decay and maggots wretched Mario's stomach—not because of the foul odour, but because of what would be the source of the smell. Mario hoped it was just the carcass of a deer at the mouth of the cave, but in his heart, he knew that wasn't true.

As Mario turned the corner of the tunnel, he came to a sudden stop. Fifteen feet in front of him sat a man. The man was completely naked, hairless, and had alabaster skin. Mario squinted in the faint torchlight to get a better look at the man and realized this was no man at all. This creature looked exactly like a man, except it had six legs. Two at the front, two at the back, and one on each side.

The creature turned around and faced him. In its mouth, hung the rotting corpse of a large rat. The beast slurped up the entire body of the rat, like one would slurp up a bowl of noodles. Mario could hear the rat's bones crunching from the powerful jaw of the creature. The monster's eyes were as black as coal and tears appeared to be rolling down his face, except the tears were crimson red like blood.

"Guys . . ." Mario whispered as he slowly reached for his sword.

Immediately, the beast let out a high-pitched wail and charged towards him with lightning quickness. The monster used all six of its legs to get to top speed in a fraction of a second. The legs flailed wildly as they bent in abnormal directions, clinging to anything that would give the monster traction. Petrified at the grisly beast coming towards him, Mario fumbled around for the hilt of his sword while having his eyes glued on the monster ahead of him. By some miracle, Mario found the hilt of his sword and held it out at full extension. The beast's momentum impaled itself on the sharp blade.

Mario breathed a sigh of relief as he pulled his sword out the creature's mouth. He could see that something was moving inside the monster's skull. He held a torch closer to the corpse to get a better look, and two miniature versions of the monster exploded from the back of the beast's head. *Obzen.*

"Run!" Mario screamed as he sprinted down the tunnel, crushing one of the small obzen underneath his heavy plate boot.

Mario's heavy breathing burned his broken nose, but he kept running. He could hear the high-pitched wails of obzen coming from behind them. He looked over his shoulder and saw a swarm of monsters crawling along the walls of the tunnel, opening and closing their jaws with ravenous ferocity.

Mario saw the snow-white head of an obzen poke its head out from one of the small holes along the wall of the tunnel. Mario severed it from its neck as he ran by. Hoping that the others would be able to run past it before the offspring would sprout from its corpse.

As Mario frantically turned another corner, he saw the end of the tunnel. It was a blinding white light that took his eyes a few seconds to adjust before he could see the foliage of the forest. *We made it. We're safe.* Mario pressed on, his eyes watering and nose burning from the pain, the howls of the obzen slowly closing in behind him.

As soon as Mario crossed the threshold out of the cave, his body filled with warmth. The sun's rays spread a soothing feeling through his entire body. But this was no time to relax, he had to make sure the others got out safe. He quickly turned on his heels to see that Deidre was only a few steps behind him. Hamish was ten feet away from the mouth of the cave while Andronikus was fifty feet behind him. The obzen mere inches behind as they snapped at his heels.

Deidre started firing arrows into the horde of monsters, but it was futile. Her arrows would only kill one, occasionally two, and there were hundreds of obzen chasing them.

Hamish tumbled out of the cave, gasping for breath. Mario quickly gave him a hand up while keeping his eyes on Andronikus and the oncoming swarm. "Come on . . . come on . . ." he whispered.

"Collapse the cave!" Andronikus yelled.

"What?" Mario whispered audibly.

"Collapse the fucking cave!" Andronikus pleaded, obzen about to overrun him.

"No," Mario barked, "we aren't leaving you. Deidre, keep firing arrows. Hamish and I will be ready to protect you two." Mario's voice wavered in confidence, yet he gripped his sword, ready for the fight of his life.

One of the obzen spewed a ball of black tar from its mouth, and it rocketed past Andronikus' ear, hitting Mario with such force that it knocked him off of his feet and sent him flying back. With a hard thud, Mario looked down at his breastplate and saw that the ball of black sludge was stuck to him. Suddenly, it started burning. Mario writhed and squirmed as the substance ate through his plate armour and began to burn his chest.

Mario howled in pain as tears rolled down his face. Through his tears, he saw Deidre was removing his breastplate as quickly as she could. Mario wriggled and squirmed as the acid began to eat away at his skin. Finally, Deidre was able to remove the armour and tossed it into the undergrowth of the forest. She poured her waterskin on his chest to help soothe the burning. Mario sat up, ignoring the pain in his chest, and saw Hamish swinging at the last rotten support of the cave tunnel.

"No!" Mario cried, but it was too late. The old wooden support snapped in half under Hamish's mighty swing. The tunnel immediately collapsed. Mario saw that Andronikus had been overrun by a swarm of obzen. One had sunk its ebony teeth in Andronikus' left shoulder. Another drove its alabaster hand through his body, exposing his intestines to the cold air. The last thing Mario saw was a third obzen, driving its bony pale fingers into Andronikus' eye sockets.

Then, in the blink of an eye, they were gone, hidden behind a wall of collapsed stone. Mario ran towards the mouth of the cave and stared at the mound of rock in front of him. Panic gripped his heart, and he frantically started to remove rocks from the pile. One by one, he lifted one of the humongous boulders from the pile and tossed it aside. Each stone was heavier than the last, but Mario pushed through the pain and exhaustion. Every fatigued muscle in his body screamed for him to stop, but he ignored their pleas. Finally, his already weak body forced Mario to stop, and he collapsed to his knees, his hands trembling violently. Tears streamed down his face as the sensations of grief and regret flooded his body.

There was a soft hand on Mario's shoulder. He looked up and saw Deidre's dirt-covered face staring back at him. Tears were beginning to well in her eyes. "Come on, we have to keep going."

Mario knew she was right. He took a deep breath and calmed himself down. Mario slowly rose to his feet and knew that he had to keep heading north. He had to see this through, or else everyone's death would be in vain.

"Nobody else will die because of me. Not Deidre, not Hamish, not anyone," Mario quietly promised himself. Sadly, he did not know of the future hardships awaiting him back in the northern kingdoms.

The Esteraks were once a respectable house. They originally made their fortune as merchants in the spice trade. They brushed shoulders with nobility, they were titans in their industry, and of course, they were enthusiastic philanthropists. But it all came crashing down when Marten Esterak III's twin sons, Otto and Bert, took over the family business. They sold all the family's assets to pursue bounty hunting, such a trivial and menial trade. This is why children should never inherit their parent's estate.

Craig Von Telverst,
Famous Families in Drussdell Vol. III

INTERLUDE

The forest was full of life. Birds were singing their beautiful songs, hidden amongst the leaves, while the rodents scurried underneath the underbrush. Insects buzzed, scuttled, and crawled over the forest path, carrying whatever goods they found back to their mound. This part of the forest appeared to be untouched by civilization, but the man knew that this wasn't true. A twig snapped under the weight of his boot. Something in the brush beside him darted in the opposite direction. *Shit,* he thought to himself as he froze in place. But there was no sign of anyone; his only company were the creatures of the forest.

The man breathed a sigh of relief and continued to stealthily sneak through the forest. His eyes darted from left to right, then right to left. Scanning the thick brush for any hidden archers, who would shoot him without a second thought. His cloth shirt was soaked in sweat to the point that it was nearly transparent.

He felt the fletching of an arrow suddenly kiss the tip of his nose. Instinctively, he fell backwards and laid along the forest floor, hoping to be hidden from the unseen assailant. Breathing heavily, he slowly raised his hand to the tip of his nose to check if there was any bleeding. To his surprise, there wasn't. *A warning shot.*

"What do you want, *dahrenn?*" a feminine voice called out from the foliage.

"I want to join the resistance!" the man responded, still laying on his back against the soft dirt of the forest.

"Ha!" the voice retorted. "Why would a *dahrenn* want to join the resistance?"

"I'm not a human! I'm a half-elf!"

"Ptui!" The woman spat. "Not much better, but we'll let Fáelan decide if you're worthy enough to join."

Emerging from the woods was a thin elven woman. Her hair was cut well above her ears, and her steely grey eyes stared at the man with condemnation. She slowly slung the bow over her shoulder and extended a hand up to the man.

To his surprise, the elf pulled him off the ground with ease. Without uttering a word, the elf swiftly turned on her heels and walked deeper into the forest. The man quickly followed.

"What's your name?" the man asked as he pushed a tree branch away from his face.

"Milandriel," she replied coldly. Neither spoke for a while.

The man swallowed nervously. "I'm Tiberius."

"Why do you have a rag on your head?"

"It's to hide my ears. Humans tend to judge me when they see them."

Milandriel scoffed, "Wouldn't know what that's like."

Tiberius watched Milandriel's feet studiously, carefully making sure he didn't clumsily step on a tripwire or fall into a pit full of spikes. Milandriel didn't utter any warnings as she led him deeper into the forest. She was walking with such speed that Tiberius thought that she was intentionally trying to lose him so he would be lost and helpless in the forest. Sweat began to sting his eyes as he struggled to keep up with the nimble elven woman. His throat began to ache for a sip of water as the dry forest air scratched it.

After what seemed like a day, but was probably only a couple hours of hard bushwhacking, Tiberius found himself in the middle of a secluded elven village. It was nothing like he imagined. Heads were on spikes, corpses were tossed onto a pyre, and multiple huts had been burned down. In one corner of the camp, Tiberius saw a mound of valuables, most likely stolen from innocent human travellers. Milandriel escorted Tiberius through the camp, and he could feel the eyes of everyone staring at him. *Appearances are everything.* He reminded himself as he walked with his head held high through the camp. They stopped at a large, wooden lodge in the middle of the camp. He could see the wood was still stained with blood.

"Wait here," Milandriel instructed as she walked into the lodge.

In front of the lodge, there was the rotten head of an elven woman stuck on a stake. Underneath the stake was a mound of dead, decaying ravens. The smell and sight were enough to make Tiberius gag. He looked around the camp nervously. He felt as if the entire camp was eagerly awaiting the chance to assault him. He saw elves smile menacingly as they sharpened their daggers on stones. A few threw their knives into an old tree trunk as they kept eye contact with him. Tiberius felt a bead of sweat run down his back.

"A *dahrenn* in my camp?" a stern, masculine voice said from behind him.

Tiberius turned his head and saw a battle-hardened elf standing in front of him. The elf had scars covering his entire face, most notably one above his left eye, which had turned the iris into a sickly white colour. Tiberius looked at the elf's hands and saw that the fingernails were jagged and covered in dried blood. Tiberius gulped nervously and looked the elf in the eyes. "I'm not a human."

"Prove it."

Tiberius kneeled down and quickly removed the red bandana around his head so the entire elven village could see his slightly curved ears. Everyone waited for the elven leader to speak. He said nothing, but his angry expression stayed on his face.

"A half breed," the leader growled. "Stand up."

Tiberius quickly shot to his feet and stood up straight, just like the headmaster at the college instructed him to do when he was addressing authority.

The elven leader bared his yellow teeth in a crooked smile. "My name is Fáelan, but the *dahrenn* know me as *Fén'Corriéadh Diobdhael,* or in the common tongue, The Silent Death." The elf's crooked smile grew wider. "Tell me, why are you here?"

"I want to join the resistance!" Tiberius exclaimed with all the exuberance he could muster.

Fáelan erupted in laughter, with the rest of the village following. The grizzled elf wiped a tear from his wounded eye. "I'm one of the only survivors from the first Elven Uprising, and I only lead those who're willing to take *dahrenn* lives. What makes you think you have what it takes, half breed?"

"The Church of the Golden Sun blames us for everything. If there is a famine, it's because the elves ate too much. If there is a plague, it's because the elves spread disease. They probably blame us for the fucking weather! I was a member of the Knight's College, but my teachers refused to deal with the church. I wanted to be a knight to protect people, and if the knights refuse to do anything, I'll find someone who will." Tiberius' voice echoed in the empty forest.

The entire village stared at Fáelan for a reaction. But his expression remained unchanged. Tiberius waited anxiously to see if his words had an impact on the elven leader. Slowly, a smile appeared on the elf's face.

"You're alright for a half breed," the elf growled. "We have two rules here. Rule number one: Everyone earns their keep. Rule number two: We don't take prisoners. Questions?"

"Yes," Tiberius answered meekly, looking at the severed head on the spike. "What did she do?"

Fáelan gave a low, throaty chuckle. "She used to be the keeper of this forest. She wanted to negotiate with humans and settle our grievances with diplomacy. She was weak and naïve, and without her, our blood is stronger. I only want warriors, not diplomats. So, tell me half breed, are you a warrior or a diplomat?"

"A warrior, sir."

"Then, let's hunt us some humans."

***

The inn was unusually quiet this particular morning. Light leaked into the musty dark room through a frost-covered window. The candles around the room had burned out during the night, leaving behind only a puddle of hardened wax. The sounds of people talking leaked into the room, as well as the scent of breakfast that was being prepared on the floor below.

The aroma of cooked venison awoke Lukas from his rest. He threw off the many blankets and walked around the room, stretching his tired muscles. He stretched his hips as he watched the locals go about their day through the frosted window. *I can't help but feel sorry for these savages,* he thought to himself, *stuck in a frozen wasteland such as this. No wonder the Northerners don't have any culture; they're just trying to survive. They're no different than the wolves that howl at their doors.*

"Are ye coming back to bed, love?" a feminine voice cooed from behind him.

Lukas turned around and saw the pale naked body of the large, homely woman lying in his bed. *She was certainly prettier last night. Damn northern wine.* Lukas bared his teeth into an awkward smile. "No, thanks, my dear. You'll find your payment on the nightstand. I prefer to perform my ablutions in solitude."

A perplexed expression stuck on the ugly woman's face. Her mouth was agape, exposing her rotten and missing teeth, as she stared blankly at Lukas. "What?" she finally croaked out.

Lukas rolled his eyes. *Simpletons.* He pointed to the coin purse on the night-stand. "That money is for you. I'm done screwing you." Lukas' voice was harsh. He had no patience for idiocy.

"Ye talk funny, not from round 'ere, are ye?" the woman asked as she struggled to put her dress back on.

"No, I'm not." Lukas sighed as he splashed some water from the basin onto his face. He felt a pang of regret surge through his body at the thought of sleeping with someone so profoundly stupid and so horrific looking. "I'm from the empire."

"Oooo, I've never been to the empire," the woman stated as she put on her slippers.

"No, kidding?" Lukas replied sarcastically.

"No, I have no kids," the woman replied; the confused look had returned to her face once more.

Lukas ground his teeth. *By the gods, is she so unintelligent that even the basic concept of sarcasm escapes her? The sooner I'm out of the North, the better.* "You just looked so worldly, I thought for sure you would've been there in your travels." Lukas could barely keep a straight face. The thought of this monstrosity travelling the world almost made him burst out in laughter. *As a travelling sideshow maybe.*

The woman giggled at Lukas' comment, unable to figure out he was lying. "No, I've been stuck 'ere me 'ole life. I 'ate it 'ere in Toldsteim; fuckin' shit 'ole."

Something we can agree upon. "It can't be that bad," Lukas lied as he put on his trousers.

"It is!" the woman screamed as if he didn't already believe her. "It's awful 'ere! Everyone's related, and it's always bloody cold."

"Well, what can you do?" Lukas said absentmindedly.

"What if ye took me back to the empire?"

"What?"

"Just ye and me, livin' in the empire."

Lukas erupted in laughter; he couldn't contain himself anymore. Tears were rolling down his face as he struggled to regain his breath. "I'm sorry." Lukas chuckled, wiping a tear from his eye. "I have no use for a whore."

The woman gave a huff, grabbed her coin purse, and slammed the door as she left the room. Lukas was on the floor, laughing. He hadn't laughed this hard in a long time. He could hear the floorboards creak under the woman's enormous weight as she stormed down the stairs.

It took several minutes for him to regain his composure. He looked at his reflection in the mirror and tidied his hair. He noticed that a small beard of stubble was starting to emerge. He quickly grabbed his razor and began shaving the unwanted hair. *Beards are for the barbarians; dignified gentlemen are clean-shaven.*

Suddenly, a loud crash came from downstairs. Lukas heard a woman scream before he heard the audible sound of someone being punched in the face. He looked out the window and saw that the street was full of saddled horses. *It seems my guests have arrived.*

"You the one sending the letters?" the bandit croaked as Lukas casually strolled down the stairs.

"I am," Lukas answered calmly. "Are you the one they call Henry?"

"Aye," the bandit replied gruffly.

"A pleasure to make your acquaintance."

"The fuck he sayin'?" another bandit called out from the crowd.

"He's saying it's nice to meet you, you imbecile," another bandit called out as he stepped forward out of the crowd. He was wearing a brown leather jacket. He had a small cap that was decorated with the feather of a woodpecker. Lukas could see the large war hammer hanging from the man's back.

"A substitute?" Lukas replied as he sat on top of the bar.

"You're a quick one, I see." Henry smiled as he pushed the first bandit out of his chair. "Had to make sure this wasn't a ruse of some kind."

Lukas smiled. *This is the first Northman who has shown any type of intelligence. No wonder he's in charge of this outfit of idiots.* "My name is Lukas Aurelius. I'm an ambassador for His Imperial Majesty, Emperor Vesuvius Vladimir Valerius. And I—"

"Hear that, lads?" Henry interrupted. "We're in service of an emperor. My how we've risen!"

The gang of bandits exploded with laughter. With a swift closing of Henry's fist, the bandits abruptly ceased their laughter. Henry slowly approached Lukas at the bar. "So why now? Why reveal yourself after all this time? You've been sending us anonymous coin and letters for months, yet now you choose to reveal yourself, why?"

Lukas stared at Henry and couldn't help but make comparisons between him and the emperor. They were of similar height and build. Both had cold, unforgiving eyes, and both had the same commanding aura that took over a room. Most people would be intimidated in front of such a man, but Lukas had spent many hours alone with the emperor and learned how to behave around such men. *The only difference between the two is the smell. These Northmen smell rancid. Have they never heard of a bath?*

"I figured you were getting curious as to where all the coin was coming from," Lukas responded calmly, trying to ignore the smell that emanated from the bandits.

Henry stopped in his tracks; he eyed Lukas suspiciously. Clearly, this was the first time that he had been in the presence of a man who showed no fear or discomfort in the presence of his gang. Suddenly, a smile crept along his face. "So, what does the emperor want us to do now?"

Lukas hopped off the bar and reached into his pocket. He tossed a large pouch of coins onto the table in front of him and the bandit leader. "Twenty-five hundred crowns now, another twenty-five hundred after the job."

The bandits started whispering to one another excitedly. The idea of receiving such a large payment filled all of their bodies with child-like giddiness. The only one that stayed cool and collected was Henry. Quickly, the bandit leader held up his hand, and the whispers from his men stopped immediately.

"What's the job?"

"You're to head north into Keten, dressed as Drussdellian soldiers. There, you will carry out a raid on a town called Blokhaven. It's a two-day ride from your camp."

"How do we get the other half of our payment?" one of the bandits interrupted.

Lukas sighed in anger but took a deep breath to calm himself down. "I'll be at the inn called The Drunken Harpy. It's in the town of Garstag, a three-day ride south from here. Any other questions?"

Henry sneered maliciously, "What about the townsfolk?"

"Do with them as you please. It is of no concern to me."

The bandits chuckled maniacally amongst one another. Henry quickly stepped forward and shook Lukas' hand. "You got yourself a deal, Southerner."

Lukas smiled politely. *Amazing what a little bit of gold can make a man do.*

***

Your Imperial Majesty,

Please consider this letter as a preliminary debriefing for my mission. Phase two of our plan is complete. The bandits, who have pompously dubbed themselves "The Hounds," have been carrying out our orders beautifully, as long as the coin keeps coming in. They continue to raid the towns that we have designated and have stirred civil unrest in Drussdell to a fever pitch. Many of the civilians no longer feel safe. Their king refuses to protect them, and I'm beginning to hear whispers of revolution amongst the crowds. This could play into our hands, but I will keep you informed if these whispers become anything more than the drunken gossiping of commoners.

After our alliance with Artanzia, Keten did not attack Drussdell as we expected. However, I have remedied the situation by employing the service of The Hounds. The bandits will now march into Keten, dressed as Drusdellian soldiers, and raid a small border town called Blokhaven. The settlement holds no strategic significance for the Kingdom of Keten; however, they will undoubtedly retaliate against Drussdell for carrying out such an attack. Keten and Drussdell will be at each other's throats, and after both forces are battle-weary, our superior army will march in and conquer both kingdoms with minimum casualties.

I would be remiss in my duties if I failed to inform you about a potential threat to our plan. A group of zealots called "The Church of the Golden Sun" have been going around, spreading their poisonous dogma to the populace. Their ideology is rooted in a foundation of hatred and racism. Their beliefs blame non-humans for the struggles that humanity face. If we do not deal with this problem, I fear it could start another non-human uprising, which may unite the northern kingdoms once more. I beg you, please send additional resources and personnel so we can take preventative measures against this potential problem.

I'll be staying at the inn in Garstag under the alias Ossypius Magnus. My cover is that I am an entrepreneur trying to start anew in the North. Please address your response to: "Ossypius Magnus at The Drunken Harpy."

I look forward to your response.

Hail V,
Lukas Aurelius

Dear Ossypius,

I thank you for your last letter, it was informative and brief. I'm glad everything is going according to plan. I have carefully thought about what you have asked of me, and I have decided not to grant your request. The worry you expressed in your letter is unfounded and circumstantial. Please pay no mind to the church and focus on the task at hand.

Sincerely,
Your Friend

Chapter Twelve

The freezing wind howled as they struggled to walk through the thick snow. Mario had heard tales about the harsh conditions in the northern part of the kingdom, but the stories didn't do it justice. The cold, dry air aggravated every injury. His broken nose burned every time he took a breath, his scarred face turning white from frostbite, but the worst was his mutilated chest. He could still feel the burn of the obzen's acid on his chest as he trudged through the blizzard. After abandoning his breastplate back at the cave, the only thing he had to protect himself from the winter wind was a cloak made of thin cloth.

Mario grimaced at the thought of his scarred chest. He hadn't had the courage to look at it when Deidre peeled off his breastplate. He didn't have the courage now. *Hopefully, it doesn't look half as bad as my face. What more can this quest take from me? It has taken my looks, it has taken my friends, and it has taken the lives of so many innocent people. I don't know how much more I can bear to lose. . . .*

Mario's body shivered as an icy gust of wind blew across his body. He had never been this far north. He didn't even think weather like this was possible until the northern part of Keten. He lifted his head and squinted so that the onslaught of snow did not attack his eyes. He could barely make out Hamish in front of him, and he had utterly lost sight of Deidre. He looked around, but all he saw was an unforgiving sheet of white. He didn't see that Hamish had stopped and walked right into him.

"Why're we stopping?" Mario called out, barely able to hear his own voice through the blizzard.

"There's torchlight up ahead," Hamish responded. "Do you see it?"

Mario squinted and stared into the blizzard, but he couldn't see anything. In fact, the only thing he could see was the snow blowing into his face. "Where's Deidre?"

"She went up ahead to investigate," Hamish replied. "If she doesn't return in five minutes, we're to go towards the torchlight and meet her there."

Mario didn't like the idea of Deidre venturing out alone in this blizzard; it would be so easy for her to be knocked off course and lose her way trying to find them. But there was no other choice, Mario had to rely upon Deidre's instincts to keep her safe. Mario decided that now was an opportune time to air his concerns with Hamish, just the two of them.

"Why'd you do it?" Mario hollered over the howling wind.

"Do what?" Hamish retorted.

"Collapse the cave."

"Are you kidding me?"

"No, we could've saved him, Hamish. We could've—"

"No, Mario, listen to me!" Hamish's voice was as harsh and cold as the winter wind. "We would've died trying to fight that hoard. You know it, I know it, and Andronikus knew it. That's why he told us to collapse the cave. I had no choice."

The weight of Hamish's words hung in the air. Mario knew that the changeling was right and waited for Deidre's return in silence. After a few minutes of waiting in the cold, Deidre's figure emerged from the blizzard.

"It's an inn!" she called out.

Mario's heart leapt up into his throat. *A warm meal, a soft bed, and some ale is exactly what I need right now!*

"Good, I could use a fucking drink," Hamish replied sourly.

"Lead the way!" Mario called out enthusiastically.

Mario and Hamish each grabbed one of Deidre's hands as she escorted them towards the torchlight. Mario put his head down and watched his feet crunch the snow beneath him. He anxiously stuck out his tongue to play with the pieces of ice that were frozen to his moustache. After a short walk, Mario began to hear the muffled sounds of music and voices. He lifted his head and saw the faint glow of torchlight. He couldn't wait to get out of this storm.

Deidre approached the old wooden door of the inn and hammered hard on it with her fist. Mario looked up at the sign above the entrance, but it was covered with snow. The door swung open and a hairy, burly man towered in the doorway.

"My goodness! More travellers? Come in! Come in!" the man called out in a more effeminate voice than one would expect.

Once Mario crossed the threshold of the tavern, his senses were immediately assaulted with the pleasant smell of roasted chicken, fresh ale, and warmth from the fire. The inn was full of people from every walk of life. Halflings, elves, humans, and dwarves. Mario smiled. After everything he experienced so far, it was nice to see that coexistence was still possible between all the different races.

The burly man escorted them to the bar where an elderly woman stood behind the counter. "Brought more guests for you, ma," the man squealed as he approached the ancient woman.

"Oh dearie," the woman croaked. "You must be absolutely frozen!" she cried out, looking at Mario. "Help yourself to a room for a bit and warm up."

Mario smiled politely and quietly shuffled to an open room on the far side of the inn. He noticed out of the corner of his eye a small pile of dirty clothes in a back room of the inn. Mario cautiously looked to see if anyone was watching him, but everybody was too busy drinking and playing games to notice the frozen knight in the corner of the tavern. Stealthily, Mario walked into the back room and hid the pile of clothes underneath his cloak and hastily made his way back towards the open room.

The room seemed cramped compared to the massive quarters he had slept in at Kartaga. There was a bed in the corner, a small wooden nightstand, and a dirty mirror hanging on the wall. Mario sat on the bed and let out a long exhale. His body tingled painfully as it slowly began to unthaw. He slowly flexed his fingers and wiggled his toes. The frozen joints popped with each movement.

Hesitantly, Mario stared at his reflection in the mirror. *I guess it's now or never.* With a deep breath, he threw the cloak from his shoulders and exposed his bare chest. For the first time since the cave, Mario stared at his injury. The entire outer layer of skin was removed. What remained was a pink, blotchy mess full of scabs, craters, and scars. It looked more like the surface of the moon than his chest. Mario felt bile rush up into his mouth at the sight. *Gods . . . I'm hideous.*

Slowly and painfully, Mario removed the rest of his armour with tear-filled eyes. He stared at the pieces of armour with hatred and resentment. Every piece reminded him of the pain he had endured since leaving the college. "You've caused me nothing but misery," he said aloud as he kicked the armour underneath the small straw bed. He then picked up the pile of clothes and began to put them on. The cloth shirt and pants seemed to be a perfect fit. While the worn, leather boots were a touch too big for his feet. Mario then swung the thick leather jacket across his back. Besides being a bit short in the arms, it fit beautifully.

Mario examined how his new wardrobe looked on him through the dirty mirror. He pursed his lips angrily. "What would Dad think?" he asked aloud. "I look like a common cutthroat, like a bandit or a thief. No, not *like* a thief, I *am* a thief." Mario instantly felt lightheaded, and the room began to spin. His body was exhausted from the past few days of hard walking. He needed rest.

Mario placed his sword on the nightstand and collapsed into bed. "Just a few minutes of shut-eye," Mario whispered to himself as he felt his body slowly drift into sleep. "Just . . . a few . . . minutes."

***

Loud banging and drunken shouting shook Mario out of his slumber. With a groan, Mario sat up on the bed and slapped his cheeks to help wake him up.

"Gods," Mario grumbled, "I need more fucking sleep." As Mario rose from the bed, the bones in his knees cracked angrily, while the muscles in his back refused to relax. Mario winced at the unexpected tightness. *Perhaps it is from being on the road too long, or is it because of all the stress?*

The banging at the door intensified and interrupted his thoughts once more. Mario grabbed his sword from the nightstand and angrily tightened it around his waist. He swung the door open and glared at the ones responsible for disturbing his much-needed rest.

Standing in front of the door were two very hairy and very drunk dwarves. The one on the left was probably only half an inch taller than the one on the right. He had a thick red beard and deep amber eyes. His hair was covered with an orange handkerchief soaked with either sweat or ale. The dwarf on the right had a long black and grey beard, which went down to about his waist. His eyes were a steely grey, and he had a bright blue handkerchief covering his head. The stench of the two dwarves was almost enough to put Mario back to sleep. They had the unmistakable aroma of ale, piss, and shit.

"What do you want?" Mario growled as he glared at the dwarves, trying to breathe through his mouth, so he didn't have to smell them.

"The name's . . . *hiccup* . . . the name's . . . *hiccup* . . . Gilbert Abernathy!" the taller dwarf slurred. "This here is my apprentice, Callum . . . *hiccup* . . . Say, what's your last name again, Callum?"

"What do you want?" Mario interrupted angrily. He could feel the blood rush to his face as his frustration increased.

"We heard yous a knight," Callum drunkenly answered, struggling to keep his balance while he did so.

Mario let out a deep sigh and pinched his brow. "Who did you hear that from?"

Both dwarves turned in unison and pointed at the table across the inn where a drunken Hamish was playing cards with a group of people. Hamish saw the two dwarves looking toward him and returned the gesture with a drunken smile and wave. Mario cursed under his breath.

"So . . . *hiccup* . . . is it true?" Gilbert slurred, turning his attention back towards Mario.

Mario took a sharp inhale, preparing to answer the drunkards' question when Deidre emerged from the crowd of people and shoved the two drunken dwarves aside. "Move!" she barked as she grabbed Mario by the hand and led him to a table in the corner of the inn.

"Have a nice nap?" Deidre asked sarcastically.

Mario could feel the anger radiating off of her body. "I was," Mario retorted, just as sarcastically. "How long was I out?"

"About an hour, an hour that we have now wasted."

"We won't be able to find the bandit camp in this blizzard. We'll have to just wait it out."

"I'd still be able to find it," Deidre mumbled under her breath.

"Would you still be able to find it while taking care of that?" Mario asked while pointing to a clearly intoxicated Hamish, who was vomiting on the card table.

Deidre shuddered. "We leave once he sobers up."

Suddenly, two men sat down at their table. Both Mario and Deidre were surprised as they didn't hear the men approach. The two men were identical to one another. Both were bald, tall, and muscular. Their eyes were as green as emeralds, and they both had thick, curly moustaches. They were dressed in the finest clothes Mario had ever seen—golden necklaces, thick fur coats, and leather gloves that were fit for a noble. The only difference between the two men was their weapons. One had a greatsword slung across his back, while the other had a mace tied to his waist.

"Greetings, friends!" One of them smiled, showing his rotten yellow teeth.

"We aren't your friends," Deidre hissed.

"Every friend is a stranger at first," the other one retorted.

"Are you mercenaries?" Mario asked, eyeing up the two men.

"We would never stoop to such a dishonourable profession!" the first man scoffed while gesturing for two more ales.

"Then, what are you?" Deidre growled, clearly annoyed by the vague answers.

"We're bounty hunters!"

"Dressed pretty fancy for bounty hunters."

"Well, our family were originally merchants, but once my brother and I inherited the business, we sold everything to pursue our love of bringing evil to justice."

"We're the same as you, Knight," the other stranger interjected, his green eyes staring deep into Mario's.

"How do you know I'm a knight?" Mario asked suspiciously.

"Well, from your drunk friend over there," the first man answered, grinning from ear to ear. "But you aren't dressed as a knight."

Mario looked down at his clothes, and the man was right. He didn't look anything like a knight. He looked like just another commoner in these clothes. Mario grew sick at the thought of being treated like a peasant instead of the son of a hero. Mario coughed nervously and held out his hand. "Mario Deschamps."

"Otto Esterak, this here is my twin brother, Bert." The first man grabbed Mario's hand in a firm shake. "And what's your name, lovely?"

Deidre shot the man a deadly glare and walked away from the table.

"Your squire needs some manners," Bert remarked while staring at Deidre's ass as she walked away.

"Oh, she's not my squire, just a friend."

"Right." Otto winked.

Mario squeezed his knuckles as his anger started to boil over. "Is there a reason you came over and disturbed us?"

"Just wanted to talk to a brother of the trade," Otto answered calmly. "Perhaps buy you a drink."

"No."

"If you're a knight, how come you don't talk silly?" Bert remarked as he scowled at Mario from across the beer-soaked table.

"What do you mean?"

"Well, knights are supposed to be all polite like. Talking with a bunch of 'thees,' 'thys,' and 'thous.'"

"Well, I don't," Mario snapped as he got to stand up from the table.

"Innkeeper!" Otto shouted. "Make a fresh meal for the knight and each of his companions on us." He tossed a hefty pouch of gold across the counter towards the old lady.

The ancient innkeeper replied with a toothless smile. Mario stopped and stared at the two brothers, inquisitively.

"Consider it payment for indulging in conversation with us," Otto answered as if sensing his thoughts.

Mario wanted to say "fuck off" or "I'm not for sale" or some other witty remark, but his stomach growled at the thought of a hot meal. Begrudgingly, he sat back down at the table.

"Excellent." Otto began, "Tell me, have you ever met a bounty hunter before?"

"Don't believe I have."

"Well, allow me to explain what we do then," Otto replied pompously. "Kings, dukes, counts, and other nobles will often put up a bounty for the capture or death of some lowlife."

"Lowlifes endanger the innocent. It's our job to protect them," Bert interjected.

"See, that's how we're the same, Mario. The only difference is you get paid from the king's treasury, while we have to fight and haggle over contract prices."

Mario gulped. He could sense that this conversation was taking a foul turn. He stealthily moved his hand to the hilt of his sword in case things turned violent.

Surprisingly, Otto smiled and threw his arms in the air. "Alas, we all can't be born from esteemed families such as you."

"Deschamps, like Pablo Deschamps?" Bert asked, even though it seemed like he already knew the answer.

Mario's muscles relaxed, and he removed his hand from his sword. Out of the corner of his eye, Mario saw Deidre glaring at him from across the inn. *Why is she so untrusting? These two seem alright, and who knows, maybe they'll have information about the bandits.* "Yes," Mario answered. "Pablo was my father."

"Hear that, Bert!?" Otto exclaimed. "We are dining with the son of a hero!"

Bert bared his rotten teeth in a crooked, disgusting smile. Shivers ran down Mario's spine. But his disgust was quickly dissipated by the lovely aroma floating out the kitchen. His mouth began to water, and his stomach growled, hungry for the delicious-smelling meal.

"A surprise that the son of the Slayer of Elves would choose one as his companion," Otto remarked while turning his head to stare at Deidre from across the inn.

"We have a common goal," Mario quickly interjected.

"Oh yeah? What's that?" Bert asked, leaning forward on the table.

"We're hunting some bandits."

"Ah, yes. Hunting bandits, now those were the good ole days." Otto recollected while leaning back in his chair.

Mario shook his head in confusion. "I thought you were bounty hunters? Surely you must fight bandits."

"We used to, back in the day . . ." Bert began.

"But after a few years, we realized that they weren't the most cost-effective source of income," Otto interrupted, finishing his brother's sentence.

"So, what is?"

Otto placed his forearm on the table and leaned forward on it. The old wooden table squeaked under his shifting weight. "Monsters," he whispered.

Mario's heart stopped. The memory of seeing Andronikus being torn apart by the obzen surged back into his head. His stomach no longer growled out of hunger but instead started churning, preparing to spew bile. Mario took a deep breath to regain his composure. "Just the ones that endanger the citizens, right?"

Bert chuckled menacingly. "Nah, that's the beauty of it. Nobles will pay out the ass for parts of a monster. Most think it is a type of aphrodisiac, or something that'll grant them eternal life."

Mario felt sick. For the second time that day, the contents of his stomach rushed up into his mouth, burning his esophagus as it did so. Mario managed to swallow his vomit while turning his head slowly to look at Hamish, who was passed out behind the card table in a drunken stupor. Mario failed to notice that the twins were watching his eyes.

"You know," Otto started, "my brother and I have been doing this for years, and we've gotten pretty good at it. We're not Order of the Swords good, but we're pretty damn good."

"Yeah. We can tell who's a monster just by looking at 'em," Bert interjected.

Mario hurriedly stood up from the table, almost knocking it over into the two bounty hunters' laps. "I'm afraid we must be going," Mario said nervously as he walked quickly towards Deidre.

"Like you said," Otto called out, "we're stuck in a blizzard." A devilish smile spread across his face.

Mario's skin went pale, and he grabbed Deidre by the elbow and dragged her across the inn towards Hamish. "Those two know Hamish isn't human," he whispered.

"What? How?"

"I don't know, but let's get out of here as quickly as we can."

"There's a blizzard outside, plus Hamish is in no condition to move."

Mario ground his teeth together nervously. He had begun to sweat; he felt the emerald eyes of the Esterak brothers watching him like hawks. "Ask the inn-keeper if there is any way through the blizzard. I'll try to wake up, Hamish."

Deidre nodded and walked off towards the bar. Mario tried to move through the crowded inn to get to his unconscious friend. His broad shoulders easily pushed people out of his way, his eyes never leaving Hamish's body.

Mario bent down and grabbed Hamish by the collar of his shirt and shook him violently. "Hamish! Hamish, wake up!" But he was unresponsive, his limp body shook lifelessly. *Fuck.* Mario looked around the room and saw a glass of water on the card table. He quickly swiped it off the table and splashed it directly in Hamish's face. As soon as it hit the changeling's face, Mario knew it wasn't water. It had the unmistakable fragrance of . . . *vodka.*

Mario looked around the room in a panic, trying to find something that would awake Hamish, then he saw it. A silver coin. Mario quickly grabbed the coin off the ground and pressed it against Hamish's bare hand. Almost instantly, his skin started smoking, and his body jolted back into consciousness.

"Mario?" Hamish slurred, confused.

"Hamish, I need you to focus."

"It is you. We should get a drink!"

"Hamish! Do you know those two men over there?"

Hamish's drunken eyes scanned across the room and eventually focused on the two bounty hunters. "Yeah, I know them. I whooped their asses at cards. I took all their money. They even threw in a silver ring."

"Did you touch the ring, Hamish!?" Mario was struggling to keep his voice at a low volume so nobody would hear, but panic was starting to take control over his body.

"How else was I to know it was silver. Looked exactly like nickel to me." Hamish hiccupped.

Fuck sakes, Hamish. Mario turned his head and saw Deidre approaching from the bar. Mario prayed that she had good news for them, but the look on her face quickly dashed his hopes.

"We have two options," Deidre whispered, making sure nobody heard her voice.

"Which are?"

"Stay here for the night with the two bounty hunters, or test our luck in the blizzard."

Mario scratched his chin nervously as he looked across the room and saw the bounty hunters watching him, smiling from ear to ear. Mario's head snapped towards Deidre. "You sure you can navigate in this blizzard?"

Deidre smiled. "Only one way to find out."

Mario quickly slung Hamish's arm over his shoulder and nodded towards the door. "Let's go."

The cold winter wind blew the door wide open as snow began to blow into the inn. Patrons yelled and grumbled as the icy air stabbed their skins. Mario quickly closed the door behind him and stared at the frozen wasteland in front of him. The wind was howling. Over the course of an hour, there were another three inches of snow on the ground.

"Where do we go?" Mario called out to Deidre.

"North."

Mario grimaced at the thought of going further into the blizzard, but he had no choice. The idea of getting into a fight with the Esteraks filled his body with dread. Begrudgingly, he trudged through the thick snow, while supporting a limp and lifeless Hamish on his shoulder. "Gods, he's fucking heavy."

"You calling me fat, boy?" Hamish slurred.

Mario turned his head and met the changeling's cross-eyed, drunken stare. "Yes." Mario smiled.

Hamish grinned as he squeezed Mario's shoulder. "Listen to me," he started, "I just want to say thanks for bringing me with you."

"Why? Ever since we left Eulway, this whole thing has been a total shitstorm."

Hamish chuckled. "True. It seems like every day we have to fight for our lives. But I wouldn't have it any other way."

"What do you mean?"

"I've lived among humans for almost my entire life, but I never really felt like I belonged anywhere. But with you, Deidre, and even Andronikus, I felt like I was finally home. I was able to be my true self with you guys, and . . . " Hamish paused to clear his throat, tears running down his cheeks, "I'm proud to call you my family."

Mario was touched; he was at a complete loss for words. What Hamish said meant everything to him. The constant feelings of regret and guilt had faded away at that moment. Someone was actually glad to be there beside him; someone who considered him a part of their family.

"Hamish . . ." Mario began, but before he could finish his thought, Hamish leaned over and puked all over Mario's "new" boots. "Come on, let's get you out of the cold." Mario sighed, but Hamish did not respond. He had passed out once again.

The blizzard had gotten worse since they stopped at the inn. The wind howled as if it were dying. There was nothing to protect Mario's face from the monstrous wind. He had to use his arms to hold Hamish upright, and the collar of his jacket stopped just below his jawline. The cold air bit viciously at Mario's cheeks. His eyes began to water as they were assaulted by the snowflakes flying directly into his face. After about twenty minutes of hard walking, Mario collapsed into the snow.

Mario heard the sound of snow crunching in front of him and lifted his head up to see Deidre glaring down at him. "What're you doing? Get up!"

"Too tired." Mario panted. "He's too damn heavy."

Deidre sighed and threw Hamish over her shoulder with ease. She extended a hand to help Mario up. "Come on, I saw a small grove of trees up ahead. We can make camp there for the night."

Mario reluctantly grabbed Deidre's hand. She instantly pulled him up to his feet. Mario stumbled, surprised by the strength of the elf. "Lead the way."

In about fifteen minutes, Deidre had led them to a secluded small grove of trees that was shielded from the harsh winds of the blizzard. Mario was astounded by how well Deidre could see during such a storm. *Must be that elven vision.* Once inside the grove, Deidre threw Hamish's lifeless body on the ground with a hard thud. Hamish let out an audible groan but was otherwise unresponsive.

"I'll start a fire," Deidre said as she gathered loose sticks and twigs from the ground.

Mario's body shivered, and his teeth started chattering uncontrollably. He couldn't wait for Deidre to build the fire so he could curl up next to it and fall asleep beside its warmth.

"Do you think we did the right thing?" Mario asked, breaking the uncomfortable silence.

"In terms of?"

"Andronikus."

Deidre let out a soft sigh as she stacked the wood in a small pyramid. "I don't know. . . . Those things, there were so many. I think Andronikus knew it was him or all of us. That's why he told us to collapse the cave mouth."

Mario swallowed bitterly. Even though Andronikus was a cold, unfeeling bastard, Mario still missed him. The past few days of travelling north had been riddled with an uneasy quiet. It felt like a piece of Mario died in that cave.

"Remember back in Riverwell?" Deidre asked, interrupting Mario's thoughts.

"What about it?"

"Andronikus knew that you can't jeopardize the group for the well-being of one. That's why he told us to leave Mile's corpse behind, and that's why he told us to leave him behind."

A tear began to fall down Mario's cheek as the image of Mile's corpse entered his mind. He quickly wiped his eyes, fearing that the tear would freeze to his skin. The roar of the fire brought Mario back into reality.

Deidre gasped. "Finally." She lay down in front of the fire.

Mario sat down opposite her and stared at her through the soft glow of the fire. "I'm sorry," he said.

"For what?"

"For everything. For bringing everyone on this stupid quest. For what happened to you with Pascal. For—"

"Hey!" Deidre snapped as she sat upright. "I *chose* to come with you because those bastards were enslaving my people. What happened to me isn't your fault. That bastard got what he deserved . . . and so will the rest."

An uncomfortable silence hung in the air while the wind howled in the distance. Deidre stared at Mario with intense eye contact. Mario's stomach began to feel queasy, and he turned his head to avoid her gaze. *I don't know what to say to her. I don't know anyone who's been through what she has.*

"Get some sleep," Deidre ordered as she cozied up to the fire.

Mario grabbed the shoulders of his leather coat and pulled it tighter around him. He slowly leaned his head down against the frozen ground and closed his eyes, the sounds of the fire and distant wind slowly lulling him into a deep sleep.

***

Distorted screaming and the sounds of flesh being cut awoke Mario suddenly from his sleep. He opened his eyes and saw Hamish, in his monstrous natural form, being attacked by two men—one with a greatsword and one with a mace. Mario shot to his feet, unsheathed his sword, and charged into the fray to try and save Hamish. His eyes were locked on Otto Esterak, whose greatsword had just pierced through Hamish's chest. Out of the corner of Mario's eye, he saw Bert emerge from the darkness and swing violently at his head. Mario quickly swung his sword to try and parry the attack, but the bounty hunter's mace crashed through his measly defence and cracked against his right shoulder.

Mario felt his entire body twist from the force of the blow. His right arm exploded with pain, but he was too angry to notice. Mario recklessly charged at Bert, hoping to catch him off guard with his rage-fuelled attack. But the bounty hunter nimbly sidestepped, grabbed Mario by the collar of his coat, and threw him back towards the fire. Mario lifted his head and saw that Deidre was missing. *Shit.*

"Well, Knight, we meet again," Otto Esterak boisterously exclaimed as he ripped his sword free from Hamish's limp chest. His brother chuckled as Hamish's body fell lifelessly to the ground. "It seems you're all out of friends," Otto Esterak continued. "We have no quarrel with you, but if you choose to fight us, I promise your body will rot beside this creature's."

Mario didn't have anything to say to them. His body was fully consumed by rage. He charged at Otto, sword in hand. Otto quickly pirouetted out of Mario's way and stabbed him as he ran by. Mario felt the cold steel of the sword puncture right below his ribcage. He collapsed into the snow in pain. He slammed his fist into the frozen ground as he slowly stood up. Blood was gushing from the wound. Mario grimaced and grabbed his sword with two hands.

A gust of wind blew through the grove of trees and kicked up a cloud of snow. Mario shielded his eyes reactively, taking his attention away from the bounty hunters. Once he uncovered his eyes, he saw an angry Bert charging towards him, his mace held high above his head. At the last possible second, Mario quickly sidestepped out of the way. But Bert used his momentum to spin himself around and swung his mace up towards Mario's head. Mario tried to block the second blow with his sword, but Bert's strength was too great. The force behind the bounty hunter's swing forced Mario's sword back up into his face, cutting him just above his left brow. Mario stumbled back blindly, clutching his sword with one hand and his wounded eye in the other.

"Gods, I thought you were a knight!" Otto laughed as he slowly approached with his greatsword. "If I had known it would be this easy, I would've woken you up before we slaughtered your friend."

Mario grimaced as he stabbed his sword into the ground. He was losing too much blood to continue fighting these two. Bert was too strong, and Otto was too fast. Together they were too much for one man to take. *Where the hell is Deidre?*

The distant wind of the blizzard howled as Mario heard the heavy footsteps of Otto Esterak crushing the snow as he approached Mario's wounded, battered body. It was eerily silent. Blood was beginning to flow from his eye down towards his lips. The metallic taste filled Mario's mouth.

"I thought knights were the best of the best," Bert mumbled as he stretched his back leisurely.

"Apparently not," Otto replied sarcastically. "If this is how difficult it is to fight a knight, imagine how easy it is to kill elves—"

Mario heard the crack of Deidre's bowstring. The next sound he heard was her arrow tearing through flesh. Then he heard Bert's body collapse to the ground as he choked on his own blood. Mario knew this was his chance and leapt to his feet and charged at the last bounty hunter.

Mario's rage reinvigorated him. He swung with such speed and fury that Otto was barely able to parry his attacks. Their two swords clanged against one another as they locked into a stalemate. Without allowing Otto to catch his breath, Mario headbutted the bounty hunter directly in the nose. The sound of his bones breaking was music to Mario's ear.

Mario charged at him once again, this time feinting a spin to the right. The disoriented bounty hunter fell for the bait. Mario planted his left foot and spun hard in the opposite direction. His sword sliced Otto's throat with ease. The bounty hunter's blood sprayed from his neck and stained the snow a dark crimson red.

Mario dropped his sword and collapsed in the snow. Exhausted from the fight, the blood loss, and the loss of his friend. It felt as if the world was spinning. Blood was slowly trickling into his left eye as he stared up at the night sky. He felt Deidre drag him back towards the fire, but he was too tired to react. He couldn't move a muscle, even if he wanted to. *Just leave me here to die.*

Mario saw Deidre's lips moving frantically as she tossed her daggers into the fire. But he couldn't hear what she was saying. It sounded like his head was underwater. His eyes started to feel heavy. Feeling left his body as he stared up at Deidre's scared face. *Is this what it's like to die? Just numb indifference?*

Mario could feel Deidre's cold hands clumsily take off his jacket and shirt. He felt her soft hands run over his bare torso as she rolled him onto his left side. *This seems like a good place to die.* His body relaxed, ready for the embrace of death.

Life surged into Mario's body once more as Deidre pressed her hot daggers against his side. Feeling returned to his body, mostly in the form of pain. The stench of burnt flesh filled his nose as he sat up, clutching his burning side while he did so. Before he could react, Deidre pressed the second dagger against the wound above his eye.

"Agh!" Mario screamed as he scuttled back away from the elf. "What are you doing?"

"Stopping the bleeding."

Mario painfully stood up and touched his side and his head and realized that Deidre was right. The bleeding had stopped, but he still felt weak. "Give me my clothes. It's freezing out here."

Deidre handed him his clothes as she walked back into the trees. Mario struggled to put on his shirt and jacket; his body screamed in agony as he pulled his arms through the sleeves. Once the ordeal of getting dressed was finished, Mario sat back down beside the fire and warmed his hands. "Where were you?" he called out without moving his eyes from the fire.

"Getting food," Deidre replied coldly as she tossed a dead rabbit into Mario's lap. "I ran back once I heard the screaming."

Mario looked down at the rabbit, then back up at Deidre. Her eyes were focused on the fire; she had two dead rabbits beside her. "We should bury Hamish in the morning," Mario said.

"The ground is frozen."

"Well, I'm not leaving his body to rot beside those monsters'. . . . We'll build a pyre then."

"We don't have time—"

"Then we make time! Gods damn it, Deidre! It's my fault everyone is dying, mine!" Mario's side ached as he screamed, but he pressed on. He'd be damned if he let another one of his friend's body rot on the ground. "The least we can do is give Hamish a proper fucking funeral! He deserved that much!"

His voice faintly echoed into the quiet night until all that remained was the cracking of the fire. He took a deep breath to calm down, his side stinging as he did so. "Deidre, I'm sorry that I yelled—"

"No," Deidre interjected. She lifted her gaze from the fire, and Mario saw that tears filled her eyes and began to roll down her cheek. "You're right. Hamish *does* deserve that much."

"Get some rest, Deidre. We have a long day ahead of us tomorrow."

"Do you hear that?" Deidre whispered.

"What?"

"Listen."

Mario closed his eyes and focused on the sounds around him. All he heard was the crackling of the fire, the howling of the wind, and the rustling of pine needles. He opened his eyes and stared at Deidre. "I don't hear anything."

"I hear horses," Deidre informed as she rose to her feet.

Mario painfully stood up and followed Deidre towards the edge of the grove. After a short walk, they found two horses, decorated with the finest tack, tied to the trunk of a pine tree. Mario slowly approached the horses and ran his hands down the creature's neck. "They're beautiful."

"Must've been the bounty hunters," Deidre replied as she carefully examined the saddlebags.

"We'll ride them tomorrow after we burn Hamish's body. Beats us walking on foot."

Deidre nodded in agreement and took the reins of one horse into her hand and led it back towards the fire. Mario stared at the other horse in front of him. "Hopefully, you will fare better than the other horses." Slowly, he led his new mount towards the fire.

Once the horses had been tied up back their camp, Mario removed all the tack while Deidre began rummaging through the Esterak's supplies. "Food, bedrolls, gold, blankets. These guys had everything," Deidre said.

Mario didn't answer. The thought of Hamish's decomposing body being only fifteen feet away made him uneasy. Mario wrapped himself up in a blanket and rested his head on one of the beautiful leather saddles. He stared at the coals of the fire while his mind raced wildly. Guilt surged through his body as he began to recollect Hamish's last words to him. *I'm proud to call you my family.*

Tears began to roll down his face. He saw Deidre's concerned face looking at him through the fire. Arduously, he rolled away from her, closed his eyes, and tried to sleep as best as one could when a friend rots fifteen feet away from them.

Toldsteim is the northmost village of the kingdom. Its people bear a closer resemblance to the berserkers of the northern isles. They endure an incredibly harsh climate, make due with minimal supplies, and are stuck between two warring nations. It speaks to the strength of the citizen's character, choosing to stay and live in such an awful place.

Master Aegius Laramonde,
History of Settlements in the Kingdom of Drussdell

Chapter Thirteen

The morning was eerily calm. The area showed no signs of being ravaged by a vicious blizzard the night before. The rays from the early morning sunlight bounced off the fresh layer of snow, making them glisten like a sea of diamonds. The only sound was the crackling of a fire from a funeral pyre. A small stream of black smoke slowly rose into the picturesque blue sky. The smell of burning flesh hung in the air.

"Should we say something?" Mario asked, breaking the lengthy silence.

"Like what?" Deidre asked.

Mario stared at the flames, hoping that the right words would come to him. He looked at his friend's monstrous body as it was engulfed by the fire. A tear rolled down his mutilated cheek. "Hamish was a good man . . ." he started, choking on his tears, "He once told me that we were the closest thing he ever had to a family. I only wish that I had more time with him. May he rest in peace."

Mario's words seemed to fall short of their mark. He felt like he hadn't said the right things. It was almost as if there was something left to be said, but the words eluded him.

Deidre quietly approached the funeral pyre and placed a bundle of sticks on the fire next to Hamish's corpse. She stepped back as the bundle of wood was swallowed by the flames. She stood beside Mario, watching the fire attentively.

Suddenly, the flames began to gradually change colour. The fire's original orange and red slowly transformed into beautiful shades of green and blue. Even the smoke itself evolved from a sombre charcoal black into a mesmerizing deep shade of purple.

Deidre let out a sigh of relief. "*Nhav'carenn*," she whispered.

"It's beautiful," Mario whispered back.

"It's an elven tradition. It's supposed to help guide his spirit back up to the heavens."

"You believe in that kind of stuff?" Mario asked, staring at Deidre's solemn face.

"No," she replied, turning her head to meet Mario's gaze. "But I figure that it's worth a try if it turns out to be true."

Mario reached down and grabbed Deidre's hand into his own. Her skin was as cold as ice. He gave it a small, friendly squeeze. He turned his head and looked at the saddled horses, who were already eager to get the day's journey underway. "We should get moving."

Deidre nodded and pulled her hand from Mario's. She threw herself onto the back of the horse and, with a swift kick, galloped out of the grove of trees. Mario sauntered over to his horse and laboriously pulled himself onto the saddle. He turned his head for one last look at the funeral pyre. He stifled a tear, gave a slight nod of his head, and rode off after Deidre.

The frozen plains looked like something out of a painting that early morning; it was beautifully barren. Because of the blizzard, all signs of life had been covered by a fresh layer of snow. Mario felt like a famous explorer, riding his trusty steed into the unknown. He watched the cherry-red sun slowly rise in the east. Sadness began to grip his throat; he wished that he could've shared this moment with more than just Deidre. He wished he could've heard Andronikus' cool indifference. He wanted to hear Roger's over-the-top enthusiasm, Finnegan's crabbiness, and Hamish's voice. But instead, he was here with Deidre and an uncomfortable silence.

"Beautiful, isn't it?" Mario asked, hoping to engage in conversation.

"Hmm," Deidre replied coldly.

"I never thanked you for healing my wounds," Mario added, ignoring Deidre's lack of a response.

"You're welcome. Your chest looks like shit, by the way." Deidre smiled, looking over her shoulder.

Mario laughed nervously. He could only imagine how disfigured his chest looked now with an extra scar. His face probably didn't look much better. *Another scar right above the left eye. What's another one for the collection?* Mario looked down at his hands and saw that they were slowly turning red from the cold. The icy leather reins were greedily stealing heat from his hands.

"How're you holding up?" Deidre asked, looking at Mario's trembling hands.

"I'm fine," Mario retorted. He clumsily tied the reins around the horn of his saddle and stuck his hands underneath his armpits for warmth.

"We'll be at the bandit's camp soon."

"What will you do once this is over?"

"Probably go back to the forest."

"Then?"

Deidre let out a sigh. "You don't understand. The forest and my clan are all I've ever known. I can't just leave that behind. So once we find these bastards, I'm going to go back to my normal, secluded life in the forest. Far from the *dahrenn*."

Mario gulped. He could hear the angry quiver in Deidre's voice when she spoke of the humans. Mario's heart ached for her. Not only had she lost as much as he had, but she lost so much more. He wondered how she was dealing with the pain. He wanted to ask her, but the words eluded him once more.

"What about you?" Deidre asked, interrupting his thoughts. "Are you going to go back to being a knight?"

Mario's body tightened. He had been dwelling on this very question for days now. It seemed like every day Mario lost another piece of himself because of his knighthood. He had lost his friends, his looks, and at times, it felt like he lost his very soul. Setting off on this quest changed him. He was no longer the bright-eyed, naïve graduate that he was a few weeks ago. No, that Mario had died. He was now a grizzled, jaded, battle-hardened veteran who ached to hang up his sword.

"I don't know," Mario answered meekly. "I took an oath, so I would be dishonouring the order and my family legacy."

"Who cares?" Deidre spat. "With all due respect, the order is a crock of shit. And your family legacy is a man who slaughtered an entire village of innocent people. Be your own person."

Mario flinched at Deidre's hateful words. Even though he was beginning to have doubts about being a knight, he still resented anyone talking ill about his family's profession. "You don't know what you're talking about."

"Your dad was called the Slayer of Elves. The great Pablo Deschamps, the hero of the Elven Uprising! Let's call a spade a spade. He was a murderer and a bastard. The only good thing he did in his life was siring you into the world."

Mario pulled back on the reins of his horse. The steed let out a sharp whinny and abruptly obeyed its rider's orders. "You shut your mouth!" Mario pointed a finger angrily at Deidre. "My father was a damned hero, not a murderer or a bastard! He protected the people against all kinds of threats. Bandits, criminals, wild beasts, and even murderous bands of elves!"

This time, Deidre pulled on her horse's reins and glared back at Mario. "*We* were the murderous ones?" Her voice was at maximum volume as it echoed throughout the open plains. "We were fighting for elves to finally be made equal to humans! We didn't want to live as slaves or as second-class citizens anymore. We wanted to live as we had for thousands of years before humanity forced us into hiding and subjugation. And yet you have the gall to call *us* the murderous ones."

The two of them stared at one another silently, both seething in their own anger. This had been the dark cloud looming over both of their heads since they met. Only now, when they were alone did the issue rear its ugly head.

Mario searched for words, but he could find none. He wanted to say things like: "Elves would be lucky to live among humans," or "Humans were doing elves a favour by rescuing them from their own savagery." But in his heart, he knew that these statements were not true. He had seen what humanity had done to elves, what it had done to Deidre's clan, and what it had done to her.

"Let's keep riding," Mario replied bitterly as he gently kicked his horse into a walk. Deidre stared at him angrily, her nostrils fully flared. Mario could tell he had struck a nerve with her, and to her credit, she was right about a lot of things. *Elves were and are treated as inferiors to humans, and humanity has done some pretty deplorable things. But she is wrong about one thing; my father was not a murderer. He was a hero and deserves to be remembered as such.*

Deidre clicked her tongue against her teeth and kicked her horse into a trot. Soon she was beside Mario, still glaring angrily at him. "No, we are going to talk about this now." Her voice was as cold as the northern air.

"I'd rather not."

"Tell me, why do you idolize your father so much?"

"'Cause he's a hero."

"He's a hero to the *dahrenn*. To us, he is a villain. He is the very personification of what humanity has done to the elves for centuries and what they will continue to do for centuries to come."

Mario lifted his head and stared back at Deidre; his lips contorted into an ugly frown. "Then why are you even here!?" The veins in Mario's neck began to protrude out of his skin as his anger took control. "If you despise us humans so much, why are you here with me!?" This time Mario's voice echoed throughout the open plains. His body was warm with rage; he felt his hands tremble as he struggled to control his emotions.

Unexpectedly, Deidre's face sank. Her skin went pale, and she hung her head. Tears were beginning to well in her eyes. "Because I thought you were different."

Shame surged through Mario's body. He instantly regretted what he had said. It felt like he had been punched in the stomach. "Deidre, I . . ."

But before he could utter another word, Deidre kicked her horse into a full gallop, leaving Mario behind and alone in the snow.

"Shit," Mario muttered to himself as he watched Deidre ride away. *She probably just needs some space and to be with herself. I'll keep riding. I'm sure she'll come back.* But with each passing minute, Mario believed that less and less.

After several hours of riding in the cold, Mario finally saw another sign of life in the distance. A small tower of smoke rose into the air, likely from a campfire. *Deidre.*

Mario kicked his horse viciously. The mount immediately broke into a gallop. The cold winter air stabbed Mario's face as he travelled at breakneck speeds. The smoke from the campfire grew as he drew closer. Soon, he was able to see the faint reflection of the flames on the snow. Mario gently pulled on his reins, and his horse gradually came to a stop.

Disappointingly, it was not Deidre at the campfire but a man. He wore a fur hat and a thick black coat. The man was warming his hands by the fire. Mario noticed that his complexion was darker than most people in the north. The man had light brown eyes that blended into his tanned skin. The man was clean-shaven and bore his shining white teeth in a friendly smile.

"Greetings, sir, please, I don't have much. But if you wish to rob me, I'll give you everything I have. I just ask that you leave me with my life." The man's voice had an accent that Mario had never heard before.

Mario stopped his horse and dismounted, his boots sinking in the fresh layer of snow. "I am no bandit. I'm looking for my friend. She is an elven woman and—"

Suddenly, the man started chuckling. "Ah, you must be the knight. Come sit down!" The man pointed to the spot on the opposite side of the fire. Mario realized that someone else had recently sat there. "Apologies for mistaking you as a bandit, Sir Knight. It's just you wear no armour, and your face is horrifically scarred."

The man's words cut Mario's ego. He hated being reminded that he was deformed and now hideous. He was accustomed to being addressed with the respect that came from being a knight, but perhaps those days were behind him. "You know Deidre?" Mario asked, ignoring the man's remarks as best he could.

"She did not give me her name, but I imagine we are talking about the same person. A few hours ago, an elven woman stumbled across my camp, it appeared like she had been crying. Against my better judgement, I invited her to sit down at my camp."

"What did she say?"

The man grinned slyly at Mario. "Not much, but she did tell me that you pissed her off royally."

Mario swallowed. He already felt guilty enough as it was; the man's words twisted a knife in an open wound. Mario reluctantly sat down at the fire. "Did she say if she was coming back?" Mario's voice quivered as he struggled to contain his guilt.

The tanned man stared into Mario's eyes intensely. It was almost as if the man was trying to learn Mario's secrets by staring at him. The strange man relaxed his body and chewed on his bottom lip. "Is this a matter of love?"

Mario's body jumped back involuntarily at the mention of love. He had never viewed Deidre in that way. Although she was very pretty and very attractive, there was no romantic spark between them. They grew up in vastly different worlds, with vastly different perspectives.

"No," Mario replied; he could feel his face turn red from embarrassment. "We're just friends."

The man frowned, almost disappointed by the news. "Shame, I enjoy a good love story. Nothing screams star-crossed lovers like an elf and human, especially if that human is a knight."

"Sorry to disappoint, but did she tell you if she's coming back?"

The man smiled coyly. "Yes, I managed to calm her down, though it was not easy. She has a fiery temper."

Mario breathed a sigh of relief. "Thank you, you've no idea how much this means to me. Where is she?"

"Not so fast," the man replied. "How about a story for a story?"

Mario ground his teeth. He didn't like the idea of this foreigner prying into his life, but he didn't have a choice. He needed to know where Deidre was. "Sure."

"You seem fairly young to be a knight, yet your scars would suggest that you've had a long and gruelling career. Which is the truth?"

Mario winced at the mention of his scars; he hated how they were beginning to define him. "I am fairly young for a knight," he responded after a lengthy silence. "Truth is, I got these scars from fighting a monster."

The stranger burst out in laughter. His accent reverberated off the snow on the plains. "I'm sorry, but did you say a monster?" the man asked while wiping tears out of his eyes.

Mario nodded his head politely.

"Do you fancy yourself as a member of the Order of the Swords? What could possibly make you think you were capable of fighting a monster?"

"I didn't set out to find a monster. I stumbled upon it. It was life or death," Mario retorted defensively.

"Ah, I see," the man replied. "Well, I'm glad you made it out in one piece . . . more or less."

Mario clenched his fist in anger. He was beginning to think that the stranger was making demeaning comments about his appearance intentionally now.

"So which beast gave you the scars? Werewolves? Necrophages? Vampires?" the man inquired, interrupting Mario's brooding.

"No, it was none of those," Mario answered. "It was some tree-like monster. The vampires were actually quite hospitable."

The stranger erupted in laughter once again. "You have to be joking, right?" the man exclaimed as he wiped tears away from his eyes. "Vampires are mindless beasts, consumed by their lust for human flesh. They're incapable of hospitality."

"You're thinking of sasabonsams," Mario corrected. "Most people tend to confuse the two monsters. Sasabonsams are the beast-like creatures that live only to feed, while actual vampires are like humans and are governed by thoughts, logic, and emotions."

The stranger stared at him, blankly. Mario could tell that the man was trying hard to comprehend what Mario had just told him.

"How do you know all of this boy?" the man asked; his voice suddenly became cold, and his eyes narrowed suspiciously.

"One of my companions. He was a member of the Order of the Swords, a monster hunter."

The stranger's body instantly relaxed. "That explains it! Tell me, where is he now?"

Mario gulped as the image of Andronikus being torn apart by the obzen flashed back into his mind. A guilt-riddled pain gripped his stomach as he remembered how they brutally ripped out his friend's innards. Bile began to rush up into his throat. Out of all the death that Mario had seen, Andronikus' had been the most horrific. "He died, in a cave-in," he said while swallowing the vomit that had worked its way into his mouth.

"I'm sorry."

"Where's Deidre?" Mario interjected, shaking the sour memory out of his head.

"Right, a deal's a deal. I was able to calm her down, but she was still upset and needed some space. She told me that she would be waiting for you in the next town. It's called Toldsteim, and it's only a few hours north of here."

Mario rose to his feet. "Thank you, I'll head there right away." Mario placed one foot in his stirrup and threw himself on the back of his horse. He was about to take off at full speed but glanced at the man once more and stopped. "Are you from the South?"

"Indeed, I am!" the man answered boisterously.

"What are you doing in the North?"

"I'm a merchant, trying to start anew. I fear there is nothing left for me back in the empire, except pain and sad memories."

"Why have you helped us? You had no reason to."

"Truthfully, I like stories. I always fancied myself as an author when I was a child. Unfortunately, I'm about as creative as the beast you're riding. Therefore, I choose to listen to people's stories wherever I go. I'm always fascinated with what one might learn through a fellow traveller or through some town gossip."

Mario was not sure what to say for some time. The Southerner seemed genuine, but Mario had the creeping suspicion that something was off. "Well, thank you for all you've done. . . . I'm sorry I didn't catch your name."

"Ossypius Magnus, at your service."

Mario nodded his head slightly. "I'm Mario Deschamps." With a swift kick of his leg, he took off in a gallop. Eager to reunite with his friend.

***

Lukas Aurelius spat on the ground as he watched the young knight ride off hastily in the distance. His frustration began to boil over as his mind frantically jumped from one angry thought to another. *Why does everyone in the North smell like they fell asleep in a stable? I would think a knight, a person of high societal standing, would know the importance of bathing oneself. I can't wait to be back in the empire, so I don't have to hold my breath while speaking to people.*

Once the knight had disappeared over the horizon, Lukas allowed himself to relax and breathe in the clean, winter air. The fresh breath seemed to soothe his frustration as he began thinking more and more about the young knight. "He's not a bad lad, for a Northman. Sure, hygiene is an issue, but other than that, it wasn't a terrible interaction," Lukas mumbled to himself aloud. "A shame really, soon chasing after his elven friends will be the least of his worries when Keten invades his country."

Lukas sat quietly for some time as he began contemplating what the young knight had told him. "Vampires . . ." he whispered, thinking about what to do with this new information. "If the boy is telling the truth, this could present some opportunities for the empire. The vampires would be difficult to control. Waging war against them would certainly be impossible; therefore, an alliance will have to be formed. The sasabonsams are like animals, and animals can be controlled with ease. Several societies have used war animals in the past, but to have a swarm of bloodthirsty beasts at our disposal, it would make the empire unstoppable!"

Lukas began to chew his bottom lip, as one piece of information from the conversation puzzled him. "Where did I hear that name before? Deschamps?" he asked himself aloud. After a few minutes of deep thought, he remembered. "Ah yes, the knight King Dryden secretly killed! I wonder if the boy knows about his father. . . ."

Lukas quickly grabbed his notebook and a small piece of charcoal from out of his pocket and began to write a letter to the emperor informing him of the new information he had just learned. He grinned as he penned his letter, describing his plans to use the monsters as soldiers. He relished in the thought about how clueless Mario and the rest of the North were to the empire's plans, and how dumbfounded they would be when they saw the empire's forces marching side by side with an army of sasabonsams. Knowing how the future was going to play out gave him great pleasure. However, even Lukas could not foresee that in a few days' time, Mario would hold a blade to the spy's throat.

***

After a few hours of hard riding, Mario came to a small settlement that he presumed was Toldsteim. A tall palisade, made from trunks of oak trees, surrounded the town. Each log was sharpened to a point, preventing anyone from climbing over the top of the wall. On top of the palisade were several men, who all wore heavy fur coats to protect them from the winter air. All of the men wielded a bow as the knight slowly approached the town.

"Greetings," Mario called out to the guards on top of the defences.

"Begone," one of the guards gruffly called out as he readied his bow. "We don't want no vagabonds!"

"I'm not a vagabond. I'm a kn—" Mario stopped himself before he could finish his sentence. He remembered that Ossypius had mistaken him as a bandit earlier, and the only reason the Southerner believed him was that he had already met Deidre. Mario knew that the guards would have a harder time believing that he was a knight.

"What are ye then if not a vagabond?" one of the guards called out, interrupting Mario's thoughts.

Mario panicked. His mind raced as he tried to think of a believable cover story. Frantically, he shouted the first occupation that came to mind, "I'm a bounty hunter!"

Silence hung in the air. A few of the guards atop the palisade got together and murmured amongst themselves. Finally, after lengthy deliberation, the one guard stepped forward. "A bounty hunter, eh? Well, you'll be in no shortage of work. Plenty o' filth' round here that needs cleaning up."

Mario smiled and nodded his head politely. "I'm supposed to meet my associate here, a she-elf. Have you seen her?"

The guards' faces suddenly went pale. Once again, they clumped for another discussion.

Mario raised an eyebrow in confusion, a sinking feeling began to take hold of his stomach. "What's wrong?"

One of the guards stepped away from his comrades and addressed Mario with his chest puffed out and head held high. "I'm sorry to inform you, Master Bounty Hunter, that the town of Toldsteim is under the protection of the Golden Sun. As a result, no non-humans are allowed entry without being accompanied by a human chaperone.

Mario frowned and angrily jumped off his horse. *This fucking church.* "Where is she!?" he bellowed as he slowly moved his hand toward the hilt of his sword.

The guard gulped meekly and looked towards his fellow guardsmen for support. There was none to be found. "Good sir . . ." the guard stammered, "threatening the guard is an offence that—"

"Where is she!?" Mario interrupted, his angry breath clearly visible in the cold northern air.

"The priests escorted her away from the city!" the guard blurted out sheepishly.

"Where!?"

"Into the forest," the man said, pointing towards the mass of trees lying just east of town.

Mario quickly mounted his horse and galloped into the forest. His heart began to race at the thought of what the priests would do to Deidre. Judging from previous experience, he knew that it would not be a pleasant encounter for her.

The snow of the forest crunched beneath the horse's hooves. Some of the low hanging branches on the trees smacked against Mario's cheeks. Blood was beginning to slowly pour out of the cuts, but he didn't care. He was trying to find any sign of Deidre and the priests. Finally, he saw it. Four horses were tied to several nearby trees, three of which he had never seen before; the fourth was Deidre's. Mario quickly rode over towards the horses and dismounted. He could tell by looking at the snow that a struggle had taken place here.

"Seems, they pulled Deidre off her horse when she wasn't looking," Mario whispered aloud. He knew very little about tracking, but he would be damned if he let his inexperience stop him from finding the elf.

Suddenly, he heard a scream from deep within the forest. Mario instantly recognized it as Deidre's. He sprinted towards the direction of the cry, sword already in hand. As he crashed the undergrowth, his mind began imagining what despicable things the priests were doing to her. His first thought was that they were going to rape her as the bandits did, but that seemed unlikely. The priests hated non-humans; surely, they wouldn't want to sleep with one. The second thought was that they were going to torture her, either for information or for pleasure. Mario wasn't sure which one he feared more.

As Mario barrelled through another set of trees, he found himself in the middle of a snow-covered clearing. His stomach immediately churned. In the middle of the opening were the three priests and Deidre. Two of the priests pinned Deidre to the ground by the arms and the shoulders, while the third, with his trousers around his ankles, tore at Deidre's pants. She squirmed violently as tears rolled down her cheeks.

Mario swallowed his disgust and let out a fierce, rage-filled roar. Before the pants-less priest could react, Mario had already shoved his sword down the heretic's throat. The man's body twitched violently as the sword severed his spine. The two other priests quickly let go of Deidre and began to run back towards the horses. Deidre shot to her feet and started chasing after her attackers with unbelievable speed. Mario followed closely behind. The one priest was quite large and, as a result, could not run away very quickly. Deidre ran past the fat priest, her eyes fixated on the faster of the two clergymen.

Mario caught up to the obese clergymen with ease. He wagered that one could hear the priest's wheezing breathing clear across the forest. He swung his sword at the man's head, but to his surprise, he missed his mark. Either the man nimbly ducked, or he collapsed from exhaustion at just the right time—Mario wasn't sure which. As a result, the blade severed only the top layer of the priest's head, removing the scalp and the hair and exposing his bloody skull to the cold northern air. The man howled in pain as he writhed on the ground. It was at this moment, Mario understood why Andronikus took his time punishing Pascal; it was empowering. Mario slowly pressed his blade into the fat priest's chest. He made sure he applied the right amount of pressure so that he only punctured the lung. He regretted killing the first priest too quickly; he was going to make sure this one died slowly and painfully. *He's going to drown in his own blood.* Mario ripped the sword out of the man's chest and walked away with cold indifference.

On the way back to the horses, Mario heard a loud thumping coming from the trees. He cautiously approached the sound, sword in hand, and saw that it was Deidre, enacting her vengeance. She had tackled the last of her attackers to the ground and had crushed his head with a nearby rock. Mario looked at the body of the priest and saw that his head was now completely flattened, yet Deidre was still smashing it with the stone.

Mario slowly approached Deidre and grabbed her by the wrist. Instantly, she let go of the rock and brought Mario in for a firm embrace. She began to sob uncontrollably. Mario wrapped his arms around Deidre and squeezed as hard as he could. He wanted to let Deidre know that everything was okay and that he was going to be there for her, but the words escaped him. He hoped that she would understand him through the hug.

"Thank you," Deidre whispered as she tightened her grip around Mario.

"I'm sorry, Deidre—" Mario started.

"Don't be. There is nothing to be sorry for. I'm just glad you're here now."

Mario smiled as he began to pull away from Deidre, but she quickly pulled him back in. "Don't," Deidre mumbled. "Just a few more minutes."

"Okay," Mario whispered as he began squeezing Deidre tightly once again.

The wind billowed through the quiet of the forest as Deidre softly sobbed, trying to move past yet another awful encounter with humans.

Thinkers prepare the revolution and bandits carry it out.

Mariano Azuela

Chapter Fourteen

The tavern smelled of strong ale, hickory-smoked pork, and burning cedar-wood. The flames from the fireplace filled the entire room with warmth and protected the patrons from the unforgiving, icy wind waiting for them outside. The main floor of the tavern was crowded and full of life. People were playing cards, drinking profusely, and making merry with one another. However, there was one patron who was not enjoying himself in the inn's revelry. Instead, he sat alone at a table in the far corner of the inn, carefully watching the door to one of the rooms. Most of the people had already noticed him, not just because he wasn't a local, but because he was accompanied by a she-elf.

Mario observed the locals suspiciously, all while keeping one eye on Deidre's room. He thought that she should have some time to herself to rest and recover from her encounter with the priests. Every now and then, Mario would hear bits and pieces of the patrons' conversations. Most were banal, meaningless chit-chat, but there were two groups of patrons that he took a keen interest in.

The first was a group of two very drunk merchants. One appeared to be from the Forsaken Lands of the Far South. He had very dark, almost black skin and spoke with a heavy accent. The other was from the North; he had pale white skin, and was covered with bright red hair. From what Mario could gather, it appeared that both men had travelled all around the world and had seen many things between them.

"I once saw a dragon gobble up an entire herd of sheep with one bite!" the northern merchant slurred.

"My friend, my friend," the southern merchant replied, "you are mistaken. There hasn't been a dragon in these parts for over a thousand years. You probably just saw a drake or a wyvern."

"Pfft!" the first merchant scoffed. "I'd think I'd know the difference between a damned drake and a fuckin' dragon!" The man slammed his fist against the beer-soaked wooden table.

"Please, I mean no offence," the second merchant apologized. "It's just that all those damned snakes look so similar, and they move so bloody fast, that I tend to get them mixed up myself."

"Ah, I suppose your right. Let's get another round!"

Mario smiled as he turned his gaze back towards Deidre's door. He couldn't help but respect how easily the dark-skinned merchant defused the tension between them. It reminded him a little about Miles, and it was a skill Mario secretly wished he could master.

The other group of patrons that caught Mario's attention was a man and a woman. Both were wearing thick fur coats made from the pelts of several small animals. Mario noticed the man carried a woodcutter's axe with him no matter where he went. The man was tall and muscular; the only hair on his body was a frost-covered thick, bushy beard. The woman was the complete opposite. She was small, frail, and her long blonde hair was neatly braided into a bow behind her head. From what Mario observed, he thought that the man was trying to woo the woman with either heroic tales or hilarious stories.

" . . . and then I walked up behind him, gave him a slap on the back, and called him the ugliest fucker I'd ever seen!" the man shouted, exploding in laughter after finishing his story.

The blonde woman smiled politely and, for the first time in a while, spoke to the man. "Tell me, have you ever seen a knight in person?"

The man scratched his neck nervously as he stared into the girl's deep yellow eyes. "No, unfortunately . . . though I do have a few stories of some!"

The woman's face lit up with excitement. "Oh, please do tell!" she squealed. "I always dreamed of being rescued by a handsome, valiant knight, who would then take me to be his bride!"

The muscular man gulped nervously and took a quick drink from his mug of ale. "Well, I once heard the story of a knight who went completely bonkers! Apparently, he thought some of the countryside's windmills were giants and tried to slay them!"

The woman giggled. "No, no. I mean stories about knights being heroes! You know saving fair maidens, getting rid of criminals, and protecting the realm from evil!"

"Well, there is the tale of the great Pablo Deschamps! He was dubbed the Scourge of Bandits and the Slayer of Elves!" the man whispered as if he was telling a secret. The woman leaned forward in her chair, as did Mario. "They say he single-handedly saved the North from the elves, and if not for him—"

"Excuse me, good sir."

Mario turned suddenly in his chair and glared at the man who had interrupted his eavesdropping. Even from across the table, Mario could tell that man had not bathed in weeks. He reeked of shit, both animal and human, and his shirt was covered in stains. "What do you want?" Mario asked annoyingly.

"Sorry for disturbing you, master . . . but are you the bounty hunter?" the man replied meekly, his eyes cast down on the floor.

"I am."

"And that elf you travel with, is she your—"

"My companion, yes," Mario interrupted angrily. "Now, what can I help you with?"

"Are you after The Hounds?"

"The who?"

"The Hounds!" the man emphasized quietly, as to not be heard by the other patrons. "They're a group o' bandits that live 'round here. They're led by a man named Henry, who carries a large war hammer with him at all times."

Mario's eyes widened, and he shot to his feet, knocking his chair over. "Do you know where to find these men?" he asked impatiently. He could feel the excitement grip his throat. *Could this lowly peasant be the key to finding the bandits and finally bring them to justice?* Mario waited with great anticipation for the man's response, his entire body weight supported by his tip-toes.

"Aye," he replied sheepishly, still not daring to look Mario in the eye.

"Do you have a horse!?"

"Aye."

"Ready your horse then. I will fetch my companion, and you will lead us to them."

The man nodded and quickly shuffled his way out of the inn, his gaze never leaving the floorboards. Mario watched the man as he left and found himself wondering about his curious nature. *Why doesn't he look me in the eyes? Perhaps he is scared or shy, or maybe he doesn't want to gaze upon my hideous face.* Mario shuddered at the thought. He quickly walked towards Deidre's room and began pounding on the door.

Deidre opened the door and wiped the crust out of her puffy, swollen red eyes. Mario could tell that he had disturbed her from a deep sleep. "What?" Deidre growled, her eyes barely open.

"I know where the bandits are!"

Deidre's eyes grew wide. She quickly turned on her heels, grabbed her bow and her daggers, and marched out of the room. "Where?"

"There's a local peasant who says he knows where to find them, and he has agreed to lead us there."

Deidre stopped in her tracks. She turned towards Mario and grabbed him by the collar of his shirt, pulling his ear to her mouth. "Did it ever cross your mind that this could be a trap?"

Mario's heart sank; he had let his excitement get the better of him. He knew that the bandits probably realized that he and Deidre had escaped from Pascal by now. He also realized that he had a very recognizable face, thanks to the scars; it would be easy for one of the bandits to recognize him. "Shit," Mario grumbled. "What do we do now?"

"I don't like the sounds of this. It's just too convenient," Deidre whispered as she looked around the tavern defensively.

"But if he is telling the truth, this is an opportunity we cannot afford to pass up," Mario retorted.

"I have an idea, but you have to follow my lead."

Mario nodded and followed Deidre out of the inn. As soon as they crossed the threshold of the doors, the cold, brisk, winter air bit at their exposed flesh. Mario shivered and pulled his jacket higher up to protect his neck. Deidre shielded her eyes from the harsh wind with her hand and began to tell him her plan.

"Tell him to fetch some water for the journey," she instructed. "When he is alone, I'll act as if I'll rob him. If he fights back with any skill, he is probably a bandit."

Mario nodded in agreement, and Deidre took off, running down the street and out of sight. He didn't like this idea, but he had no choice. Deidre's conclusion about the man was just as likely as his. This could very well be a trap—one they very well wouldn't be able to escape from.

When Mario reached his horses, he saw that the man was already there waiting for him, his horse saddled and ready to go. He sized up the stranger as he approached. The man was thin and covered in dirt. His mangy beard was just starting to turn grey. *He certainly does not appear to be a bandit, but appearances can be deceiving. Andronikus was practically skin and bones; nobody would think that he was as gifted a fighter as he was.*

"Where's your companion?" the man called out from atop his horse.

"Still getting ready," Mario replied. "We need you to go fetch us some water for the trek." He hoped that the man would take the bait and fall right into his and Deidre's trap.

"Absolutely!" the man exclaimed as he jumped off his horse and ran down the street to where Deidre was hiding.

Mario decided to take time and check over his horse. Despite all that Mario had asked of the beast, it still appeared to be in great shape. It was not lame, nor had any visible injuries, and its hooves weren't splitting. It appeared to be in overall good health. *The Esteraks sure knew how to pick a mount.*

Mario then turned and looked at the stranger's horse. It was a sickly bay that looked like it hadn't been fed in weeks. The ribs were clearly visible, and the animal's head hung low, as if it were trying to uncover the frozen grass beneath the thick layer of snow. *Surely, this horse won't survive the journey there and back.* Mario pitied the animal. He wondered what his dad would've said if he saw a creature in such a destitute condition.

Suddenly, Mario heard wailing coming from down the street. He turned his head and saw that Deidre was dragging the stranger by the ear towards Mario as he wept like a small child. When they arrived at the horses, Deidre threw the man on the ground.

"Well, he's not a bandit." Deidre smiled as she watched the man struggle to get up. "Poor fool erupted into tears the minute he saw my dagger. I'm surprised he didn't piss himself."

The man quickly rose to his feet. "Is this how you accept someone's help!" he yelled, brushing the snow off of his shirt.

"I'm sorry, but we had to make sure that you weren't one of the bandits and leading us into a trap," Mario replied as he helped remove some of the snow from the man's shoulder.

The stranger's eyes darted between Mario and Deidre as if he was trying to figure out their intentions. After long contemplation, the stranger shrugged his shoulders and hopped onto his dying horse. "The camp is half a day's ride from here. We should be there by nightfall."

"What's your name?" Mario asked as he slowly mounted his own horse.

"Howard, Howard Blackley."

"Nice to meet you. Now lead us to the bandits," Deidre replied coldly.

Despite their urgency, the party of three travelled at a very sluggish pace. Howard's horse was struggling to walk through the thick snow, while Deidre and Mario's horses were ready to break out into a full gallop at any given moment. Mario noticed that Howard was slowly leading them north, towards the border of Drussdell and Keten. The further they went, the deeper the snow became, slowing them down even more. The frozen plains of Drussdell started disappearing gradually. What was once barren and icy fields were slowly transformed into dense, snow-covered forests and impressive mountain ranges. When the sun began to fall behind the mountains to the west, Deidre's frustration began to boil over.

"Move it!" Deidre barked. "We want to arrive at their camp before we are a hundred!"

Howard chuckled quietly to himself as he ran his hand down the neck of the sickly horse. "Ole Blue takes his time wherever he goes, but rest assured, he always gets you there!"

"Yeah, in three centuries from now," Deidre grumbled under her breath.

"So, Howard, what do you do?" Mario asked, eagerly wanting to change the subject.

"I used to be a farmer," Howard replied. "We had goats, sheep, chickens, and even a few oxen . . ." he trailed off as he looked ahead.

"What happened?"

"The Hounds," he replied. "They raided our town and took everything from me. My wife, my children, my farm . . . everything."

His words hung in the air. For a while, they quietly listened to the crunch of snow as it crushed beneath their horses' hooves. Mario turned his head to look at Deidre. He saw that her face had turned red from embarrassment.

Mario cleared his throat and turned his attention back on the farmer. "How did you escape?"

Tears began to swell in Howard's eyes, and his face began to contort.

Mario recognized it as the face of guilt and regret, feelings he's had many times before. "How did you escape?" Mario asked again.

"I . . ." Howard began, "I made a deal."

"With who?" Deidre growled, her blue eyes glaring at the back of Howard's skull.

"The Hounds, they . . ."

"Spit it out!"

"I gave them what they wanted. In return, they let me go, and I took Ole Blue here with me."

Mario's stomach began to churn; he already had a sense of what the bandits would've wanted from him. His hands began to tighten around the reins of his horse with frustration and anger. "What did you give them?"

For the first time since they met, Howard lifted his head and stared into Mario's eyes. Tears were streaming down his face as his lips quivered uncontrollably. "Everything! I gave them everything!" Howard confessed, his voice cracking as he did so. "I told my family to hide in the cellar, and that I would try to lead the bandits away from our home. Blue was our only horse, and they caught up to me quickly. Henry, he gave me a choice, give up my family and live, or die and have them find my family anyway."

Mario's body began to fill with disgust, but it was overshadowed by the amount of rage that was emanating from Deidre. He could hear her furious, rapid breathing from behind him. He knew that she was about to come unhinged. This time, however, he did not feel compelled to intervene. *Deidre needs to blow off steam, and Howard certainly deserves a berating.*

"Your own kin!" Deidre shouted. "Your own flesh and blood, you gave them up just like that!? What kind of a father does that!?"

Ole Blue came to a sudden stop as Howard let go of the reins. He started sobbing uncontrollably in his saddle, his face buried between his two hands. Mario almost began to pity him. "I know, I know!" he wailed, finally lifting his head out of his palms. "I've done wrong by my family, and I will surely be punished for this, but I'm trying to fix it!"

"How?" Deidre growled, her hands slowly reaching towards her daggers.

"If I lead you to The Hounds, you will kill them, and then my family will be avenged. I know it won't bring them back, but it is the best I can do for them now."

Deidre's fingers were around the blade of her dagger, ready to surgically throw the weapon into Howard's spine when Mario suddenly cleared his throat. "It is not our place to pass judgement. Let's just ride to the camp in silence. We don't want to lose the element of surprise."

Deidre stared at him and reluctantly sheathed her blade.

Mario's disgust began to fade as he stared at Howard. *This is the type of man I'm supposed to bring to justice as a knight, yet he clearly regrets his cowardice and is actively trying to redeem himself. For the rest of his life, he has to live with what he did to his family. Is that punishment enough?*

It wasn't long before the sun hid behind the mountains. The last of its orange rays of light bounced off the snow-covered peaks of the mountains before disappearing entirely. The pine trees of the forest became more and more scarce as they journeyed north. Some were stripped of their needles, others had their branches cut off, and several were chopped down completely. Mario noticed that some of the tree trunks had deep claw marks in their trunks. He grew uneasy.

"What happened here?" asked Mario, pointing to one of the marked trees. "Did a bear do this?"

Howard stopped his horse and looked carefully at the claw marks. "Nah," he mumbled. "Too large for a bear."

"Well, what are they from then?" Deidre asked with an annoyed tone.

Howard leaned down and grabbed a tuft of fur that was dangling from a low branch. He slowly brought the piece of hair to his nose and took a deep breath. His face immediately contorted into disgust, and he spat on the ground as he tossed the piece of hair away from him. "Werewolf."

"You're kidding," Deidre asked as she folded her arms across her chest.

"I've smelled one before when I was a young lad. Once you smell a werewolf, you never forget the scent." Howard radiated an aura of calmness as he brushed the snow off of his pants, which reminded Mario of Andronikus. Whenever he talked about monsters, it was always as if he was describing a cat or a dog. That calmness always seemed to soothe Mario, no matter what ungodly beast they were about to face.

"Do you have any silver?" Howard asked suddenly as he mounted his horse.

Mario already knew the answer to that question, but he looked towards Deidre anyway to see if, by some miracle, she had acquired some silver-forged weapons without him noticing. When she shook her head, Mario's heart sank. He could feel the hair on the back of his neck stand up with fear and paranoia. "Hopefully, we find the bandits before the werewolf finds us."

Immediately their pace doubled; even Ole Blue managed to go faster. The threat of being mauled by a werewolf seemed to be a good motivator. Mario and Deidre's heads were on a swivel as they rode deeper in the forest, watching, waiting for the beast whose territory they were entering.

Suddenly, Howard came to a halt. Mario and Deidre pulled up on their reins and listened carefully. In the distance, they could hear the cracking of fire, laughter, and drunken shouting. Mario could even smell the cooked meat on the spit. Slowly, they all dismounted their horses walked closer towards the camp.

At the edge of the trees was a small ledge, only a five-foot drop to the bottom. Resting at the bottom of the cliff was the bandit's camp. To Mario's surprise, it was larger than he imagined. He saw at least a half-dozen huts, three wagons, over twenty horses, and a countless number of men. Most of the bandits appeared to be wearing army uniforms, all drenched in blood.

"Why are they dressed like that?" Deidre whispered as she pulled her bow off of her shoulder.

"I'm not sure," Mario replied, "but it can't be for anything good." Out of the corner of his eye, he saw Howard begin to slink away back towards the horses. "Where are you going?"

"Home."

"Why?"

"I'm not a fighter, sir," Howard answered as he rubbed his hands together for warmth. "I'm just a farmer. If I try to help you, I'll only get in your way."

Mario sighed and thought about Howard's words carefully. *He's right, the last thing we need is an untrained man fighting alongside us. But we could also use all the help we could get.* "Alright," Mario uttered after some deliberation, "but before you go, take this." Mario pulled out a small pouch of coins and set it down into Howard's hands. He could feel Deidre's icy, disapproving stare in the back of his skull. "Get that horse some good food," Mario instructed. "Horses are magnificent creatures, and they deserve our respect. That means feeding them well and riding them hard only when you have to."

Howard frantically nodded his head. "Thank you, sir! Thank you!" With a quick turn of his heels, he shuffled off, back towards the horses.

"That was awfully kind of you." Deidre frowned.

"I know what it is like to regret something that you've done, to not be able to escape your past. I felt sorry for Howard. His decisions will haunt him until the day he dies. Besides, I figured you wouldn't want to share any of the bandits more than you have to," Mario joked as he eyed Deidre slyly from the side. He could see a big, malicious grin spread across her face.

"You're right, more for you and me."

"So, how're we doing this?"

Before Deidre could answer, they heard a bone-chilling howl. Mario saw that the bandits had the werewolf inside a cage. The beast growled and snapped its jaws at anyone who passed by the pen. But whenever the monster touched the bars of the cage, it screamed in pain and retreated. The bandits walked by and tossed bones, rocks, and anything else they could find in the camp to antagonize the creature.

"Let that thing out, and let it do the work for us," Deidre snickered.

"What's stopping it from turning on us?" Mario asked and saw that Deidre was disappointed that he had found a flaw in her plan. *She probably would've enjoyed watching the carnage.*

"Well, well, well," a familiar voice cooed from down into the camp.

The bandit leader, Henry, emerged from one of the huts, his war hammer in hand. "Amelia, Amelia, Amelia," he sarcastically boasted as he watched the werewolf through the bars of the cage. "Why all the anger? We have fed you and given you a comfortable little kennel to call your own, yet still, you try to bite the hand that feeds you."

The werewolf snarled in anger. Her beady yellow canine eyes followed Henry wherever he went. Henry laughed at the beast's response. "Are you upset that I outwitted you? It wasn't hard. You weren't a very clever girl. You gave us too many warnings about the wolf that lurked in these woods. Only one person could know so much about a werewolf, and that's the beast itself."

Henry's voice was just as charismatic and captivating as Mario remembered it. He saw how the entire company of bandits had their eyes glued on their leader as he conversed with the caged monstrosity.

"Tell you what," Henry announced loud and boisterously, "stick your claws through the bars and try to slash my throat." The bandit leader leaned forward so that the column of his throat was only a few inches from the bars of the cage, well within slashing distance. "Go ahead, take your best shot." The leader smiled as he leaned closer towards the cage.

Without a moment's hesitation, the beast lunged forward. Her arm surging towards Henry's neck at lightning speed. But, unexpectantly, the bandit did a quick and nimble pirouette out of the way and swung his hammer down hard on the creature's paw, pinning it to the ground. Mario could hear the sounds of bones shattering from the edge of the camp. He cringed as he listened to the werewolf yelp in pain.

"He's fast," Deidre growled as she drew her bowstring back, ready to let her arrow fly.

"Wait!" Mario whispered, but it was too late. Deidre had already shot her arrow, and it struck Henry in the back, right between the shoulder blades.

With a gasp, Henry collapsed to the ground and let go of his war hammer. The monster in the cage immediately pulled her paw inside and began licking the injured limb. With great effort, Henry rolled onto his side to see where the mysterious arrow came from. In the blink of an eye, the second arrow struck him as it landed right below his sternum. The bandit coughed blood and went limp.

The rest of the bandits were frozen in place by a state of shock. Mario leapt from the small ledge and decided to use the opportunity to his advantage. With a giant swing of his sword, he severed three of the bandits' throats. The repetitive snapping of Deidre's bowstring echoed in the night as several bandits fell, with elven arrows embedded in their necks, heads, and chests.

By this time, most of the bandits realized that they were being attacked, and with their leader incapacitated, they decided to flee the camp. However, they did not make it far. They were quickly shot dead from Deidre's arrows or cut down by Mario's blade. One of the bandits tried to sneak away, but Mario had spotted him at the last second. Mario swung his sword wildly and severed both of the tendons in the bandit's heels. Before the rogue could cry out in pain, Mario split his head in two. Bits of skull fragments and brain matter splashed up in Mario's face, but it didn't affect him. He was entirely consumed by his rage. All the people he lost, all the pain he had endured, was finally being served to the people who deserved it. A few times in the battle, Mario caught himself in a state of euphoria. The act of carrying out vengeance lifted him to a state of complete joy. It was a high like he had never experienced, and he let the sensation consume him.

The ambush took only a minute before the slaughter was done. Most of the bandits perished; only a handful were able to escape with their lives. Deidre hopped down from the ledge and began removing arrows from her victims' bodies. Mario stabbed his swords into any of the bandits who groaned or moved in the slightest. It appeared that their vengeance was finally carried out when they heard an exhausted cackling coming from the edge of the camp. Mario turned his head and saw, despite having been shot with two arrows, that the bandit leader lived.

"Do my eyes deceive me?" Henry coughed. "Or is that really you two? I thought you would've been sold into slavery by now."

Mario marched angrily towards the bandit, his bloodied sword gripped tightly in his hands. He couldn't help but think about how much he was going to enjoy butchering the scoundrel.

"Oh my, you've gotten even uglier!" Henry exclaimed as he wiped the blood off his face. Mario froze instantly in his tracks. Despite seeing his demise a few feet in front of him, the bandit leader still showed no fear and was as charismatic as ever. "What happened to your friend, the town guard?"

Mario slowly paced towards the dying man and shoved his sword deep into the shin of the bandit. Henry winced, but he refused to utter a sound. "His name was Hamish."

"Ah, so dead," Henry replied. "But at least you still got your elven whore." Instinctually, Mario punched the man as hard as he could in the mouth. He felt some of the bandit's teeth getting knocked loose from the force of the blow. Henry laughed as he spat out some of his dislodged, rotten teeth onto the frozen ground. "You're just like me."

"I'm nothing like you!"

"Please, look at yourself! You have no armour, you look more like a brigand than a knight, and you slaughtered an entire camp of people without giving them a chance to surrender and arrest them. The worst part of it is I bet you enjoyed cutting down my men like dogs."

Once again, Mario punched Henry. The bandit's words hurt worse than any dagger or sword ever could. He didn't want to believe any of it. Yet, when he looked objectively at himself, he realized that the rogue's arguments had some truth to it. Mario shook his head in denial. "You don't know what you're talking about."

"I know that look," said Henry as he grinned his toothless, blood-stained smile. "That's the look of a killer, a scoundrel . . . of a good for nothing bastard."

A sinking feeling emerged in Mario's stomach. It felt like he had lost all the air out of his lungs, and he felt uncomfortably nauseous. Despite the awful feeling, Mario pressed the tip of his blade against the bandit's throat. "Tell me about the letters!" his voice cracked under the anger and sadness. The euphoria that consumed him in battle had left him. It was replaced by despair, anger, and guilt.

"We both serve a higher power, Knight," Henry stated as he looked up towards the night sky. "You serve the king, and I serve whoever pays me. The letters were from a Southerner who paid us to carry out raids on certain towns and villages. We just got back raiding a small village in Keten."

"Why Keten?"

Henry smiled coyly and chuckled to himself before he looked Mario in the eyes. "We're going to start a war."

Mario dropped his blade in disbelief as the bandit's words sank in. Mario felt his blood turn cold as he thought about a Keten invasion. It would be a long, bloody, and gruelling battle between the two kingdoms. One he would be obligated to serve in.

"Where's this Southerner?" Deidre asked as she aimed an arrow between the bandit's eyes.

"He's in a town called Garstag, staying at the inn called The Drunken Harpy. We were supposed to meet him there to get the second half of our payment."

The three of them sat in silence for some time, thinking heavily about the information that was just shared. Finally, Henry decided to break the silence. "So, what now? You going to kill me, Knight?"

Mario stood up, dusted the snow off of his pants, and sheathed his sword. "No," he replied calmly as he began walking back towards the horses, "she is."

As he walked back towards the horses, all Mario could hear were the sounds of Deidre's daggers piercing the bandit's flesh and Henry's tortured screaming. A smile broke out on Mario's face, a smile that made him disgusted in himself and forced his stomach to churn.

In all my years, I have never met a race as vindictive and vengeful as the elves. One would think that a race of people can't survive and succeed as a society if the people all bear grudges against one another, but that is just the thing. Elves settle their disputes with one another rather quickly and peacefully. It's the disagreements with other races, primarily humans, that result in violence and an inability to bury the hatchet between the two.

Yancy Provid,
A Life Among Elves: A Half-breed Story

Lycanthropy is a terrible disease. Once infected, every full moon a person transforms into a mindless beast. The person is no longer governed by logic, feelings, or even morals. No—the only thing controlling the beast is its insatiable hunger.

Lucius Volpe,
Lycanthropy Vol. I

CHAPTER FIFTEEN

The soft orange glow of the rising sun sparkled off of the snow-covered treetops. The warm rays gradually hit Mario's face, gently waking him from his slumber. He slowly opened his eyes and looked around. To his surprise, he saw that both horses were still tied up; there was no sign that Deidre had returned from the bandit's camp.

Mario quickly shot to his feet. Panic began to grip his heart. *What if one of the bandits survived? What if they took Deidre?* He cursed himself for falling asleep before Deidre had returned. As he was readying to venture back into the bandit's camp, Mario heard the sudden snap of a twig behind him. He quickly spun around, sword brandished at full length, and saw a blood-soaked Deidre staring blankly back at him.

"We have a problem," Deidre said monotonously before walking back towards the bandit's camp.

Mario quickly sheathed his sword and followed her. Something didn't feel right. Deidre's expression, the flatness of her voice, the fact that she didn't return to the horses till morning, everything about the situation was off. Mario started to grow uneasy, not sure what to expect once he had returned to the bandit camp.

"What happened?" Mario asked, trying to prepare himself for what awaited him.

Deidre remained silent and kept walking towards the camp. Mario gulped nervously.

Upon reaching the camp, Mario immediately vomited in his mouth. The carnage looked even more horrific in the daylight. Bodies of bandits were scattered across the frost-covered plain, and the ground was stained crimson from the blood. The snow in the camp had turned to slush, it squished and gurgled from the over-saturation of blood. Crows had descended and began feasting on the rotting flesh of The Hounds. One of the birds stabbed its sharp, pointed beak into a man's eye and effortlessly ripped it from the socket. Mario winced at the sight. Although he had seen grizzlier things in his travels, he still could not find a stomach for them. Deidre, however, seemed completely unbothered by the experience. She maintained the same slow, stiff walk that she had in the forest.

"There," Deidre said, pointing toward the silver cage that housed the werewolf the night before.

Mario gasped, as he saw a completely naked woman huddled in the cage. She was covered with cuts, scars, and a multitude of bruises. The woman lifted her head from her knees and exposed her tear-filled eyes to the world. She looked Mario in the eyes, and in a raspy voice said, "Help me."

"We should let her out of the cage," Mario responded while taking a step closer to the woman's cage.

"No!" Deidre snapped. Mario instantly stood still. He turned his head to meet Deidre's gaze but instead saw that her eyes cast down. "We can't."

"Why not?"

"Mario, she's a werewolf. Every full moon, she transforms into a monster and hunts the innocent."

"Yes, but surely we can't condemn her to die in a cage next to rotting corpses."

Deidre sighed as a tear slowly rolled down her blood-stained cheek. "We have to."

"So, this is how she is to meet her end?" Mario retorted, his breath hot with anger. "To starve in a cage, to die with no dignity whatsoever? That's how you wish to leave her?"

"We have to!" Deidre screamed, her fists shaking violently. "Mario, we can't let her loose. Either she starves, or she slaughters everyone nearby."

"No!" the woman pleaded from within the cage. "I won't hurt no one! I'll leave, far away, and live off berries, deer, and squirrels!"

Deidre slowly turned her head and looked at the woman with eyes full of regret. "We can't . . . werewolves have no control of themselves once they turn. Everyone knows that."

Mario looked between the two women; his heart began to race as he realized he had to make the final decision. Every fibre of his body told him to free the woman. Condemning someone to die in a cage was as cruel of a punishment as Mario could imagine. However, he knew Deidre spoke the truth. People with lycanthropy have no control over their monstrous side; it was common knowl-edge. Because of this, he knew the woman's promises were empty. *If only I had a silver sword, then I could end this quickly and painlessly.* Mario turned his gaze to the silver cage. "I'm sorry, but we can't risk the lives of many for the life of one."

As Mario and Deidre turned away to walk back towards the horses, they lis-tened to the caged woman scream and howl after them. They heard her skin sear against the silver bars of the cage, as she desperately reached out to them. Mario wished that he had never returned to the bandit's camp because this time he left more disgusted in himself than before.

The walk back to the horses was a long and quiet one, but it was far from peaceful. Mario noticed that something had changed in Deidre; she was differ-ent. She was avoiding eye-contact, conversation, or any other forms of interac-tion. She cast her head down, no longer her vigilant self, searching for threats lurking in the distance, but instead almost welcoming the embrace of death. Mario had seen this behaviour in her before—after her encounter with Pascal.

Once they had reached their horses, Mario stopped and placed a hand on Deidre's shoulders. "Deidre, what's wrong?"

"It's nothing," Deidre replied, still avoiding eye contact.

She's a terrible liar. "You said it yourself; we had to leave her in the cage for the sake of everyone."

Deidre began to sob uncontrollably and pulled Mario into a deep embrace. Her head shook on his shoulders as she struggled to control her emotions. The cold, sticky blood that covered her clothes clung to his beard and face. He felt the cold substance seep through his clothes and onto his mutilated chest.

"I don't know what's happening," Deidre said. "I don't know what's wrong with me."

"Nothing is wrong with you."

"Yes, there is! Look at me!" Deidre cried as she pushed Mario away. "I'm a fucking monster! I just sentenced a young girl to starve in a cage, a girl who has done nothing wrong except contract an awful disease."

"Deidre, that wasn't your fault—"

"And I'm still not better. . . .I carried out my vengeance. I did everything I dreamed of to that bastard and more, but nothing's changed. I still feel this hollow emptiness in me, like a piece of me is still missing. I thought it would all go back to normal after we found them. . . ."

Mario grabbed Deidre by the hand and pulled her to a nearby collapsed tree, then sat down beside her on it. He wrapped his one arm around her and let out a long, heavy sigh. "I don't think it will ever go back to normal. I think our old lives are long gone. I'll never go back to being a knight, and you'll never go back and be a forest elf again."

Deidre lifted her head and looked deep into Mario's eyes. He was mesmerized by how her blue-grey irises sparkled as tears welled from her eyes. He felt her warm breath on his neck. Her hands tightly gripped his, palms covered with calluses and blisters. Mario could see Deidre's throat move as she struggled to find her words.

"So, what do we do then?

"We have to keep moving forward. We have to learn to live with what has happened to us. We must not stop living because of our pasts."

"How do we begin to do that?"

"You could ride with me to Garstag, in search of the Southerner that Henry mentioned."

Deidre smiled bashfully. "You still wish to travel with me?"

"I wouldn't have made it this far without you, and it seems fitting that we see this through together. Plus, us monsters have to stick together." Mario chuckled softly.

Once again, Deidre pulled Mario into a hug. She gently kissed him on the cheek and whispered into his ear, "Thank you."

***

"Shut that cunt up!" Fáelan barked as he viciously freed his sword from the merchant's spine.

Tiberius turned his head to see an arrow puncture the wailing woman's neck. Blood erupted from the wound; streams of red leapt from her body and stained the roadside. He knew Milandriel shot the arrow; her fletchings were unique and easily recognizable, the feathers of nightingales. He remembered when he first joined the resistance that he used to wince and cover his eyes at such grisly sights. But now, he was used to it. Fáelan once told him: "Humans don't learn from talking. They can only learn through bloodshed."

A high-pitched squeal turned Tiberius' head to the left. He saw that one of his brethren was bashing in the skull of the merchant's infant child. The baby's head burst open, and brain matter scattered across the ground. The sinister chuckle of the elves filled the air. Tiberius' stomach began to churn, but he quickly reminded himself of the first lesson Fáelan taught him: "Every dead human means one less dead elf."

"*A Thiarna rí!*" one of the elven scouts called out as he removed a heavy wooden chest from the tipped over wagon.

Fáelan quickly marched towards the chest and kicked it open. He stared at the contents with great disappointment. "The fuck is this?" he exclaimed as he picked up the loose sheets of paper in the chest. "Nothing but deeds, bills, and other useless *dahrenn* documents."

"Fáelan, ya blubberin' fuck, don't ye know anything 'bout smugglers?" a gruff, gravelly voice called out. Tiberius turned his head and saw the dwarf stroking his beard as he examined the merchant's cart. He was hesitant when Fáelan mentioned that Donovin's band of dwarves would be joining the resistance, but so far, they'd proven themselves invaluable. Although they all had a fierce temper, and an unquenchable thirst for ale, they were unmatched on the battlefield. Tiberius was always in awe about how the dwarves willingly threw themselves into harm's way when attacking. They were reckless and unpredictable, a dangerous combination.

"Speak to me like that one more time Donovin, and you'll join the *dahrenn* in the ditch," Fáelan growled as he glared at the dwarven warrior.

Donovin grinned ear to ear, Tiberius knew he had faced tougher foes than the elven leader. Almost nightly, he would tell the tale of how he fought and killed the griffon of Grimm Mountain single-handedly. With each retelling, the story got more and more outlandish, but Donovin always had the scars to support his claims. The dwarf knocked on the hard wooden floor of the wagon and began hacking the floorboards away with his axe. "See?" Donovin replied. "If you shut yer yap for more than ten seconds, ye'd realize ye could learn a thing or two from me and my lads!"

The dwarves began the arduous process of removing the hidden cargo from the false bottom of the wagon. Tiberius' eyes grew wide when he realized that all of the cargo was weapons. Swords, axes, bows, maces, spears, lances, and even a few shields. Tiberius knew that with these, they would be able to arm everyone in the resistance with their own weapon and bow, and finally be able to attack some of the *dahrenns'* outposts.

Fáelan slowly walked up to the dwarf, his frown furrowing with every step. When he was only a few inches away from Donovin, a smile broke across his lips. "Well done, Dwarf."

"So, what now?" Donovin asked coarsely as he spat on the ground. "We're just a wee ways from the town of Garstag. Why don't we give these new weapons a test with a good ol' fashion raid?"

"No," Fáelan responded quickly. "We will return to camp and rest. Tomorrow is another day."

Donovin grumbled under his breath but ultimately agreed with the elven leader. Tiberius was relieved that he would not be carrying out a raid tonight. They had been marching nonstop for days. The only rest that he had was when they were looting after an ambush or battle. He had never been this tired before; he thought that if he closed his eyes for only a few seconds, he would fall into a deep sleep. Suddenly, he felt a hard slap on the shoulder. "Not a bad day, huh, Half-breed?" Milandriel laughed as she ran her hand down his muscular arm.

"Any day we kill a *dahrenn* is another day we save our people," Tiberius responded immediately. He had learned that phrases like these always went over well with Milandriel and Fáelan.

"When I first met you, I didn't think you'd last an hour with us, but yet, here you are. And with a few kills under your belt as well."

Tiberius blushed. He looked down at his necklace of severed human ears. He hated wearing severed flesh around his neck but knew it was a symbol of status within the resistance, and with it came respect. Looking at each of the three ears brought about the memories of killing their owners'. The sounds of their screams still echoing inside his head.

"Remember why we wear them?" Milandriel asked, interrupting Tiberius' thoughts.

"Because during the uprising, they did the same to us," Tiberius replied. Milandriel smiled and patted him on the cheek softly with her hand. She then turned on her heels and began to follow Fáelan back towards the camp. Tiberius couldn't help but admire the view as he followed in behind her.

***

The closer they came to reaching Garstag, the more Mario wondered about Deidre's kiss. *Was it a friendly kiss? Or did she mean it more romantically?* His stomach began to contort anxiously. He had never seen Deidre as a potential romantic partner until now. Ever since the kiss, Mario couldn't stop thinking about her. He daydreamed about them running away together. Living their lives contently in solitude, far from the judging eyes of human society. On several occasions, he caught himself fantasizing about spending the night with her. He quickly shook the idea out of his head. *Snap out of it, Mario. It'll never happen; she hates humans. Plus, she could never be attracted to someone as hideous and disfigured as me.*

"What're you thinking about?" Deidre inquired, interrupting his thoughts. "You've been pretty quiet during the ride."

Mario scratched his neck, nervously. "Nothing, just absent thoughts. Nothing important." He grimaced as the words left his lips. He found the idea of lying to Deidre unbearable, but he knew he had to. She was not ready for a conversation like this.

"I don't believe you," Deidre said playfully through narrowed eyes. "Tell me, what are you thinking about?"

Mario began to panic. He felt sweat droplets form on his brow, and his mouth became incredibly dry. His eyes darted from one side to the other rapidly, desperately trying to find something that he could construct a lie out of. Finally, he saw it: Deidre's clothes. "I was thinking about how we are going to talk our way into Garstag when we look like we just slaughtered a small family of pigs."

Deidre looked at Mario's clothes and then down at her own. She chuckled at the sight. "Fair enough, I almost forgot I was caked in blood. But where are we going to wash? All the rivers are frozen this far north."

"A hot spring, maybe?"

"Possibly, but it'll take forever for our clothes to dry. They'll freeze as soon as they leave the water."

Mario turned around and saw the corner of a fine fur coat sticking out of one of the Esterak's saddlebags. A fiendish smile spread across his face.

"Oh no," Deidre said.

"You have to. Otherwise, you'll freeze," Mario replied teasingly.

"*Bloede Caern,*" Deidre cursed as she began to ride her horse off of the road into the forest in the direction where she suspected a hot spring to be. Mario eagerly followed, giggling quietly to himself along the way.

As they ventured off of the main trail and deeper into the surrounding forest, Mario noticed that the further they ventured in, the more the trees became bare. Leaves, branches, and even some of the bark had been stripped from the trees. The snow around the trunks of the trees had been trampled flat by several sets of footprints. Mario stopped his horse abruptly and dismounted.

"What's going on?" Deidre asked once she saw that he was no longer following.

"Look at the trees," Mario responded. "They're stripped bare like someone was collecting material to build a shelter."

"Bandits," Deidre hissed as she hopped off her horse.

Mario nodded his head and dismounted so he could examine the tracks around the trunk of the tree. *The prints are shallow in the snow, which means none wore heavy armour. However, some have no boots at all and instead leave a perfect outline of their feet. Slaves?*

"Mario!" Deidre called out in a hushed voice.

Instantly, Mario left the tree trunks and quickly scuttled towards her. "What?"

"Elven arrows." Deidre pointed to an arrow embedded in the side of a pine tree.

"Do you know of any elven clans this far north?" Mario asked as he eyed the brown-feathered fletchings.

"No," Deidre responded coldly, "which only means they were forced to move."

Mario's heart sank. After all that they had been through, after she had carried out her revenge, Deidre still loathed humanity. It was bittersweet knowing that he was the only living human that Deidre could tolerate. She was important to him, and he was glad that they had become close. But he secretly wished that she could see that not all humanity was like Henry or Pascal, that there was, in fact, some good in everyone.

"We better leave the horses; best to investigate on foot," Deidre commanded as she nimbly shuffled through the trees.

Mario nodded his head and stealthily followed.

The sound of a bowstring snapping echoed in the empty, winter air. Mario instantly froze in place, as he knew it was not Deidre's. The elven arrow missed the tip of his nose only by an inch. The wind cut his face as it flew by.

"Deidre!" Mario called out as he quickly jumped behind the cover of a tree trunk. As he scanned the trees for more hidden archers, he heard a stern, masculine voice shouting from within the forest. He couldn't understand what was being said, but he knew it was elvish.

"Do my eyes deceive me, or does an elf travel with a *dahrenn*?" the voice exclaimed, hidden amongst the snow-covered foliage.

"So?" Deidre replied smugly as she took cover behind a rotting log.

"Come out. I wish to talk," the voice replied.

"No thanks," Deidre replied sarcastically. Another bowstring snapped, and this time an arrow struck the log that Deidre was hiding behind. Three inches from her throat.

"I insist," the voice replied menacingly.

Deidre and Mario faced one another and exchanged looks of helplessness. Seeing as they had no other option, they begrudgingly abandoned their cover and stood in the middle of the forest, their hands raised in the air. Out of the trees emerged a small band of non-humans. Mainly elves, but there were a few dwarves among the ranks as well. Suddenly, a tall elven man walked into sight. Mario could see that he held a magnificent elven sword at his side. The elf's face was covered in scars, and his one eye was completely devoid of colour. An ugly sneer broke across his face as he approached.

"Well, I'll be damned," the elf growled. "It is an elf and a human, and a free elf to boot!"

"Who are you?" Mario asked gruffly, trying to mask the fear slowly consuming his body.

The elf slowly turned his head and glared at him. During his travels, Mario had been on the receiving end of Deidre's glares on many occasions. However, the glare coming from the scarred elf forced Mario to sweat profusely.

"They call me Fáelan," the elf replied, through a clenched jaw.

"Wait, as in the Fáelan that fought in the first uprising?" Deidre asked in disbelief.

"The very same," the elf replied dryly, "but I'm more interested in your story. How did a free elf end up with a *dahrenn*? Are you his captive, sister?"

"No," Deidre replied, eyes slowly narrowing. "He's my friend."

The gang of non-humans erupted in laughter at her remark—except for Fáelan, who had a look of pure disappointment on his face.

"Tell me, sister, have you forgotten what they've done to us?" Fáelan said, interrupting his band's laughter. "How they slaughtered our people? How they hunted us like dogs?" Fáelan's voice was starting to rise, and Mario was beginning to see the veins in his neck bulge through his pale skin.

"I remember," Deidre replied sourly.

"And yet you still choose to travel and befriend one of them?"

"Yes."

"Might I implore why?"

"He's not like the others. He has a good heart. He's different."

"The hell he is!" another voice called out among the gang of non-humans. Suddenly, another elf emerged from the crowd. He was considerably younger than the rest and wore a red bandana on his head, covering the top part of his ears. Mario's heart sank.

"Tiberius?"

"Wait, you two know one another?" Fáelan asked coarsely.

"Unfortunately, we do," Tiberius replied. "We were in the Knight's College together, although he certainly is uglier than I remember."

"Nice to see you too," Mario replied sourly as he stared at his best friend.

"This man and I saw an elf in need in the town of Redfern," Tiberius shouted out, loud enough so everyone could clearly hear him. "The helpless elf was being beaten, and he chose to do nothing. He walked by, pretending that he hadn't seen the elf. But I chose to take action, to protect my brethren from the filth—filth like him."

Deidre turned her head in shock, and she stared at Mario through tearful eyes. Mario swallowed solemnly and hung his head in shame. The mass of non-humans began chanting wildly, demanding his head. Suddenly, Deidre stepped forward and cleared her throat. "That may be true, but that is not the man I know. He has grown a lot since those days. He's changed—"

"Please!" Fáelan exclaimed. "*Dahrenn can't* change. They just say that to manipulate us. You're falling for his tricks, sister."

"I'm not!" Deidre yelled. "I swear he's different! Please trust me—"

"Trust!" Tiberius interrupted. "How can you talk about trust when you are travelling with the son of the man who slaughtered our people!"

The forest suddenly fell silent, with everyone in a state of shock, including Mario.

Tiberius glared at his former friend with cloudy eyes of hatred. "This is the son of Pablo Deschamps! The Slayer of Elves!"

The forest instantly stirred into a frenzy as Tiberius' words lingered in the air. Mario began looking around and saw that he was surrounded. He felt like reaching for his sword, but he knew that he would be shot with an arrow before he could ever touch the hilt. He turned his head and surprisingly saw Deidre pointing her bow at him through tear-filled eyes.

"I'm sorry," Deidre said softly, as she drew her bowstring back to her ear.

Mario looked around helplessly, desperately trying to find a way to escape. He felt like a rabbit trapped in a hunter's snare. As he felt tears beginning to well, he turned his head to look at Deidre one last time. He looked at her blue-grey eyes, her blonde hair, and then her lips. There, he noticed that she was mouthing something: *"Run."*

Mario's eyes widened, and as if on cue, Deidre turned sharply and shot an arrow directly into Fáelan's shoulder. Mario instantly sprinted deeper into the forest, zig-zagging between the trees, hoping to get out of the elven archer's line of sight. As he ran, he heard the sounds of swords clashing and skin being sliced open. He cringed at the thought of Deidre being outnumbered, but he couldn't afford to think about that now, he had to get out of this forest. Crashing through the underbrush, he heard the sound of footsteps beside him. He turned his head and was immediately tackled to the ground.

Quickly rising to his feet, Mario saw that the person that tackled him was Tiberius. "Please, I don't want to fight you," he pleaded.

Tiberius wordlessly unsheathed his sword, preparing for a fight. Mario begrudgingly did the same. Suddenly, a dwarf and a she-elf emerged from the undergrowth, both armed with daggers. Mario cursed under his breath and waited anxiously for one of them to make the first move. Wasting little time, Tiberius instantly lunged forward. Mario quickly sidestepped, and instead of swinging his sword, he chose to punch his friend square in the jaw with his left hand. Tiberius turned around and swung wildly at Mario's throat, which he easily parried.

The she-elf suddenly jumped into the fray, her daggers glistening through the air as she swung them violently at Mario's throat. Every swing seemed to have more power behind them and were much harder to block and parry. As Mario began backpedalling from the onslaught in front of him, he noticed the other elf leap at him from the side. Mario kicked the she-elf in the knee and pushed himself out of harm's way. He tripped over a stump and quickly rolled backwards and onto the balls of his feet.

Already gasping for air, Mario stared at his three opponents as they began to surround him. His eyes darted from the she-elf to the dwarf, and then to Tiberius. Slowly with his left hand, he reached down and grasped a clump of dirt and snow. When the she-elf leapt from the side, he threw the ball of mud at the eyes, blinding her. As she fell to the ground, clutching her eyes, Mario powerfully drove his sword through her midsection and severed her spine. Her body began to convulse uncontrollably on the edge of his sword.

Out of the corner of his eye, Mario saw Tiberius charging towards him. He quickly turned his hips and kicked with his right foot. He heard the sound of Tiberius' ribs cracking. On the opposite side, the dwarven warrior barrelled towards him. Mario tried to pull his sword free, but it was stuck in the elf's spine. He reluctantly let go of his blade and sprinted towards the dwarf. The dwarf froze in place. When Mario was only a few feet away, he lowered his shoulder and collided with the stunned dwarf. Both crashed against the hard, frozen forest floor. Mario rose to his feet and saw that the dwarf was holding his nose as blood began gushing out of it.

Mario grabbed one of the dwarf's daggers off the ground and plunged it deep into the warrior's right eye, piercing his skull. The dwarf's body spasmed as Mario twisted the blade further into the brain. Tiberius, meanwhile, had slowly risen to his feet, his left hand tenderly supporting his ribcage. Mario marched over to the elven corpse and managed to finally free his sword.

"Please, Tiberius," Mario pleaded. "I don't want to do this. We are brothers!"

Tiberius' face hardened. "You were never my brother."

Tiberius let out a menacing battle-cry and rushed his former friend. Mario was able to parry and block his attacks with ease. During the onslaught, Mario realized that there had been countless opportunities where he could've ended the fight with a single swing of his sword. It was no secret that he was more gifted with a blade than Tiberius. However, he couldn't bring himself to deliver the fatal blow. This was not a monster or some fanatical elven warrior—Tiberius was his best friend. And he could not stand the idea of ending his life.

Amidst the skirmish, both of the young men's swords intertwined in a stalemate. Mario stepped forward, powerfully pushed Tiberius back out of the grapple, and readied his sword in another defensive stance.

"Why won't you fight me!?" Tiberius screamed as he wiped the sweat from his brow.

"I can't . . ." Mario whispered as he felt the fingers around the hilt of his sword loosen.

Tiberius shook his head in disappointment. "You always were weak." He lunged at Mario once again. However, this time Mario did not parry nor block the attack but instead ducked underneath the swing of the deadly blade. Mario then drove his sword up through Tiberius' skin, just underneath the right collarbone.

Tiberius dropped his sword and fell to the ground in pain. Mario gave a swift kick to the temple and knocked his friend unconscious. Mario quickly removed his sword and looked back, where he last saw Deidre. Every fibre of his body screamed for him to keep running into the forest, but his heart ached at the thought of leaving her. He sheathed his blade and began running back towards the spot of the ambush. With every step, he felt his heartbeat quicken. His mind began to imagine all the horrible punishments the elves would inflict on a traitor. His stomach began to churn but managed to charge forward despite the sickly feeling.

Mario gasped once he returned the clearing. Several bodies covered the forest floor. He quickly started investigating the corpses to see if any were Deidre. Mario held his breath every time he turned a body over, scared that he would see her face. Every time, however, he breathed a sigh of relief. None of the dead elves were Deidre, which meant that Fáelan had taken her somewhere. But there was too much blood and footprints to track which way they went, and Mario was far from an expert tracker.

He wandered the battlefield aimlessly, looking for some sort of lead until he came across a familiar-looking bow. After a few seconds, he recognized that it was Deidre's. Tears began to flood his eyes as he picked up the hand-carved bow off the bloody ground. Deidre was gone, either dead or a captive of the elven resistance. His body wretched at the idea of him being helpless to save her. Wiping the tears from his eyes, Mario grabbed a few undamaged arrows and threw the bow across his back, taking it as a memento. Whether he liked it or not, he would have to finish his quest the way it began—alone.

Magi are charlatans that travel the countryside, claiming to wield unimaginable magical powers. I have been on this world for centuries and have yet to see a single magus with any magical ability. Save your hard-earned coin, folks. They are nothing but deceitful conmen, no better than the bandits and thugs that live on our city streets.

Luth Cottonworth,
Magi: The Festering Tumour in Our Society

Magi are not like other wizards and mages. They are not bound by some archaic code. They travel town to town, helping desperate people with their magic, for a price.

Lord Arnold Culsworth,
Magi: The True Magical Heroes of the Realm

Chapter Sixteen

The iridescent silver moonlight glistened off of the snowy ground, making it look like a sea of diamonds. Every individual snowflake twinkled and sparkled when the gentle rays of light struck them. It was unnaturally calm. No wind, no rustling, no signs of life. It was the kind of night where the slightest sound would carry for miles. Mario crawled out of the frozen earth, with icicles dangling from his beard. He slowly rose to his feet and brushed the snow off of his clothes. Looking back, he cursed himself for thinking an abandoned badger burrow would make a good hiding spot. It managed to successfully hide him from any of Fáelan's elves that were potentially tracking him, but it failed to protect him from the harsh northern elements.

In the distance, Mario could see the faint glow of torchlight and the muffled sounds of music, laughter, and merrymaking. His heart panged painfully with sorrow. He wished that he could partake in the festivities; he wished he could leave everything behind and start anew. But he knew he had to see this through, not only for his own sake, but for everyone else's too. Mario slowly walked out of the forest and exposed himself to the blinding white moonlight. He reactively threw his hand up to protect his eyes from the barrage of light. Once his eyes had adjusted, he saw that the town of Garstag lay just beyond a frozen river.

Suddenly, the crack of a whip came from down the roadside. Mario quickly turned, hand already on the hilt of his blade. However, it was not an enemy, but rather a humble merchant. The man had a small wooden cart, which was pulled by an albino donkey. Mario relaxed as the stranger approached.

"Greetings."

"Evening stranger!" the merchant cheerfully replied. "What are you doing out so late?"

"I could ask you the same thing."

"I'm delivering goods to the festival!"

"Festival?" Mario asked, taken aback.

"Gods, boy, do you not know what day it is today?" the merchant responded in complete disbelief.

Mario shook his head, since he left Kartaga all the days had blurred together.

"It's the day of Thuul. Winter is almost at an end!"

Mario looked around the snow-covered landscape and found it hard to believe that winter was ending. "Now that you mention it, it does look like springtime."

"Pah!" the old merchant spat. "You youngin's always quick with the back talk."

"I'm sorry. I've been travelling for a while and—"

"No worries, lad!" the merchant boisterously interrupted. "Who amongst us hasn't had a bad day, eh? Plus, it is unfit to bear a grudge on such a merry day. Do you need a ride to town?"

Mario nodded politely. "I'm looking for a friend at an inn called The Drunken Harpy."

"Ah, you've come to the right place! That's where all me cargo is goin' to. Hop in!"

Mario climbed up on the cart and sat beside the old merchant. He could see that the man had only a few winters left. The man's face was wrinkled and frostbitten, his eyes were beginning to lose colour, and his beard was almost as white as the snow on the ground. His hands shook uncontrollably as he held onto the reins.

"What's your name, lad?" the merchant asked politely.

"Mario, yours?"

"Gavin."

"Nice to meet you, Gavin."

"What brings you to these parts? Hardly anyone travels here unless they *need* to be here."

"Like I said, I'm looking for a friend." Mario's voice suddenly grew cold. "He has something for me."

Gavin cleared his throat. 'Sounds like grave business, but remember, spilling blood on the day of Thuul is forsaken."

"Why's that?"

"Well, according to the old tales, 'if blood is dropped on the day of Thuul, demons will come and create a fool. So, stay your hand and turn the cheek, else your future will turn bleak."

Mario snickered under his breath. "And you really believe that?"

"Aye, with me life. I've never spilt a drop of blood and have had no hauntings or demons show up."

"Do you know anyone who has been haunted by a demon?" Mario asked bluntly.

"Well . . . no, but that doesn't mean—"

"Trust me, Gavin, demons are the least of your concerns. It's just a stupid rhyme told to children."

Gavin fell uncomfortably silent. The rest of the cart ride into town was as awkward as it was quiet. Mario felt bad for criticizing and ridiculing the old man's beliefs. Plus, Mario was far from an expert on the existence of mythical creatures. Mario turned his head to the sky and couldn't help but think about Deidre. He hoped with all of his heart that she was safe, but he knew that was unlikely. Fáelan had probably either killed her, tortured her, or worse.

A sudden bump in the road jolted Mario from his trance-like state. He looked around and saw that they were in front of a crowded inn. People were outside of the inn, drinking, gambling, fucking, or some other form of debauchery. Mario saw the silhouettes through the windows of the inn and saw that the inside of the tavern wasn't any more decent.

"What's going on?" Mario asked as he glanced at a young couple having sex out in the open.

Gavin turned his head and stared at the couple in joy. A small, playful smile broke out on his face. "The day of Thuul is about rebirth and making merry. The weather will soon bring new life into the world, and we do the same."

Mario scratched his neck uncomfortably. "But what about privacy?"

The old man chuckled at Mario's innocent question. "Today, we are free from the bonds of society. Tonight, we can do what we want, where we want, with who we want. Just as the gods intended."

Mario was about to ask another question when he saw a second man join in on the couple's activity. He was in disbelief how nobody objected, how it was welcomed and embraced.

Gavin saw Mario's disbelief and calmly stated, "There is only one rule tonight."

"Don't spill blood."

Gavin nodded his head and hopped off the cart. He grabbed one of the bags of food out of the back and struggled to throw it over his shoulder. "Would you mind giving an old man a hand, Mario?"

Guilt forced Mario to agree; he still felt bad for mocking the man's beliefs, especially now that he saw how much joy it caused everyone. Mario picked up and threw a bag of food on each of his shoulders. As he walked towards the inn, he felt the hands of men and women alike grabbing at his clothes, begging him to join their festivities. He ignored their please and kept walking towards the door.

"A shame really." Gavin sighed.

"What's that?"

"That I can no longer join them. Oh, how I miss the days of my youth where I'd fuck and drink for hours! But alas, the old body can no longer keep up with the activities."

Mario nodded, pretending to listen to the merchant's whining, but secretly he was thinking about Deidre. He felt a little bit relieved that Deidre wasn't here with him. Although it was unlikely that she would join in the festivities, his heart couldn't bear the idea of her being with someone else.

As the door to the tavern was opened, the aroma of freshly cooked food and bodily fluids assaulted Mario's nostrils. The air inside was hot, musty, and thick. He quickly walked to the bar and threw down his two bags of food. He saw the lovely young bartender walk towards him. Her fiery red hair was tied into pigtails, her eyes were a lovely hazel, and her face was covered with an adorable set of freckles. He was surprised to see that she was barely wearing any clothes, most of her skin exposed for all to see.

"What can I get ya, love?" she asked in a unexpectantly hoarse voice.

"I . . . um . . . I . . ." Mario stammered as he struggled to ignore what was happening all around him.

"Ah, perhaps ya want me? Well, just say the word, stranger. I love me a man who looks a little dangerous," the bartender purred as she slowly grabbed Mario's hand.

"I'm looking for someone!" Mario blurted out.

"We're all looking for someone tonight—"

"No, I'm looking for a man; he's a Southerner. He's supposed to be staying here."

The young woman's face sank as she let go of his hand. "I never would've thought ya swung that way, darlin', much less with a borin' ol' sack like 'im." She turned her head and pointed disappointingly to the room in the corner of the inn. "He's in there."

"Thank you," Mario replied nervously and quickly walked away from the bartender. As he waded through the mass of drunken bodies, Mario felt his blood beginning to boil. The thought of having the man responsible for all the death, destruction, and violence that he had endured trapped in a small room filled his body with a sick sense of joy.

Mario opened the door to the room and quickly closed it behind him, making sure to lock it. When he turned around, he saw that the man was sitting in the corner of the room smoking a pipe, his face completely concealed by darkness.

"As I've said before, I'm not interested in participating in any barbaric forms of indecency."

"You mistake me for someone else," Mario growled through a clenched jaw. He felt the pounding of his heartbeat in the front of his skull. It was taking every ounce of self-control he had to not unsheathe his blade and skewer the mysterious foreigner.

The man set his pipe down on the end table and rose from his chair. As the man moved toward Mario, his face became illuminated from the moonlight pouring in through the nearby window. Mario was stunned to see that he recognized the man's face and had seen him before. It was the southern merchant that helped him find Deidre—Ossypius Magnus.

"You," the Southerner mumbled in disbelief. Before he could utter another word, Mario pounced on him, pinning him to the floor.

Mario had lost all of his restraint, and the rage had fully consumed him. Ossypius squirmed helplessly as a cascade of furious blows struck his face repeatedly. Every punch was harder than the last, and Mario never seemed satisfied. Even when the merchant's face began to swell uncontrollably, Mario did not stop. Nor did he stop when the sounds of teeth being knocked loose and bones breaking filled the room. He didn't even stop when he heard the sounds of his own knuckles cracking from the force of the blows. Mario only stopped when he was completely exhausted. He stood up on the blood covered floor and wiped his stained hands on the sheets of the bed.

"Before I kill you, tell me why," Mario demanded as he removed his sword from its scabbard.

"Wait, wait!" the man garbled. "I know who killed your father!"

Mario's blood ran cold. His hand went limp, and his sword fell from his grasp. Tears began to well from his eyes. He quickly grabbed Ossypius by the collar of his shirt and pinned him against the wall. "How do you know this!"

"I heard it!"

"From who!?"

"King Dryden himself!"

Mario's grip tightened around the man's bloody clothes. "You lie."

"No, I swear I'm telling the truth!" Ossypius pleaded. "I work for the emperor, and my job is to listen to the conversations of key individuals."

"You're a spy?"

The Southerner did not reply and avoided Mario's furious gaze.

"Answer me!" Mario yelled as he slammed the man's head into the wooden wall of the room.

"Yes! I'm a spy!" the man confessed. "I heard King Dryden say that he ordered your father to death!"

"Why?"

Ossypius gulped nervously. "Because your father slaughtered an entire village that the king deemed traitors. Then the king killed your father to stop the commoners from finding out that he ordered the death of royal subjects!"

Mario released him. He couldn't believe what he was hearing, yet it all made sense. How his father never returned home after the uprising, and how the elves feared him and called him a murderer—all to protect the king's reputation. Mario's head was spinning from the news. He stumbled out of the inn, covered in blood, and started walking. His mind was racing uncontrollably as he started to contemplate the conspiracy. *Did the college know about this? Did they hide it from me? Why would nobody tell me?* As he reached the climax of his downward spiral, Mario collapsed in the middle of a crossroads, sobbing uncontrollably.

Suddenly, an eerie fog began to roll in. It covered the ground in a grey haze and blocked out majority of the moonlight. Mario lifted his head and wiped the tears in his eyes. Then, he heard a familiar sound that sent a shiver down his spine. The ominous jingling of bells. Goosebumps covered his skin, the air became unnaturally cool, and fear gripped his lungs. The bells were getting closer, and with each passing second, Mario felt his body succumb to the sheer terror slowly enveloping him.

Out of the dense, supernatural fog emerged a man. He was wearing a thick set of clothes decorated with bells along the seams of his shirt. The toes of his shoes were curled with a single bell at the tip. The man had a shaved head with a small amount of stubble that complimented his jawline. He also carried a walking stick eerily similar to a wizard's staff. The man's irises were a bright, unnatural shade of crimson. They glared at Mario menacingly.

"Greetings," the man called out.

Mario slowly rose to his feet and lowered his right hand to his sword's scabbard only to find that it wasn't there. He cursed as he remembered dropping it in the inn, and then thoughtlessly leaving it behind.

"Tell me," the man continued as he approached Mario carelessly, "what troubles you, my son?"

Mario's heart began to race. He recognized the man's voice. It was the same voice he heard on the river, and in the caves. It was the ghastly voice that had been haunting his dreams ever since the pogrom in Riverwell. Mario felt his skin begin to lose colour. "What . . . what are you?"

The man smiled wickedly. "The name's Alistair Belial. I'm a magus."

Mario narrowed his eyes skeptically. "Everyone knows magi are charlatans. Good for nothing conmen."

Alistair laughed ominously. "My dear, dear Mario, how else would I be able to communicate with you if I wasn't magic?"

"How do you know my name? Why have you been talking to me?"

With the snap of his fingers, the magus conjured two chairs out of the thick grey fog. The man promptly sat in one and gestured for Mario to have a seat. Reluctantly, he joined the stranger.

"Now allow me to explain," Alistair began as he leaned forward in his chair. "I'm very much real, and I'm very much magical, so please do not take me as a conjurer of cheap tricks." Mario nodded. The man leaned back in his chair. "To put it simply, my profession is to lend my magical abilities to anyone who needs them—for a price."

"What do you charge?" Mario interrupted.

Alistair chuckled sinisterly. "I have no need for gold. I much rather prefer deals." The magus' eyes suddenly intensified their unholy glare. "According to my count," the man said as he created a large ledger out of the surrounding smoke, "you already owe me a favour."

Mario shot out of his chair. "What? No, I don't. I've never seen you a day in my life!"

"Tsk, tsk, tsk," Alistair clicked. "Let's refresh your memory, shall we? Ahem. 'Gods, if you're listening, I've come to ask a favour of you . . .'" Alistair said while perfectly imitating Mario's voice. "'None of these people deserve to die because of me. I'm the only reason any of them are here.' Do you know that you whine a lot? It's a wonder how anyone can stand you with all of your incessant moaning. Where were we? Ah, here we go! 'Please, I beg that you allow me and my friends to survive this fall.'"

Mario's heart sank as he remembered the prayer he made when he went over the waterfall. Slowly, his body collapsed into the chair, and his arms went limp. He couldn't remember the last time he had been this overwhelmed. First, he loses his last remaining companion, Deidre, then he learns that the king had secretly murdered his father, and now, almost inexplicably, he learns he owes a favour to a magus.

"I assume that satisfies your curiosity?" Alistair asked, interrupting Mario's thoughts. "Besides, after all my hard work of keeping you four idiots alive, what do I have to show for it?" The magus stood up from his chair and gestured at the empty crossroads surrounding them. "All I have left is a miserable, whining, pathetic, child. Hamish is dead. Andronikus is dead, Miles is dead. Finnegan and Roger are most likely dead, and then there's the elf, Deidre."

Mario glared at the man with tears in his eyes. The way Alistair said her name was riddled with condescension and disapproval. Mario clenched his fists angrily at the mysterious magus.

The man smiled viciously. "She was the one person whose life you didn't need to destroy. Instead, she joined you, and as a result, she was raped, beaten, raped again, and finally butchered by her own kin—all because of you!"

"Shut your mouth!" Mario screamed as tears began to leak from his face.

"No!" Alistair barked back, with a voice twice as loud. "I will not shut my mouth. It is about time someone put you in your fucking place, you miserable little shit! Look at everything you've done, all the pain you've caused, all the lives you've destroyed. And for what? You had the man responsible in your hands and you let him go!? All of your friends' lives were ruined for nothing! All because you weren't man enough to finish the job."

Mario's knees grew weak and his heart began to ache with sadness. In his heart of hearts, he knew Alistair was right. He'd known it all along. He was solely responsible for ruining his friends' lives. Tears flowed down Mario's cheeks as guilt and regret began to consume him. Alistair slowly walked over to him and placed a hand on his shoulder.

"Let me give you some free advice, kid. Don't let this all be for nothing."

"What do you mean?"

"I mean go and kill the son of a bitch that killed your father. You can't bring him or your friends back, but vengeance is the next best thing."

Mario wiped the tears from his eyes. "How do I do that? I can't demand an audience with the king. I'm nobody."

Alistair let out a deep throaty chuckle. "Are you forgetting who you are? You're Mario Deschamps! An *ordo equestris pro tem*! You've completed your first quest, and by tradition, the king has to dub you a knight."

"But I have no proof. I—"

The magus let out an exasperated sigh, and with a snap of his fingers, emerged Ossypius Magnus bound in shackles. "Now go, fulfill your destiny."

Mario begrudgingly grabbed the cold, iron chain that was connected to the shackles clasped around the Southerner's wrists. "But how did you—"

"No more questions," Alistair barked. He turned away from Mario and reached into the fog surrounding them. With great artistry and elegant movements, he began crafting something out of the mist. The supernatural vapours swirled in the magus' hands and began to take shape. After a few minutes, Alistair was done. What was once nothing more than an eerie cloud of grey fog, had now turned into two majestic large grey steeds. "These horses will take you straight to the king's keep and will stop for nothing. Not food, not water, not rest. You'll be at the doors in one day."

Mario couldn't help but smile. Completing his quest and avenging his father would bring him some desperately needed closure. *At least this way, it'll all mean something.* "Thank you," Mario whispered as he helped his prisoner mount a horse.

"Mario."

"Yes?"

"No more free favours."

Mario nodded his head, hopped on his horse, and with a hard kick, broke off into a gallop, vanishing in the dense fog.

***

Alistair chuckled in joy as he watched the young knight ride away. The guilt radiating from Mario nourished him. Every heartache, every painful thought that Mario had brought new life into the demon's body. Nothing gave Alistair Belial more pleasure than successfully manipulating a mortal into becoming a host. He needed a host to keep him on the mortal plane, and Mario was riddled with guilt and regret—the two emotions that gave him power. Alistair knew that the young knight still had some more guilt that could be milked out of him, and with an incredibly delicate hand, he could be the key that allows the demon to stay on the mortal plane for good.

Revenge is an act of passion; vengeance of justice. Injuries are revenged; crimes are avenged.

Samuel Johnson

Chapter Seventeen

The walls of Drossberg were enormous and made out of thick grey stone. Banners of azure and gold flickered atop the palisade, rustling violently from the wind. Guards walked along the battlements while archers watched the horizons diligently. Inside the castle walls, the populace were stirred into a frenzy. They had been talking about today for months; the king had finally had a son. Gossip had already begun spreading about how the boy looked more like the king's brother, Dredden, than it did the king. Rumours about Queen Othelia being unfaithful to King Dryden were not a new thing within the city. After the prince's birth, however, they began to gain some legitimacy. An eerie fog descended on the city suddenly and without any warning. The guards instantly stopped their patrols and froze in place.

"Where'd that fog come from?" one of the guards asked his commanding officer.

"Not a clue, but 'tis a bad omen for sure. The gods are displeased," the captain replied.

"How could the gods be displeased today!?" the younger guard replied. "Today, they brought Prince Conrad into the world. It's nothing more than bad weather."

"Perhaps," the captain retorted, chewing on his bottom lip fiendishly.

"Captain! Come quick!" a guardsman shouted from the gate.

Without wasting a single second, the captain and his men sprinted along the battlements to see what the commotion was all about. Upon reaching the gate, the captain placed his hand on his panting recruit's shoulder, trying to hide his own fatigue. "What is it, lad?"

"Someone's approaching the gate."

The captain's face dropped into a frown. "That's what all that hollerin' was about? A couple o' riders?"

"I . . . I—" the guard stammered.

"Spit it out, boy!"

"I thought it was suspicious, with the fog and all."

"It's probably just another envoy to congratulate the king on his new child. They sent messengers out as soon as Queen Othelia went into labour."

"Shall I open the gate then?" the man replied.

"Standard procedure, recruit," the captain barked as he desperately tried to see through the thick, unnatural fog.

The sounds of horses riding at full speed grew nearer with every passing second. The melodic jingling of the tack echoed in the air. Then, out of the fog, two riders emerged. One was wearing tattered, bloodied rags with a bow slung across his back, while the other was bound in shackles. The horses came to a sudden stop at the iron bars of the gate. Without uttering a single word, both riders dismounted. Then, as if by design, the horses turned around and charged back into the fog.

"Who . . . who goes there?" the young guard meekly asked.

"Let me talk to 'em," the captain growled as he shoved the recruit aside. Bad omens be damned, he was still going to do his job with as much bravado as he could muster. "Hey!" the captain yelled. "Who are you? Answer me, or I'll dump hot tar on you!"

The man with the bow across his back lifted his head and stared directly up the castle wall to meet the captain's gaze. The man cleared his throat. "I'm Mario Deschamps. I'm here to see King Dryden."

The guardsmen stood silently, anxiously waiting for their leader's response.

"What business do ya have with the king?" the captain asked gruffly.

The man grabbed the shackles of his prisoner and shoved him forward. "I've completed my first deed and demand that he dubs me a knight. As evidence, I've captured an imperial spy."

"King's busy today. Doubt he'll have time for anyone, even a knight." The captain snorted.

"He'll make an exception," the man replied grimly.

The captain turned around and looked each of his men in the eyes. They all stared back with curiosity. Even though his heart told him not to let the man into the city, the captain had no legal authority to deny him entry. "Open the gate!" he ordered, albeit begrudgingly. "And you," he said to Mario, "my men will escort you to the keep."

Mario nodded his head politely and walked inside the castle walls.

***

Mario had only been to the capital once when he was a small child. He remembered how big everything seemed back then: the walls, the keep, the houses, everything. However, now they paled in comparison to the buildings of Mnildrom and the ingenuity of the forgotten dwarven architects. As he was being escorted through the narrow, crowded streets of the city, he noticed how happy and jovial the people were. Men were singing songs, women were weaving wreaths and putting up garlands, and children were dressed in their best clothes. It made his stomach churn. It sickened him how happy the people were while a bloodthirsty tyrant ruled over them. It appeared that the whole city was anticipating a party or celebration of some kind, but he didn't care to ask. All he wanted to do was tear down the decorations and scream about the atrocity that King Dryden had committed. Suddenly, there was a lump in his throat, and he felt the blasphemous words on the tip of his tongue.

"Where'd you get them scars?" one of the guards asked, interrupting Mario's thoughts. He quickly relaxed and turned his head to meet the guards gawking gaze.

"Which one?"

"The one's on your face."

Mario chuckled to himself. "I have so many scars at this point, I sometimes forget that they're there. If I'm being totally honest, I can't even remember what I look like without them."

The guard stared back blankly. Then turned his head to Ossypius, bound in shackles. "Why doesn't 'e talk?"

Mario had found himself wondering that same question himself over the last day. When they first met, the Southerner was incredibly talkative. But ever since he had met Alistair, Ossypius had become abnormally silent. His skin had turned a sickly pale instead of the lovely tanned colour Mario had seen when he first met him. His eyes had turned into a milky white, and every breath seemed laborious, as he let out an awful wheeze with every exhale.

Mario had tried to talk to him while they were riding the magus' horses, but he never got a response. *Alistair probably threw a hex on him or casted a spell to make him a more agreeable travel companion.* Although, Mario knew that wasn't true. Something had changed inside of Ossypius; something had died.

"Eh?" the guard probed again. "Why doesn't 'e talk?"

"He's shy," Mario lied.

"He looks sick," the captain replied.

"Why do you care?" Mario snapped. "He's an enemy spy sent to destroy us from the emperor."

The captain nodded his head in agreement. "To hell with him. Feed him to the dogs."

"You said your name was Deschamps, right?" one of the younger guardsmen asked.

"Yes," Mario replied painfully, already knowing where the conversation was heading.

"You're . . . you're the son of Pablo Deschamps, the Slayer of Elves!?"

"I am."

Suddenly, the entire escort of guards came to a halt. Each one of them turned and stared at Mario with amazement, including the captain. It was as if they were looking at a dragon or another fabled beast. Mario glared back with annoyance. "Well?" he asked, clearly aggravated. As quickly as they had stopped, the guards resumed leading him to the keep.

"Perhaps the king will make an exception for you today," the captain called out.

Mario bit his lip angrily.

The keep in the centre of the city was built with the exact same stone as the outer walls, except that they were painted white, no doubt to represent the purity of the nobility. Mario felt like he was going to jump out of his skin. Everything he had admired and dreamt about as a child now filled him with disgust. The keep was no longer the home of a divine ruler; instead, it housed a pretentious, homicidal child that never had to face any consequences. Mario knew that today that was all going to change.

The halls of the keep were much like the halls of the Knight's College. The nostalgia only angered him more. It was as if Mario had been lied to his entire life about how elegant, grand, chivalrous, and amazing life as a knight and noble would be. But, as he learned, that was not the case. He hated how naïve he used to be. He hated how easily the wool had been pulled over his eyes, that he had foolishly believed every word people said. "Soon this will change," he quietly muttered to himself. "Soon this will change."

King Dryden's throne room was widely regarded as the most elegant and beautiful room in the kingdom. The floor was made out of polished white marble; the pillars that were supporting the conical roof were made entirely out of gold. A single carpet dissected the room from the doorway all the way to the king's chair. It had an azure body with gold tassels along the side. The throne itself was made out of solid oak, with golden accents along the armrests. Despite the breathtaking reputation the room had, Mario was underwhelmed. In his eyes, the throne room in Kartaga was wildly superior and much more magnificent.

"Wait here," the captain ordered. "I'll fetch the left hand of the king."

"I don't want to see a dignitary," Mario retorted full of rage. "I want to see the king!"

"The left hand is more than capable of bestowing your knighthood on you, Sir Deschamps."

Mario's eyes widened. "On behalf of my father's legacy and the great service he provided our kingdom, I demand to be dubbed a knight by King Dryden himself!"

The throne room fell silent. A couple of the guards whispered sheepishly amongst themselves. Finally, the captain broke his stunned silence. "I'll see what we can do. Come on, men."

As the guards left the room, Mario helped himself to examining all the art on the throne room walls. Every painting reeked of privilege and crude exaggerations. Several depicted the king, clad in armour, leading his men onto the battlefield. Some showed the king cutting down hordes of enemies with a mighty longsword, while others depicted him shooting arrows directly into the invaders' breasts.

Finally, there was one picture that caught Mario's eye that he didn't immediately sneer at. The painting was of a man fully clad in magnificent plate armour. Both the man's sword and armour were covered in blood. The knight was kneeling on the ground, and his blade was stabbed deep into the earth. He was completely surrounded by bodies—bodies of both men and elves alike. Ravens were flying overheard, and some had begun feasting on some of the corpses.

The knight appeared to be the only survivor of the battle. Mario lowered his eyes and saw that the plaque on the painting read *"Pablo Deschamps: Drussdell's Greatest Hero."*

Tears began to leak out of Mario's eyes—some out of sadness and some out of anger. Mario wished that this painting was in the halls of the Knight's College because, in this painting, the life of a knight did not look glamourous. It was not clean, easy, respectful, or dignified. It was ugly and bloody. If this picture had been hanging in the college, perhaps Mario would've reconsidered being a knight, perhaps all of his friend's lives could've been spared.

Suddenly, he heard angry voices coming from the stairwell. Mario quickly wiped the tears out of his eyes and walked back to where the guards had ordered him to wait. The king and an entire retinue of royal guards stormed into the throne room. Mario's hands turned into fists at the sight of him, but he managed to keep his emotions under control.

"Where's the man who has the gall to rip me from my family?" King Dryden yelled angrily as he plopped down atop his throne.

"I'm right here." Mario snarled, unable to hide his emotions.

The king leaned forward and eyed him severely. The echo of their angered breath filled the room with incredible tension. "You have quite the spine on you," he began. "First you tear me away from my kingly duties, and then address your rightful ruler with such insolence! I've beheaded men for less offences."

"I bet those men didn't capture an imperial spy," Mario retorted, tugging on Ossypius' chains.

The king leaned back in his chair and pressed his fingers against the bridge of his nose. "Alas, no, they did not." Dryden sighed exasperatedly. "Well bring him forward. Let's get this over with."

Mario's heart began to race wildly. The moment that he had fantasized about over the last day was finally here. His hands suddenly became clammy. Nausea gripped his stomach. With his right hand, he pulled one of the scavenged arrows from the forest out of the quiver and hid it up his jacket sleeve. "Do you know who I am?" he asked, waiting for the opportune moment to strike.

"Yes, you're the insolent pup that Pablo Deschamps sired. A shame he couldn't teach you any manners before he passed."

"You mean before you murdered him?"

To Mario's surprise, the king's expression was the only one in the throne room that didn't change. He sat on his throne with the same annoyed look on his face. No fear, no shock, and no horror. *He is a good liar.* Rage began to consume his body, and his hands started to shake.

"Bring me the spy, boy. I don't have time for such nonsense," the king commanded.

Mario began to shuffle forward. When he handed Ossypius' chains over to the royal guards, he quickly removed Deidre's bow from his shoulder and readied the arrow. Before anyone could react, the bowstring was already drawn back, and in the blink of an eye, the arrow was shot.

King Dryden slumped down into his throne and began to squirm wildly as blood squirted out from the wound in his neck. The royal guards and some of the servants desperately tried to stop the king's profuse bleeding, but it was no use. The arrow had severed the carotid artery. The perfect shot.

Mario watched the king spasm wildly in a pool of blood with a smile. His father had been avenged. He dropped the bow on the ground and held his arms high in the air while most of the guards were frantically trying to save the king's life. A few tackled Mario against the hard marble floor. They shouted unpleasantries and cursed him as they threw the shackles around his wrists, but he paid them no mind. Instead, he kept staring at the king. Watching his frightful eyes as they realized that his life and reign had been snuffed out in a matter of seconds.

The guards' cold metal gauntlets gripped Mario's arms and legs with great force. There was no way he could escape even if he wanted to. The guards quickly removed him from the throne room and began dragging him down the stairs towards the dungeon, arguing amongst themselves while they did so.

"I say we just kill 'im here and now!" one of the guards yelled.

"No, we behead him tomorrow in front of the people. Then everyone can see his worthless body squirm."

Once the cell door in the dungeon had been opened, the guards threw Mario down onto the piss-soaked, shit-covered hay. While he was laying helplessly in the cell, each of the guards took a turn beating the knight, not stopping until they could no longer throw a punch or kick their legs. Then they unlocked the shackles and slammed the door to the cell shut.

It was then, and only then, that the gravity of Mario's actions dawned on him. Bloodied, with numerous broken bones, horrifically scarred, and all alone, he realized he made a grave mistake. He had just killed the king—he was a regicide. When he realized that the last of his days were going to be spent locked up in a filthy cage, he began to weep. Mario pulled his hands over his face and sobbed like a child. Through the tears, coming from the musky long dark corridor, he heard the distinct, ominous sound of bells jingling.

EPILOGUE

The sewer stank of shit, piss, and other unspeakable things. Ever since the riots, the people of Riverwell were throwing anything into it that would've implicated them on the night of the pogroms. Gustav and his brothers were charged by the town council to clean out the sewer of any unnecessary garbage. Gustav hated that him and his brothers were tasked with such a demeaning job. They were hard working farmers, barely getting by. And this was their punishment for letting off some steam in town.

"Gods does it fuckin' reek down 'ere!" Anders squealed as he pinched his nostrils together.

"This is yer fault!" Timil screamed as he waded through the water full of unpleasantries.

"My fault, 'ow the 'ell is it my fault?"

"It was yer idea to come tah town and git right shittered!"

"Fuck you. If it's anyone's fault it's Gustav's."

"The fuck you goin' on about?" Gustav snapped at his younger brother. "Mama shoulda tanned yer hide more. Maybe then ye'd have some brains."

Anders hung his head low while Timil exploded in laughter. Suddenly, the scent of rotting flesh filled the small stone passageway. All three brothers had to cover their noses to protect themselves from the malodorous smell. Their eyes began to water as they slowly approached a small mound of corpses. Monsters had already started feeding on the dead bodies, as some were partially devoured and teeth marks covered majority of the remains.

"By the gods . . ." Timil gasped.

"What do you think happen'd to 'em?" Anders asked.

Gustav couldn't help but look at two corpses in particular. One was of a halfling, who appeared to be a simple commoner, judging by the rags he wore. The other was a dwarven warrior, whose body had been torn apart by beastly claws.

"Probably folks who tried to flee the sewers," Gustav said, announcing his conclusion aloud. "The dwarf was probably a guard for 'em. Only he was no match for the beasties."

All three brothers nodded in agreement with one another. Suddenly, they heard ungodly wails coming from down the corridor. All three men froze in place out of sheer terror. The sources of the sound appeared to be getting closer.

"What . . . what was that?" Anders asked nervously.

"Corpse eaters," Gustav replied.

"What do we do?"

"Run."

***

The dried leaves cracked and popped under the elves' heavy footsteps. Blood slowly dripped from the prisoner's broken face staring at the cold, dreary, frozen ground. Her entire face burned with pain; it hurt to even breathe. Her legs dragged behind her lifelessly as she was carried deeper and deeper into the forest; her captors silent as they ominously marched forward.

At the edge of the treeline, there was a large, unnatural hole. Through blurred vision, Deidre could see that the hole was full of corpses—human corpses. Tears slowly began to leak out of her swollen eyes and down her bloodied and battered face.

"*Dhoirse, e'tal urilla vacht. Dahrenn,*" one of the captors growled as they tossed her broken body into the pit, alongside the other corpses.

Deidre gingerly caressed her own face. Shockwaves of pain gripped her body with every touch. Slowly her hands made their way to her ears. She immediately began trembling violently when she didn't feel their tips. The realization that Fáelan had cut off the point of her ears sent her into hysteria. It was a death sentence among elves—to be cast out and forever marked as someone who betrayed their kin. Deidre slowly curled up in the fetal position and wept.

***

The scene was the personification of absolute carnage and slaughter. Limbs were viciously hacked off their bodies, blood had permanently stained the cave walls a dark shade of crimson, and alabaster bodies riddled the passage. Alone, among the pile of corpses, was a man. He was completely naked and covered in the monsters' black acidic blood. The man let his battle-worn sword fall aimlessly to the ground. He scratched his thin, patchy beard as he began to laugh maniacally to himself.

"Eight hundred . . . you killed me eight-hundred and ninety-four times." He slowly grabbed the severed head of one of the monsters and held it close to his grisly face. "But you should've known," the man whispered, "you can't kill an immortal."

ABOUT THE AUTHOR

A.J. Rettger lives on a farm near the small town of Aberdeen Saskatchewan with his dog, Zeke. He has a bachelor's of education degree, as well as a certificate from a private vocational college. His hobbies include playing Dungeons and Dragons, listening to heavy metal, and reading and writing fantasy books. *Oathbreaker* is his first book.

Printed by Libri Plureos GmbH in Hamburg,
Germany